HAILEY'S
TRUTH

BOOK THREE IN THE *BODYGUARDS OF L.A. COUNTY* SERIES

CATE
BEAUMAN

DEDICATION

To my pal Hank. Thank you so much for everything!

CHAPTER 1

Redding, California
December 2003

THE SKY WAS DARK, THE stars winking in the frigid cold. Hailey snuggled under the blanket Daddy had handed her, tense in the heavy silence filling the car. Jeremy leaned against her shoulder, oblivious, worn out, and asleep after the exhausting fun of Tyson Miller's Welcome Home Party. Ice glazed the roads—a rare occurrence in Redding, but she knew Mom and Daddy were watchful for the deadly sheen on the treacherous mountain pass.

"Mom, do you think we should turn around? I'm sure the Miller's wouldn't mind if we stayed."

Mom turned in her seat, smiling, reaching out to hold Hailey's hand. "We'll be all right, sweetheart. We're taking it slow. We'll be home before you know it. Close your eyes. I'll wake you when we get there."

Hailey nodded, giving her mom's small, soft hand a gentle squeeze before she let go. Resting her head against the seat, she closed her eyes, listening to her brother's breathing, the whir of heat pumping through the sedan. She dozed off, drifting toward deep sleep.

"Harold, watch out!"

Hailey's eyes flew open, her heart pounding as the car skidded toward a dense patch of trees.

Her father over-corrected, finding purchase just inches from a formidable pine. The car came to a dead stop.

"Damn." Daddy's breath rushed out in rapid heaves

as he white-knuckled the steering wheel.

"That was too close, Harold." Mom clutched the door handle, her voice shaking. "I think we should turn around. We're closer to the Miller's than we are home. I don't want to risk the children..."

"All right, honey. We'll turn around." He took Mom's hand, kissed her knuckles the way he always did. "Are the kids okay?"

Hailey slammed her eyes shut as her mother turned. "Yes. They didn't even flinch."

Daddy chuckled. "I guess they wore themselves out." He shifted into reverse on the desolate road. The wheels whirled, spinning in place, before they found traction and the car finally moved. "We'll have quite an adventure to tell them about in the morning."

When the car accelerated, Hailey opened her eyes and stared at Daddy's big hands on the wheel, focusing on the gold wedding band wrapped around his finger. She was so lucky to have this, to have them—a home, a family.

She stared at her mother's pretty profile as she sat up straight in the passenger seat, looking out the windshield, forever watching. They were almost back to the Miller's. Hailey settled her head on the rest, closed her eyes again, content, safe. She blinked them open as the bright lights of an on-coming vehicle blinded her. Hailey threw her arm against her forehead in defense.

"What's this guy doing?" Daddy swerved to the right, toward the shoulder, catching another patch of ice.

"Harold! Harold!"

The car spun once, twice, gaining speed as her mother gasped and her father swore. Metal slammed against tree trunk with a deafening smash. Hailey flew forward as she heard her mom scream. Jeremy woke on a strangled cry as the oncoming vehicle collided with the driver's side door, sending the car flying again, crushing Jeremy and

Mom against another tree trunk.

Dazed, Hailey sat back. The car was silent but for her sobbing breaths. She glanced around in the dark. Daddy was slumped over the steering wheel. Mom leaned forward, her body sagging against the seatbelt, her head dangling. Hailey stared at her brother, at the blood oozing from his temple.

"Mom. Daddy," Hailey said in a whisper, unable to find her voice. Her breathing came in spasms as she tried to sit up, but the seatbelt held her in place. She fought the confinement, reaching, stretching for Jeremy. "Jeremy!" She jumped, startled by her own scream. "Mom, Daddy, Jeremy's bleeding! Wake up and help me. I'm *stuck*!"

No one moved. No one rushed to help.

She struggled against her belt again, fumbling with the release. It was jammed. Hands shaking, she tugged and pulled, but the thick strap wouldn't budge. "Mom, help me! Daddy." Why wouldn't they move? Why wouldn't they help?

Tears coursed down her cheeks. "Mom!" She scraped and clawed at the thick fabric trapping her in place, her fingers aching as she ripped the skin from the tips, desperate to free herself from her prison.

Just then, another set of lights blinded her. A pickup came to a screeching halt yards away. Two people ran forward, shouting, peaking through the spider-cracked glass.

"Help me! I'm stuck!" Hailey couldn't allow herself to focus on her family. They lay there as if they no longer lived.

In the back of her mind, somewhere dark, somewhere deep, she knew; but she wouldn't let herself believe. Instead, Hailey concentrated only on her belt, on her need to be free.

"We'll get you out of there, honey. Hold on. I'm going

to call for help," a man's voice said before she heard him run off.

Hailey stared at her mother again. The headlights of the pickup showcased the streams of crimson dripping from her ear, from her nose, from her mouth. Daddy's face still lay pressed against the deflated airbag, its white cloth smeared with blood. She looked at Jeremy, willing him to move, to make a noise, to do *something*. "Jeremy, please wake up. Please."

He didn't respond.

She tried again, her voice desperate, pleading on a sob. "Please, Jeremy, *please*. Don't let me be here alone. Don't leave me by myself." She remembered being by herself before Mom and Daddy saved her all those years ago.

The men ran back, peering into the window again. The one in a ball cap tried the door, shaking the vehicle with his effort to open it. "It's stuck. We're going to have to bust the window, Billy."

The bearded guy, Billy, cupped his hands around the glass, making eye contact with Hailey. "Honey, do you have something you can cover your face with? We have to break the window."

She stared into his eyes, trying to focus on his words before she looked around at her silent family. Why couldn't she concentrate?

"Honey, cover your face with the blanket so we can get you out of there."

Hailey picked up the end of the fleece Daddy had handed her, pressed the soft fabric against her cheeks.

"That a girl." Billy pounded at the glass and Hailey screamed, jolted by the noise. Within seconds, cold air slapped her face as warm hands brushed her forehead. Billy used a tool to slice her free from her seatbelt prison. "There we go, honey. Let's get you out. The door's stuck. Let me help you climb through."

"My family—what about my family?"

The guy with the ball cap peered in, meeting her eyes before turning to Billy, shaking his head. "Let's get you out first."

She didn't want to leave, but she didn't want to stay. Billy reached in as blue lights and sirens approached in the distance. She heard the faint whimper behind her and turned. Jeremy lifted his hand to his temple and winced.

"Jeremy?" Fear and relief washed through her as a tear spilled over her cheek. Was this real? Was Jeremy really moving, or did she need to believe he wasn't going to leave her behind? Tugging out of Billy's grip, Hailey crawled over broken glass to her brother. "Jeremy. Oh, Jeremy." She clutched at his blood-soaked fingers. "You didn't leave me."

"Hailey?" Her brother stared at her, his brows furrowed.

"Yes, it's me."

"I want Mom."

She glanced at her mother, who was still bleeding, still silent. Despite her own trickles of grief, her instinct to protect kicked in—the one she developed the day the social worker dropped off her badly bruised new little brother. "We'll see mom soon."

Jeremy touched his wound, dropped his hand, closed his eyes again.

"Jeremy?" Panicked, Hailey shook his arm. "Jeremy?"

Billy reached in, grabbed her shoulder. "Don't shake him, honey. You don't want to hurt him more than he already is. The fire trucks are here. The firemen will take care of him. Let's get you out so they can help him."

Hailey clutched at her brother, refusal on her tongue, but the man's kind eyes and gentle voice coaxed her to put her brother's hand back on his lap. She covered Jeremy with her blanket, moved toward the calm, encouraging voice. "That's a girl. Come on now." He grabbed her under the armpits, freeing her from the wreckage of the car.

Firemen rushed to her family's vehicle, and the one still smashed into its side. Police officers spoke into radios. A paramedic crouched in front of Hailey, settled a thick blanket over her shoulders. "Are you hurt?"

"I—I don't think so." She glanced down at her fingers, torn and bloody from her seatbelt battle.

"Let's get you on a stretcher anyway." He lifted her to the bed.

Hailey stared at the mangled maroon sedan. "What about my family? Is my family going to be okay?"

"I'm not sure." The paramedic wrapped a blood pressure cuff around her arm as a police officer walked up to the ambulance.

The officer stared into her eyes. "They're getting your brother out now. How old is he, sweetheart?"

"He'll be ten in March."

"How old are you?"

"Fourteen—almost fifteen."

"The deceased's car is registered to a Harold and Loraine Sturgis," the officer's radio belched. He pressed the button and "ten-foured" dispatch.

Deceased. The word hung in the frigid air. Her parents were deceased. In her heart of hearts, she'd known, but the word gave her a truth she didn't want to hear. *Deceased* changed everything. "My parents are dead."

"Why don't we get you down to the hospital?" the paramedic said.

Hailey grabbed the policeman's hand before he could walk away. "My mom and dad are dead."

He nodded. "Your parents didn't make it."

Foggy shock fuzzed her brain as a cooling numbness took over, a defense mechanism she'd learned many years before. She hadn't needed the layer of protection in almost a decade, but she needed it now, so clung to it.

"What will happen to me and my brother? Will they split us up? We're foster kids."

"I don't know. Let's get you to the hospital. We'll figure things out from there."

The firemen pulled Jeremy from the mangled car, unconscious, his neck in a brace. Why couldn't he be okay? Why couldn't she take his hand and run with him into the forest? Her parents were dead, the only parents she had ever known. Now they were gone.

Hailey's veneer of cold was slipping; the crushing weight of grief was taking over. Mom and Daddy—the only people who'd ever loved her. The only people who'd given her a chance.

Jeremy was whisked into an ambulance. "Can I ride with him?"

"No. He needs to get their fast."

Two hours later, Hailey sat behind a curtain in the ER, listening to the murmurs in the cordoned off areas around her. Booted feet stopped outside her enclosure before a hand with painted pink fingernails yanked the light blue fabric back. "Hailey Roberts?"

Hailey clammed up. The dull, overtired eyes, the cheap suit—it all screamed social worker. Ten years in the system told her she was about to be given her fate.

"You are Hailey Roberts, correct?"

"Yes. Where's Helen? Where's my brother?"

"Helen is away on vacation for the holidays. She'll take over your case again once she returns next week, but in the meantime, you're stuck with me. I'm Denise Schlotter."

"Where's my brother? Where's Jeremy?"

"He's down the hall. He just came from x-ray."

"I want to see him."

"You can't right now. We've found you a place to stay until Helen comes back. It's a good, Christian family. They have three young children of their own and two foster kids. They said they would be happy to have you for the time being."

"What about Jeremy? Is he coming too?" That was all she cared about—her brother. She couldn't lose her family. He was all she had left.

Denise glanced at her paperwork. "He has to stay here for now. He has a concussion."

Hailey fiddled with the bandages covering her aching fingers, trying to keep her nerves at bay. "When will he come? Tomorrow? The day after?"

Denise blew out a heavy sigh. "Hailey, let's be straight with one another here. You've been in the system a long time. You've been very lucky to have what you did. You're a good girl. You make excellent grades. You never get in trouble. By some miracle, you've risen above your first four years. Your brother, however, has not. He's a young man with several problems. Your parents have had their hands full with him."

Instantly on the defense of her brother, Hailey sat up. "Jeremy's making progress—that's what his therapist said. You can't take him away from me. We're all each other has." Fear clogged her throat as she saw the refusal in Denise's dull brown eyes. Hailey cloaked her terror in anger. "If you take him away from me, he'll only get worse. My parents would want us to be together."

"Unfortunately, I don't see that as an option." Denise blew out another long breath. "Let me give you some advice. You have just over three years left in the system. You're birthday's next week. Play your cards straight; keep doing well in school. You might actually make something of yourself." She gave Hailey's shoe a pat. "Mrs. Frazier, your new foster parent—for the time-being—should be here soon. I need to speak with the doctor about your release. I'll be back."

The curtain snapped shut and she was alone. The carousel ride she'd avoided her whole life was about to begin. Her stomach clutched with nausea, not only from losing her parents—which she still couldn't fully grasp—but from the loss of a brother who might as well be dead. What would being tossed from home to home like someone's old trash do to him?

Hailey hopped to her feet, panicked, terrified. She had to see Jeremy, to tell him what was going on, to say goodbye before Denise told him with as little compassion as she'd told her. Lips trembling, Hailey sniffed and wiped at a tear threatening to fall. She had to be strong for him.

Hailey peeked from the side of the drab blue curtain. Denise was speaking with someone at the nurse's station and Hailey made her escape.

Walking hurriedly down the hall, she prayed she was heading in the right direction. She gasped as the doctor who'd treated her turned the corner. Hailey whirled, rushed into the small bathroom, crossing her fingers he hadn't noticed her.

Knees trembling, hands shaking, she twisted the lock. Closing her eyes, Hailey rested her back against the door, trying to get a grip on her shaky emotions. After three deep breaths, she still couldn't settle.

She opened her eyes, stared at her reflection in the mirror. Her honey-colored eyes were wide with fear and sorrow. Pretty light brown ringlets hung at her shoulders. Mom had helped her curl her hair for the party.

You're such a young lady now, Hailey, and so beautiful. I'm so lucky I have you.

Her mother had hugged her one-armed as she released the iron from a tendril of hair. Hailey choked on a gasping sob, desperately wanting that moment back.

She shook her head, growing frustrated. She couldn't go to Jeremy like this. How would she convince him everything was going to be all right if she couldn't believe it herself? *Think of Jeremy, Hailey, only Jeremy. He needs you.* With a last steeling breath, Hailey turned away from the mirror. She opened the door a crack and left the bathroom when she was certain the coast was clear.

Hailey peered into each room until she found the little boy with his arm taped and boarded, an IV stuck in place, a brace snug around his neck. Shiny brown curls stood in wild tufts against bright white bandages. His eyes were closed, his sleeping face angelic and pale.

Hailey stepped forward, gathering her strength. She touched Jeremy's warm little hand and his lids fluttered opened.

"Sissy?"

She smiled, brushing the hair from his forehead. "Hi." How would she say goodbye? How would she tell him they couldn't be together anymore?

"I can't move my head." He tugged at the brace.

"The doctors are keeping your neck safe. It'll be okay." She stared into Jeremy's chocolate brown eyes, shades darker than her own, and his light beige complexion, so much like hers. If only they shared blood, the State would keep them together.

"Where's Mom and Daddy, Hailey?" Jeremy clutched at her sore, bandaged fingers. "My head hurts. I want mom and daddy."

She twisted the pretty pearl ring on her finger—the heirloom their mother had given her for her fourteenth birthday—desperate for the right words, willing their mother to send them to her. Mom had always known just what to say. "Mom and Daddy had to go away. They had to go to heaven and be angels."

Tears leaked from the side of Jeremy's eyes, coursing

into the bandages wrapped around his head. "I want them to come back."

"They can't. They have to stay there."

Jeremy's lips trembled. "I'm scared."

"Me too." She had no choice but to admit it.

"I want to go home. When can we go home?"

"We can't go home anymore, Jeremy. We have to live somewhere else now."

Wild terror filled his eyes as he tried to sit up. "I want to go *home*."

Hailey held him down. "We can't. We're going to live with different families. They'll be nice to us and help us, just like Mom and Daddy." She desperately wanted to believe it.

Jeremy started to wail. Hailey ran over and shut the glass slider. If they found her in here, they would make her leave. She hurried back, shushing Jeremy, trying to be patient. They didn't have much time. "Hush now, Jeremy." She stroked at his forehead again. "I have a plan, but you need to quiet down and listen."

Jeremy's crying turned into gasps of unsteady air. "Okay."

"We have to go away from each other for awhile."

He clutched her fingers again.

"I'm going to come back for you when I turn eighteen. That's not too long from now. When I turn eighteen, I'll find you and take you away. But you need to be good. You have to stop doing bad stuff at school and try hard. Mom and daddy are going to be watching you from heaven and they want you to be a good boy. It'll make it harder for me to get you if you don't behave. Do you understand?"

"Yes. But I'm going to miss you."

"I'm going to miss you too, but I'll think of you every day. I'll never stop loving you. I won't forget you; I promise." She hooked her pinky with his. "I promise I won't forget you. I promise I'm going to come get you. Do you believe me?"

He sniffed. "Yes."

"Good." She kissed his lips, then tried to smile.

The glass door slid open. Hailey whipped a glance over her shoulder.

"There you are, Hailey. I was afraid you'd run off." Denise stood next to a tall, thin woman with black hair and a dower face. She clutched a maroon bible in her bony left hand.

Her time was up. Hailey ignored the tired looking women and turned her attention back to her brother. "I have to go, Jeremy. Remember my promise."

Jeremy began to sob as he held her arm in a vise-like grip. Desperate to give comfort, frantic to stay, she stared down at her ring. It was her only link to Loraine, the only mother she would ever have, but she took it off. "Here. I want you to have this. This will help you remember me. Every time you look at it, think of me and know I'm thinking of you. Don't forget that I'm coming for you. I love you, Jeremy."

"I love you, too."

"It's time to go, Hailey." Denise wrapped her arm around Hailey's shoulder, tugging against the strength of the determined and frightened boy.

"Don't leave me, Sissy! Please don't leave me!"

"I don't want to, Jeremy." Her voice broke, as did her heart. "I don't have a choice. I love you." Denise dragged her away and out the door, shutting the glass, silencing the wails of her brother as Mrs. Frazier mumbled scripture from the Bible.

Hailey stared over her shoulder, looking into her brother's shattered eyes, until she rounded the corner and lost sight of him. And lost hope.

CHAPTER 2

December 2013

HAILEY BENT DOWN AND PICKED up the deflated remains of two pink balloons. She tossed them in the trash along with pale yellow streamers and white baby duck confetti.

"Thanks, Hailey. I'd do that myself, but..." Sarah shrugged and brushed her hands over her enormous belly.

"Take a load off, Sarah. I've got this."

"You don't have to ask twice." Sarah blew out a breath as she settled herself in a dining room chair. "I'm ready for little Emma here to make her debut. I want to bend down again, to tie my own shoes. I can't wait to be able to see my toes," she chuckled.

Hailey grinned. "Three more weeks...or less," she added quickly when Sarah's smile faded. "I bet she'll be here before your due date." She swiped up another balloon, shoved it in the trash bag. "Are you still going away next weekend?"

"We're planning to. Our last weekend away—just the three of us. We want it to be special for Kylee. Everything's about to change. Can you still take care of Bear and Reece?"

"Yeah, absolutely. I just wasn't sure. You seem really uncomfortable."

"After Emma drops a bit I'll feel better." Sarah rubbed her palms in circles over her mound of baby. "How's the new apartment? How are things working out with Jeremy back in your life?"

"So far, so good." Hailey beamed. "He found a job—a pretty decent one, in fact. He already bought a car and hasn't been late with his half of the rent yet. I think that baby face of his helps him clean up in the tip department. I want him to get back to school, but we'll start with steady employment first."

"*You're* still going back to school next month, right?"

"Of course." Hailey sat in the chair next to Sarah, met the worried look in her eyes. "This is a good thing, Sarah. Having my brother back in my life makes me happy. I know Jeremy's had some trouble, but he's trying to change. I have to give him a chance. He hasn't had anyone."

"Oh, honey, I know."

Hailey picked up a piece of confetti, fiddled with the pink paper, feeling like a broken record. She'd had the same conversation with her old roommates yesterday at their once-a-month lunch bunch. "My parents died before Jeremy had an opportunity to turn himself around. I haven't had a moment's trouble with him over the last two months."

"I just worry a little bit because I love you so much." Sarah took her hand. "You're so good at taking care of everyone else. I want to be sure you're taking care of yourself, too."

Hailey gave her fingers a squeeze. "I am. And I love you too."

"Have you heard anything about Project Mexico?"

"No." Hailey blew out a frustrated sigh. "I'm starting to think it isn't going to happen. I really wanted to go, but the application pool is enormous. I could've made a difference, and the free credit hours wouldn't have sucked either." She jerked her shoulders, trying not to wallow in the gloom of a missed opportunity. "I'm going to sign up for two of the counseling classes I need when campus opens Monday morning. That's what I can swing this semester."

"Hailey, we can lend you—"

"No," she cut Sarah off. "Sorry," she smiled, her voice becoming gentler. "I appreciate the offer, but it's important to me that I pay my own way. You and Ethan are more than generous with my wage." She already owed them so much. They included her in holidays, birthdays, vacations. She'd been a bridesmaid in their late-summer wedding. She was always made to feel as if she belonged. For that she owed Ethan and Sarah everything.

"You're excellent with Kylee and she loves you. We all do. As far as I'm concerned, you're priceless." Sarah jumped slightly, smiled. "Emma's awake."

"Can I feel?"

Sarah took Hailey's hand, pressed her palm to her stomach. Emma jabbed and kicked about.

Hailey grinned, thrilled, fascinated. "Was that a foot, an elbow, or a knee?"

"I think a foot." Sarah beamed.

Hailey felt the jab again and yearned to know the joy of a life growing inside her, to know the bond a mother feels for her child—or most mothers, anyway. "She's spunky. Emma's gonna give us a run for our money."

"I think you might be right. She is a Cooke after all." Sarah chuckled.

"Hey, I heard that." Ethan entered the room, sweaty in his workout clothes. "Wow, look at all the loot." He walked over, pressed a kiss to the top of Sarah's head. "Did you have fun?"

"Yes, I did. Did you, Austin, and Hunter enjoy punching each other?"

"Boxing each other," Ethan corrected. "And yes, we did. I'm just sorry Morgan and Hunter had to leave so quickly. I owe him a right hook to the jaw." He gave his own jaw a testing wiggle as he smoothed a hand over

15

his chin.

"Where's Austin?"

That's what Hailey wanted to know. It never sucked to get a good look at Austin Casey. His tall, powerful build, strong square chin, and firm lips on a killer face gave her heart a solid pitter-pat every time. Not only was Austin a hottie, but he was teddy bear-sweet with just a hint of bad boy to keep things interesting—a lethal combination in her mind.

He walked through the doorway, brown hair damp from a shower. "Hey, Sarah. Hey, Hailey."

A slow smile spread across his face, and, as predicted, Hailey's heart gave a good solid thwack against her ribs as butterflies danced in her stomach. She brushed a hand against her tummy, trying to quiet the flutter. "Hey," she said casually as she reached for the black trash bag and stood.

Hailey had known him over three years, had spent weeks with him behind the walls of Ethan's estate during Sarah's nightmare stalker experience, yet Austin never failed to tie her stomach into knots when he grinned at her like that. Instead of standing and staring like an idiot, she stooped forward, snatched up more pieces of baby shower confetti, sneaking glances at his dark green eyes. She loved the color, could look into them for hours. They reminded her of a forest of pine trees.

"Wow." Austin scanned the room, whistling through his teeth. "I think Emma has everything she'll need."

"And then some," Sarah said, smiling.

He leaned in and kissed Sarah's cheek. "How are you feeling?"

"Like I'm ready to have this baby. How's your sister? The stork is circling around her place these days, too."

"Actually, my mom called an hour ago. Christie went into labor. I should be an uncle again by

16

tomorrow morning."

"Don't make me hate her, Austin." Although Sarah's tone sounded serious, humor brightened her pretty blue eyes.

"Emma will be here before you know it," he reassured her.

"You're very sweet. Do you want some cake?"

He eyed the remains of the two-tiered work of art. "It's tempting, but I've gotta run. I told my mom I'd give my great aunt a ride to the airport. She's getting too old to drive, and I don't want her on a bus or taxi."

Hailey all but melted as she walked to the kitchen for plastic wrap and a plate. How could she resist a man who worried about little old ladies? She hurried back, cut a huge section of pink fondant ribbon and white cake, wrapped it, and handed it off to Austin. "Here you go. I would hate to see this go to waste. I'm pretty sure Wren drove the baker crazy concocting this design." Their fingers brushed as he took the plate, sending skitters of heat along her skin while he appeared completely unaffected.

"Thanks." He smiled. "This definitely won't go to waste."

Sarah yawned. "I hate to be a party pooper, but I'm going to catch a quick nap while Kylee's still taking hers."

Ethan rubbed her shoulders. "Can you wait one second? I have some news."

"Sure. Is everything all right?"

"More than. I got a call before I came in—from the University. The Dean wanted to tell me they've accepted Ethan Cooke Security's bid to oversee Project Mexico."

Hailey couldn't help but feel excitement for Ethan and a tinge of disappointment for herself. "Awesome. Congratulations."

"There's more. I probably shouldn't say anything, but I'm going to anyway. My secretary faxed over the student roster, and I couldn't help but notice Hailey's name among the winter semester participants. Your letter should be in the mail."

The trash Hailey picked up fell from her fingers. "What?"

"You're going to Mexico, señorita." Ethan winked.

She pressed her lips together as Ethan's news sunk in. "I'm going to Mexico?" She clasped her hands to her chest as her heart galloped wildly. "I get to go?" She let out a squeal and launched herself into Ethan's arms. "Oh, my God. This is so great. I'm going to Mexico!" She leaned down and smothered Sarah in a tight hug. Overcome with excitement, she grabbed Austin around his muscular waist and held on. His arm came around her.

"Congratulations, kid."

"Thanks." She was too amazed by her stellar luck to acknowledge the inner-cringe that usually accompanied 'kid'. Austin was barely four years older, yet he seemed to think of her as a pimply-faced adolescent.

Small footsteps padded down the hall, stopping in the doorway. Kylee, with her sleep-pinked cheeks, held Mr. Ruff, her stuffed dog. "Hi."

Hailey broke away from Austin and scooped her up. "Hi, pretty princess. I'm going to Mexico." She spun in two quick circles, making Kylee laugh.

"I guess I'll nap later," Sarah said, letting out another yawn.

"No way. Go up to bed. Rest. I'll take care of Kylee for awhile." Hailey gave Kylee a noisy kiss. "Jeremy's working at the restaurant tonight, and I have nothing waiting for me at home."

"Hailey, you don't have to," Ethan said, as his cell phone started to ring. He checked the readout. "It's dispatch. Hold that thought." He stepped from the room, popped his head back in. "Would you mind staying for a few minutes after all? Spain just called. They're having an issue."

"Not even a little. Sarah, go to bed. Kylee and I are going out to play on the swings. I'll throw some dinner together after."

Sarah pushed off the back of the seat in her attempt to stand. Austin rushed forward and took her arm, helping her up. "Thanks," she said to Austin. "I owe you one, Hailey."

"No, you don't. Let's go play," she nuzzled Kylee, grabbed their jackets from the entryway closet, and headed out the door with Bear and Reece, Ethan's golden Bullmastiffs, at her heels. There was nothing she loved more than being needed. Right now, she was exactly where she was supposed to be.

Austin caught the door before she could close it. "I'm heading out too."

"Oh, sorry." She smiled. "See you around."

He walked down the steps to his honey of a sports convertible, giving her and Kylee a quick wave. "Yeah, see you." He got in, started the engine, and drove off.

Hailey huffed out a wistful sigh as she watched the taillights disappear down the long drive.

Two hours later, Austin pulled into his reserved parking spot at Palisades Luxury Apartments. He grabbed his huge slab of cake from the passenger's seat and headed for the door. He swiped his card, let himself into the posh lobby, with its elegantly draped windows, ornate wood furnishings and potted palms scattered about. He stopped at his mailbox, snagging the free pizza advertisement taped to his box, before the uptight building manager spotted the florescent fliers and threw a fit for dicking with her ambiance. As he continued, he spotted the bright orange paper stuck to Hailey's box as well. He plucked it up and kept going.

Instead of taking the elevator, Austin started up the stairs, pushing through the glass door to the second floor hallway, contemplating what he would add for toppings to his free large pizza with his order of breadsticks and two-liter soda—chicken and onion or ham and pineapple?

He crouched down next to Hailey's door, ready to send the flyer under, when he heard a crash. *What the hell?* Austin abandoned his cake as he pulled his gun free and stood.

"What the fuck, man? Why'd you fucking hit me?"

Austin stepped closer, recognizing Hailey's brother's voice.

"You're lucky I'm only hitting you, punk. I should slice your throat. You try to undercut me again, homeboy, and I'll take your dick too. This is the big time, man. These motherfuckers aren't fucking around. Consider this your warning—your *only* warning. Next time, you're dead. You sell what I give you, then you get your cut. That's how this works. I won't tell you again."

Bone cracked against bone and something fell to the floor, shattering.

"All right. Okay. I get the point," Jeremy said in a groan.

"Not yet." Another punch was thrown. "I'm still educating you. Hopefully, you'll learn, or you won't live very long."

Jeremy took another blow and coughed.

"You work for me now. There's no going back."

Austin's hand hovered over the doorknob. He wanted to listen to the conversation play out, but they would kill Jeremy if this kept up. He gripped the knob as the room fell silent.

"I think we understand each other now, don't you, homeboy?"

There was no answer.

"I said, don't you?"

"Yes," Jeremy wheezed.

Footsteps started toward the door. Austin holstered his weapon, grabbed the plate of cake.

"Wait a minute. Wait a minute. Hold up here, brother. Who's this fine piece of ass? This your girl?"

Silence.

The man landed another blow. "I said is this your ho?"

"No," Jeremy coughed. "My sister."

"Well, well, well. You watch your step, man, or I'll be helping myself to her before I kill you." Something clattered to the floor and glass broke. "You be at the drop spot tomorrow, and don't be late. I better see you at two, homie."

The knob twisted. Austin hustled to his apartment, pulled his keys from his pocket as if he'd just gotten home. Hailey's door opened. A man as big as he was, wearing sagging jeans and a long basketball jersey, stepped into the hall. Every inch of his exposed skin was intricately inked with devils, skeletons, and words Austin couldn't make out without staring. A shorter man, dressed similarly, looked over his shoulder, making eye contact before he stared forward again.

Gang bangers.

Austin set the plate on the floor, searched through his keys, stalling, catching small glimpses as the shorter man punched the button for the elevator. A boldly colored S-1 tat extended from his raw knuckles to his wrist. As the elevator slid open, Austin shoved his key in the lock, twisted it, waiting for the door to slide closed.

Alone in the hallway, he hurried to the stairwell, watching from the window until the men got in their car and took off. He doubled back and knocked on Hailey's door. When no one answered, Austin knocked again.

Jeremy opened the door a crack. His curly brown hair stood in wild tufts. His raw face swelled with nasty gashes and severe bruising. "Hey, Austin. This isn't a good time."

Austin pushed the door open, ignoring Jeremy's not-so-subtle hint. Jeremy appeared to be mixed up with the wrong crowd, had dragged his sister into it. Right now was a very good time. "Wow, buddy, what happened to you?"

"I got mugged. I brought in good tips today; somebody must've been watching—followed me home." Jeremy's lip dribbled blood as he spoke. His eye puffed shut as Austin watched.

"Looks like I'm in the wrong line of work. You must've had some wad." Austin scanned the trashed space. The coffee table leaned haphazardly, two of its legs splintered to bits. Glass vases and knickknacks lay smashed and scattered over the area rug. Amongst the chaos of the living room, the cracked photo of Hailey caught his eye.

"Yeah." Jeremy coughed, wincing, holding his boot-scuffed ribs. "Look, I need to lie down."

"We should call the police and report this. Let me grab you a shirt. I'll take you to the hospital."

"No," Jeremy said quickly. "My boss already took care of it. I called him as soon as this happened. I just need to lie down."

"You sure?" Did Jeremy really expect him to buy this?

"Yeah." He grimaced.

"Okay. Oh, this was stuck to your mailbox." Austin held up the florescent orange flyer. "I wanted to drop it off before Linda took them all down. They make a damn good pizza. Knock if you need anything—2H."

"Uh huh." Jeremy hobbled forward and grabbed the paper as the door closed.

Austin stared at the chrome 2E on dark wood for several seconds, rubbing his fingers over his tensed jaw.

What the hell was he supposed to do now? That kid was bad news—the scum of the earth. Austin was familiar with his type—saw them every day. Jeremy would suck his sister dry before he vanished again.

He turned, wandered back to his apartment, thinking of Hailey, trying to ignore the tug of desire her striking face and siren's body always brought with them. All that smooth, golden skin...her top-heavy lip that begged to be nibbled...those enormous honey-colored eyes and dainty nose...an odd combination with mouthwatering effects. He struggled not to notice every time he saw her. And he saw her a lot.

When she had thrown her arms around him in a hug hours before, he'd breathed in her peachy scent, felt her small, firm breasts against his side, and fought to keep things casual. Closing his eyes, he clutched the doorknob, trying to find a grip on his hormones, determined not to let his attraction to Hailey affect him. She was in trouble and oblivious to the whole thing. He was going to have to keep an eye on her until they left for Mexico. Hopefully, when they got back, Jeremy would be long gone.

Steadier, Austin picked up his plate of cake and let himself into his living room. He twisted on the lamp, looked around, sniffing at the hint of lemon scenting the air. The cleaning lady had come. The week's worth of dust had been swept away from the dark heavy wood. The plants he didn't bother with, but Wren had insisted on, had sprung back to life with a little water.

Ethan's sister had more or less taken over his space with her high-end designs, but he couldn't complain. She'd done a hell of a job decorating his bachelor pad. He sighed a thank you every time he sat in the chunky brown leather couch or recliner. It beat the hell out of the milk crates and cheap futon he'd had before.

Austin set the plate on the coffee table, along with the

flyer and his keys, and powered up his laptop. He had one goal at this point: to find out just who Jeremy was.

What was his last name?

He sat against the buttery, soft leather, sighed, punched Ethan's number into his cell phone.

"Cooke."

"Hey, what's Hailey's brother's last name?"

"That's random."

"I think Hailey's in trouble. I'll explain tomorrow. Let me do a little digging first."

"I think it's Kagan. Yeah, I'm pretty sure it's Kagan."

"Thanks."

"Should I have her stay here tonight?"

He thought of the state of Hailey's trashed living room, of Jeremy's battered face and body. It would be better if she stayed away, but she would see her living room and brother eventually. "No, but she's in for a hell of a shock. I walked by her apartment. Heard a couple of bangers beating the shit out of Jeremy. Her place is trashed. You might want to give her a heads-up."

"What the hell is he doing with people like that?"

"That's what I'm hoping to find out. Let me look into this. I'll get back to you." Austin hung up, and quickly got to work hacking through firewalls, just the way Ethan showed him years before.

He started by tracking down Jeremy's date of birth and social security number. From there, he searched court documents, sealed juvenile records, let out a quiet whistle when he hit pay dirt with a police rap sheet. "You've been busy, kid," he muttered. Breaking and entering, multiple drug possession charges with intent to sell, four simple assault convictions, DUI, underage drinking, petty theft, possession of a deadly weapon. "Two visits to the 'big house'. Looks like you're on strike two. One more and you're out, buddy."

Did Hailey know about this? He couldn't believe she did. Over the years he and Hailey had become friends. She was a sweetheart with a good head on her shoulders; her brother didn't fit with the life she'd made for herself.

Rubbing his fingers over his jaw, Austin blew out a long breath. He needed to find out how deep Jeremy's ties were with S-1. There was nothing more he could do until tomorrow.

He exed out of the files, sat back, picked up his phone again, and ordered a large pizza with grilled chicken and onion. He turned on the TV, flipped to the Raiders highlights, all the while thinking of Hailey.

CHAPTER 3

USTIN BATTLED L.A.'S MID-MAY TRAFFIC on his way to Yoshoris, the trendy Japanese restaurant he'd overheard Hailey say Jeremy worked at. This wasn't exactly how he'd planned to spend his day off. A run along the beach, a few laps in the pool, and a Skype session with his sister to welcome his newest niece had been the original idea.

He came to a dead stop on the 405—again—in a clusterfuck of vehicles as far as the eye could see. Thank God he only had one more exit to go. He rubbed his fingers against his temple, along his jaw, blew out a long breath, more tired and less patient than usual.

He hadn't slept much last night. When Ethan called at nine, he'd waited by the window until he saw Hailey pull into the parking lot. He'd watched her race into the lobby. He cracked his door, listening to the elevator slide open moments later.

Austin knew Hailey had found the mess in her living room and her beaten brother when her door slammed closed, followed by a shocked, "Oh, my God." He'd walked to 2E, standing close to the door, listening to snatches of Jeremy's bullshit story. Of course, Hailey had eaten it up. When Austin heard all he could stand, he went back to his apartment, sick inside, concerned, and more involved than he wanted to be.

As a result, there he sat, stuck in traffic, trying to get to the bottom of a situation that was between Hailey and her brother. Except he truly believed she had no idea Jeremy was mixed up with the big time. Austin remembered the thug with the S-1 tattoo commenting on Hailey's photo. He still couldn't believe her jackass brother hadn't tried to leave her out of it—selfish bastard. Hailey was in danger; he would do what he could to help. That's what friends were for.

The traffic inched forward, enough for Austin to hug the shoulder and get to his exit. He took the off-ramp and drove the ten blocks to Yoshoris at a crawl, smiling when he actually found a space to parallel park. He stepped from his vehicle, crossed the street, peeked into the empty restaurant, glancing at a small, stylish sign that said they didn't open until five.

Austin knocked on the glass when he spotted a woman sitting in the corner of the dining area surrounded by a pile of papers. She glanced up as he took his wallet from his pocket and pressed his badge to the window. It was only his bodyguard identification, but it looked official enough to get her to unlock the door.

"Hi." He smiled. "I'm sorry to bother you. I'm looking for a friend. Is Jeremy here?"

The woman's brows furrowed as she shook her head. "I'm sorry, sir, I don't know a Jeremy."

Austin scratched his cheek as if contemplating and looked up at the restaurant sign. "This is the only Yoshoris in L.A., right?"

"Yes."

"And you don't employ a Jeremy Kagan?"

"I do the hiring myself. I've never heard of him."

Just what he'd thought. "I'm sorry I took up your time, ma'am."

"Not a problem." She closed the door and twisted the lock.

Austin glimpsed his watch. Twelve fifteen. He had less than two hours to get through traffic and back to the apartments. He fully intended to follow Jeremy and find out what he was really doing to bring in an income, although he had a fairly solid idea.

Austin pulled into the parking lot at one fifteen, relieved that Jeremy's car still sat in its spot. He reached into the bag of fast food he'd stopped for, grabbed the grilled chicken, no mayo. His phone rang as he took a huge bite of the sandwich. He checked the readout; it was Ethan.

"Hold on," Austin said over a mouthful.

"Stuffing your face as usual."

He swallowed. "It's after one. I have to eat lunch sometime."

"Did you sleep in, princess?"

He grinned, took another bite, talking with his mouth full. "No, I've been in my car for most of the day. I'm following Jeremy. Brother dear is definitely mixed up in some serious shit. I'm pretty confident he's dealing drugs."

"Son of a bitch."

"It gets better. Not only is he dealing, but the bangers who kicked his ass last night are S-1. They were covered in gang tattoos. There's definitely a connection."

"You've gotta be fucking kidding me. Hailey went ape shit when I told her that Jeremy had been injured. I can't imagine what she'll do when she finds out about this."

"Thanks for keeping it discreet. I don't want to say anything until I know exactly what we're dealing with."

"I figured as much. So, what's the plan?"

"I overheard one of the guys tell Jeremy he'd better be at some drop spot at two. I'm going to follow him to the location—whenever he decides to get his butt out here."

"I'm glad Sarah and I decided to leave early."

"Oh yeah?"

"Yeah, Sarah had some mild contractions last night. We're thinking we should take Kylee to California Kids now or her indoor water park adventure isn't going to happen anytime soon. It works out well that this is the perfect excuse to keep Hailey out of the way. She'll be staying here for the next few days, provided Emma doesn't decide to join us before then."

Austin didn't miss the excitement in Ethan's voice. His little girl would be here soon. Ethan and Sarah had been friends for years before their relationship changed into something more serious several months back. They'd gotten off to a rough start when that crazy bastard, Ezekiel, put everyone through hell. But that was over now, and things had smoothed out for two of his closest friends. "Well, at least Hailey's safe for the time being. One of the men made a threat against her."

Ethan steamed out a weary sigh. "What a goddamn mess. Sounds like it's a good thing she'll be leaving town for a while."

"That's what I was thinking." The lobby door opened. Jeremy stepped out. "I have to go. Our man of the hour just arrived."

"Be careful. S-1 is nothing to mess around with."

"Oh, honey," Austin sniffled into the phone, "I'm so glad you care."

"Fuck you."

Austin chuckled as he hung up. His smile disappeared as he watched Jeremy take the steps from the lobby to the parking lot one at a time, wincing the entire way, holding his side. The kid's solid boxer build lost a bit of its intimidating effect as he walked hunched over, like Great Aunt Lucy.

Austin polished off his last bite of sandwich, following it up with a deep swallow of water as he studied Jeremy's swollen eye and the colorful bruising over most of his right cheek. His bottom lip was double its normal size. Austin almost felt bad for him. Almost.

Several minutes later, after a ginger walk to his car,

Jeremy got in and took a left out of the lot. Austin waited thirty seconds, then did the same. He followed Jeremy's black BMW through the tidy upscale neighborhoods of the Palisades to the mean streets of South Central L.A.

Graffiti-covered sidewalks and abandoned buildings gave way to ramshackle houses, proudly displaying green spray painted S-1 emblems over every inch. Austin's stomach sank as the reality of Hailey's situation became more apparent. After some quick research the night before, he'd discovered that S-1 was rumored to be the foot soldiers of the Mexican Mafia, pulling off grisly hits, drug trafficking, and kidnappings, among other criminal activities. Valid information had been hard to come by. Every reporter or blogger who had stuck their nose too deep either mysteriously vanished or ended up dead.

Jeremy pulled up to a dilapidated house and stopped the car. The two men Austin recognized from the night before stood from their perches on the sorry-looking stoop and walked toward him as he got out. As Jeremy exchanged knuckle bumps, Austin drove in the opposite direction; his sports car was too flashy not to be recognized if he got too close.

Austin circled the block, parking two hundred yards down, still within camera range with the long distance surveillance lens. He glanced at the burned out houses along the tired looking street, the thugs standing around, waiting to find trouble—or make it. He took his Glock from the center console, released the safety, set his weapon on the floor by his feet. Even with his training, it never hurt to be careful.

Austin picked up the camera, focused on Jeremy and the men still standing by the BMW. He zeroed in on the shorter man's tattoos, snapping away at the green and black emblems mirroring the markings painted on the houses. He tightened his focus on the elaborate slashes of red forming a 'ZU' on the inside of his forearm.

Satisfied he had enough on guy number one, Austin studied guy number two, noticing the same slashes of red among the ink of skulls and devils. He snapped several more photos for good measure. Just as Austin was about to set down the camera, a movement in the window of the derelict house caught his attention. He refocused, zooming in as far as the lens would allow. Through his grainy view, he captured images of a man in a black suit, surrounded by several well-armed bodyguards. Who the hell was this? *What* the hell was this? He clenched his jaw, knowing that whatever was going on, it wasn't good.

Austin honed in on Jeremy again when the muscled hulk covered in devils patted him down. Seconds later, they walked into the house. It was tempting to get out and move closer, but that wasn't a good idea in broad daylight. Instead, Austin scooted further forward in his seat and focused on Jeremy shaking the suited man's hand.

He muttered a curse as a guard moved, blocking his view. He waited patiently, eager to get more pictures, but Jeremy and the two men came back out not even five minutes later. Austin took more pictures of Jeremy carrying a black duffel bag. Jeremy popped his trunk, shoved the bag in the compartment where he kept his spare tire, then replaced the carpeted panel.

Any lingering doubts about Jeremy vanished. The kid was up to his eyeballs in gang and drug activity. Austin snapped more pictures until Jeremy got in his car and drove away.

Austin sighed as he set Ethan's surveillance camera on the passenger seat. "What a fucking mess." He turned the ignition, thought of Hailey. She'd been so happy when Jeremy walked back into her life a few weeks ago. What would it do to her when she found out her brother wasn't who she thought he was? From the small snatches of conversation he'd overheard, Hailey was nothing but proud of Jeremy. Austin imagined the truth would wound her deeply.

Austin blew out another breath and released the parking brake as his driver's side window smashed in fragments around him and the cold barrel of a 9 mm was pressed against his temple.

"Sweet ride, man. I want it. Get the fuck out."

Son of a bitch. "I've gotta engage the break." Austin tried to keep his voice easy as his heart rate accelerated.

"Don't try anything funny. Real slow or I'll fucking ax you, punk."

"Real slow, just like you said." Austin glanced down at his gun he couldn't reach, yanked up the break, and placed his hands on the wheel.

"Now get out."

"I'm getting out." The banger holding him hostage couldn't have been any more than seventeen, but that didn't make him less dangerous. The gleeful power radiating in the kid's voice made it worse. There was no value of life here. The same scenario could've played out over a pair of shoes. This was just a bonus.

"Bet your ass you are. Now, move."

He put his hands higher in the air as the kid with the green bandana knotted around his head reached in and unlocked the door. Austin unfolded his powerful body from the driver's seat and stood.

"Man, oh man, you're a big mother fucker." The banger licked his lips, radiating with nerves as he aimed at Austin's face again.

Austin kept his hands half raised as four other men, older, their eyes more brutal, moved in to surround him. *Well, shit.* As the odds quickly turned against him, he focused on staying steady, on keeping calm. He'd been in worse situations, but this one sucked pretty bad right now.

As long as he allowed them to think they had the upper hand, he would stay in control.

"Move forward." The kid gestured with his pistol.

Austin took two steps closer to the gun aimed at him.

"What we got here, Little G?" one of the men said as he continued to advance. "This your new ride?"

"Hell yeah."

Little G took another step toward Austin, cocky now. Austin saw his opportunity.

"We gonna—"

Before Little G finished, Austin grabbed the gun and put the kid in a sleeper hold. He was unconscious before the four gangsters could draw their knives or pistols from their pockets. He held the gun to the kid's temple. "I'd hate to have to shoot your pal here. Go ahead and back yourselves up."

"You're outnumbered, homie."

"Maybe." He aimed the pistol between one of the banger's feet and pulled the trigger. A bullet sparked less than an inch from his foot, landing in the dingy yard behind him. Austin repeated himself three more times, aiming within inches of each man's sneakers. "Or maybe not."

Two backed up, two turned and ran away.

"We just want your car, homie." The kid drew his gun, challenging.

"Yeah, but I want it more." Austin aimed at the kid's saggy jeans. "I bet you want to keep your balls, so I'm gonna suggest you drop that and stay back while I get in *my* car, or I'll shoot and I won't miss. I promise." He wiggled his finger on the trigger to send his point home, and the kid dropped the pistol.

Austin loosened his grip on Little G, sending him crumbling to the ground, still unconscious. He eyed the two remaining gangsters as he walked to his car, got in, and peeled away, ducking as a stray bullet shattered the glass of his back window. "Damn it."

He took the first turn, then another and another, until he was sure no one followed. Sweat beaded on his forehead, dripped down his back, as his sheen of calm vanished and adrenaline took over. He brushed the dampness away with his forearm, stretched his tensed shoulders as he drove closer to the 110 onramp. He accelerated onto the interstate, swearing profusely as wind surged through the broken windows.

This whole situation was a fucking nightmare. He glanced at the glitter of glass littering his floor, his seats, and clenched his jaw.

Enough was enough. It was time to get to the bottom of this, get a good look at the pictures he'd taken, and find out just what Hailey knew.

CHAPTER 4

A USTIN PULLED AROUND THE CIRCLE of Ethan's large driveway, stopping next to Hailey's car. The dark green compact had seen better days. The rust spot above the bumper had grown since the last time he'd parked behind the secondhand Ford.

He got out of his own damaged vehicle, swore again at the lack of glass in his driver's side and rear windows. He circled the car, running his fingers over the body, searching for bullet holes. When he didn't find any, he relaxed a fraction.

Luckily Sarah's sedan was parked in the garage. He would have to borrow it until he could get his windows fixed. With one last glance at the mess, Austin grabbed the camera through the gaping hole and let himself into the house with the key he'd been given.

Bear and Reece didn't greet him, nor did Hailey. They were somewhere among the ramble of rooms in the spacious home. Austin took advantage of going unnoticed, heading straight for Ethan's office. He shut the door, locked it, and booted up the state of the art computer system. Computer Forensics was Ethan's game. His equipment was top notch.

Austin sat in the comfy leather chair and uploaded the card of photos he'd captured. He flipped from one shot to the next, stopping on the picture of the intricate red 'ZU' inked into both of the men's arms. He turned his chair toward the second computer, called up information on the S-1 gang until he found a hit on the suspected affiliation between the S-1s and the Zulas—one of the most dangerous players in the Mexican Mafia. As he advanced his search, he discovered image after image of the same red tattoo, confirming that the symbols inked into the men's arms indeed held importance to the gang and cartel itself.

Austin flipped through the next few pictures, paused, staring at the grainy image of the man in the black suit. He played with the computer functions until he had a crystal clear picture of a surprisingly good-looking guy who couldn't be much older than he was. Who the hell was he, and what about him warranted bodyguards with assault rifles? Austin pressed a button on the keypad and the computer began a photo identification scan. Within twenty seconds a flashing green box popped up telling him a match was found.

Austin's heart froze as he scanned INTERPOL's information, realizing he stared at Donte Rodriguez, the Zulas second highest-ranking man—or rumored to be, anyway. Only one other person ranked higher; he was so elusive, INTERPOL had nothing more than a handful of scattered details about the most powerful figure in the Mexican drug cartel.

Donte Rodriguez was known and feared throughout the drug rings for his brilliance and ruthlessness— speculatively, of course. He was so well guarded, so well connected with corrupt officials, he had little fear of being apprehended. And Jeremy had shaken his hand.

Sitting back, Austin rested against the plush chair, closed his eyes, rubbed his hand over his chin. How the *hell* had this happened? Even in his wildest imagination he couldn't have come up with a bigger worst-case scenario.

Jeremy was hanging around with frontrunners of the Mexican Mafia. How was he supposed to tell Hailey that? Now that the men knew Hailey existed, she would be the bait used to keep him in line.

Hailey's trip to Cozumel couldn't come fast enough. They needed to get her away from her brother. Hailey's need to honor her family was going to cost her her life.

Austin stared at Donte's unsmiling face for several more minutes before he shut down the computer. There was nothing he could do for Hailey until he knew what she knew. At least she would be safe behind the walls of Ethan's estate for the next few days.

Austin got up and wandered through the house. He followed the murmurs of music pumping from the speakers in the massive game room. Hailey sat curled in the corner of the couch, reading, with Bear and Reece flanking each side. Their heads shot up and tails wagged when they spotted him.

Hailey did a double take before she set her book on the arm of the couch and stood. "Um, hi."

Austin tried to ignore the hitch in his pulse as he took in her snug blue jeans and a form-fitting black turtleneck over the subtle curves of her compact body. "Um, hi yourself." He smiled.

Smiling back, she ran long, graceful fingers through the mane of her ponytail. "I'm not sure if Ethan told you, but he and Sarah decided to leave early."

He couldn't stop staring. Whenever she pulled her hair back like that, her big, almond-shaped eyes looked impossibly huge. They were her best feature, hands down, and she had plenty of amazing attributes. The fun and energy in the depths of golden honey captivated him. "Yeah, Ethan called me earlier this afternoon. Kylee better hurry up and have fun. Emma's going to be here before we know it."

Hailey grinned fully, beautifully. "I can't wait." She sat down on the edge of the cushion.

He took the cushion next to her, breathing in her peach blossom scent. "What are you reading?"

She looked at her book, feathering the pages. "Oh, I want to learn to snorkel while I'm in Mexico. I've always wanted to scuba dive, but since that's way out of my budget, I'll have to be satisfied with snorkeling."

"I could teach you." The offer was out of his mouth before he'd thought it through.

Her gaze whipped up to his. "You could?"

He couldn't back out now, not when excitement brightened her eyes. "Sure."

"I imagine you did a lot of diving as a SEAL."

"I did my fair share." He all but lived in the water for seven years of his life, pulling off top-secret missions for the Department of Defense.

"How would we do it? I mean practice?"

He glanced out the window toward the heated pool. "I see a perfectly good pool right out there."

"But I don't have any equipment."

"I have some stuff we can use."

"This is really great, Austin. I can't wait to get started."

"How about tomorrow?"

"Tomorrow sounds good." She pressed her lips together, fiddled with her book again.

It was time to get down to business. "I saw your brother this morning. He looks pretty banged up."

The light dimmed from her eyes. "Someone beat the crap out of him—mugged him for his tips."

"That's what he said. What did the police say?"

She frowned. "What do you mean?"

"Did the police come by and get his statement?" He felt like a dick for asking questions he already had answers to. "He'll want to call and do a follow-up on his report. Hundreds of people are mugged everyday in L.A. If he doesn't stay on top of his case, he'll get lost in the shuffle."

"I don't know. The cops never came by while I was there. I'll give him a call later and find out. He was planning to work the lunch shift today, even with his injuries. I threatened to talk to his boss myself, but he insisted I back off. Sometimes it's hard being the big sister." She flashed him another smile.

She didn't know the half of it. "Where does Jeremy work again?"

"Yoshoris."

"Nice place." He nodded his approval. "Trendy. Have you ever been there?"

"No. The menu's a little on the pricey side."

"Yeah, I guess it is, but I thought..." he trailed off frowning. "No." He shook his head, hating himself for playing this game.

"What?"

He shook his head again. "Hmm. I just thought Yoshoris was a dinner spot. I didn't think they served lunch."

She shrugged in an "I don't know what to tell you" manner. "They must. Jeremy works the lunch shift all the time."

"Hmm."

She firmed her lips, stood. "Another 'hmm.'"

"Well, yeah. I'm pretty sure they're all about dinner."

"Austin, it kinda sounds like you're questioning me. Like you don't believe me— or more like you don't believe my brother."

He'd hit a nerve. "I didn't say that."

"Your 'hmm' did." She paced away, heating up. "Why do I feel like my brother's always under attack? Why do I constantly have to defend him?"

Austin got to his feet. "Hailey—"

"I know my brother's had some trouble in the past," she interrupted. "I know that you're all aware of it and are keeping an eye on me, but you don't need to. It isn't necessary. He's changed—Jeremy's changed," she said again, as she rounded back his way. "He's made his mistakes and is working hard to fix them. He doesn't have to keep paying for them."

"Okay," he said, hands up, letting her know he was backing off.

"You don't get to judge him. You don't know what his life has been like, what it's like to grow up a victim of the system—being tossed here and there at the whim of someone's generosity...or lack thereof. So you go ahead and keep your 'hmm.'" She started toward the door.

He snagged her elbow. "Whoa, killer. Take it easy."

"Don't." She freed her arm, crossed them, stood hipshot, her eyes shooting daggers at him. "Jeremy hasn't been able to catch a break. I'll do everything I can to make sure he gets one now."

From the little he knew of Hailey's childhood, she hadn't been able to catch a break either, but she wasn't selling crack for the Mexican Mafia. She'd made something of herself. He seethed to tell her this, but bit his tongue instead.

This whole situation was going to be even messier than he thought. It was going to take time to crack through her knee-jerk habit to stick up for her brother. Her love and loyalty ran deep here. He wouldn't get anywhere or convince her of anything with her hackles up. "I'm sorry if you thought I was judging Jeremy. I have no idea what it's like to grow up in foster care. It can't be easy."

Her gaze left his. Hailey stared at the floor as she gave him a jerking shrug. "Yeah, well, it's over for both of us." Her voice became gentler. "Let's forget it. I have some stuff to do, so I'll see you later." She turned to leave again.

"Hailey, wait."

She kept walking.

"Please."

She stopped.

"I really am sorry." Not for raising questions about

Jeremy, but that she loved someone who clearly didn't deserve it. He walked to her, hesitating before he ran his hand over her soft ponytail.

She turned to face him. "You're forgiven." Sighing, she closed her eyes. "I'm sorry, too. I know everyone's trying to help."

Although she said everything was okay, her rigid stance told him otherwise. He glanced at the pool, and inspiration struck. "Are you up for your first lesson now?"

"Now? It's cold and almost dark."

"I'm pretty sure the pool has a light, and I'm positive the water's heated. It'll only suck when we get out." He scanned the vintage arcade games placed throughout the room before he looked at Hailey again. "Or I can kick your butt at Pac-Man, Donkey Kong, or skee-ball like I always do."

The guard she'd put up vanished as she smiled slowly. "Do you have a swim suit?"

"I'll borrow some trunks from the pool house."

"I'll meet you in ten minutes."

As she left, Austin rubbed his jaw. Yup, this was definitely going to be a goddamn mess.

Hailey wandered to the pool in her gray sweats. The lights were on in the twelve-foot depths, casting a blue tint to her skin. Austin had turned on the outdoor speakers, filling the brick and potted palm space with the same jumpy beat playing in the game room. She sat on one of the lounge chairs, waiting for him to emerge from the small changing area in the pool house.

She was finally going to learn to scuba dive. A childhood dream was about to come true. She'd always been drawn to the water, fascinated by what lived in its boundless depths. And how lucky was she that Austin offered to teach her? He would be endlessly patient, and it never hurt that he was fabulous to look at—a bonus for her.

Hailey sighed smugly, perfectly content with the world around her. She stared into the distance, watching the lights of the city wink while she listened to the waves crash against the cliffs below. Life didn't get any better than this. Ethan and Sarah's house was a testament to beauty with a fair share of luxury. When Sarah and Kylee moved in several months before, Sarah and Wren did a lot of redecorating, adding more feminine touches, but Ethan's spaces had remained the same—masculine and full of toys.

She loved the game room, with its pool and foosball tables, arcaded games, and home theater that rivaled any of the megaplexes downtown. When Sarah asked her if she would mind watching the dogs a couple weeks before, Hailey had jumped at the chance. Staying here was like living in a miniature resort—not that she didn't stay here most of the time anyway.

Jeremy would love it, but she'd hesitated to bring him. *Why?*

Hailey took a deep breath of sea air, trying to dismiss the nagging thoughts that kept sneaking into her bubble of serenity. Small pieces of her conversation with Austin continued to pop into her mind. Why had Austin questioned Jeremy's work schedule? Why did the seed of doubt he'd planted seem so ready to bloom?

Shame weighed heavy in her stomach. After changing into her bathing suit, she'd barely been able to resist the urge to confirm Yoshoris' business hours. Jeremy deserved more trust, more faith. If she wouldn't give him that, who would?

She fiddled with her fingers, sick with guilt. At

moments like this she couldn't suppress the mixed feelings of having her brother back in her life. For years she'd searched for him, longed for him, aching for the special bond they used to share. Now he was here, and at times it tore her apart.

Having him back forced her to dig up the past. She'd buried the pain years before, finding a way to move on and be happy. In the eight weeks since he'd returned, she found herself remembering things she wanted to forget, found herself questioning who she was.

It frustrated her that she seemed more focused on the negative than the blessing of having him with her again. Perhaps that was why she was growing more resentful of everyone's inquiries into Jeremy. Each time they asked about him or hinted something might not be quite right, she wondered. Didn't that make her ungrateful? Was she a hypocrite?

Her mind kept wandering to the last time Jeremy popped into her life two years before. At eighteen, he'd come straight from a short stint in a jail cell, promising her he wanted a fresh start, that he was ready to change. He was ready to go back to school, but needed a place to stay and some money to get started. She'd withdrawn two thousand dollars from her meager education fund to help with his legal fees and court costs, had given it to him without question, proud that he wanted to turn his life around. She had woken the next morning to a quick note telling her that something had come up, but he would pay her back.

She never told Sarah, and made excuses for taking the semester off; she hadn't been able to pay for the classes she'd planned to take, putting her almost a year behind. Hailey remembered being furious, but under the embers of frustration and anger had been a deep well of guilt. If she could've stayed with him all those years before, if she hadn't left him, he wouldn't be where he was. Their parents had died and she'd abandoned him the same night. He'd been so small, so scared, and she left without a fight.

Hailey stood and walked to the rail, holding on, letting the cool wind rush across her face. She needed to believe that the sweet parts of Jeremy she'd loved so much as a child were still there, that he really wanted a better life than the one he'd led over the last several years. If he vanished again, she couldn't be sure she would help the next time he came around, and wouldn't that be like abandoning him all over? She pressed her fingers to her temple, let out a long breath as she turned, and flinched. Austin stood in front of her. "I didn't hear you come out."

"You seemed lost in your thoughts."

She was, but she wanted to forget them. "I guess I was." She tried not to stare at Austin's magnificent body. His broad, chiseled chest and powerful arms sent her heart racing. Her fingers ached to touch him. She made the mistake of glancing at navy blue swim trunks, a tad too tight for his athletic build. In defense she focused her gaze on his stellar face, her eyes refusing to leave his. Man, why did he affect her like this *every* single time? Instead of standing there drooling, she walked to the water. "You wanna get started?"

"Yeah, sure." He dove in, surfaced almost immediately.

She pulled her top over her head and tugged her pants off. Goosebumps puckered her skin from the cool breeze blowing from the cliffs. "Holy cow, it's cold."

Austin treaded water lazily. "It's perfect in here. Come on in."

Hailey jumped in and was instantly enveloped in warmth. She pushed off the bottom, surfacing a foot from Austin. "You're right, it's perfect." Smiling, she tipped her head back, slicking the hair away from her face, catching a glimpse of stars. "So, how do we practice scuba diving or snorkeling without any equipment?"

"There are things I need to know you can do before we get to the equipment. You need to show me you have good, basic swimming skills, that you can hold your breath for a reasonable amount of time. What do you want to start with, a few laps or underwater exercises?"

She was suddenly nervous, knowing Austin would be scrutinizing her every move. "Uh, underwater exercises."

"All right. Let's focus on swimming to the bottom a few times, see how long you can hold your breath."

"I can't hold it very long."

"You'll be surprised how long you can stay under when you're relaxed. Let's try." He took a breath and somersaulted, making his way to the bottom with effortless movements. Before Hailey could blink, Austin sat against the blue and white tiles, Indian-style, moving his arms with smooth, graceful motions. She was swimming with the next thing to a mythical sea god, and she sure as heck wasn't a mermaid.

Hailey took a breath and swam to the bottom, much less gracefully than Austin. She crisscrossed her legs like he did, but started to rise. He pressed his hand to her shoulder, keeping her in place. Hailey felt her need for a breath but fought against it. Lungs screaming for air, she pushed off the tile, gulping in the sea breeze as soon as she broke the surface. The cool night was like a shock to her skin as she grabbed hold of the side of the pool.

Austin surfaced next to her.

"I didn't stay under very long." She was already discouraged, and they'd just begun. The water had always called to her, but that didn't mean she was any good in it.

"That's because you're not relaxed."

"No, I'm not. I'm wasting your time. I've wanted to learn to do this for as long as I can remember, but the

truth of the matter is, I'm not very good in the water."
Why am I acting like this? Why am I so tense and serious?
This is supposed to be fun.

"I'm a farm boy from Iowa. Do you think I was a
natural when I joined the Navy? I worked my butt off to
get good. Luckily, you won't have to try as hard as I did.
Just relax, Hailey." He touched her shoulders and she
did the opposite of relax when a sizzle of molten heat
engulfed her skin.

She nodded, trying to appear as unaffected as Austin.
This would never work if she fed into his belief that she
was a giggling, foolish child.

His fingers kneaded her tensed muscles. "Close your
eyes and breathe."

She stared into the dark green depths of his eyes,
hypnotized, before her lids fluttered closed. Her breath
shuddered out once before she fought to control it.

"There you go. Now, keep that up. In slow, out slow."

Austin's knee kept brushing her thigh as he kicked to
stay afloat. His magic fingers continued to press against
her skin, turning her muscles to mush. His deep voice
soothed and her lips tingled with an ache to feel his
mouth against hers.

"Take a breath, hold it. Keep your eyes closed."

She did what he said, feeling the solid wall of his chest
press against her breasts as he wrapped his arm around
her waist and took them under. Her feet touched the
bottom, but he tugged until she knelt on the pool floor.
She was anchored against him, thigh-to-thigh, stomach-
to-stomach, as he continued to hold her tight.

Hailey no longer focused on taking her next breath as
Austin's hard, smooth body fit snug to hers. She placed
her hands on his waist, skimming slippery, firm skin,
until her palms rested on his hips. The current from
his muscled arm moving, planting them to their spot,

46

brushed against her cheek.

The urge for air crept back again. Hailey moved, trying to break free of Austin's hold, but he held her still. She opened her eyes, meeting the dark green of his as he stared into hers, his face an inch away as he kicked, bringing them to the surface.

Hailey expected him to let her go as they breathed in each other's breaths along with the cool night air, but he continued to hold her, smiling. "You did it."

"Huh?" She couldn't break away from his gaze.

"Thirty seconds. Good stuff, Hailey."

"Thirty seconds?" And then it registered. She'd stayed under water for thirty seconds. The most she'd ever been able to accomplish before she panicked was fifteen. "I made thirty seconds?" She beamed. "Not bad."

"Not bad at all, kid."

The smile froze on her face before it vanished. They were back to kid. She'd all but disintegrated into a puddle of sexual mush, and he was once again unfazed. "Thanks," she said with less enthusiasm.

He let her go and swam to the edge. "Why don't we get a few laps in before we call it a night? Remind me to write down the name and address of a good dive shop to check out. Miranda can hook you up with everything you'll need."

She could've *sworn* she saw desire in his eyes on their ascent. Had she imagined it in her oxygen-depleted state? Apparently so. Hailey let out a long breath. "Yeah, sounds good." She swam to the side, feeling like a fool.

CHAPTER 5

HAILEY SAT UP IN BED, bleary-eyed, exhausted. She'd tossed and turned all night. Between her Jeremy dilemma and the constant replay of her pool time with Austin, she'd barely caught a decent hour of sleep. Her stress level was at an all time high; her hormones raged. She was miserable. She pulled her covers back, swung her feet over the edge of the bed, almost stepping on Bear and Reece. "Oops. Sorry, boys."

They stretched, yawned, and stood in unison.

"Guys, I'm not gonna lie. That's a little weird. Do you want to go outside?" Tails wagged as Bear and Reece dashed through the bedroom door. "I'm taking that as a yes."

Hailey got to her feet and wandered downstairs to the noisy commotion of two excited dogs. "I'm coming. I'm coming." She opened the door and they ran out like a shot. "And they're off." She watched them water the trees and bushes around the plush front yard before they lay in the grass and rolled about. "I'll leave you to it, men."

She went to the kitchen, grabbed a bowl from the cupboard, a box of cereal from the pantry, and milk from the refrigerator. As she took her first bite of Cheerios, she passed a glance over her phone before she looked at the clock—nine thirty. Jeremy would be up and around she assured herself, as she retrieved his number and pressed 'send'. She wanted to know how he was feeling, to confirm he'd gone to work, but, ultimately, she needed to extinguish the doubt Austin had planted the night before.

"Yeah?" Jeremy said groggily.

"Hey, how's the face today?"

"Rosa?"

Hailey frowned. *Rosa? Who the heck was Rosa?* "It's Hailey. You know, your big sister?"

"Sorry. What's up?"

"I just wanted to check in, see how you were doing. How's the lip and ribs?"

"Still pretty sore, but getting better."

"I'm glad you're on the mend. Are you working this afternoon?"

"Tonight."

"Maybe I'll stop in and visit."

"No—that's not a good idea."

She heard the trace of hurried panic before he smoothed himself out. Her stomach sank as the seed of uncertainty grew another sprout. "Why? I want to see my little brother in action."

"I'd get all flustered knowing you were watching me. It would mess with my flow. Besides, it'll be impossible to get a reservation for tonight. They book up fast."

Jeremy loved to be the center of attention—since when did he worry about his "flow"? Hailey closed her eyes, swallowing hard against disappointment. "All right. Maybe some other time."

"I've gotta go, Hailey."

"What's your favorite dish on the menu?" She couldn't let this go. She wanted Jeremy to convince her Austin was wrong. She needed to know her brother hadn't been lying to her for almost two months.

"Huh?"

"I asked you what your favorite dish is."

There was a long pause before he sighed. "The steak's good."

"The steak? How do they prepare it?" She pushed now that she didn't believe him.

"What do you mean how do they prepare it? It's a steak," he snapped. "They cook it like they cook a steak. What the hell is this?"

"Nothing." She pressed her lips firm as she rubbed her fingers against her temple. "Nothing. I'll let you go."

"Are you coming home today?"

She continued to knead at the throbbing in her head. "I'm not sure. Why?"

"No reason. I was just wondering."

"It'll depend on my errands."

"Okay. Talk to you later."

"Yeah, later." She hung up and shoved her cereal bowl away, feeling sick. Jeremy was lying; she couldn't deny it any longer. She picked up the phone again, found the number for Yoshoris.

"Thank you for calling Yoshoris. Can I help you?"

"Yes, I hope so."

"I'll do my best," the gentle female voice said.

"First, do you serve lunch?"

"I'm afraid we don't, but I'd be happy to book you a reservation for this evening."

Hailey stared at the silver spoon glinting in the sunshine as the woman confirmed what Austin told her.

"I'll have to call my friends and find out what they want to do."

"Okay. Will that be all?"

She no longer needed to ask, but made herself anyway. "No. If we do decide to come in this evening, can we request Jeremy for our waiter?"

"Jeremy?"

"Yes, Jeremy Kagan."

"I'm sorry, we don't have a Jeremy Kagan working here. How odd. You're the second person to ask for him."

She stopped tracing frantic patterns on Kylee's Sesame Street placemat. "I'm sorry, did you say someone else has been looking for Jeremy?"

"Yes, just yesterday. A man came to the door, showed me some badge of sorts, and asked if he could speak to Jeremy Kagan."

"Was he a police officer?" She cringed.

"No, he was a bodyguard, I believe. Or at least that's what his identification said."

"Could you describe him?" Although Hailey was sure she already knew.

"Um, tall, muscular, brown hair—handsome."

"Green eyes?"

"Why, yes, now that you say that, I do remember his eyes being green—very dark. Striking."

"Thank you for your time. I'll get back to you with our reservation."

Hailey set down her cell, continuing to stare at the spoon as she dealt with the shock of her short phone call. Not only had Jeremy lied to her, but surprisingly, Austin had too. It hurt her more that Austin hadn't shared the truth. She'd come to expect Jeremy's constant pattern of deception, but Austin...Why hadn't he told her he didn't believe Jeremy worked at Yoshoris? Better yet, why had he taken the time to find out?

Standing, confused, ill, Hailey filled Bear and Reece's food and water dishes before she left the kitchen, leaving her mess where she'd made it. Both Austin and Jeremy had some explaining to do.

An hour later, Hailey stormed through her front door. Jeremy sat on the couch in his boxers with a bag of doughnuts and a glass of OJ, watching Jerry Springer.

"Give me one reason why I shouldn't pack your bags and throw you out on the street."

Jeremy stood, wincing, holding his ribs.

"You lied to me, Jeremy."

"What are you talking about?"

"I called Yoshoris after we hung up. They've never heard of you. Explain—and it better be good."

He sat back down, put his head in his hands. "When're you gonna stop checking up on me?"

"When are you going to grow up and stop lying about every darn thing?"

"I didn't want you to be disappointed that I haven't found a job yet, so I made it up."

She steamed out a breath, walked to the door and back again, trying to get a grip on her nonexistent patience. "Where are you getting the money?"

He didn't answer.

She marched over to the couch, loomed over his hunched form, struggling not to shout. "I *asked* you where you were getting your money. If you're mixed up with drugs, Jeremy, I'll never forgive you."

His gaze snapped to hers, his eyes full of wounded shock. "Sissy, how could you think that? Why would you throw my past in my face? I know I had some trouble before, but that was a long time ago. How can I forget if you won't? Don't I get an opportunity to change? Or am I going to pay for the same mistakes over and over?"

Guilt swamped her as he stood and hobbled toward his room. Lying about a job was a long way from selling pot. Hailey stared at the ceiling, trying to regroup. "Look, I'm sorry. Just tell me where you got the money for your fancy car and your half of the bills and I'll drop it."

He turned to face her. "I've been doing some odd jobs here and there under the table, but nothing illegal. I didn't want to tell you that I don't have a full-time job yet; it's embarrassing. I didn't want to let you down again. I'm on the straight and narrow. I don't know how else to tell you to make you believe me."

Jeremy stared at her with defeated, pleading eyes, so much like the night in the hospital when he'd been a boy...when she'd left him to fend for himself.

"You can start by telling the truth," she gentled her voice. "Not having steady work doesn't make me ashamed of you, but the lying bothers me a lot. Can we make a deal from here on out?"

He shrugged, looked away.

She took that as assent. "You tell me the truth, no matter what, and I'll do my best to stop checking up on you."

He shrugged again, nodded. "I can live with that."

"Good. I'm sorry for jumping to conclusions." She reached out to him but dropped her hand when he didn't make a move to take it. "That was unfair."

"I can't change who I was."

She'd really hurt him with her accusations. "I know. I can only apologize again."

"Let's forget it." He smiled. "Come give me a hug, Sissy."

Her heart melted every time he used his childhood nickname for her. It brought back so many good memories. It reminded her of the sweet little boy she and her parents had drawn out of the lost, troubled shell he'd arrived with when Mom and Daddy took him in all those years before.

She hugged him gingerly, careful not to touch the ugly rainbow of colors against his ribs. As she breathed in his aftershave and felt his strong arms around her, the familiar tug of shame came rushing back. How could she regret having Jeremy in her life when they had so many moments like this? It was *good* to have him here—her family. She drew away. "Can I ask you a couple more things so we can put this behind us and move on?"

"Sure, come sit down, have some breakfast." Jeremy

turned off the TV and handed her a doughnut covered in powdered sugar—her favorite.

"Thanks." She relaxed now that the air was clear once and for all, took a bite, licked the sugar from her lips. "Who beat you up?"

"Some guy from the garage where I've been picking up hours. He's been pretty damn resentful I'm getting time when he's not getting enough. He thought he'd teach me a lesson."

"Did you report it?"

He glanced away and back. "No. I want to leave it alone. I lied to you about that too." He let out a heavy sigh. "I don't want the police involved. It'll only make things worse."

"All right, we'll leave it alone. Do you want me to help you find a steady job?"

"No. I think I'm onto something. Some rich guy up in the hills needs an assistant or what not. He may give me a chance. I kinda mentioned I know Ethan Cooke. I'm hoping that'll do the trick."

She took her last bite, brushed her fingers together before reaching for the roll of paper towels Jeremy had brought with him instead of the napkins that sat on the small table in the kitchen. "Last question: Now that we're figuring this out, is there anything else I should know? Is there anything else you want to tell me before we drop this whole thing?"

"No. That's it." He took her hands, stared into her eyes. "I'm sorry I lied, Hailey. I'm working so hard to be a better person. I want you to be proud of me, to honor mom and dad for everything they tried to give us. From this moment forward, no more lies." He locked his pinky with hers, an old childhood gesture. "I'm going to call that guy again and try to get the assistant job. If not, I'll keep my hours at the garage until something else comes around. The money's pretty good."

Her eyes watered as she nodded. "I love you, Jeremy. I *am* proud of you for trying. Mom and Daddy would be too."

He hugged her again and she held on. "Do you want another doughnut?"

She eased away, grinning. "No. I have stuff to do. I need to go."

"I'll be at the garage this afternoon. You can come check on me if you want. It's down in South Central."

"No, I don't need to check on you." She frowned. "South Central? Jeremy, that's a really dangerous place."

"I've been a street kid for years. I can handle myself."

She took in his bruises, his swollen eye and lip. He hadn't handled himself so well two days before, but she kept her comment to herself. "I know you can. I'll see you soon."

"Bye, Sissy."

She blew him a kiss at the door and closed it behind her. It was Austin's turn.

Austin hurried to the front door as whoever was outside continued to pound a fist against it. He yanked it open, stared at Hailey, flinty-eyed and arms crossed.

"You lied to me." She pushed passed him and walked to the center of his living room, carrying her peachy scent and a hell of an attitude with her.

He shut the door.

"I said, you lied to me. Why?"

"Why don't you tell me what I lied about, then I can give you an answer." He assumed this had to do with Jeremy, but he wasn't offering up any information without knowing what she did.

"Why did you act like you didn't know Yoshoris' business hours, especially after you went there yesterday to check up on my brother?"

He suppressed a wince—just barely. She'd been busy this morning.

"And the bigger question is, why were you checking up on my brother in the first place?" She folded her arms again, all business.

"Take a seat and I'll explain." He gestured to the huge leather cushions.

"I think I'll stand, thanks." Her arms tightened, her hip shot out to the side.

He shrugged and leaned against the door. The best way to deal with this was to meet her fire with a wall of calm. "Suit yourself."

"I want answers, Austin."

"Fine. After I talked to your brother the other day, his story didn't add up, so I thought I would check it out."

"Why?"

"I just said, his story didn't check out, and I was right."

Her brow raised a fraction. "Well, score one for you. Why didn't you tell me that last night instead of dancing around the truth?"

This was a side of Hailey he'd rarely seen. She was always so bubbly, so cheerful. But her claws were out today, and she was looking for blood—his blood. If she wanted the truth, he'd give it to her—or most of it anyway. "Because if I'd told you I heard your brother getting beat up and that the story he fed me afterwards was a bunch of bullshit, you would've reacted exactly as you had last night, like you are right now."

"How dare—"

"Your instinct's to protect," he cut her off, his own voice going edgy. He knew where this was going and didn't like defending himself against a liar's word. "A natural reaction, but sometimes it's hard to see the truth when it's staring you right in the face."

"And what truth is that, exactly?" Her foot began to tap.

"He's a criminal, Hailey."

"A brush with the law doesn't make him a criminal. He's paid for his mistakes."

A *brush* with the law? Was she fucking kidding? "Your brother's bad news. Nothing good will come from having him back in your life."

She gaped at him before she turned away and walked to the window, her hands fisting at her sides.

He clenched his jaw, already wishing he could take his comment back. Not because it wasn't true, but the delivery had been bad.

"Wow, you've got a nerve," she whispered in a hiss of fury.

"Hailey, Jeremy's messing with drugs." He would leave it there.

She whirled around, cheeks flushed. "You saw him using drugs?"

"No."

"You saw him selling?"

"No."

"Then how can you say such a thing?"

"I have my reasons." God that sounded lame and condescending.

"You have your reasons," she spat back. "Let me get this straight. You haven't seen him using, and you haven't seen him selling, but Jeremy's mixed up with drugs. That's quite an accusation without any proof. Who *are* you and what did you do with the real Austin Casey?" She took two steps closer, then stopped.

"I'm right here."

"Not from where I'm standing," she scoffed.

The hell with this. He moved until they stood toe-to-toe. "Take a closer look. Nothing about me's changed. Jeremy's mixed up with S-1."

"S-1? What the heck is S-1?"

He saw it click as furious incredulity blazed into her eyes. "A *gang*?" She laughed, bitterly now. "This is getting good. He's a gangster and a what—what—" she flung her arms around wildly "—a drug dealer or user? You haven't actually seen him do either, but you have your reasons for accusing. I think you should concentrate on being a bodyguard and leave your P.I. aspirations behind." She sidestepped him and marched to the door. As she twisted the knob, he put his hand against the wood, holding it in place. "Where are you going?"

"Back to Ethan and Sarah's. Don't worry; I'm not about to confront Jeremy. I wouldn't dream of insulting him with questions when your facts are so baseless. Get out of my way; I'm angry enough to hit you."

"Hailey, what I'm telling you *is* the truth."

She turned again, her body brushing his as her breath trembled in and out. "Jeremy and I just had a long talk. He confessed everything to me—working as a mechanic under the table, lying about Yoshoris, not really calling the cops when he got beat up. He looked me in the eye and told me there was nothing else when I asked. As far as I'm concerned, he has a clean slate. Not even Jeremy can hose me that badly."

More fucking lies. That sent him over the edge. "Then you're being a fool."

"Oh...my...God." She spaced out each word, her eyes popping wide. "How *dare* you?" Hailey tried for the door again. "Get out of my way."

"Not yet." He kept his hand against the wood.

"I don't have *anything* more to say to you."

Stubborn determination creased her brow. Her

mind was made up: Hailey wouldn't believe anything else he told her so he would keep the rest to himself. If she couldn't grasp Jeremy's involvement with S-1, she certainly wouldn't be open to hearing that he was playing Russian roulette with the Mexican Mafia. He stared down at her as she trembled with fury. She was all but ready to blow her top.

Austin gained a slippery grip on the tethers of his temper. "Look, we're both pissed off. Why don't you sit down a minute and take a deep breath?" He needed to take one himself. He took Hailey's arm, tried to lead her to his couch. "I don't want you driving when you're this upset."

She pushed him this time. "What, are you going to get me a glass of milk, maybe a cookie too? Why do you treat me like a damn child? I'm almost twenty-five for God's sake." She shoved at him again. "I'm more than capable of taking care of myself. I've done it most of my life. Now let me go!" She ripped free of his hold, yanked the door open, slammed it behind her with a solid crack.

"Hailey. Son of a bitch!" Austin started after her, stopped, slammed his fist into the door. He leaned against the wood, closed his eyes, and steamed out a heavy breath. "That went well."

CHAPTER 6

HAILEY POPPED UP FROM THE water, choking—again. She yanked her flooded mask from her face and flung it, watching it sink to the bottom of the pool. "Damn it," she snapped, slapping her hand against the warm liquid, creating a splash and rippling waves.

She was still rip-roaring after her confrontation with Austin, and now she could add a healthy dose of frustration to her list. Why couldn't she get this *right*? She'd watched forty-five minutes of 'How to Snorkel' videos on YouTube. They'd assured her it was so simple; well, apparently it wasn't. She glared at her mask, slapped at the water again, unable to rid herself of the choking rage and confusion threatening to overwhelm her.

Enough was enough. Hailey swam to the edge of the pool and rested her head against her arms on the smooth cement coping. The wake she created slapped over the naked skin of her waist. She concentrated on the sounds of the waves hundreds of feet below, trying to relax the aching strain in her shoulders and neck. With each breath in and out, she counted—or attempted to—until her busy mind wandered back to Austin's wild accusations. Why would he say such horrible things? He had to have known he was hurting her.

She remembered Austin's solemn eyes staring into hers. Could it be true? Was Jeremy mixed up with drugs and a *gang*? She too had jumped to the conclusion that Jeremy was into drugs again because of the quick cash for his car, designer clothes, and his half of the bill, but a *gang...* The very idea was so absurd. She vehemently shook her head. No, of course not. Gangsters weren't clean cut; they were covered in tattoos, wore funky sagging clothes and bandanas around their heads. That definitely wasn't Jeremy. And besides—he'd promised. Austin was trying to be a good friend, to help, but he'd made a mistake; he was running with the wrong information and overreacting.

She still couldn't believe Austin had called Jeremy a criminal. Ted Bundy was a criminal. Selling a bag of pot at a party and being caught with a beer in your hand at the age of eighteen was teenage stupidity. Jeremy had moved past that mistake. He didn't even drink anymore.

Calmer, steadier, she stood again in the shallow end, using her foot to retrieve her mask and snorkel. She was going to get this right, by God, without Austin's help. She doubted he would be rushing to her aid anymore.

Hailey spit into her mask, rubbed her saliva about, and rinsed. She slipped it on, adjusted the strap. "I can *do* this," she said before popping the snorkel piece in her mouth. Determined to get it right, she submerged herself, kicking her flippered feet. As she took her first breath through her snorkel, she sucked in a mouthful of water and her mask filled. She thrust her head out of the water clumsily, coughing, losing her balance. As she fell backward, she tossed her mask off. "I give *up*. That's *it*. Some people just aren't meant to be scuba divers," she said to no one. She yanked off her flippers, winged them through the air, and gasped when Austin caught one in his hand.

He stood, staring at her with a full grocery bag in his arm.

Oh, great. She closed her eyes as humiliation burned her cheeks. This just wasn't her day. With as much dignity as she could muster, Hailey walked through the shallow end, up the stairs and grabbed her towel. She wrapped herself in the soft cotton, fighting the urge to shiver in the cool breeze.

"Your mask's too tight." Austin tossed the flipper on the nearest lounge chair as he continued to look at her.

She glanced up and back down at the brick inlay of the patio. How should she respond to his calm observation? Should she pretend this afternoon hadn't happened? She reminded herself Austin was only trying to help, that he would never be intentionally cruel. But he'd said horrible things that weren't true. *Your brother's bad news. Nothing good will come from having him back in your life,* played like a mantra in her head. "It didn't feel too tight."

"Trust me. I know what I'm talking about."

Her eyes flew to his, fully aware of his double entendre. She wasn't going there again today, especially not when her temples were starting to throb. "I'll have to loosen the strap, then." Her teeth started to chatter, partly from the cold, mostly from nerves. He would continue to insist that her brother was the symbol of everything she stood so firmly against—drugs, useless violence.

Her world was imploding around her—a good man, a person she trusted implicitly, told her what she couldn't allow herself to believe, while her brother, a man she *wanted* to trust the same way, to believe in wholeheartedly, told her something different. Her stomach clenched from her mental tug-of-war.

Hailey pressed her fingers against her head. *No.* She couldn't do this anymore today. She'd always believed herself strong enough to handle anything. For so many years, she'd had no choice. But this was too much right now. The possibilities were too disturbing. "I need to get dressed. I'm cold."

"Okay," was all he said as she walked away.

He'd hated seeing Hailey like that—eyes vulnerable and weary, body braced as if waiting for his next verbal attack. He despised knowing he'd caused her misery.

Austin cringed as he thought of how he'd handled things at the apartment. He couldn't have screwed it up more if he'd tried. There were a hundred-and-one ways he could've presented Hailey with the facts.

He shook his head, muttered a curse. Had he really expected Hailey to respond any differently than she had? He'd more or less called Jeremy a loser, a druggie, and a gangster. True, Jeremy was all three, but Austin had totally screwed up nonetheless.

Austin scrubbed another asparagus shoot and placed it in the olive oil and herb marinade he'd prepared for the mix of vegetables he would grill later. He needed to make things right with Hailey, but wasn't sure how to go about it. A simple apology wouldn't get him out of this one.

He picked up a zucchini next, ran it under tepid water. Should he tell her he'd made a mistake? She didn't believe him in any case. Austin shook his head, immediately dismissing the idea. He wasn't a fan of lies. The fact of the matter was, everything he'd said was the truth. But how did he make someone see what they were determined to ignore?

He would start with an apology for hurting her, for his poor delivery of hard facts, and go from there.

"You're still here."

He glanced over his shoulder. Hailey stood at the island, hands braced and tense against the marble countertop, her face slightly pale.

"Yeah, I wanted to talk to you."

"I'm not really in a talking mood. I have a headache." She rubbed at her temple.

"I don't like the way we left things. You and I are going

to be spending a lot of time together over the next few months. We're off to a rough start."

"What do you mean?"

"Jackson and I have been assigned to Project Mexico."

"Oh." Hailey dropped her hand, walked to a cupboard, pulled a glass from the shelf, stood next to him as she filled it with water. Her peach blossom scent surrounded him, even after she'd gone back to stand behind her island barrier.

Austin shut off the tap and turned to face her. "I know I hurt you with the things I said this afternoon, and I'm sorry for it."

"The content or the delivery?"

"The delivery." As he stared at her, he could only be truthful. "I wish I could apologize for both, but then I'd be lying. I stand behind the information I shared with you."

Austin debated whether to show her the pictures he'd taken, but what good would it do? He could tell by her steady, staring eyes and her stubbornly lifted chin that she still wasn't willing to believe him. The pictures didn't show Jeremy doing anything more than hanging around sketchy-looking characters and carrying a black duffel bag. He wasn't technically doing anything wrong, according to the photographs. It was only implied. Until he had something absolutely solid, Hailey would dismiss what he said. She would find a way to see the innocence behind the truth. Her need to protect Jeremy was too ingrained.

"I don't know what to say, Austin. You'll believe as you choose, and I'll believe in Jeremy. I owe him that at least." Her voice strained and quiet, she sunk to the wooden barstool, resting her forehead against her fingers.

Hailey's defeat undid him. Austin walked to her, hesitated before he took her hand clenched on the marble counter. He was always careful not to touch her. It made him feel things he knew he shouldn't. "Let's table this conversation. I came over to apologize and throw a couple of steaks on the grill."

Her eyes filled and she closed them.

He'd never seen her cry before. "Hey," he said gently, pulling her to her feet.

"Hey," he said again when she wouldn't look at him.

Hailey pressed her forehead against his chest, surprising him. She stood in silence, her hand limp in his, her other clenched at her side.

Sarah and Ethan had shared with Austin small snatches of Hailey's rough upbringing. Who had she had all the years after her parents died? Hailey protected Jeremy, but who protected her? No one, he imagined.

Austin freed her hand and wrapped his arms around her rigid back, loosely, absorbing the shock of her body against his as they mirrored their intimate stance from the pool floor. Hailey's vulnerability affected him differently than the sexual punch last night, but no less potently, as she cautiously accepted the comfort he offered. Austin tightened his grip, pulling her more truly against him, holding on until she relaxed. As her body pressed against his, he moved his hands over her slender back. "I'm sorry, Hailey."

The heat of her breath seeped through his shirt, warming his chest as her forehead stayed pressed there. Her arms came up and wrapped around his waist. She moved until her cheek rested against his heart.

He closed his eyes, playing his fingers through her soft, damp hair as his stomach tied itself in knots. Words escaped him as something changed. Knee-jerk desire turned to longing.

Moments later, Hailey eased back, staring into his eyes. He skimmed his knuckles against her cheek as her gaze darted to his mouth. She tilted her chin up, inviting him to make a move. The heated look passing between them kicked his heart into a gallop, but he resisted, stepping back, preventing himself from making a mistake.

Although he didn't think of Hailey as a child like she'd accused, he did see her as Kylee's nanny and Sarah and Ethan's friend. Crossing the line into something more was bound to end badly. Long-term relationships couldn't exist in his line of work. His dedication was to his job. He knew what Hailey sought, and it was nothing he would ever be able to give. "Are you okay?" He asked, taking another step back.

"Yeah." She looked down and fiddled with her fingers before she hurried to the patio door, letting Bear and Reece inside.

Austin turned to the counter, needing something to do. He busied himself with the marinating vegetables. He cleared his throat in the awkward quiet. "I was going to grill up a couple of steaks, throw some veggies on too. If you'd rather, I'll leave."

"No, you can stay." Hailey went to the cupboard, took plates from the shelf, pulled a drawer open, grabbing silverware. She set the table in silence.

Austin's cell phone vibrated against his hip. He glanced at the readout and answered. "Casey."

"It's Phillips. I know it's your day off, but I need a favor."

Austin pulled the platter of steak from the fridge. "What is it?"

"Jerrod Riley decided he wants to spend the night on the town. We're leaving from an early dinner out and are heading for Club LAX. I'm a little concerned about crowd control."

"Do you need backup?"

"I wouldn't turn down an extra hand."

"When?"

"As soon as you can. The women were all over him. His songs are number one and two on the charts right now. He's a hot commodity, and the crowds are treating him like one."

Hunter wouldn't ask for help if he didn't need it. "I'll be there." Austin put his phone back and turned to Hailey. She was already gathering up the dishes.

"I'm sorry. We'll have to take a rain check on the steaks. Hunter needs my help tonight. Jerrod Riley decided he wants to spend a night on the town."

"Okay. I'll see you around."

Her voice was still strained, still too quiet. She looked so sad, so alone. Austin reached for his phone, tempted to call Hunter and tell him he couldn't come after all, but changed his mind. That would be the first step down the wrong path. "I'm on duty for the next few days. Why don't I give you a call next week. We'll schedule a snorkel lesson. You have to be a solid snorkeler before we can move to free diving."

"Okay, that'll be fine." She gave him a small smile that didn't reach her eyes.

He stepped toward her again but didn't touch her. If he did, he would break all the rules. "I really am sorry about today. And about dinner."

She shrugged. "It's over. I was planning to curl up with Bear and Reece and watch a movie on the big screen anyway."

The idea was so cozy, so appealing. This was the first time he'd ever considered putting work on the backburner to eat a slab of steak and sit through a movie with a woman.

Not good.

Austin reassured himself it was only because he couldn't stand to see anyone hurting. He felt himself losing his footing as he stared into Hailey's sad honey eyes. In defense, he turned away. "I'll see you around."

"Yeah, see you."

Austin walked down the hall, then pivoted back, remembering his cap on the counter. He stopped cold in the kitchen doorway.

Hailey leaned against the huge panel of glass, arms wrapped around herself, staring out at the city lights far in the distance. She was so small against the massive windows and view beyond.

Austin took another step forward as a tear tracked down her cheek. "Hailey?"

She whirled, dashing her hand over her face. "I—I— just leave me alone." She backed toward the door, feeling for the knob as she went. When she found it, she fumbled, pulled, turned, and fled.

His instinct was to follow, but something told him Hailey was used to dealing with her tears, with her pain all by herself. Tonight he would let her go, would let her be as she'd asked, but that was going to change real soon.

Helpless rage chewed at Austin as he drove down the freeway on his way to help Hunter. Jaw clenched, shoulders tight, he dialed Ethan's number and waited.

"Cooke."

"It's Austin. We have a problem."

"What's up?"

"Hailey." He gripped the wheel tighter as he thought of her—small and alone by the big window. "She's in bigger trouble than I initially thought. Jeremy *is* dealing drugs. He *is* mixed up with S-1, but more than that, he's also in deep with the Mexican cartel—the Zulas. I captured footage of him shaking hands with Donte Rodriguez, the

68

number two man in their organization. We need to get her out of here."

The line stayed silent.

"Are you there?" he spat into the receiver.

"Yeah, I'm here. I'm trying to take it all in. Project Mexico doesn't leave for another three weeks. There isn't much we can do about that tactical problem."

The urgency to do something left Austin restless. "We could send Hailey early. Send her on a vacation. That kid brother of hers is a fucking loose cannon. The organization knows Hailey exists. I heard them threaten him with her. She's in trouble, Ethan."

Ethan blew out a long breath. "Yeah, I know. Let me think about this tonight. We'll come up with a game plan first thing in the morning."

It wasn't good enough—not nearly good enough, but it would have to do. She was safe behind the walls of Ethan's Estate. Between the supermax-like features of his security system and Bear and Reece, no one was getting to her. The dogs wouldn't let anyone touch her. "Okay. I'll talk to you first thing. Oh, by the way, I have Sarah's car. Some little fucker shot up my windows."

"Well son of a bitch. You're just full of great news." Ethan's voice lacked good humor.

"Yeah. I do what I can. I'll call tomorrow." Austin hung up and took his exit. He pulled into Club LAX's parking lot, struggling not to turn around and head back to Sarah and Ethan's. Hailey was safe for tonight, he reassured himself, and he had a job to do.

He got out of his car on a sigh, and met Jerrod Riley's limo as it pulled up to the building's curb.

Someone pulled the black bag from Jeremy's head.

69

He sat in the dimly lit office of a skeezy warehouse surrounded by guards and a man known to few—Zulas Rodriguez, the leader of the Zulas Family.

Jeremy swallowed hard, trying to keep his nerves and dinner down as his gaze skimmed over a samurai sword on the dingy table in front of him.

The guards pulled a bag from the man sitting next to him. Jeremy glanced over, realizing it wasn't a man sitting inches away, but a kid who couldn't be more than seventeen, eighteen tops. The kid muttered in Spanish, sweating profusely and on the verge of tears.

Jeremy stared straight ahead, choosing to focus only on Señor Rodriguez and Donte, his son. He sure as shit wouldn't live long if he carried on like that. He knew he would either impress his leader tonight or die a very painful death. Jeremy kept silent as Señor Rodriguez stood across from him, staring, measuring.

"This is the young man who will change my route?" Señor Rodriguez said to Donte.

"Yes, Papa. After a conversation with Mr. Kagan, I believe he is just what we need. Let's see if you agree."

"I'm listening." He nodded his go ahead, his eyes never leaving Jeremy's.

"You see, Papa, Jeremy has a young, beautiful sister who will be taking part in Project Mexico, a University program based in Cozumel." Donte tossed several photographs of Hailey on the same table as the sword.

Jeremy's tongue darted across his lips as he stared at the pictures Señor Rodriguez spread out. In some shots, Hailey played with Kylee at a park, in others she stepped from the apartment building on her way to her car. In another, Hailey walked the aisles of a dive shop, buying snorkeling equipment. In yet another she put groceries in a cart. Jeremy swallowed hard. He had no idea they'd been watching Hailey for days.

"Yes. Quite nice, quite nice." Señor Rodriguez nodded again.

"I believe this is the perfect opportunity to create our new shipping route while staying under the radar. Jeremy, being the dedicated brother that he is, can assist his sister with a most noble cause. Of course, the details are still in the works, but the front is perfect and slightly poetic. We'll be helping Mexico while we help ourselves."

Señor Rodriguez smiled slowly, his face splitting with a grin. "I like this plan, Donte. Well done, my son. And what about him?" He gestured to the kid sitting next to Jeremy, his smile fading.

"Oh, I brought him along as an example. He has betrayed our organization."

"No—no, Señor, I have not," the young man protested, sweat flying from his face as he sputtered desperately. "I have *not*," he repeated in an impassioned shout as he tried to stand.

A guard slammed a high-powered rifle against his shoulder, knocking him back in his chair, groaning.

Jeremy curled his toes in his shoes, mindful to appear relaxed, aware that eyes were on him.

"So, this man has betrayed us, Donte? Mr. Kagan..."

Jeremy's gaze flew to Señor Rodriguez. "Yes, sir?"

"Do you know what happens to those who betray my family? Our organization?"

"Yes—"

"No." He interrupted, frowning, and Jeremy struggled not to squirm. "Do not answer. Watch instead. We will trust you with some of our biggest secrets. You will want to avoid the same fate."

The kid fought to stand, but his hands were tied to the chair. He screamed and begged in equal measure. "I did not betray you, Señor Rodriguez. I did *not*."

"Have dignity on your way to death," Señor Rodriguez

demanded sharply.

Donte took the huge knife from the beat up desk.

Jeremy's pulse pounded as cold sweat dribbled down his back.

The kid screamed, trying to move away, as Donte advanced forward, holding the sword to the tip of the kid's nose. With a ruthless whack, Donte sliced it off. Blood poured from the hollow as the office echoed with primitive shrieks until the kid began to choke on his own fluid.

Jeremy took several slow breaths, fighting the urge to vomit.

"Now you look like the pig that you are," Donte said calmly. "But we aren't quite finished." He sliced off the boy's ears slowly, drawing it out as if he cut two pieces of bread. The kid no longer begged for his life. He stared in a trance, mumbling in Spanish.

A guard yanked Jeremy from his chair, tugging him back to stand by Señor Rodriguez. His legs trembled beneath his jeans as Donte held the kid's hair with one hand, now matted with clots.

"Death to those who betray the Zulas," Donte shouted as he swung the knife with great force, severing head from body. Blood spit from arteries, spraying across the room, landing on Jeremy's face and his clothes. He wanted to wipe the warm drops away, but didn't dare. Instead, he swallowed bile as his stomach shuddered.

Donte held the head in his hands, smiling triumphantly, before he set it on the table as if it were a gruesome Halloween prop. "Send this, along with his other parts to his mother," he ordered to one of the guards. "She'll be looking for her boy."

Jeremy bit the inside of his cheek as gray dots danced before his eyes. If he passed out, he would die the same way.

"This, Jeremy Kagan, will be your fate and the fate of your beautiful sister if you betray the Zulas. There is no going back now. You are one of us." Señor Rodriguez held out his hand. "You should feel honored. Welcome."

"I do. Thank you." Jeremy nodded, ill, as he returned the firm handshake. He had not only bound himself to a life he no longer wanted, but Hailey too. And there was no way out.

CHAPTER 7

HAILEY LET HERSELF IN THE front door of Ethan and Sarah's house and was instantly surrounded by dogs. She crouched down, giving both Mastiffs an affectionate rub. "Hi, guys. How are my boys?" She was rewarded with warm, slobbery kisses against her cheeks. "Aw, guys, you shouldn't have." She grimaced as she wiped saliva away, brushing her damp hands on her slacks. "I mean really shouldn't have."

"You're here!" Kylee bolted down the hall, overdressed in her frilly pink party dress. Friday night pizza and movies at the Cooke's was turning into a fancy affair. "Come with me." The pretty little angel with big blue eyes and golden hair, the mirror image of her mother, grinned, pulling on Hailey's hand. "I've been *waiting* and *waiting*."

Hailey stood before she fell. "What's the hurry?" She looked at her watch. "I'm not late. Is the pizza here already?"

"Just *come*, Hailey." Kylee tugged impatiently.

"All right, bossy." Hailey smiled as she let Kylee pull her down the hall. The last week had been a whirlwind. Between helping Morgan with a massive filing project at the Bureau and staying with Sarah and Kylee on 'stork watch,' she hadn't had a moment to herself.

Ethan had called Sunday night, soon after Austin left, to ask if she would be willing to stay at the house for the week, since his schedule was jammed with security details. Twenty minutes later, Morgan phoned, wondering if Hailey wanted to make some extra cash by helping her overworked secretary at the office. When Morgan named her price, Hailey couldn't say no.

Other than the quick phone conversation with Jeremy mid-week, Hailey hadn't heard from or seen him. Despite her best efforts to get to the apartment, she simply hadn't had time. She'd planned to go home tonight after a full day at the Bureau, but Sarah had mentioned pizza and movies with the gang the night before. How could she miss out on an evening with her favorite people?

"Come on. Come on." Kylee all but vibrated with excitement.

They walked around the corner, stepping into the dining room.

"Surprise!"

Gasping, Hailey stumbled back.

Hunter stood behind Morgan, clasping his hands around her waist, both of them grinning. Ethan smiled, holding Sarah's hand as she sat in a chair, also beaming. Kylee jumped up and down, still gripping her fingers.

"Are you very excited?" Kylee shouted.

"Yes, I am." Hailey glanced around the room, shocked. Colorful balloons in all shapes and sizes were tied to each chair. A large 'Happy Birthday' banner hung from the door leading to the kitchen. The fun, funky cake on the buffet was perfect. They had done this for her. She didn't think anyone would remember her birthday. She barely had herself.

Tears threatened to spill as she pressed a hand to her heart. "You guys..." She sniffled, grinning. "Thank you."

"Happy birthday." Sarah got to her feet and wrapped Hailey in a hug. "You didn't think we were going to let your twenty-fifth birthday pass without a party, did you?"

"I—I never thought anything. Thank you," she repeated in a whisper.

After a round of hugs for everyone, Morgan disappeared into the kitchen with Hunter at her heels. Moments later,

Hunter carried out a huge dish of Morgan's famous lasagna. Morgan trailed behind with a large salad bowl and basket of steaming garlic bread—Hailey's favorite meal.

"Take your seat, birthday girl," Hunter said, as he plunked the bubbling cookware inches from her plate.

"Absolutely." Hailey smiled and sat down. As everyone took their seats, she noticed two empty settings. "Who else is coming?"

"Mommy called your brother, but he didn't come," Kylee supplied.

"Kylee, have some bread." Ethan plunked a thick, buttery piece on her plate.

The room fell silent. Hailey stared at the empty spots, trying to ignore the stabbing disappointment.

This would've been the first birthday she and Jeremy celebrated together since her fourteenth. Their lives had turned upside down the week before she turned fifteen. The foster family she lived with after her parents' deaths didn't think it necessary to recognize the day of her birth—a day that had been no more than an acknowledgement of sin, according to Mother Frazier. After all, Hailey had been born to a crack whore, and out of wedlock at that. The Frazier family reminded her of that often, but especially on her 'special day'.

"He must be busy." Hailey shrugged, picking at the piece of bread Sarah served her.

"I'm sure that's it." Sarah gripped Hailey's arm, holding on.

"Sorry I'm late."

Hailey's gaze snapped up. Austin stood in the room, big, gorgeous, and casual in his blue jeans and Adidas sweatshirt, gripping a wrapped box in his hand.

"The traffic was awful."

Hailey stared, fighting tears again as her heart thundered. She hadn't expected this, especially after she hadn't heard from him since Sunday. She'd assumed he'd forgotten about his offer to help with her lessons, or just hadn't been interested after the way they left things.

But he was here, now. Austin had rushed to be on time for her party.

"Happy birthday," he smiled, his gaze never leaving hers as he made his way to her chair.

"Thank you." She pushed back from the table, standing, and he pulled her into a hug. Her pulse kicked into a frenzy as Austin held her just as he had Sunday evening. Hailey closed her eyes, breathing in his soap, feeling his body pressed firmly to hers.

He eased away, meeting her gaze, staring, sending her pulse scrambling again.

Hailey cleared her throat as she realized everyone was looking at them. She gave Austin a smile, struggling not to feel awkward as she remembered him catching her with tears on her cheeks. "I'm glad you could come." She took her seat as Austin went to his, smiling again as his gaze flicked to hers. "Let's eat."

Hailey picked up her water, sipped, quenching her suddenly dry throat. As Hailey set down her glass, Sarah caught her attention with a look. Morgan did the same across the table. Hailey stared down at her plate, plucked up a forkful of leafy greens, and took a bite, knowing she, Sarah, and Morgan would talk later.

An hour later, the crew sat around the cozy living room. They chatted and laughed while waiting for Sarah's return from the bathroom.

"Sorry I held things up," Sarah said as she waddled in, stopping halfway to the couch, holding her stomach and wincing.

Ethan rushed to his feet. "Are you okay?"

She nodded, still pressing her hands against her large belly. "Yeah, just a couple of contractions—a little stronger than the past few days, but nothing to worry about yet. I don't think."

Ethan led her to the sofa. "Sit down. Relax."

"I'd rather stand."

"Okay." He kissed Sarah's forehead, turning her until her back rested against his chest. Ethan rubbed his hands over Sarah's belly. Hailey's heart melted from his tender gesture. Ethan was so handsome, so strong, and he adored his wife and children. Hailey wanted that more than anything—exactly what Ethan and Sarah had, what Morgan and Hunter had.

She snuck a peak at Austin as he held Kylee on his lap, bumping his leg up and down, zig-zagging, making Kylee laugh as she was zoomed left and right wildly.

Hailey looked at Sarah as Sarah pressed her lips firm, frowning. "Sarah, are you having another one?"

Austin stopped bouncing Kylee and her laughter ceased as Ethan turned his wrist, glancing at his watch. "I think we should time these."

After several breaths, Sarah relaxed her head against Ethan's shoulder. He murmured something close to her ear and she nodded. "I'm all right. Hailey, go ahead and open your gifts."

Hailey looked at the small stack of boxes and bags on the coffee table. "My presents can wait. Maybe we should call your dad."

"I have plenty of time." Sarah gave her an encouraging smile.

Kylee scrambled from Austin's lap, handing Hailey a bold floral gift bag. "Open this one. It's from me and mommy and daddy."

"Okay. Do you want to help?"

Kylee's eyes widened with glee. "Yes."

"Sit next to me." Hailey patted the spot on the cushion next to her. Hunter scooted over, moving closer to Morgan.

Hailey placed the bag between herself and Kylee. Eager to assist, Kylee yanked the bright blue paper from the top. Peeking in, Hailey smiled and pulled out a wide-brimmed sun hat. "Looks like I'll be set for my trip."

Kylee reached in, taking out a bottle of sun block.

"Yup, definitely ready for my trip." Aloe Vera came next, along with hand sanitizer, a calling card, hair ties, barrettes, chewing gum, and various other knick-knacks she'd need for her three months away. When the bag was empty, she hugged Kylee tight. "Thank you for my wonderful gifts. Now, I have everything I'll need for Mexico."

"You're weltom." Kylee patted Hailey's back.

Hailey smiled at Sarah and Ethan. "Thanks, guys."

"You're welcome, but I think you missed something," Ethan said.

Hailey peeked in the bag, frowning. There was nothing but blue and purple paper. "Um, no, that's everything."

"Try moving the tissue," Sarah suggested.

Hailey tugged at the colorful paper, her frown deepening as she pulled out a brochure for Grand Cozumel Luxury Resort and Spa. "What is this?" She opened the pamphlet, catching a plane ticket before it fell. Her name was printed across the top. She scanned her welcome letter, focusing in on her cabana number for her weeklong stay. Her heart pounded as her eyes welled and a tear spilled over. "I—I don't know what to say. This is too much. I can't... I can't—"

"Yes you can because you deserve it." Sarah walked to her.

Hailey stood, gripping her tight in a hug. She never in her life had been given such a gift. "How can I possibly thank you?"

Sarah kissed her cheek. "Have fun."

"Who needs a tissue?" Morgan snagged one, wiping at her own eyes as she passed the box to Hailey.

Hailey took one, as did Sarah before setting down the box.

"I need one too," Kylee insisted, plucking one free. She blew her dry nose enthusiastically before she dashed for the next gift. "Here. Open this. It's from Auntie Morgan and Unke Huntee." She shook her head, looking at Hunter. "Uncle Hunter."

"That's a girl." Hunter tweaked her nose, earning a grin.

"I'm not sure I can take any more surprises." Sitting down, Hailey took the prettily wrapped box from Kylee. "Go ahead, present helper. Give the paper a rip."

Kylee tore at the giftwrap with relish, then helped pull the lid from the box. Hailey stared at a beautiful camisole and matching robe. The stunning blue reminded her of a tropical paradise. She fingered the soft silk. "This is amazing. Thank you."

"I thought it would be the perfect indulgence for six nights of luxury."

"I agree." She could hardly wait to wear her new nighty. She was about to replace the lid but stopped, spotting the two envelopes peaking from the robe. Hailey pulled them free, opened the first—a gift certificate entitling her to an afternoon of horseback riding along Cozumel's beaches. "This is awesome." She'd never ridden a horse, but she was darn well going to on her dream vacation. She peeled open the next envelope and gaped—a full day at the spa offering her 'the works'. Another new adventure. "I can't believe this. I really can't." She rushed up, giddy with disbelief as she hugged Morgan, then Hunter. "Thank you so much."

"You're welcome," they answered in unison, smiled at each other.

"One more." Kylee handed her the gift box Austin had been holding when he walked in. She couldn't wait to see what Austin had been thoughtful enough to pick up for her.

"Go ahead." She gestured toward the present, giving Kylee the green light.

Kylee gave the paper a rip, pulled the top off the box and Hailey grinned. A weight belt and top-notch mask she'd tried on but hadn't been able to afford. "Hey, thanks. How did you know which one to get me?"

Austin smiled. "I have my sources."

"Oh?"

He shrugged. "I called Miranda, asked her to keep an eye out for you."

Hailey struggled with her smile. Miranda the friendly shop owner—the redhead with her amazing body and stunning complexion had been off-the-charts beautiful. Miranda had hinted, very subtly, that she and Austin knew each other well. "Thank you, Austin. This is great."

"There's one more thing—two actually—but you won't find them in the box. I'm taking you jet skiing, and we'll definitely have to spend some time skin diving."

"Sounds fun." Both opportunities sounded amazing, but she wasn't going to hold her breath. It wouldn't be easy for either of them to get a day off once Project Mexico began. "We'll have a busy semester with Project Mexico, but I'm sure we'll find at least one afternoon to get to an adventure."

"Actually, I have a little vacation time scheduled before Project Mexico. I'm taking the week at the resort as well."

Staring, Hailey concentrated on keeping her jaw from dropping. *Keep it casual, Hailey.* "Cool," was all she could manage. They probably wouldn't bump into each other much anyway.

Sarah sucked in a sharp breath and squeezed her eyes shut as she clutched Ethan's forearms. "Oh, God, this one hurts."

"Deep breaths in and out, Sarah," Ethan whispered calmly next to her ear, as he rubbed his hands over her belly.

Hunter glanced at his watch, holding up six fingers to Ethan. Sarah's contractions were getting closer.

Morgan stood. "I'm calling your dad, Sarah. Tonight's probably the night."

"I'll get her bag." Hailey got to her feet.

Kylee's lip wobbled. "Mommy."

Austin scooped her up. "It's okay, sugar plum. Emma's ready to come meet you."

"My baby?"

"Yup." Grinning, he walked to the dining room. "Let's go check out Hailey's birthday cake. You can show me what piece you want."

"Okay."

Hailey dashed upstairs, heading to the nursery. Flipping on the light, she grabbed the diaper bag Sarah filled yesterday. She glanced around the beautiful room with its pink, yellow, and pale green touches, excited that by tomorrow or the next day, the newest member of the Cooke family would be sleeping there. She couldn't wait to meet baby Emma.

Flicking off the light, she went to Ethan and Sarah's room for the suitcase just inside the door. She hurried back downstairs, entering the living room to a quiet argument.

"We're not leaving yet."

"Sarah, your contractions are six minutes apart. It's Friday night. The traffic's going to be a nightmare."

"I'm not leaving until Hailey has her cake. Oh, another one already." She pressed her forehead to Ethan's shoulder, groaning. "Oh, Ethan, it hurts."

He rocked her gently. "I know, baby. Just breathe."

As the contraction ended, Hailey stepped further into the room. "Bags are here. Time to go. Call us when we have a baby."

"Hailey, it's your birthday. You haven't had cake yet."

"We'll save it—eat it later. Maybe we'll add Emma's name, too."

"But this is your moment...for now." Sarah smiled. "Let's sing. You can make a wish, blow out the candles, then I'll go."

Ethan's eyes pleaded his urgency.

"Um, okay. Let's do this. Everyone, come on," Hailey hollered, wanting to get this over with quickly. "Dining room, stat," Hailey demanded as she gave Austin, who was holding Kylee, a gentle shove.

Morgan set the two-layer cake, decorated with funky purple daisies, bold blue zig-zags, and swirls, on the table. Morgan brought the lighter to the candle as Sarah gasped. "My water just broke and here comes another contraction."

The cake was quickly forgotten as Ethan coached Sarah through her pain and everyone scrambled into action. Morgan hurried for the phone and dialed. Austin left the room with a crying Kylee. Hunter hollered something about getting the Rover ready as he dashed down the hall.

Hailey stared at the small puddle on the hardwood floor, just inches from where Sarah had been standing before Ethan pulled her against him. Poor Sarah's maternity jeans were soaked between and down the legs. Hailey hurried upstairs, grabbed panties from the drawer and a loose, flowing skirt from her closet. Sarah would be more comfortable without the restriction.

She ran down the stairs to Sarah. "Here, Sarah,

something to change into."

"Thanks."

Ethan helped her into the bathroom. Minutes later, Ethan walked with Sarah to the entryway, but she soon stopped for another contraction. She moaned as Ethan encouraged her to breathe. "We have to go, Hailey. Hunter and Morgan are going to drive us. You'll stay with Kylee, right?"

"Of course."

Sarah stopped with her hand on the doorknob. "I need to say goodbye to Kylee."

"Austin," Ethan hollered, "can you bring the big sister out here?"

Austin stepped into the hallway. "The big sister fell asleep while we were reading 'I'm Going To Be A Big Sister.'"

"Poor thing wore herself out waiting for Hailey's party. It's probably for the best." Sarah gripped Ethan's hand. "Okay, I'm ready to have this baby."

Hailey gave Sarah a quick hug. "Everything's under control here. Call us when she comes. Good luck."

CHAPTER 8

H AILEY PULLED KYLEE'S LIMP ARM through her yellow pajama top and covered her with the pretty pink quilt. "Night, night," she whispered, kissing Kylee's forehead. Hailey switched on the nightlight and the state of the art monitor that would allow her to hear Kylee no matter where she was in the house.

Wandering to the room she slept in more often than not, Hailey pulled a pair of jeans and long-sleeved, black v-neck from the drawer. She'd been in office attire for too long. Hailey slid into her relaxing outfit and went downstairs. She had quite a mess to clean up, but it didn't matter. This was the best birthday she'd ever had.

A week at a resort and spa with all the extras. Hailey smiled. How could she ever thank her friends for giving her such an amazing gift? She would definitely be sending something special back for everyone—except Austin, because he was going too.

Hailey tried to ignore the twinge of excitement. Just because he was going didn't mean they would spend time together. The resort was probably huge, and things between them were still a little...weird. Twice now, she'd sworn she saw desire in his eyes; twice she'd been wrong. Austin wasn't interested. It was time to face facts, time to stop hoping for something that wasn't going to happen.

She rolled her eyes, frustrated. How many times had she declared that before?

As Hailey passed Kylee's playroom, she sighed. Project Mexico was such an exciting opportunity, but she was going to miss everyone so much. An entire semester away from Kylee. And Emma would grow so much over the next three months.

Hailey stepped into the dimly lit kitchen and stopped. Her stomach fluttered as she watched Austin wash the dishes. He looked yummy with his sleeves pushed up over his muscular forearms, his jeans snug over his amazing... She closed her eyes, shook her head. This wasn't exactly a great start at overcoming her unrelenting attraction.

Breathing deeply, Hailey squared her shoulders. This was the perfect opportunity to practice being unaffected. Raising her chin, determined, she moved to the island. "You never fail to surprise me."

He turned, wiping his big hands on the dishcloth. "I wasn't going to let you clean up. It's your birthday."

She smiled. "I certainly won't forget this one, that's for sure—a surprise party, amazing gifts, and a new baby all in one night. I couldn't ask for more."

He smiled back. "Sounds pretty perfect—except for one thing."

Hailey shook her head, unable to think of anything they'd missed. "What?"

"You never got to your cake. You have to make a wish and blow out the candles. It's part of the whole birthday deal. You don't want to start off the big two-five on the wrong foot."

"I can wait." Hailey didn't mention that until she met Sarah, she'd gone years without making wishes and blowing out candles, and she'd done all right.

"No, you can't." He took her hand, pulled her into the dining room. Dim light from the kitchen threw the dark room in shadows. Austin picked up the lighter, bringing the flame to life. The bright flicker cast his skin in gold light, illuminating his dark green eyes...his straight white teeth as he gave her a slow smile.

Oh, lord, he was breathtaking in candlelight. Her

stomach churning, Hailey gripped the chair in front of her as Austin touched the flame to each wick and began to sing. His smooth tenor's voice surprised her, sending skitters along her skin, giving her goose bumps.

With the candles lit, he set the lighter down and finished singing. "Happy birthday, Hailey. Make a wish."

Her mind went blank. She was supposed to make a wish, but everything she wanted stood across from her, staring into her eyes.

"Did you make your wish?"

"Uh..."

"Your cake's about to go up in flames."

Breaking free from her trance, she looked down. The candles were burnt to the bold blue frosting. "Crap." She huffed out several breaths until the room went dark and a small cloud of smoke surrounded them. Hailey moved her arm about, waiting for the smell of melted wax to dissipate. "Do you want a piece?"

"Of course. This looks amazing."

"It really does." She pulled the stubs from rich vanilla frosting and licked her finger. "Mmm, good."

"Let me get us some milk. We can't eat cake without milk."

"So true." Hailey cut a huge slice of sinful chocolate cake, layered with a rich ganache center. "This is going to be heaven." She cut another smaller piece for herself, turned with both plates, and smacked into Austin. The plates collapsed against her shirt. She gasped as ice cold milk sloshed forward, spilling over her front, adding to the mess.

"Shit. Shit. I'm sorry, Hailey."

Hailey stared at the heaps of chocolate and frosting, at the stream of milk puddling on the wooden floor.

Austin set the nearly empty glasses on the table, then pressed the plates against Hailey's abdomen as he pulled her forward. "Let's get into the kitchen before we make this worse."

"I'm not sure it could be worse." She smiled sheepishly. Why? *Why*, did this stuff happen to her?

"A situation can always be worse. I wasn't carrying coffee, right?"

She chuckled. "You've got me there."

They stepped on cool marble tile, stopping by the sink. Hailey pulled the dishes away and more cake fell with a splat. She laughed, unable to help herself. "This has been some night."

"I'd say. You have to take off your shirt." Austin pulled his sweatshirt over his head. "You can put this on after you get that off." The Under Armor he wore underneath molded against his solid chest and chiseled abs. "Ready?"

"As I'll ever be."

Austin turned as Hailey tried to pull off her top carefully. She removed her arms from the sleeves first, attempting to free her head without wearing any more cake than she already did. The flimsy cotton caught on her nose as she tugged her shirt up and over. Cold milk and sticky sweets left a trail over her stomach, chest and face. "Darn it."

"What's wrong?" Austin said, his back still to her.

"What *isn't* is a better question." She threw her soiled shirt in the sink, grabbed at her hair with chocolaty fingers. Ganache and crumbs matted her brown locks. Hailey stared at her chest, her stomach, realizing streaks of blue dyed frosting and soggy chocolate stuck to her skin.

Her most memorable birthday was becoming more unforgettable by the second. She couldn't put Austin's white sweatshirt on without staining it, and she refused to walk through Sarah and Ethan's gorgeous house dripping goo everywhere. "This is *unbelievable*."

"What's going on?" Austin turned, his eyes growing wide as he let out a snort of laughter. "Good God, Hailey. Look at you."

She glanced at the mess again, trying to hold onto dignity in her black bra and chocolate crumbs.

"It's everywhere. You kind of look like a raccoon," Austin said, strangling on suppressed laughter. "You have frosting all over your nose, all over your cheeks." He pointed, losing his composure on a burst of laughter.

Turning, Hailey stared at herself in the reflection of the microwave, horrified. She *did* look like a raccoon, and Austin was still struggling to control his mirth with a phony cough. Hailey turned back as Austin coughed on a chuckle again. Before she thought it through, she stepped over, wiped her filthy hands on his cheeks. "There. We're both raccoons."

"Hey." He grabbed her wrists, trapping her palms against his face.

She beamed. "Now you look as foolish as I do."

"I'm not sure that's possible." Grinning, he let go of her, then ran a strand of her matted hair through his fingers. His smile disappeared as he stared in her eyes.

As his breath warmed her lips, she saw it: his desire unmistakable. Screw her vow to get over him. What she'd always yearned for was right here. Her heart stuttering, Hailey moved in, closed her eyes.

"Uh, Hailey..." Austin eased back. "What're you doing? We can't do this."

Blinking her eyes open, she stared.

He stepped away completely. "Let's keep it simple, keep things friends."

She still stared, too confused to be horrified, yet... What just happened? He'd wanted her. She *saw* it.

Austin stepped forward again. "Friends, right?" he said gently.

Hailey's cheeks burned bright as she struggled to keep tears of humiliation in check. "Yeah. Yeah, of course." Suddenly cold, she looked down at herself, realizing she was still half naked. She pulled her dirty shirt from the sink, yanked it over her head, no longer caring that the milky, chocolaty mess felt like ice against her skin.

Stomach churning, Hailey turned on the hot tap, ran a sponge under the molten water, barely registering the painful heat. How was she going to turn around and look at him? How could she have been so wrong? Why hadn't she just stuck with the *plan*?

Granted, she hadn't dated much and didn't have a lot of experience with men, but how did she mistake Austin's signals so severely? She now knew, in no uncertain terms, that Austin was *not* interested, not even slightly, not even a little bit.

A good man will never want the likes of you, Hailey Roberts. Your pretty face and pretty body are a sin. You're trash, nothing but a whore like that sinning woman who made you. Mother Frazier's stinging words raced through her mind, as they had frequently over the last two months. She tried to remind herself that they weren't true.

Shaken to her core, Hailey eased the water off, wrung out the sponge, braced herself before she faced Austin again.

He leaned against the fridge, staring at her. "I'm sorry if I've—"

"Please don't apologize." She scrubbed at the sticky fingerprints on the marbled countertops, unable to meet his eyes. "If anyone should apologize, it's me." Why wouldn't he leave?

"I'm just not in a place right now—"

"You don't have to explain, Austin." She scrubbed harder, until her arm ached. "You're not interested. I get it." God, this was beyond mortifying.

The phone rang and she hurried to answer. "Hello."

"Hailey, she's here. All six pounds, seven ounces of beautiful baby."

Hailey's eyes misted as pride lightened Ethan's voice. "Congratulations, Dad."

Emma let out a wail of protest in the background and Sarah laughed. "Sounds like everyone's perfect. Can we visit in the morning?"

"You better. We want Kylee to meet her new sister. She's so beautiful," Ethan repeated.

"Give Sarah a hug for me and kiss Emma. I can't wait to hold her."

"All right. See you in the morning."

Hailey hung up. "Emma's here."

"Yeah." Austin rubbed a hand over his chin, then picked up the sponge she'd dropped.

If he thought he was staying to help clean and drag out her agony, he could think again. "It's pretty late. I'll get this. Go ahead and grab a piece of cake. I'll wrap it for you to take with you."

"Are you kicking me out, Hailey?"

"No. I'm giving us both an out from a very awkward situation."

"It doesn't have to be."

"But it is."

"Hailey—"

He was trying to be nice, trying to keep her from having hurt feelings. She turned back to the sink, afraid she would humiliate herself further with tears. "Austin, please go. It's been a long day, and I want to go to bed."

"If that's what you want."

"It is." She clutched at the counter.

"Good night, then."

She closed her eyes. "Good night."

Austin's footsteps disappeared down the hall.

Hailey held Kylee's hand and carried the gift bag in the other as they walked to the nurse's station. "Remember what we talked about—nice and quiet. Lots of babies are trying to sleep."

"I be quiet."

She picked Kylee up as they approached the front desk, waiting for the nurse's acknowledgement.

The harried woman glanced up from a chart. "Good morning, can I help you?"

"Yes. We're here to see Sarah and Ethan Cooke. They had a baby girl last night."

The nurse looked back at the big duty board hanging on the wall. "Room 321. Down the hall and to the right."

"Thank you." Hailey smoothed a strand of blonde behind Kylee's ear. "Are you ready to meet Emma?"

"Yes!" She beamed, clapping.

"Me too." Hailey smiled, brushed her nose with Kylee's—eskimo-style—and started down the hall. When they stopped at room 321, Kylee bunched her knuckles. "I knock."

"Okay."

Kylee banged her small fist on the door, hardly making a sound.

Ethan pulled the door open, grinning. "Hi, big sister."

Kylee held out her arms. "Hi, daddy."

Ethan took Kylee, kissed the top of her head. "I missed you last night. Are you ready to meet your baby?"

"Yes. We bought her a present."

Ethan glanced at the gift bag Hailey still held. "That was very nice." He snuggled Kylee on the bed next to Sarah and Emma.

Sarah wrapped her arm around Kylee as Emma

suckled greedily at her mother's breast. "Hi, sweetheart, I missed you this morning."

"I missed you too." Kylee moved her head, trying to peek at her new sister. "She's very small."

"Yes, she is. We have to be gentle. Do you want to hold her?"

Kylee's eyes brightened. "I will be careful."

"Oh, I know you will." Sarah broke Emma's latch and covered her breast. She placed Emma in Kylee's eager arms.

Kylee stared at Emma, grinning, as Emma suckled in her sleep. "You are my baby." Kylee kissed her sister's forehead and Hailey sighed. How was she going to leave her girls for three whole months?

"I have to get a picture. I'll look at it every day while I'm away." Hailey set the gift bag down and dug in her purse for her small digital camera. "Kylee, look at me and smile."

Kylee did as she was told and Hailey captured the moment. "Sarah, Ethan, I want one with all of you."

Ethan moved to the side, flanking his daughters as Sarah did the same. "Big smiles." Hailey snapped another picture, studied the screen. The perfect family: two stunning, loving parents and their beautiful little girls. Hailey felt a tug of envy as she powered off the camera. "I'm so happy for you."

Emma began to fuss, and Kylee gasped. "I was gentle."

Sarah took Emma from Kylee. "Yes you were. Emma's telling us she wants to eat some more."

Ethan scooped Kylee up. "I think the big sister and I should get something to eat. I bet we could find you a doughnut."

"Ooh, a doughnut. I want a doughnut."

Ethan smiled as he looked at Sarah. "One doughnut isn't going to kill her, Sarah. We'll be back later." He pulled the door open and they left.

"I can't tell you how many times he's said that." Sarah grinned as she shook her head.

"I'm pretty sure I've heard the same thing a few times myself." Hailey gave Sarah a hug. "Congratulations." She sat on the edge of the bed next to her, staring at sweet-faced Emma. "She's beautiful."

"Do you want to hold her?"

"Of course. I hardly slept last night; I was so excited." She left out the part about tossing and turning every time she thought of her disastrous situation with Austin.

Sarah handed Emma over.

Hailey brushed her fingers over soft skin, breathing in the scent of baby powder as she snuggled Emma close. She played with the black peach fuzz on Emma's head. "She has her daddy's hair color."

"For now. We'll see if it stays that way."

As Hailey stared at the pretty baby, doubts took over. What if going to Mexico was a mistake? What if Sarah and Ethan needed her help? How was she going to deal with Austin? Each time they saw each other it was bound to be awkward.

"Hailey, what's wrong?"

She shook her head. "Nothing."

"I don't believe that for a minute. I could tell something was bothering you the minute you entered the room."

She skimmed Emma's curled fist. "I guess I'm having second thoughts about Mexico. I'll be gone for such a long time. What if you need my help with the girls? Ethan's busier than ever."

Sarah wrapped an arm around Hailey's shoulders. "We're going to miss you so much, but I want you to go. I want you to do this. What an opportunity. You spend so much time taking care of everyone else. I want you to take care of Hailey for a change. Just think, twelve free semester hours. You're so close to finishing school."

"I know." But school wasn't what she wanted. Completing her degree was necessary, but what she dreamed of was a family of her own. She yearned for babies to treasure and love, a husband who would stand with her and build something lasting and strong.

"I thought you really wanted this. What's going on?"

She nuzzled Emma's warm, smooth forehead against her cheek as she prepared to confess all to Sarah. "I—"

The door opened and Morgan popped her head in. "Am I interrupting?"

Sarah smiled. "No, come on in."

Morgan walked over, joining Hailey and Sarah by the bed. "I can't get enough of that beautiful face. She's perfect."

"Do you want a turn?" Hailey held Emma out to her.

"If I must." Morgan took Emma and smiled.

Sarah pushed over. "Have a seat. Hailey was just about to tell me why she doesn't want to go to Mexico anymore."

Morgan's gaze snapped to Hailey's. "You don't want to go? I thought you were excited."

Hailey shrugged. "I was. I am. I was." She huffed out a breath. "I made a complete idiot out of myself last night." Blushing, she covered her face with her hands. "Just thinking of it makes me cringe. I'm such a moron." She peeked through her fingers.

Sarah's brow shot up. "Are you going to tell us or keep us in suspense?"

"I tried to kiss Austin, and he didn't try to kiss me back."

Morgan wrinkled her nose. "Ouch."

"Yeah, ouch."

"I'm sure it was a simple misunderstanding." Sarah rubbed a hand over Hailey's stiff shoulders.

"It was *definitely* a misunderstanding. I thought he

was interested, but he cleared that notion right up."

Morgan frowned. "Then I've misunderstood too. I've seen the way he looks at you, Hailey. He's definitely interested—make no mistake about it."

Hailey smothered the flicker of hope as she thought back to the awkward scene in the kitchen. She shrugged. "I'm afraid not. He said, and I quote, 'Let's keep it simple, keep things friends.' He all but patted my head."

Morgan scoffed and rolled her eyes. "Why are men so stupid?" She kissed Emma's forehead. "You might as well learn right here and now, Emma. Men are completely stupid...sometimes...most of the time."

"And sometimes they're just confused," Sarah added as she smiled at Morgan.

"Let me assure you both. Austin was not confused. He doesn't want me." Saying so hurt.

"Oh, honey, I agree with Morgan on this one. You don't leave Austin unaffected. I can see it in his eyes. I think he's a little shy and very sweet. Maybe you need to give him a push."

"Give him some time, Hailey," Morgan encouraged. "If he doesn't come around, go get him. In fact, I'm pretty sure I know just the thing to wear. I believe you received it for your birthday. It's a beautiful blue nightie."

The thought of trying to seduce Austin was too much. She couldn't even make the guy kiss her, and now she was supposed to get him into bed? Maybe if she was as stunning as Morgan or as classically beautiful as Sarah, but she wasn't either of those things. She was cute enough and smart, and she was okay with that.

Austin could do worse. Maybe she didn't want him after all... And snowflakes flew in hell. "You know, I'll probably be so busy with Project Mexico, I won't even have time to think about Austin."

Morgan and Sarah exchanged a look and smug smiles.

"Good luck with that," Morgan said.

Hailey gave Morgan a playful swat on the leg. "If you two are finished teasing. I have to go. I have a plane to catch in two days and a crap-load of packing to do."

"Are you going home?" Sarah asked, sobering.

"Shopping first to pick up a few last-minute supplies, then yes. Do you need me to take Kylee instead?"

"No. My dad's releasing us this afternoon if I promise to take it easy. You know you can always stay with us until you leave." Sarah glanced at Morgan. "I would love to have you. Having you close might help Kylee with the adjustment."

Hailey had planned to stay home, to spend time with Jeremy before she left him for three months, but if Kylee needed her she would be there. "I can make that work. Most of my stuff's at your house anyway. Let me get to my errands, then I'll come over."

"Hailey, you're great."

"I do what I can." She smiled, feeling better after time with her two closest friends.

"Wait," Morgan snagged Hailey's arm as she stood. "I'm actually glad you were both here this morning. I have something I want to tell you."

Hailey sat back down. "What's up?"

"I guess I'll come right out and say it. Hunter and I are pregnant."

Humming silence filled the room, until Hailey and Sarah hugged Morgan gently, since she was still holding Emma.

"Oh my God, Morgan!" Hailey hugged her again. "This is amazing news. You let me go on and on about my foolish troubles when you actually had something important to say."

"I liked listening to your 'foolish troubles.' I'll like listening more when you call Sarah and me to tell us the little blue number worked."

Hailey chuckled. "Don't hold your breath. How far

along are you?"

"We think about five or six weeks. I took a test this morning; I have a doctor's appointment later this afternoon."

Sarah dabbed at a tear. "Hunter must be thrilled."

"We both are. Hunter still might be sitting on the toilet seat staring at the test." Morgan smiled as she looked at Emma. "I can't wait to hold my baby. I had no idea I could feel like this. I'm in love already. I'm looking forward to calling my parents tonight."

"Congratulations, Morgan. I'm so happy for you and Hunter. I have to get going. I'll leave the mommies to it." She hugged Morgan and Sarah, then kissed Emma on the forehead. "I'll be back to help with Kylee later. Morgan, I'll swing by and say goodbye to you and Hunter tomorrow afternoon."

"Let's have dinner—all of us, if you think you're up to it, Sarah," Morgan said. "I feel like cooking. I could bring some stuff over. We'll eat at your place. That way, you can keep Emma home."

"Great."

Hailey grabbed her keys from her purse. "Can I pick anything up while I'm out and about?"

"I think I have everything we'll need."

"All right. Until later, then." Hailey walked to the door, pulled it open. With a last wave, she stepped out and slammed into Austin. His hands flew to her arms, steadying her. "Oh sorry." She stepped back from the shock of his touch.

"No problem." He cleared his throat, shoved his hands in his pockets.

They stared at each other in awkward silence until Hailey cleared her own throat. "I have to go."

"Yeah, okay."

Hailey walked off, rolling her eyes. She really had to stop running into him that way.

CHAPTER 9

AUSTIN STEPPED FROM THE JET way onto the plane. He nodded at the flight attendant's sunny welcome, murmuring a thank you as he made his way down the aisle. He passed Hailey settling in and paused, making brief eye contact with her before she looked down and he moved on.

They hadn't spoken since Saturday morning when they'd bumped into each other, literally, at the hospital. If Morgan and Sarah hadn't been watching—carefully—he would've pulled her into a corner and straightened out the 'kitchen incident' right then and there.

He had planned to try again in the airport, but as he walked to the boarding gate, Hailey had glanced up from her magazine, doing a double-take, swearing. He was an excellent lip-reader. She'd gathered her carryon and purse casually—or so she must have thought—and wandered off in the opposite direction toward the food court. She'd managed to stay gone until their second boarding call.

Austin stowed his carryon and sat down. He looked out his window, watching men load luggage on the conveyer belt. He glanced at Hailey's ponytail peeking over her seat. The next three months were bound to be awkward if they didn't clear the air.

Sighing, he stared out at the suitcases again. An apology was definitely in order. He'd sent Hailey mixed signals, then embarrassed her with rejection. What a shitty-ass move. He never should have touched her hair, never should have stared into those honey-colored eyes.

Austin pressed his head against the seat and closed his eyes. He couldn't remember the last time a woman had affected him the way Hailey did—on every level. She thought he'd pulled back from lack of interest. Quite the contrary. He was *beyond* interested. He *wanted* her, but if he had kissed her Friday night, they would've done a hell of a lot more than that. The sparks of need had been there, waiting to combust into bright, hot flames. He would have eaten her alive and that would have been unfair.

Every time he watched Hailey interact with Kylee, he knew that was what she wanted—children, home, something stable of her own. At times he could all but see her yearning. And that was the problem. He had no plans to go there—not anytime soon. Kids, family, and the responsibilities that came with the package weren't on his list right now. He didn't want what Hailey wanted, so that was the end of the story. Why waste her time?

He liked things as they were—great friends, a lucrative job he loved. He answered to no one but himself, and that was the way he wanted it.

All his life he'd played by someone else's rules. His childhood had been consumed by his parent's dairy farm. Although he'd had a wonderful, loving family, his father's dreams had never been his. Austin had craved action, adventure, the sea.

On his eighteenth birthday, he'd packed a bag, walked into the United States Navy recruiting office, and never looked back. He'd traded one form of demand for another, but the new one he had loved—until he and his SEAL team ran with the wrong information and killed a building full of innocent civilians. After that, he struggled through his last six months of service, choosing not to reenlist.

Following several weeks of soul searching, he signed on as Security Expert for Ethan Cooke Security. He was good now—fine, exactly where he wanted to be. Nothing was missing from his life.

Austin glanced at Hailey's ponytail again, slightly weary of his own lack of conviction.

The flight attendant welcomed everyone, pulling Austin from his thoughts. She began her speech about exits and cabin pressure, which he largely ignored. He spent so much time on planes, private and commercial, he could've given the spiel himself.

Austin reached for the magazine he'd picked up at the Media Store, pausing mid-stretch as he watched two men enter the plane before the attendant closed the door.

"Fucking-A," he muttered.

Jeremy and the banger who beat him up made their way down the aisle to Hailey. She stood, beaming, giving her brother a hug. Jeremy kissed Hailey's cheek, then said something to her. Austin strained to hear snatches of their conversation as the attendant voice projected through the speakers.

The man with the tattoos took Hailey's hand, his eyes all but devouring her as he smiled. Austin caught his name. Mateo. Mateo looked far more respectable in his blue plaid shorts and polo shirt than he had stepping from Hailey's apartment, but designer clothes didn't hide the thug beneath.

Sighing, Austin rubbed his hand over his chin. So much for vacation; the next seven days were going to be another workweek. He wouldn't be able to let Hailey out of his sight with those two hanging around.

Jeremy, Mateo, and Hailey took their seats as the plane pulled back from the jet way. Within minutes, the jet taxied down the runway and was airborne. As the plane reached cruising altitude, passengers settled into sleep or their magazines and the cabin quieted, but not enough for Austin to keep up with the murmurs of

Hailey's conversation.

He secured his laptop case and slid into the empty row of seats diagonal to Hailey.

She glanced up midsentence, her eyes cool, before she dismissed him and looked back down. At least he didn't have to worry about introductions.

Pulling his laptop out, Austin flipped open the lid. He clicked on "games" and started a round of "free cell" while he listened.

"I still can't believe this. What a great surprise." Hailey beamed. "So, Mateo, tell me more about yourself. How do you know Jeremy?"

"We both work for Mr. Rodriguez."

"I haven't had much time to hear about the new job." She smiled at her brother. "We've both been so busy. What exactly do you do?"

"Simply put, Jeremy and I are Mr. Rodriguez's right hand men. We help him with anything he needs. Our goal is to ensure his businesses remain successful."

"Mr. Rodriguez lives in the Hills? I'm afraid I've never heard of him." Hailey shrugged apologetically.

"He's actually from Mexico," Jeremy spoke up, voice tight. "That's probably why. He's—"

"He's from a very wealthy family—old money," Mateo cut him off. "The Rodriguez family likes to stay in the background, but they oversee several quiet organizations that help others. They're big believers in giving back."

Austin clenched his jaw. This guy was good.

"How admirable." Hailey's voice rang with delight.

"I think so." Mateo winked. "In fact, after Jeremy told Mr. Rodriguez of your plans to participate in Project Mexico, he insisted we come help."

"Amazing. Really." Hailey shook her head. "You don't hear of many people like that anymore. I would love to meet Mr. Rodriguez."

"I know he would like to meet you." Mateo grinned, then his smile slowly faded. "I owe the Rodriguez's everything. They saved my life."

Hailey leaned in closer, her eyes swimming with compassion.

"I haven't always been a good person." Mateo gestured to his arms, the gang symbols decorating his skin. "I've lived a life I'm not very proud of." He looked down, then raised his eyes to meet Hailey's gaze again. "But I've put all that behind me. I met Mr. Rodriguez three years ago. He changed me into the person I am today. I believe in his mission, fully, and hope to be half the man he is someday."

Austin rolled his eyes, shook his head. What a load of bullshit.

Hailey reached for Mateo's hand. "It takes courage to change your life. If there's anything I can do to help..."

"You can enjoy a day of sight-seeing with Jeremy and me tomorrow. I've been to Cozumel several times over the last few months."

Hailey nodded, smiling. "Okay."

Like hell she would. Austin rubbed at the tension squeezing his jaw. He couldn't believe this. Hailey was actually eating it up. He unfastened his belt, needing to stand before he reached over and knocked someone, anyone out. Hailey might as well write 'sucker' on her forehead.

"Where will you guys be staying?" Hailey asked.

Austin planted his butt back down, wanting to know the answer himself.

"At the resort—a few cabanas over, I believe. Jeremy wanted to be close—in case you need him."

Austin ground his teeth. How the hell was he going to keep Hailey safe when his room was in the hotel? Thank God the flight had WiFi capabilities. Ethan would have to pull some strings. He sent Ethan a message:

It just keeps getting better... You'll never guess who joined the party. He and a roommate will be in the cabana suites. You know what to do.
-Austin

Within seconds, he received a response.

Let me make some calls. I'll keep in touch.

With that settled, Austin got to his feet. He couldn't listen to one more second of Mateo's fake sob story about his personal struggles and triumphs as a former drug addict and gang member.

Austin wandered back to the bathroom, glancing around at sleeping passengers, at people reading or typing away on their computers. He almost missed a step when he recognized the two men from the photos he'd taken in South Central, who had stood guard over Donte Rodriguez.

Son of a bitch. Austin locked himself in the small commode and scrubbed his hands over his face. What the *fuck* was he going to do?

Jeremy and Mateo's every move was being watched, and more than likely Hailey's too. They were 30,000 feet in the air and surrounded by the Mexican Mafia. The whole point of this vacation was to *remove* her from the situation. It would only be worse when they landed.

Austin squeezed his fingers against the base of his neck, rolled his shoulders, attempting to relieve the sharp clenching ache. *Damn.* This was a nightmare and there was no way out.

This entire mess couldn't be fixed by putting Hailey on the next plane home. If the mafia wanted to find her, there would be nowhere she could run. The Zulas' connections ran far, wide, and deep.

Austin pressed at his temple, struggling to think over the pounding. All he could do now was wait. He needed to talk to Hunter and Ethan.

He stepped from the bathroom, staring at the back of Jeremy's head, struggling with blood scorching rage. Jeremy had sentenced himself to a life of danger and death, and in his greed, he'd brought his sister along too.

A grin split Hailey's face as she stared at her accommodations for the week. "Holy crap! This is *amazing*." Her cabana suite was cozy, elegant, and fifty yards from crystal blue water. She rolled her bulging suitcase further into the room and let out a hoot of delight. Her bed, cloaked in pale green and yellow bedding, was big enough for four. The small whicker sitting area sat across from huge panels of glass, giving her a view of vibrant pink flowers, bright green palms, sandy white beaches, and the bold, blue ocean. It took her breath away. "I can't believe this."

Hailey abandoned her luggage, sighing as she stood in her bathroom doorway. The room was stark white but decorated beautifully. Massive conch shells and coral pieces accented beach wood and lush tropical plants. Tan candles sat in threes along the lake-sized tub. She pressed a button by the light switch and gasped as a curtain silently moved up, exposing a view of ocean waves as far as the eye could see. "Oh, I am *so* taking a bath in here while the sun sets...tomorrow night." Hailey had plans to meet Jeremy for an overdue birthday dinner in three hours. She was going to make the most of her time.

Sliding her sunglasses in place, Hailey grabbed her

small digital camera and locked the door behind her. The warm sea breeze caressed her cheeks as she breathed deeply, unable to believe she was truly here in this tropical paradise.

Gasping, she stared at a yacht miles out. She'd never seen a boat so big; it was practically a small-scale cruise ship. Zooming in as far as her camera lens would allow, she pressed the shutter button several times, watching the towering white vessel grow small before she continued down the beach.

"Hailey."

She paused, startled by Austin calling her name from the cabana next to hers. "Oh *great*." She wasn't ready to deal with him, especially when he was shirtless. Hailey turned and kept walking, picking up her pace. If she was being rude, she didn't care. Austin had embarrassed and confused her; now she was pissed off. Was she being unreasonable? Maybe. Did she feel justified? Absolutely.

Over the past three days, she'd done little but replay their evening in the kitchen. She couldn't forget the way Austin had stared into her eyes as he played with her hair, his lips a whisper from hers. Flutters churned in her stomach, her heartbeat quickening as she remembered the moment now. It still annoyed her.

Austin said "friends," but she had *seen* something else in those few seconds by the kitchen counter. She had never thought Austin the type to play games, but maybe she was wrong. She wasn't about to stick around and find out.

"Hailey, wait up," Austin said, as he hurried into step beside her.

"This isn't a good time." She quickened her pace further, but his long legs were no match for her shorter strides. She huffed out a breath, came to a stop , trying to ignore the light sheen of sweat over his amazing, tanned muscles. "I said this isn't a good time."

"Yeah, I heard you. I've been wanting to talk to you."

"Well, I'm busy." She turned to leave, but Austin stopped her with a hand on her arm.

"How about later? I changed rooms. I'm your neighbor. You could knock on my door when you have a free minute."

Not on your life. "Okay, yeah, sure, fine."

"'Okay, yeah, sure, fine,'" he repeated, wincing, as a pained look settled on his face. "All 'red flag' words of a pissed off woman."

Her lips twitched. Why did he have to be so damn cute?

"Wait." Austin held up a hand and took a step back "Is that a smile? Are you going to smile?"

"No, I'm not." She would make the inside of her cheek bleed before she gave him the grin that so desperately wanted to escape. She refused to be affected by his charm.

"Will you have dinner with me?"

If she could count the number of times she'd wished he'd ask this very question... But he wasn't interested in her romantically. He confused her too much right now, but she still wanted him despite everything that had happened. Staying away from Austin for the next several days was the best thing she could do for herself. "I can't; I'm having dinner with Jeremy."

"How about lunch tomorrow?"

"I'm sightseeing with Jeremy and Mateo."

He clenched his jaw before he relaxed it. "How about dinner after?"

She remembered her plans for her candlelight bath. Dinner with Austin sounded even better, but a bath was safer. "Austin, I really think..." she stopped, smiling suddenly as Mateo approached. She was happy to have a distraction. "Mateo, how's your suite?"

"Freaking awesome."

She chuckled. "I thought the same thing. Mateo, this is Austin Casey. Austin, Mateo Flores."

Mateo stuck out his hand. "Nice to meet you, Austin. Have I seen you before?"

Austin shook Mateo's hand. "Yeah, coming out of Hailey's apartment."

Hailey stared at Austin, shocked by his unfriendly tone. In the last week, she'd seen a side of him she didn't know existed. The rigid set of his body and the hard light in his eyes were new, and she didn't like them. "Mateo, I'm heading up to the main hotel to look around, maybe get a snack," she improvised. "Do you want to join me?"

"Sure."

"See you around, Austin." She turned her back, dismissing Austin and his ugly attitude.

"Hailey, wait." Austin snagged her arm.

She pulled free of his hold, wanting nothing to do with him at the moment. "I said I'll see you around."

As Mateo took a step forward, Hailey placed a hand on his chest. "Mateo, can you give us a second? I'll catch up."

"Yeah, sure." Mateo gave Austin a warning stare before he wandered down the beach.

Hailey waited until Mateo was out of earshot before she rounded on Austin. "What is *wrong* with you?"

"Nothing. I just think you should be careful." He gestured toward the path, his implication clear.

Hailey's eyes widened as irritation turned to a quick, burning anger. Austin didn't know anything about Mateo. He was judging on nothing more than appearances. "What should I be careful of, exactly?"

"Of who you're hanging around with," Austin's voice grew edgy.

She remembered not too long ago Austin's accusations of Jeremy's gang affiliation. Was this what he'd been talking about? Austin saw Mateo come out of her

108

apartment and jumped to the conclusion Jeremy was a dealer and gangster?

Hailey glared and crossed her arms. "And what's wrong with Mateo? His tattoos? Maybe if you took the time to get to know him instead of making rash judgments, you would realize the ink on his arms is part of a past he's trying to leave behind. You're something else."

Hailey spun away, turned back, unable to let this go. "Mateo is a friend of Jeremy's, so that makes him a friend of mine. You, on the other hand, have made your feelings toward my brother more than clear."

She gave Austin a shove, just because she could. Not that he moved, but it felt good to place her anger somewhere. "I know we can't all be as perfect as you, Austin Casey, but if your snobbery is considered perfection, then I don't want to be."

Hailey stormed off, hurrying down the beach to catch up with Mateo. If she saw Austin before the week was over, it would be too soon.

CHAPTER 10

AUSTIN LAY ON HIS BED, staring at the ceiling fan, fuming. He'd handled things on the beach worse than he had the night in the kitchen. Lately, every time he was around Hailey, she jumbled his brain until he couldn't think.

It might as well have been amateur hour while he stood in the sand, losing his cool. His open hostility toward Mateo had been completely foolish and broke every rule in the subtle art of reconnaissance.

He couldn't gather information if he alienated Mateo and Jeremy before vacation even began. And he wouldn't bring Hailey around to who her brother really was if he made her angry every time he saw her.

Hailey was a champion of the underdog. If he continued to express his dislike for her brother and Mateo, he would never be able to keep her close. Mateo was the real deal—a first-class con on top of everything else.

But Mateo didn't know Hailey the way Austin did. That's where he had the upper hand. He had three years of interaction, of friendship. He had visits to the zoo, arcade battles, movies with popcorn and debates at the end, holidays, long weekends away—with Ethan, Sarah, Morgan, and Hunter.

If Austin wanted that to continue, he had to stop alienating her. His inability to control his shaky emotions was going to get Hailey killed.

Austin sat up, sighed, and glancing at the clock—seven thirty. He needed to eat. He hadn't had anything decent since his early morning breakfast. The clerk at check-in said the beachfront dining room had a five-star rating. If he was going to eat, he planned to eat well.

Austin pulled a pair of khaki slacks from the small closet along with a dark green polo. Dressed and ready, he locked up and strolled down the beach. Minutes later, he climbed the steps to the restaurant, his stomach growling as he breathed in the scent of well-prepared seafood. He walked in the upscale dining room, stopping at the bar.

"Good evening, sir." The bartender placed a cocktail napkin in front of him. "What can I get you to drink?"

"What do you have on tap?"

"Pretty much anything you want, including our house brews."

Austin was always willing to try something new. "Give me your most popular homebrew."

"Right away, sir." The man was true to his word. He slid a pale ale in front of him within seconds.

"Thanks." Austin glanced around at well-presented entrees. A vivid blue sundress on the outside deck caught his attention. Hailey's light brown hair billowed in the gentle breeze as she sat at a table—alone—stirring a straw in her beverage instead of eating the salad before her.

A waiter stopped at her table and she glanced at her watch, shaking her head. The man pulled the menu from the empty setting and walked off.

Austin wanted to feel smug; her asshole brother had shown his true colors once again. But as he stared at Hailey, alone and beautiful at a table set for two, he couldn't feel anything but sadness. Austin slid a five on the bar, then wandered out to the deck, stopping behind the vacant chair.

Hailey glanced up.

"Hey," he said, looking at her. She took his breath away. Hailey had pulled her hair back in a barrette, leaving her face unframed, the way he liked best. She'd curled the ends; loose spirals fell to her naked, slender shoulders.

"Hey." She looked at her Sprite, starting to stir it again.

She wasn't going to give an inch, even though her eyes were sad. He hated seeing her upset because it was so rare—except lately. "Can I sit down?"

Hailey shrugged. "I guess."

He took the empty chair and the waiter came over.

"Señor, let me get you a menu."

Austin looked at Hailey, waiting for her to object. When she stayed silent, staring back, he gave the waiter a nod. So, they would have dinner after all.

Within moments, the waiter handed him a menu. "Thanks." Austin set it down without looking at the offerings. "Nice night."

"Mmm." Hailey stopped stirring her soda and rested her hands on the table.

Austin took a chance and snagged her fingers, holding them firm as they stiffened against his palm. "Hailey, do you want me to leave?"

"Kind of."

No, she definitely wasn't going to give an inch. "Tell you what. If you still look like you want to strangle me by the time you finish your salad I'll leave."

"Fine."

"I'm sorry—" He tightened his grip when she tried to pull free. "It'll be easier to apologize if you actually look at me."

Her gaze lifted from the table, meeting his.

"I'm sorry about this afternoon. I was rude to both you and Mateo. I'll apologize to Mateo when I see him." He would choke on it, but if two simple words helped keep her safe, he would get over it.

Hailey's fingers relaxed in his hand. "I appreciate it."

"Then it's done."

The waiter wandered back. "What can I bring you this evening, Senor?"

"I'll have what the lady's having."

"Very good." The waiter plucked up the menu and left.

"I ordered calf brains, you know."

He grinned at the teasing light warming her eyes. Now they were getting somewhere. "Then you'll have leftovers to bring back to your room."

She smiled.

"What are we really having?"

"Grilled salmon topped with a lobster, mango salsa, herbed brown rice, and sautéed vegetables."

"That's more like it. Do you want a glass of wine?"

"No, thanks. Alcohol makes my head fuzzy." She wrinkled her nose. "I know, not very sophisticated."

"Sophisticated is boring. I like you just the way you are."

Hailey's smile disappeared, and she pulled her fingers free.

"Should we clear up the night at Ethan's while we're at it?"

"No."

He wanted to, but she clearly didn't. "Will you share your salad?"

She pushed her plate to the center of the table.

Austin stabbed a bite of lettuce and a cherry tomato, intending to keep their conversation light. "Do you like your room?"

"I love it. It's beautiful. The view's sensational." Her eyes brightened, unable to conceal her enthusiasm. Hailey fiddled with her straw again. "What about you? Do you like yours?"

"I can't complain. We should definitely enjoy ourselves while we're here. Ethan sent me pictures of our accommodations for the next few months.

They're very…basic."

She chuckled. "That nice, huh?"

"Yeah, that nice." He smiled, relieved they were on the right track. "We could drive over and get a firsthand peek this week, or we can enjoy a little piece of paradise and deal with reality when we have to."

"Let's deal with it when we have to. I don't want to leave. The resort's too beautiful, too perfect."

Hailey was describing herself and didn't even know it. The sun sunk low along the horizon, casting her creamy skin golden in the last of day's light. White Chinese lanterns glowed, dancing about in the wind, lending an air of romance to the warm tropical evening.

"How pretty." She sighed, smiling.

Austin made a sound in his throat as he chewed, trying and failing to be unaffected by Hailey in candlelight.

She set her fork down. "So, what are your plans for your first full day of vacation?"

"I'm not sure." He would be tagging along wherever Hailey and her pals were going. He just didn't know where that was yet. "What about you?"

The waiter came back, taking the empty plate.

She shrugged. "Everything's up in the air. Mateo told me he and Jeremy might have to work. I guess Mr. Rodriguez called after they landed."

Austin noticed Hailey had nothing to say about Jeremy's absence this evening.

Colorful plates were set before them, and she breathed in deeply. "Oh, *look* at this. I can't wait to try it."

"Go ahead." Austin was enjoying her pleasure for the simple things.

Hailey picked up her fork and cut a small piece of salmon, picking up a chunk of mango and lobster with it. She brought the bite to her mouth, closed her eyes, and moaned. "This is *so* amazingly good. Here, try." She cut another piece of fish and held it to his lips.

Austin stared at her as he took the food from her fork. The sweet mango and subtle Cajun spices created a delicious contrast of flavors. "Wow, really good."

He picked up his own silverware and dove in, pretending that her quiet moan moments before hadn't sent his hormones into overdrive.

After several bites in silence, Hailey met his gaze, smiled. "So...I guess I'm glad you happened by my table tonight."

Austin grinned as he swallowed another sensational bite. "I'm pretty glad too."

"If Mateo and Jeremy can't sightsee tomorrow, I'm thinking about doing the horseback tour. I've never ridden a horse. It should be—"

The boisterous hoots and hollers of a small crowd below cut her off. The group strolled by, laughing, as they made their way into the resort's casino.

Mateo had an arm slung around a pretty woman's waist. Jeremy was talking loudly, holding a young blonde's hand, a beer bottle in the other, with a cigarette dangling from the corner of his lips.

Hailey set down her fork and stared as Jeremy disappeared through the door. "What is he doing? Jeremy doesn't drink. He gave it up."

"Apparently not."

Hailey's heated gaze snapped to his.

Austin shrugged, trying to keep it casual. "He's over eighteen, Hailey. There's nothing saying he can't have a beer down here."

"But Jeremy told me he doesn't drink anymore."

Austin stared at Hailey, running his tongue over his teeth. Did she finally see? Did she finally get that her brother was a liar? "I don't know what to tell you."

Hailey held his gaze for a moment, then got to her

feet. "I'm not doing this with you."

"Doing what?" He sat up taller.

"Give me a break, Austin."

"What? I didn't even *say* anything."

"You didn't have to. Your self-righteous smirk says it all." Hailey stormed down the balcony steps.

He hadn't been smirking, had he? Austin raised his hand for their check, then noticed the man in the corner, eating his meal, watching Hailey's hurried steps along the beach. Austin scrutinized the burly diner as he continued to study Hailey. Was this guy being paid to keep an eye on her, or was he simply intrigued by a beautiful woman?

Unsure, Austin committed the guy's face to memory before he scribbled a twenty percent tip on the bill, signed his name, and took the stairs in twos before he lost sight of her as she rushed to her cabana. "Hailey, wait up."

She glanced over her shoulder, walking faster, finally breaking into a run.

"Damn it." Austin started to run himself, catching up with her steps from her room. "I said wait up."

"I don't want to wait for you. I have nothing to *say* to you." She continued to her miniature porch and jammed her key in the lock.

"*Wait* a minute." Austin followed, placing his hands on her rigid shoulders.

Hailey's hand stilled on the knob. "Don't touch me," she said, her voice unsteady. "Just leave me alone."

He couldn't leave her alone now—not when she was on the verge of tears. "Hailey." He moved his thumbs back and forth over her soft skin, trying to suppress his frustration for taking hit after hit while Jeremy stayed forever in the clear.

"It's been a long day."

Austin turned her to face him. Tears swam in her miserable eyes. "Please don't cry."

"I'm not. I'm fine." Her lip wobbled, and she sniffed.

"No you're not." He pulled Hailey against him, wrapping her in a hug. Austin thought back to the moment at Ethan's when she stood by the big window, alone, with a single tear running down her cheek. Hailey wasn't going to be alone this time. "I'm sorry," he murmured close to her ear.

Hailey eased back. "You didn't do anything wrong. I'm mad at Jeremy and took it out on you." She pressed her fingers against her temple. "Just when I thought he was on the right track..." she shook her head.

Austin took her hand and tugged until she sat beside him on the step. "He's a grown man, Hailey. You aren't responsible for the choices he makes."

"I'm not ready to give up on him. There's a good person underneath the rough exterior. I've seen it. I *remember* it." She shook her head again as she tried to stand. "I don't want to talk about this."

He did. Austin snagged her fingers, tugging her down again. He wanted to understand why Jeremy deserved so much love and loyalty, especially when he clearly didn't give her any in return, so Austin pushed. "How old were you when your parents passed away?"

"They died the week before my fifteenth birthday. Jeremy was nine, almost ten. His birthday's in March."

"What happened?"

"We were on our way home from a welcome home party. One of Daddy's friend's sons had come back from some sort of military training. It was a big deal. We lived in Northern California and it was cold—colder than any of us ever remembered. The roads were icy. Daddy swerved to avoid a car that came into our lane. We hit a tree." She squeezed his hand. "It didn't occur to me until a couple years later that everyone was still alive after that initial impact. We all would've walked away, but then the car hit

117

us and we collided with another tree. That's what killed my parents. I thought Jeremy was dead too, but all I cared about was my seatbelt. I remember that more than anything else; I couldn't get out of my seatbelt. I stared at the blood dripping from my mother's face, at my dad hunched over his airbag, and Jeremy so still against the window. But all I wanted was out of my seatbelt."

Austin stared at Hailey's profile as she spoke quietly, lost in her memories. "You were just a kid."

"I've never been just a kid." Her lips curved in an absent smile. "When you grow up in the system, you don't have a chance to be *just* a kid."

"What was it like?"

She looked at him for a long time before she answered. "I don't usually tell people about my past. I think it changes who I am in their eyes, and I hate that."

"I like who you are now. Your past can't change that."

She held his gaze until she turned back to stare in the dark. "My first four years were bad, as bad as they get, or so my mom told me when I was old enough. My biological mother was a drug addict and prostitute—a pretty way of saying crack whore." She raised her chin, meeting his eyes, waiting to be judged.

"I came home to fresh-baked cookies after school and ate a hot breakfast every morning after I milked the cows. That doesn't make me better than you, Hailey. It just makes me damn lucky."

She rested her head against his shoulder in what could only be a moment of weakness. His arm came around her shoulders, pulling her closer.

"When the State stepped in and took me away, I was malnourished and didn't speak. They found me nibbling stale bread in a crib, sitting in my own waste. I was covered in sores from the ammonia in my urine and infected bug bites. My mother said it took them a year to

118

finally get me to come around. The State hadn't held out much hope. The doctors told my parents I would more than likely have severe emotional and cognitive setbacks, but Mom and Daddy didn't listen. My parents loved me unconditionally. They never gave up. They saved me with love."

Austin took her hand, kissed her palm. If he'd thought Hailey remarkable before, he had no words for what he thought of her now. And he finally understood her need to protect Jeremy. Her parents had saved her; now she needed to save Jeremy. "What about Jeremy? What was it like for him?"

"My parents brought Jeremy home when I was seven. I fell in love with him the moment I laid eyes on him. He was so bruised and broken, literally. His mother's boyfriend sexually abused him as often as he could and ended up breaking his arms and leg in a fit of rage. Jeremy wouldn't let Daddy near him for weeks, but he responded to me and mom. His eyes were so tortured, so sad—sadder than a two-year-old's should be. When I got off the bus each day after school, he would be waiting for me, ready with a big hug. I would get out my homework book and practice reading it to him until mom called us for dinner. The first word he spoke was 'sissy.' I adored him, treasured him, until the day my parents died and the State separated us. I still do."

Austin couldn't begin to imagine what Hailey and Jeremy must have gone through. "That's cruel. I'm sorry."

"What's cruel is that I didn't do enough to protect Jeremy." Self-loathing sharpened her voice.

Austin skimmed his thumb over her knuckles, attempting to sooth the deep pain away. "You were fourteen."

She shook her head. "It doesn't matter. I should've fought harder to keep us together, but I didn't. I left him alone, small and scared in his hospital bed. I walked away. I can still hear him crying, calling for me, and I can't stand it." Hailey freed her hand from his, stood, and stepped into the sand.

"You can't blame yourself, Hailey." Austin toed off his shoes, pulled off his socks, and followed.

"But I do." She walked closer to the waves. "I don't want to talk about sad stories anymore. This is supposed to be paradise. There are no sad stories in paradise."

He took her hand again, wanting to touch her. "Did you get enough to eat? Do you want to try dinner again?"

She smiled. "Nah, unless you're hungry. You didn't get to finish your meal."

"What about dessert? We could try the dessert bar in the west lounge."

"Do you want dessert, Austin?"

He wanted *her*. Her story still played through his mind. This strong, beautiful woman came from hell, and she'd risen above it, not only because her parents had loved her, but from sheer strength. At the heart of her sweet center, Hailey was a fighter. He'd always found her attractive, but their last hour on the porch changed something. "Uh-uh. Have you gone swimming yet?"

Hailey's eyes widened as she looked toward the black water in the moonlight. "No, and I'm not about to go now. You couldn't get me to swim in the ocean at night." She shuddered. "I have no intention of being some shark's dinner."

He smiled. "Are you brave enough to get your feet wet?"

"That I can handle."

They walked into the warm surf. Austin nudged Hailey out three inches above her ankles.

She tugged on his hand. "This is as far as I go."

"We'll have to work on that. There's something elemental about night swimming."

"You'll have to be elemental on your own. It's not happening."

He chuckled.

Hailey tipped her head to the stars, letting out a deep breath. "The water's so warm. It feels different here—softer, I think, than in California."

"Oh yeah?"

"Yeah." She nudged him with her elbow. "Don't laugh at me, Casey."

"I wouldn't dare. Rumor has it you have a mean right hook."

Hailey laughed. "Hunter told you about that?"

"Yeah." He chuckled again. "I don't think he'll be giving you another pair of boxing gloves anytime soon."

"He said, 'Swing on go.' I simply confirmed the word 'go,' and he repeated it back to me. I thought he was giving me the signal." Hailey bent forward with another peal of laughter. "I swung with all my might and knocked his head back. He stared at me, rubbing his cheek and cursing the room blue. I think I saw a hint of bruising at my birthday party."

Austin loved to listen to Hailey laugh. The sound was so full, so strong. She still chuckled as they wandered from the water toward her cabana.

"You don't sound very sorry about the whole thing."

"No way, I'm not. Hunter said 'go,' so I did. And he's also a what—twelfth degree black belt or whatever? He should've blocked me."

"You have a point."

"Darn right, I do." She flashed him a grin.

They climbed the steps to her room.

"Thanks for an...interesting evening," Hailey said, still smiling.

"Wow," Austin stumbled back, as if Hailey had struck him. "I think you just bruised my ego."

She grinned again. "No need for a bruised ego. Interesting doesn't mean bad, it just means...interesting."

Austin stared at Hailey, not wanting the night to end. The breeze blew a curl of hair against her cheek. He scooped the soft tendrils back, skimming his finger along her skin, testing both her and himself. "Interesting's okay, but I think we can do better, don't you?"

Hailey's smile disappeared as she stepped away. "What are you doing?"

He wasn't entirely sure, but it felt right. Closing the distance, he skimmed his knuckles against her temple, her cheekbone, watching the dim outside light play over her confused gaze. "What I've wanted to for a long time."

The heat of their breath mingled as he brushed his fingers down her neck and over her shoulder until she shuddered.

Hailey snagged his hand as his fingers wandered to her hair again. "I don't understand. I thought you said you wanted to keep things simple."

Her shaky whisper tickled his lips as he clasped his fingers with hers. Caught up in her honey eyes, Austin grazed her chin, his desire spinning out of control. "I don't want simple, Hailey, anymore than you do." He pressed gentle kisses along her jaw until her lids fluttered closed on a sigh.

Her hands wandered up his arms, over his shoulders. She brushed her fingers through his hair.

He had to taste her. Unable to wait any longer, Austin took her mouth. Soft lips met his, clinging, parting, as tongues touched and tangled. He held her cheeks in his hands, taking them both deeper as he pressed her to the door and plundered, drowning in the sweet flavor of Hailey.

She wrapped her arms around his waist, pulling him closer, until her small, firm breasts pressed against his chest.

More. He wanted more. He couldn't get enough. Austin picked Hailey up and set her on the wooden beam of the tiny porch, nestling himself between her legs. He nibbled at her top lip as he'd fantasized doing since the moment he met her.

She moaned as he ran his palms up and over smooth thighs, under her blue dress, until he cupped her butt and scooted her forward, pressing heat against heat, causing her to whimper.

Austin moved his hands to her face again as his mouth grew hungrier. *This is too much, too fast*, he thought, but as he did, cool fingers tracked down his arms and gripped at his wrists, sending shivers along his skin as she pulled him closer in her eagerness. He needed this, needed her—wanted, craved. Why had he waited so long?

Austin's mouth left hers with a trembling breath as he traced her ear with his tongue, breathing in the peach scent of her hair. "Hailey." He nuzzled her neck, ready to ask her to give him everything, knowing she would. He eased one slim blue strap down her shoulder, leaving open-mouthed kisses in its place as Hailey tugged his shirt free of his waistband. "Hailey," Austin said again, as he twisted the key she hadn't taken from the lock. The door opened and he wrapped his arms around her, ready to pick her up, to bring her inside and take what he'd craved for too long.

A movement by the docks caught his eye. Instantly on alert, Austin pulled Hailey closer and wrapped his arms tighter around her, rubbing his cheek against soft curls as he scrutinized the dark.

Austin kissed Hailey's forehead as he watched a figure fade into the shadows. He eased back, trying to ignore the discomfort of being watched.

Hailey stared up at him, eyes dark, full of passion. "I

CATE BEAUMAN

definitely wasn't expecting this."

Austin fought to stay in the moment. "Neither was I."
And he meant it. He'd fully intended to stick to the plan
and keep his hands to himself, but now that he'd tasted
her, now that he'd felt her soft skin against him, he knew
he didn't have the strength to resist her again. He twisted
a curl around his finger. "Do you want to come to my
place and watch a movie?"

She smiled. "Is that code for, 'Do you want to have sex?'"

Austin smiled back. "No. It's code for, 'Let's order in
some snacks because I'm hungry and watch a movie.'
Something action-packed and funny, like usual."

"Okay, but why don't we just stay here?"

His gun was in his room. He wanted it. Although he
no longer saw anyone by the docks, his gut told him
someone was there.

Austin helped Hailey down from the wooden beam. "I
want to change."

"Me too. Go put on some shorts and meet me
back here."

Damn it. He didn't want to leave her alone, not even
for the time it would take to grab his gun and change his
clothes. "Nah, I'm all set."

"Austin, don't be silly." She poked him in the belly.
"You can't relax in slacks and a polo. Go change."

He was stuck. "Okay, I'll be back in five minutes."

"Take ten, take fifteen. We're on vacation. I'll order us
something to eat. What do you want?"

"Surprise me." He hurried down the steps and started
across the sand. "Lock your door. I'll be back in a second."

When Hailey shut her door, Austin rushed to his own
cabana, let himself in and unlocked the padlock on his
suitcase, taking his Glock from the small lock box he'd
brought along. He took bullets from a box, loaded his
clip, shoved the magazine in the weapon.

124

Austin secured the safety and put the box of bullets back in the lock box before he yanked off his clothes and pulled on gym shorts and a white t-shirt. With few options, he settled the gun in the waistband of his shorts. He couldn't exactly wear his holster and not expect questions.

As he made his way back to Hailey's, Austin scanned the darkened beach. The small patches of palm trees and tall grasses gave the cabana suites privacy from the hotel. He looked toward the docks, still not seeing anyone. But someone was there; his instincts told him he and Hailey were surrounded.

Vacation had just begun, yet Austin no longer shared Hailey's enthusiasm for their six days in paradise. He wanted it over. He was looking forward to picking up Jackson at the airport—eager for the backup—and getting on with Project Mexico. But Hailey's problems wouldn't end in three months when everyone packed up and went home. They never would. Hailey was as bound to the Mexican drug cartel as Jeremy, and she didn't have a clue.

Jeremy stood by Mateo, sweating, queasy, waiting for what he knew was to be his next rite of passage. When one of his buddies offered him a 'prime opportunity' two months before, he had no idea it would lead to this. Selling a little rock, a little dope was one thing, but this...

He wiped his damp palms against his jeans as he tried not to breathe in the rotting trash piled high in the shadows of the alley. Jeremy looked left, right, trying to think of a way out, but Señor Rodriguez showed him death was the only option. Because Jeremy didn't see that as a choice, he kept his mouth shut, attempting to

125

ready himself to do what he had to.

The junker pulled into the dark space, lights off, and rolled to a stop.

"Time to make him pay, homie. Let's go." Mateo walked to the vehicle as two men got out of the front seats.

Jeremy followed.

"Rio, you got him?" Mateo asked.

"Fuck yeah, we got him. What kinda question is that?"

"Well, let's see him."

Rio, one of Donte's hulking guards, opened the back door, reached in, and pulled a bound and gagged man, still dressed in his police uniform.

"Yeah, there you are, mother fucking pig." Mateo spit in the officer's face. "You don't want to work for the Zulas? You too good for us?" He kicked the man in the balls, making him groan and crumble forward.

Rio chuckled, pulling the officer to his feet. "We're just getting started."

"Bring him inside." Mateo opened the door to the crumbling two-story building. "You're going to help us send a message to your little pussy friends, just in case they're having second thoughts about whose side they're on."

Rio shoved the officer into a seat in front of a video camera while the other guard closed the door and stood outside.

"Here, put this on." Mateo tossed a black mask to Jeremy as he secured one over his own head.

Jeremy pulled the wool hat over his sweaty hair and down his damp face while Rio tied the man to the chair.

"Hit record, Rio. Homeboy," Mateo said to Jeremy, "you're on, man."

Rio pressed record and Jeremy swallowed hard. *There's no way out,* he reminded himself, as he shoved the leather gloves on his hands, took the pistol Mateo handed him.

Jeremy read the officer's tag. His name was Sanchez, and he was about to die because he refused to bend to the Zulas.

Sanchez tilted his head up, his eyes boring into Jeremy's as Jeremy held the gun to his temple.

Mateo stepped in front of the camera, shouting to the lens in Spanish, pointing wildly.

Jeremy caught specific words: police, Sanchez, family, Zulas, death.

Mateo, still on his tirade, rushed to Sanchez, yanking his head back by the hair. "Beg for your life. Beg like the pussy you are."

Sanchez remained stoically silent as he waited for death.

Mateo rammed his elbow into the officer's face. "Beg, fucker."

Silence filled the room.

"Fuck this shit. Do it, homie. Show them what happens when they cross the Zulas."

Jeremy's hand sweat on the handle of the pistol as he stared into Sanchez's brown eyes. The drumming beat of his heart echoed in his head. He barely heard Mateo's shout to 'fucking do it now'.

He had to. Jeremy glanced at the madness dancing in Mateo's eyes, at the gleeful smile on Rio's face behind the camera.

"You fucking pull that trigger, man, or you're next," Mateo whispered harshly.

Jeremy swallowed again and pressed the barrel more truly to Sanchez's forehead. He pushed his index finger against the trigger. The deafening pop echoed through the rundown room as blood and brains flew through the air.

Rio shut off the camera, laughing hysterically, as Mateo pumped his fist with a cry of triumph for the Zulas.

Staring down at what was left of Sanchez, Jeremy struggled to keep the pistol from trembling in his hand. That could just as easily be him if he didn't man up.

"Here." Mateo handed him an ax, before he handed one to Rio, keeping one for himself. "We've gotta drop off a few presents, courteous of Officer Sanchez." Mateo kicked the half-headless man to the floor, the chair toppling with a crash, and began to hack off the officer's foot. "There's a lot of him to spread around. His wife will want a piece, his fellow officers, his mother." He chuckled. "Come on, man, hack an arm. We've gotta get this finished before daylight."

Jeremy stared at the gore, numb, as blood spurted and pooled on the scarred cement. He cut Sanchez's hands free from their binding; the dead man's arms flopped against the concrete. Jeremy glanced at Mateo, found Mateo measuring him through narrowed eyes. Jeremy swung the ax, biting into flesh, cracking bone, and ultimately severing a hand.

"That's it, homie. Looks like you have the chops to be one of us after all. I had my doubts. I was starting to think you were a bleeding heart like that hot sister of yours," he sneered.

"Fuck no," he said, with as much disdain as he could muster.

There's no way out, Jeremy reminded himself again. He hacked into Sanchez's elbow joint next, ready to do whatever he had to stay alive.

CHAPTER 11

HAILEY BLINKED IN THE DIM light, staring at Austin. The TV murmured in the background. Dirty plates and glasses lay stacked on the whicker table by the bed. Austin's cheek pressed against the pillow next to hers, his brown hair tousled from sleep.

Not even a week before, she'd given up any dredges of hope Austin would ever take notice of her, but he'd certainly done more than that. He'd kissed her silly in the lamplight, and here he was asleep in her bed.

When she sat down to dinner last night, realizing she'd been stood up, she had no idea the evening would turn out be one of the best in her life: conversation, a moonlight walk on the beach, Austin's firm, inviting mouth pressing against hers, those big magical hands moving over her body, and a movie to top it off.

Hailey smiled, sighing with the memory. She'd loved hearing Austin's deep chuckles mix with her own as they watched the action-packed comedy. He'd surprised her when he set the empty plates aside and pulled her against him.

As the credits rolled two hours later, Austin stunned her further when he curled her closer, whispering next to her ear, sending shivers down her spine, asking if she was up for a double-feature. She'd been exhausted from the day of travel, from the initial upheaval of the evening, but there was no way she could have turned him down.

Somewhere during the second flick, her eyes drooped and she'd dozed until the drone of action on the screen disappeared into silence. She'd slept soundly through the night, having no idea Austin lay there too.

Hailey studied the pale green comforter covering them both. They lay as if they were any normal couple, but she reminded herself they weren't. They were pals, friends, but certainly not a couple. They had shared a molten kiss, a movie-and-a-half, and a bed, but that didn't mean by any stretch of her imagination that Austin was ready to change his mind. In Los Angeles he'd said "friends." "Simple." Period. No gray area. Now, as she stared at his sexy face relaxed in sleep, nothing was simple. The line had definitely been blurred.

How in the world did this *happen*? Had Austin been caught up in the tropical atmosphere—a warm night, stars twinkling, the hypnotic ebb and flow of ocean surf?

Another thought occurred to her and she tensed, going cold. Had he felt sorry for her after what she told him? It would certainly explain everything.

Hailey closed her eyes. There was nothing she wanted less. Life hadn't always been easy, but who needed easy? She was happy with who she was, pleased with what she'd made herself into—someone Harold and Loraine Sturgis would've been proud of. She didn't want or need Austin's pity.

Hailey pushed the covers back and sat up, building a wall of mad. Anger was better than hurt. She wasn't some poor orphan child, she was an intelligent, strong woman who would and could do anything she set her mind to.

She huffed out a sigh of frustration. She *knew* she shouldn't have told him about her past. Why did her childhood always come back to haunt her? She rarely spoke of it, but somehow, it came around. She lost out on two nannying positions before she met Sarah. The families had been ready to welcome her aboard until they ran background checks. Both couples had politely refused her services, saying she was an unacceptable candidate due to her "unstable" past. "Foster child" seemed to mean trouble, even years removed, even when she'd never done anything wrong.

That's why few people other than Morgan and Sarah knew her whole story. The only man she ever told, her first and only serious boyfriend, had dumped her promptly after her confession. Todd's father had had his eye on the Governor's seat. Her biological mother's unsavory lifestyle could've jeopardized his chances of a win if the media ever found out.

It had never mattered that she was nothing like her mother, that she barely even remembered the woman.

Hailey muttered that mantra each day of her three years with the Fraziers. Mother Frazier had been determined to undo every ounce of effort her mom and dad had put in to making her whole.

Mother Frazier had punished her with backbreaking chores, impossible demands, and constant childcare duties for her biological children, all because Hailey was 'too beautiful'—whatever that meant. Beauty was the work of the devil. Her taut, curvy body drew the wandering eyes of men—a sin against the Lord, in Mother Frazier's eyes. Hailey had been reminded daily that she would burn in hell like her whore mother.

She put up with each verbal blow until the day she turned eighteen. At 12:01 a.m., Hailey stepped from their door with a backpack full of the few items she had and walked the five miles to the bank, where ten thousand dollars plus interest waited—her inheritance from her parents.

She'd dozed on the steps of First Bank and Trust, waiting for nine a.m. When the time came, she cashed out her account and took the bus to L.A., celebrating every mile the Greyhound put between her and the Fraziers', knowing she would never have to go back.

Alone and overwhelmed in the big city, she took the first job she found, waitressing by day, and when that didn't put her far enough ahead, she scrubbed toilets at the university, third shift.

She'd saved for two years, adding to her tiny little account, until she could afford to take a class or two and move into the huge house in the Palisades, splitting the rent and bills with five other women, all the while paying a private investigator to find Jeremy, with no luck.

She continued to work her fingers to the bone until she met Sarah the year before Kylee had been born. Sarah had offered her odd jobs for a generous wage. Eventually, she'd been able to give up her janitorial duties and cut back her waitressing shifts to three nights a week. After Kylee came and Jake died in Afghanistan, she and Sarah had grown closer. Hailey was there for Sarah during her darkest hours, and Sarah had returned the favor a million times over.

Hailey got out of bed, still staring at Austin, as she made her way to the bathroom. Now that the night was over and the magic of the evening gone, she doubted he would be here when she got out of the shower.

Closing the door, Hailey brought the shower to life, pulled her pajamas off, and stepped under the warm spray, hating that she felt so defensive and suspicious. Closing her eyes, she blew out through her mouth as streams of water cascaded over her face.

Why were these insecurities rushing back? She'd put all of this away, burying her emotional baggage so many years ago, but now that Jeremy was back, now that Austin was confusing her, changing everything, her past was never far from the surface.

As much as Hailey wanted to believe her past didn't affect the woman she was today, she knew differently.

Mother Frazier had successfully planted small doubts all those years ago, and Hailey still wasn't fully able to dismiss them. Was a part of her like her biological mother? Did the need for mindless sex and an urge for drugs lay dormant somewhere deep?

Todd had dumped her because of her past, and Hailey had dumped the only other man she'd allow touch her after a casual romp in his dorm room. Each kiss, each touch, had filled her with shame, fearful that Mother Frazier's words were the absolute truth—she was nothing but a good for nothing whore.

Ugh, enough. Hailey washed quickly and stepped from the shower, eager to dress and walk on the beach, eager to shut off her racing mind. She needed the sun to bake away her troubling thoughts. She wrapped herself in a towel and opened the door. Austin still lay in bed, awake.

"Good morning."

"Morning." She heard her own stiff reply.

He sat up, frowning, turned off the TV. "You okay?"

"Yeah, fine." Hailey hurried to the dresser, pulled a black bikini, jean shorts and a red tank top free.

"Are you mad I stayed?"

"No."

Austin got out of bed. He ran his hands up her arms, back down—an intimate gesture that only confused her more. This wasn't simple and this wasn't friends. She took a step back.

"Did I steal the covers or something?" He smiled.

She didn't return it. "What are you doing, Austin? Why are you still here?"

"Because this is where I want to be."

The ease of his answer left her leery. She took another step back. "Why? You said this wasn't what you wanted. You very distinctly told me you didn't want me, that you weren't attracted to me."

"No, I didn't. You told *me* I didn't want you, that I wasn't attracted to you. I said I wanted to keep things friendly between us."

Her brow shot up. "Last night was more than friendly."

He stepped toward her again, his warm hands resting against her shoulders. "If I did anything to make you even a little bit uncomfortable—"

Hailey closed her eyes, sighing as she saw the concern in his. "You didn't make me uncomfortable; I just don't understand."

"What?"

She broke free of his grip, sat on the edge of the bed.

He followed, plunking himself next to her.

"Why the sudden change?" She fiddled with her fingers. "You seemed pretty content with simplicity. Then, we talk on the steps, and you decide you want to walk on the beach and hold hands. Then you kissed me." Unable to remain still, she stood and began to pace. "If this is some sort of pity thing or if you have some sort of notion that I'm easy like my biological mother—"

Austin rushed to his feet. "*What*?" He whirled her around. "What the fuck, Hailey?"

She tried to smother the guilt of her accusations as she stared at the shocked hurt all over Austin's face.

"I don't know what the hell you're talking about, but I'm going to try to ignore the fact that you just insulted both of us."

Jutting out her chin, Hailey's eyes filled, already knowing she was completely wrong.

Austin jammed his hands in his pockets. "Is this what you think of me? Is this what you think of yourself? I can only like you or want you because of pity, because I think you're what—what a slut like some woman you don't even know?"

She flinched at the truth of his words, and shame

quickly replaced guilt, her stomach curdling with it. "I'm—"

"I'm not finished," he interrupted, rushing forward, pulling her against him, his eyes smoldering. "I wanted you long before I ever knew your story. I still want you, but not because I feel sorry for you or think I can use you for some cheap lay. If anything, I only admire you more for what you've made out of the really shitty hand you were dealt." He let her go, leaving her cold as he headed for the door.

"Austin, wait."

"I'll see you around." He opened the door, shut it solidly behind him.

Hailey stared after him for several seconds as her breath came in tearing shudders. She clutched her towel in a vice grip as the first tear raced down her cheek. Why did she do that? What had she been thinking? She eased herself on the bed, put her face in her trembling hands, and gave in to her tears.

Austin didn't deserve the filthy, vile accusations she threw his way. How would she make things right? Would an apology be enough?

Hailey took several steadying breaths, trying to find her way through her emotional storm. Her door opened again and Austin stepped back inside. She stared at the firm set of his jaw, the steel in his eyes, before she crumbled. Hailey turned away, trying to stifle her desperate crying.

She stood and started toward the bathroom, fully intending to lock the door until she had herself under control. Her tears were for her and her alone. Regrets and apologies would have to wait until later. The emotional upheaval of the last two months was all hitting her this very morning. She would deal with it and move on—alone.

"Hey," Austin said, taking her arm.

She shook her head, unable to do more.

"Hey," he said again, his voice gentle, as he followed her to the bathroom.

"Please, Austin. Please go away."

He sat on the lip of the tub pulled her down on his lap, snuggling her against him until her head rested against his chest.

Hailey pressed her face to his shirt as Austin cocooned her against him, resting his cheek on her hair, skimming his hand up and down her arm.

When her sobs turned to sniffles, Hailey wiped her palms over her cheeks and sat up, feeling foolish for so many things.

Austin swiped his fingers through her hair, brushing wisps away from her forehead. "Better?"

"Mostly." She wiped at her eyes. "Except for the part about feeling awful for the things I said to you. I'm so sorry, Austin." She wrapped her arms around him, hugging him close. "If there was any way I could take it back, I would."

"I guess I don't understand where it came from. I had no idea you thought stuff like that."

She shrugged, wishing she *didn't* think stuff like that. "Sometimes. Not very often." She confessed to Austin what she'd been too ashamed to tell anyone. "Having Jeremy back in my life has brought up a lot of things I didn't know still bothered me. In a lot of ways, I've had to take out my past, dust it off, and replay it. I don't like to; I don't want to; but it seems to be something I have to deal with regardless."

"I'm right here." He brushed her hair back again. "You're only alone if you choose to be. You can talk to me about any of it. It's not my place to judge. We all have skeletons, things we aren't proud of."

Where did this man come from, and how had she gotten so lucky? If she wasn't careful, she would fall in love—if she hadn't a little already. She hugged him again, smiled. "Thanks."

"You're welcome." He touched his warm lips to hers, then again, adding pressure before he eased back. "You ready to get this day started?"

She studied him, still trying to get a handle on this sudden change between them. "Yup. What should we do first?"

"Well, I'm thinking you might want to get dressed." He gave her one of his slow grins, sending her heart racing.

She glanced down at her towel-clad body and returned his smile. "That would definitely be a good place to start."

They wandered out to the bedroom. Hailey grabbed the outfit she'd left on the bed. "I'll be right back."

"I'll be right here." He sent her another smile before she hurried to the bathroom, happy, settled for the first time in too long.

Hailey brushed her teeth and hair in five minutes flat and headed out to Austin, not wanting to waste one moment of the day. He was shirtless in swim trunks. She stared at bulging biceps, firm pectorals, chiseled abs.

"Wow, and I thought I was fast. You went over and changed?"

"And brushed my teeth." Austin held up the bottle of sun block the Cooke's had included in her birthday gift bag. "Sun block first, then what's on the agenda?"

"Uh..." Was she actually supposed to think when he stood in front of her looking like that?

"You said something about horseback riding."

"Um...yes, I did. Let's go horseback riding."

"Horseback riding it is." He squirted a glob of white into his palm and made a circling motion with his finger.

Hailey pulled off her tank top and turned, gathering her hair in her hands. She closed her eyes, bit her lip as Austin rubbed his big, slippery hands over her shoulders, along her shoulder blades, and down her lower back. He snuck his fingers below the waist of her shorts, leaving a trail of fire wherever he touched. Hailey struggled not to shudder as the gentle pressure of callused palms tied her stomach into tight coils of need.

"I think you're good." Austin stepped back, squirting more lotion in his hand. He rubbed SPF-30 over his arms, chest, and stomach. "Do you mind returning the favor?"

"Huh?"

"Will you do my back? The last thing we want is to turn into lobsters on our first day of vacation."

"Mmm."

He held her gaze. "You okay?"

"Yes." Her brain all but sizzled in her sexual fog. "Definitely. Turn around." Hailey poured lotion in her hands, rubbed them together, pressed her palms to Austin's smooth, muscled skin. She stood on her tiptoes, squeezing his neck and shoulders, making him groan. Her hands froze against his shoulder blades.

"I officially think you should change majors. Forget social work, Hailey—become a masseuse instead. I'll be your number one client."

She ran her fingers along his spine firmly, testing herself, testing him, as he let loose another grumble in his throat.

"I'm serious, Hailey."

Was he *trying* to drive her crazy? Because it was working. Her own shoulder blades ached from the sexual tension radiating through the room. If they didn't get out of here soon, she was afraid she might explode. "Uh, I think you're all set," she said a bit too breathily.

Austin turned, staring, as she added more lotion to her hand and smoothed it over her naked stomach, her chest, her neck. He pulled her against him, skimmed his knuckles along her cheekbone, lifted her chin with his thumb until they breathed each other's breath.

Hailey clutched his wrists. She wanted him, wanted this, but not right now, not when she hadn't left Mother Frazier completely behind. The bitter woman wouldn't be allowed to mess with whatever this was she had with Austin. "We should go. Right this second."

Austin stared into her eyes as he played the pad of his thumb over her top lip. "Later, Hailey. We're going to pick up right here, later."

She couldn't hold back the shudder his promise brought. Nodding, she eased away.

Austin took the key from the side table, locked up behind them, and snagged Hailey's hand as they made their way to the hotel lobby.

CHAPTER 12

USTIN WRAPPED HIS ARM AROUND Hailey's waist. Glancing up, she smiled. He winked and tugged her closer, relieved to be back on solid ground.

When he woke an hour before, he'd anticipated a lazy, relaxing morning. He'd expected to open his eyes to Hailey lying next to him, warm and flushed from sleep. Instead, her side of the bed had been empty, the shower running.

Content to lay back and wait, Austin had flipped through American sports highlights, pleased with the night he and Hailey shared. The evening had started off a bit rough, but by the time they settled in with their movie, he found himself relaxed, enjoying the weight of Hailey's head against his shoulder, the scent of her soft hair surrounding him as he held her close.

When Hailey emerged from the bathroom with guarded eyes, a rigid stance, and a cool clip to her voice, he'd been completely unprepared. Her accusations had been so shocking, so outlandish he hadn't known how to react, but raising his voice had been wrong, and walking out had been worse.

As he slammed the door and walked away, fully intending to say "screw it" to the whole thing, Austin remembered the figure by the docks, watching in the dark. For that alone he would've turned around, but the real clincher had been Hailey's ridiculously un-Hailey like behavior. He'd marched back to her room, wanting an explanation.

Austin was glad they'd worked it out. Hailey was relaxed again, happy. He planned to make sure she stayed that way.

He broke his own rules when he kissed her last night, but since he couldn't take it back—didn't want to take it back, he figured he could relax a little, on that front, anyway. They had the next six days to enjoy each other, to see what they would see. A week of fun didn't bind him to a lifetime commitment.

But her wounded strength intrigued him like nothing ever had. There was more to Hailey than kindness and humor. Although she'd shared parts of herself, Hailey was still a mystery. He didn't want pieces of her story; he wanted the whole thing.

"Excuse me," Austin muttered when he bumped a woman on the crowded path. "Sorry," he said as he clipped another guest. Austin stepped behind Hailey and placed his hands on her shoulders, enjoying her soft skin against his palms as an influx of Resort patrons shuffled out of the hotel lobby. "We should make our reservations for horseback riding before we eat."

"Good idea. I'm so excited." She beamed at him, her eyes bright.

"We're going to have a great—"

"Hailey, wait."

Austin felt her stiffen as Jeremy came running up the path. Damn, they'd been so close.

Hailey stepped off the busy walkway, turning toward her brother as he moved closer.

"Do you want me to give you a minute?" Austin asked, watching the pleasure vanish from her face.

"No, thanks. It isn't necessary." Her voice had gone cool and quiet, much like it had that morning in the cabana.

"Hey, sissy." Jeremy smiled. "I thought we were doing something today."

"And I thought we were having dinner last night."

Jeremy's smile disappeared as he shifted

uncomfortably. "Yeah, sorry about that. I got hung up with some—"

"Save it."

Jeremy glanced at Austin before he pulled on Hailey's arm, tugging her further into the sand. "Hailey, I—"

"I really don't have a whole lot to say to you right now." She freed herself from his grip. "I saw you and Mateo go into the casino. You lied to me. I'm so passed sick of it."

"What, are you following me now?"

"Give me a break, Jeremy. I was waiting for you at the restaurant you said you would meet me at. I was on the deck, eating with Austin after you stood me up."

"I'm sorry."

"Apology not accepted. I may've been able to overlook your rudeness if I hadn't seen a beer in your hand and cigarette hanging from your mouth. You told me you stopped drinking and smoking. More lies."

"I don't have to answer to you." His voice grew hard with indignation.

"No, you don't. But I don't have to stand here and listen to your endless excuses." Hailey turned her back on her brother and started toward the lobby.

"So you're walking away from me? You're really good at that, aren't you?"

Hailey's stride faltered as pain radiated across her face, but she kept going, entering the hotel and hurrying down the hall.

Austin choked on rage as Jeremy, his eyes alight with triumph, turned to leave. Storming forward, Austin whirled Jeremy around and gave him a shove, knocking him on his ass. "You little bastard."

Guests stopped along the path, gasping and murmuring.

"What the fuck, man?"

"I'll tell you what the fuck. You hurt your sister."

"It's none of your fucking business." Jeremy got to his feet and charged forward, madness contorting his face.

Austin pivoted and knocked Jeremy down again. Bending, he yanked the little asshole up by the collar of his shirt. "I've made it my business. You listen up and listen good, you son of a bitch. You're going to start playing things straight with Hailey, or I'll kick your ass."

"You don't know who you're messing with, shit head."

"I know you don't deserve one moment of your sister's time, and that's all I care about." He pushed Jeremy away.

"You'll pay. I'm gonna fucking *kill* you, prick. Don't ever touch me again."

Austin walked to the lobby, more than finished. "Treat your sister right and we won't have any problems." He opened the door, made his way down the hall as Jeremy continued to spew threats and profanity.

He found Hailey in the restaurant sitting on the bench by the huge picture windows. Austin sat next to her, tilted her chin up until her eyes met his. "You okay?"

"I made our reservations for the horses," she said, voice stiff.

He leaned closer. "Are you all right, Hailey?"

"Yeah." She nodded.

"Want to talk about it?"

Hailey fiddled with her fingers as she took a deep breath. "There isn't much to talk about. Jeremy gets pretty mean when he's angry."

Crazy was more like it. If Jeremy had been armed, he would've made good on his threat to kill; Austin had seen the blinding rage in his eyes. "That's not an excuse."

"I'm not making excuses for my brother. It's a fact, but he was still way out of line." She looked down and stared into her lap for several seconds. "What if it's too late, Austin? What if it's too late to help him?"

How could he tell her it was way past too late to help

143

Jeremy? "You can support your brother, Hailey, but at the end of the day, he's all grown up."

"I know." She shook her head. "I'm not going to give up on him, though. I feel guilty because sometimes I think I might, but I can't."

Austin clenched his jaw, trying to tamp down his frustration. For a second, he thought they were getting somewhere. He needed to stand, to walk the helplessness away.

Hailey took his hand before he could get to his feet, rubbed his knuckles against her cheek, her eyes pleading with his. "I don't expect you to understand. I know what you see, Austin. I know who my brother is, but I have to try."

She didn't know the half of it—not even close.

Austin skimmed his thumb over her jaw. "Okay." They would leave it alone for now.

"Do you still want to go with me today?" She looked down before she met his gaze.

There it was again, the small traces of vulnerability under her strength. "You couldn't stop me. Let's get some breakfast, get on with our day."

"One...two...three... *Go!*" Austin shouted, giving his horse a nudge. He took off like a shot, as did Hailey.

Hailey's laugh carried on the wind as they soared down the beach. For someone who'd never sat a horse before, she was a natural. After he'd paid off their guide, wanting to be alone, Austin spent half an hour giving Hailey basic instructions. From there, she'd been good to go.

"You're toast, Casey," Hailey taunted as she pulled ahead, looking behind her, grinning, her hair flying around her face. She took his breath away with her carefree beauty.

Austin stopped staring long enough to realize Hailey was, indeed, kicking his butt. He gave Blaze another nudge and passed her. "I don't think so, rookie," he tossed at her as he flew by, leaving her in his dust.

"Hey." Hailey gave her horse a bump, speeding up.

Laughing, they both pulled up on reins as ocean surf met sand.

"I think we tied," Hailey said breathlessly.

"I think you're delusional. You were half-a-length behind." Grinning, Austin guided Blaze into step beside Ginger, leading the horses through the ebb and flow of white foam.

"Fighting words. Do you remember who you're messing with?" Hailey held her arms up, flexing her barely-there biceps, as she puffed out her chest. "Let's not forget about my killer right hook," she said in a terrible imitation of Arnold's Terminator voice.

Austin's brows winged up as he snorted, shaking his head. This was the sweet, fun Hailey he was used to. He was glad to have her back. "What the hell was that?"

Hailey's eyes narrowed under the pale amber tint of her sunglasses as she balled her fist. "Don't you know?" she continued in her wretched accent. "I'm your worst nightmare. Don't make me show you, Austin Casey." She tossed a playful punch his way as she struggled not to laugh.

He took the gentle jab on his shoulder. "Wow, you *are* my worst nightmare. That's some pretty tough stuff. I'd hate to run into you in a dark alley."

She switched gears, swearing at him in an inventive string of Spanish.

Surprised, he let loose chuckle. "I had no idea you were bilingual."

"I'm not." She beamed at him.

"You could've fooled me."

"One of the girls I played with when I was younger spoke Spanish. English was her second language. Her older brother educated us on the finer points." A smile lit her face again.

"I see." Damn, if she wasn't irresistible. Why hadn't he offered to take her out before this week? Hailey all but lived with Ethan and Sarah, and he was there more often than not when he wasn't on assignment. Sure, they'd watched movies together in the game room, had taken Kylee on an adventure or two, but this was different—so much better. He couldn't help but feel like he'd been missing out on something special.

"Oh, look."

He came to attention when she gasped. "What?"

"Look at the shell over there. I want it. It's beautiful." She scrambled down from her saddle awkwardly.

Austin winced, certain Hailey would end up on her ass in the water, but she settled on her feet, hurrying forward before the waves carried away the fist-sized conch.

Hailey snatched it up as another wave rushed in, soaking her to her calves. She held the shell high, smiling her triumph. Drops of water ran down her arm, glistening as they caught the sun. "Isn't it beautiful?"

She was beautiful. "It's nice."

"Nice? It's a conch shell." She turned the shell in her hand. "And it's perfect—no holes or broken pieces. I'm going to give it to Kylee. What do you think?" She held the shell up for his inspection.

"I think Kylee will love it."

"Can you hold it while I get back on Ginger?"

"Sure."

Her damp fingers brushed his as she handed him her treasure. "Thanks." She turned, reaching for the horse's reins. Ginger sidestepped her. "Hey." Hailey made a grab for the reins again and Ginger repeated herself. "Ginger," Hailey scolded, "behave yourself."

Austin gave Blaze a nudge, ready to help.

"No, stop. I can do this myself," she said, as she took a step closer to the horse cantering ahead ten yards, all but taunting her.

"Okay. If that's what you want." Austin leaned back in his saddle, ready to enjoy the show.

Hailey walked toward the mare. "Your carrots are on the line here, Ginger. Come back." The horse wandered further ahead. "Please?"

Austin bit his cheek, fighting to stifle his grin, as Ginger trotted away and Hailey ran after her.

"Oh, you can *totally* forget the carrots now, Ginger."

Austin nudged his horse into action as Ginger galloped back toward the stables, and Hailey slowed to a walk. He approached Hailey and brought Blaze to a stop.

She glanced up. "Say nothing and live."

"I was going to offer you a ride, but since I'm not allowed to say anything, I'll let you walk the mile back. It's pretty damn hot out here with the sun beaming down." Austin pulled his water bottle from the small saddlebag, took a long swallow of tepid liquid before he put it away. He clucked his tongue, starting his mount moving again. He kept his pace slow, smiling when he eventually heard Hailey's huff of breath.

"Oh, all right. Austin, I'll take the ride."

He peered over his shoulder. "What, I didn't hear you. The surf's kinda loud."

"I said I'll take a ride."

"What? You just learned how to ride today and could've used a hand with Ginger but were too stubborn to ask and now you need a ride back to the stables?"

Hailey stopped walking and crossed her arms. "I just

thought of a great place to shove the carrot Ginger won't be eating when we get back."

Austin burst out laughing, delighted with her, as a reluctant smile tugged her lips. He'd definitely been missing out on something by keeping Hailey at a distance. Scooting back in the saddle, he reached down for Hailey's hand. "Step on my foot and I'll hoist you up."

She did as he said and in one efficient move, Austin pulled Hailey into the saddle in front of him.

"Tight fit," Hailey wiggled herself against him.

"Yeah." He clenched his jaw, waiting for her to settle. Her firm bottom was driving him crazy.

She fidgeted again. "Thank God it's only a mile back to the stables."

He grunted his agreement.

"Blaze is so much taller. Look at this view, Austin. I was so preoccupied with riding, I wasn't really paying attention. The water is so *blue*. It's breathtaking."

He'd spent a lot of time in prime vacation spots while on duty. He was usually so busy doing his job, he rarely had time to relax and enjoy the sights and sounds. "Not much to complain about in a place like this."

"Definitely not." She tilted her head back to look at him. Hailey's brown hair tangled in the breeze, her eyes shining bright with fun.

This felt perfectly right, sharing this moment with her. An easy wave of contentment washed through him. Austin rested his chin on top of her hair, wrapped his arms around her waist, happy to have her close.

She sighed. "I feel wonderfully lazy right now. Should we jet ski or say the heck with it, plop ourselves in a couple of shaded lounge chairs, and take long naps?"

"Jet ski. Definitely. You're going to love it. We'll bum around tomorrow."

"Lazy slob day tomorrow, check."

"Check, but today we jet ski. There's nothing like being out on the water—the wind in your face, the spray coming back at you as you fly over the waves."

"You really love it, huh?"

"I do."

"If you love the sea so much, why did you give up the Navy? You must've seen a lot of neat stuff, done a lot of cool, top-secret things."

"I love the water, always have, but when it came time to re-enlist, I was more than ready to throw in the towel."

"Oh."

Her 'oh' asked a thousand questions without saying another word. As he held her against him, her peach blossom scent mingled with the coconut of their sun block. He found himself wanting to tell her what he typically left in his past. "Six months before my reenlistment date, I was sent on a mission that went catastrophically wrong. We ran with bad intelligence—really bad intelligence. A lot of people died who shouldn't have."

Hailey covered his hand on the reins. "I'm sorry, Austin."

"Me too."

She reached her arms back, clasping her hands behind his head, bringing his face down as she looked up, and kissed his cheek. "You know, the door goes both ways. I'm a great listener if you ever want to talk about it."

He pressed his lips to her hair, touched by her sweetness. "Thanks."

She rested her head against his chest, laced her fingers with his.

Austin stared at the creamy gold of her small, graceful hand lying on his, wrapped his arm tighter, trying to tuck his past away and enjoy what he had right now.

He looked out at crystal blue waters glistening like a gem in the sun, listening to the ebb and flow of surf—a sound that always soothed. His shoulders relaxed by degrees as the horse lazily walked them closer to the stables. They were about to have a blast on their next adventure. He was eager to share with Hailey another experience she'd never had before.

The everyday noises of civilization began to mix with the ocean waves. Austin turned his attention to the crowds further down the beach. His shoulders tensed as he recognized the man from the restaurant. He was holding a pair of binoculars. The blinding reflection of sun on glass beamed in their direction. Austin no longer questioned the man's purpose. He'd been there to keep tabs on Hailey, just as he was doing now.

Austin instinctively tightened his grip around her and nudged the horse along. A grove of palms blew in the breeze just ahead. That's where he wanted to be, out of the line-of-sight.

Scanning the area now, he spotted Jeremy and Mateo well up the beach, hanging on the girls who they'd wandered into the casino with. Austin's eyes tracked further up, noting the two bodyguards he'd seen on the plane.

Hailey chattered about something cheerfully, but he didn't pay attention.

"—on that. Isn't it amazing?"

Austin scrutinized the mass of resort guests occupying the white sand, studying the men and women frolicking in the water or lounging about in the sun or shade. Dread clenched his stomach as he picked out the arsenal of close protection agents scattered about the beach, each dressed as any other vacationer. He counted well over a dozen agents casually speaking into wrist pieces or pressing at their ears. What the hell was up?

Hailey wouldn't be worth all this to the Zulas. They wouldn't waste this much effort on one person; they would simply kill her. Something big was going on.

"Hello, Austin. I'm talking to you." Hailey tilted her head up again, smiling.

He tore his attention from the full-scale security detail, trying to focus. "What?"

"Isn't it absolutely stunning? I saw it yesterday. It's coming back."

"What?"

"The yacht, Austin."

His gaze flew to the massive boat Hailey pointed at, then to the men on the beach. "Son of a bitch," he muttered.

"I know. Amazing, huh?"

"Yeah." Everything made sense now. Someone on the mini cruise ship was a big fucking deal. Austin glanced at Mateo and Jeremy, putting the pieces together. He knew exactly who was on that boat, and the stakes had just gotten higher.

The gelding wandered to the stable, stopping as the guide took the reins. Austin climbed down from the saddle effortlessly, grabbed Hailey at the waist, and set her on her feet. She beamed, hugging him, oblivious to the danger surrounding them. "Thanks, Austin. This was really great."

He held her against him. "You're welcome."

"Do you want to give Blaze his carrots?"

He wanted to get her away from here. "Nah."

"He deserves them—unlike Ginger over there." She glared in the runaway horse's direction.

Hailey took the carrots from the guide and held them flat in her palm for Blaze to eat. She rubbed behind his ear with her free hand. "You're very sweet, Blaze. Maybe you can teach Ginger a thing or two."

Austin struggled to smile as he grew impatient. He wanted her on a jet ski, miles out in the water, as far away as he could get her from the prying eyes of the guards.

Blaze ate the last bite from Hailey's palm. She thanked

the guide as she moved to wash her hands in the small outdoor sink.

While she busied herself with soap and water, Austin walked over to the groom who was taking the saddle from Blaze. "Excuse me, Señor."

"Yes, sir."

"We just watched a honey of a yacht anchor down. Do you know who owns it?"

The man's gaze faltered with what may have been fear. "No, sir, I do not."

Huh.

"If you will excuse me, sir." The groom hurried off with the saddle.

Hailey threw her paper towel in the trash and headed over. "Are you ready to jet ski?"

The excitement was there, in her eyes, in her voice. He was sorry he no longer shared Hailey's anticipation. "You bet." Austin wrapped an arm around her, shielding her as if she were a client being harassed by overeager paparazzi.

He glanced over his shoulder. The man with the binoculars still watched. Austin turned back to walk with Hailey down the beach, eager to get them out to sea.

CHAPTER 13

THE MUSIC WAS FAST AND sultry on the outdoor dance floor. The warm winds blew in from the sea as Hailey spun in her black halter sundress, laughing. Austin pulled her back to him and wrapped his arms around her waist, smiling as they missed their step for the hundredth time. Her pulse kicked into overdrive as she placed her hands on Austin's hips, never wanting the night to end.

She faltered another step, tripped against him. "Holy crap, we totally suck at this."

"Can't argue with you there," he said as they spun again. "But who cares?" he added when they faced each other.

After dinner and a fun-filled round of karaoke, they signed up for an hour-long dance class. The mambo hadn't gone well, so they were improvising.

"I'm definitely going to need band-aids." Hailey winced when Austin's sandal made contact with her toes again. "Lots and lots of band-aids."

"Shit, Hailey. Sorry."

She limped a little into the next spin. "No problem. I didn't like my toes on that foot anyway."

A lightning grin flashed across his face as he pulled her off the dance floor. "Are you ready to call it a night?"

"My feet are, but I'm still wired."

"Let's head back to the cabanas." He took her hand as they started down the path to their rooms.

"Thank God they're close." Hailey stopped abruptly as the blister on her pinky toe screamed at her. "Hold on, I need to take off my heels." She held Austin's arm, balancing as she undid the thin black strap just below her anklebone. She pulled her foot free, sighing with pleasure, until her toes curled in a tight involuntary ball. "Oh my God. Oh my *God*. Cramp. Really, really bad cramp." She bent further forward, flexing her toes with her fingers, trying to alleviate the sharp, achy pain.

Austin hooked an arm around her waist. "Are you okay?"

When the discomfort left her foot, she wiggled her toes, waiting for the cramp to return. "I think so. This happens when I wear heels sometimes—most of the time, actually. I'm waiting for round two. It's usually a sneak attack."

She peered up at Austin, shrugging. For a fleeting moment, she wished herself sophisticated and elegant. Austin was used to women who possessed those qualities, not only at his job, but in his personal life. She thought of Miranda, the gorgeous dive shop owner Austin seemed very friendly with. The thought made her sigh on an inner cringe. Hailey quickly tried to shake her feelings away. She would never be elegant *or* sophisticated; she could only be who she was.

Hailey looked down at her other heeled foot with trepidation. She wanted to take the sandal off, but didn't dare. Falling to the ground with toe cramps would be as bad as the blue frosting, raccoon-face fiasco.

Austin's brow rose. "Are you going to take the other one off?"

"Uh, no. It's just a few more yards." She took two steps in her awkward gate and stopped as her toes curled tight and painful. "Ouch, *ouch*. See, I told you. Sneak attack." She bent down again, waiting, looking up through her curtain of hair. "This could be a minute. Why don't you go on ahead?"

"I'll wait."

HELLO

Several seconds later, Hailey righted herself. "I think I'm good this time."

"Let's be sure."

She let out a startled gasp as Austin scooped her up in his arms. Butterflies fluttered in her belly as she stared into his eyes. What girl didn't dream of being swept off her feet like this—and on a warm, moonlit night in a tropical paradise? "You don't have to carry me. It's not much further."

"Your toes may very well be bloody stumps. I have to take some of the responsibility."

"I stepped on your feet just as often as you stepped on mine."

"But I outweigh you by a good hundred pounds... Unless you're saying you want to carry me back." He bent low, as if he were setting her down.

Chuckling, Hailey wrapped her arms around his neck. "I don't see that going well. I think I'll stay right here." In his arms—exactly where she wanted to be.

"Good choice." Austin started down the lighted concrete path. With each step, something solid connected with Hailey's outer thigh. "Austin, what is that?"

His gait faltered and his eyes changed, hardening, as he scanned their surroundings. "What's what?"

"The thing that keeps bumping my leg." The magic of being in Austin's arms faded as she concentrated on the thick strip under his shirt on his left shoulder. Curious now, she ran her finger along the outline, following it over the left side of his chest. "Is that your holster? Are you carrying your gun?"

The porch light of her cabana burned dim as they turned the corner and kept moving forward.

"Yes."

"You've been wearing it all night? I had no idea."

"That's the whole point."

"Why?"

"You kind of lose the element of surprise if everyone knows you're armed."

He was being purposely evasive. "I get that part. Why do you have your gun with you?"

He shrugged as he took the steps to her suite. "I always carry my gun. It doesn't feel right if I don't."

She rarely saw him with his weapon in L.A. unless he was coming off duty, and even then, he usually didn't wear one. "But you don't need it here. We're safe."

"Just because we're staying at a resort doesn't mean bad things can't happen." He set her on her feet. "Not everyone has good intentions."

She was sorry when he set her down, but more sorry that Austin's light mood had fallen away. "I know." She walked into the room, and he followed, shutting the door.

"Sometimes I wonder."

She frowned as his tone grew more serious. "I like to see the good in people, but that doesn't mean I'm clueless about the world around me."

"Sometimes the criminal element is closer than you think." Austin flicked the lock closed and wandered to the picture window, turning his back to Hailey.

"Now you sound overly paranoid."

"Maybe you're not paranoid enough."

"I sincerely believe there are more good people than bad. Sometimes you have to dig a little to find it, but it's there. Your job makes you cynical."

"Yeah, well, cynical keeps me alive," he muttered.

She sat on the bed, staring at his back as she took off her other heel. What was going on? What had changed his mood so quickly?

Hailey stood, expecting her toes to cramp, but they didn't. She walked to Austin's side, unsure of what to do next. She took in the view, staring out at the bright lights of the yacht in the distance, trying to figure out her next step. "It's—it's so big, so beautiful in the moonlight." She slid him a sidelong glance when he had nothing to say. "Earlier this afternoon, I saw Jeremy talking to a man docking one of the powerboats that comes and goes from the yacht. I would love to get on that boat."

A grunt was Austin's only response.

Hailey brushed her fingers down his forearm, studying him as his jaw clenched tight in the cast of light. "What's wrong?"

"Nothing."

"We both know that's not true." She ran her hand up, back down, trying to soothe. "I thought we had fun tonight. What changed?"

He met her gaze in the dim porch light filtering into the room. The intensity of his stare made her swallow. She wanted to step back from the heat scorching his eyes, but instead stepped closer. "Tell me what's bothering you."

"*You're* bothering me, Hailey. Everything about you is driving me crazy."

She dropped her hand. "I don't understand."

He took a step toward her. "No, *I* don't understand. You've been through hell. You've been surrounded by the scum of the earth, yet you're still so sweet, so kind, so *naive*. How is that possible? The truth is right in front of you, but you don't see it."

She shook her head, confused. They'd spent the entire day together. She'd never enjoyed anything more, but his sudden mood had come out of nowhere. "What are you talking about?"

"Look." He turned her to the window, toward the massive boat on the water. "Why can't you *see* it?"

Baffled, she stared at him instead. "See what? What are you *talking* about?" She repeated, growing more frustrated.

"The truth, for God's sake." His voice rang sharp, and she broke free of his hold.

"Austin, I don't know what's wrong with you, but I'm leaving." She never did well with angry men. Hard eyes and harsh male voices left her uneasy. She made her way to the door.

"No, you're not. It's dark, and despite what you think, it's far from safe to be alone out there."

Exasperated, she whirled as her own temper began to heat. "Did you get too much sun today? What the freak is wrong with you? You clearly have something to say, so say it. Drop the cryptic crap and get on with it, or get out. Better yet, I will. I'm going to Jeremy's."

Austin let loose a humorless laugh as he sat in the whicker chair, scrubbing his hands over his face.

Bubbling with confusion and a healthy dose of anger, Hailey turned the knob. "I've had it. I'm outta here." She stepped into the night, taking the steps in a hurry, stopping when she spotted the huge man leaning against a palm tree in the shadows. His cigarette smoke stung the air, curling until the wisps vanished.

Why was he so close to her room? Goosebumps prickled her skin as he gave her a small nod. She didn't know him, but she didn't like him.

Hailey backed up, rammed into a solid wall of man and whirled, stifling a scream as Austin's arms came around her, steadying her. Her breath shuddered in and out as she glanced behind her.

The guy was gone.

Did she imagine him? With her next breath, she smelled smoke still lingering. Hailey looked to the beach, the water, the docks. Where did he go? He had all but vanished. She tried to break free of Austin's grip. "Let me go."

He held firm. "Not until I know you're coming back in

the room."

She didn't feel safe in the dark, not like she had just minutes before. "I'm going back." She stormed up the steps, tried to slam the door closed, but Austin caught it. She pivoted before he turned the lock. "You knew that man was out there. You knew he was watching me, and you still said nothing."

"I saw him at dinner last night."

"And?"

He shrugged. "And that's it."

Her eyes narrowed. "I don't believe you."

He shrugged again. "I don't know what to tell you."

"Oh, there's plenty to tell me, but you won't. I'm starting to recognize the machismo crap you, Hunter, and Ethan pull when you think the 'little women' can't handle something."

Sighing, Austin moved to the whicker couch.

"What are you doing?" Hailey rushed to him. Dark night stared through the big window, making her shudder. She yanked the curtains closed. Is this how Sarah felt during her ordeal? Violated? Disgusted that someone scrutinized her every move?

"Sitting down."

"Huh?" Hailey rubbed her hands over the goose bumps on her arms, fighting to find the thread of their argument. "Go sit in your own room. I don't want you here tonight." That wasn't exactly true, but she had her pride, didn't she?

He closed his eyes and blew out another long, steaming breath. "Hailey."

"Don't 'Hailey' me in that placating tone. I said, get out. If you aren't willing to explain the completely bizarre-o, one-eighty turn this evening just took, I won't have you here."

Austin rubbed at his jaw. "I'm damned if I do and

damned if I don't."

"Once again, I have no idea what you're talking about, but it sounds like you have a personal problem." She wasn't going to bend, even if the thought of being here without him creeped her out.

"You say you want the truth, but you don't. Not really."

"Don't tell me what I want."

He stared at her for a long time. "Some men are watching us. I think they're locals that know we're connected with Project Mexico."

"How would they know that?"

He shrugged. "Information was sent down to Dr. Lopez, the Site Director, from the University last week. The files were hacked into. Everything short of your social security number was up for grabs: GPAs, financial aid status, home addresses, telephone numbers, work history, etcetera, etcetera. Whoever accessed the data would know we aren't flying into Cozumel with the rest of the group on Saturday. It's documented that one of the guards is already here, as is one of Project Mexico's participants. If they have our names, it wouldn't be hard to track us down. The island's tiny."

She shook her head, unable to find the connection. "Why would anyone be threatened by Project Mexico? We're here to help."

"Not everyone wants help, Hailey. Some people are happy with who they are, happy with the choices they've made in life."

She couldn't help but find a parallel between his statement and Jeremy. She wasn't ready to give up on him, so she immediately dismissed it. "Are you saying I'm in danger?"

"I'm saying I want you to stop digging for the good in everyone, because sometimes, there's just more bad, even after you've scraped away a few layers."

"That doesn't answer my question. Am I in danger?"

"Possibly."

She tried to ignore the stirrings of fear. No international mission was without risks. The cause was more important. "What should I do?"

"Stay close to me."

She crossed her arms. "I can't stay glued to your hip for the next three months."

"No, but you can stay cautious—keep your eyes open." He blew out another long breath and glanced down at the floor before he met her gaze. "I don't want anything happening to you. I care about you, Hailey."

That took the wind out of her self-righteous sails. She opened her mouth to speak, snapped her jaw closed, surprised. How could she stay mad after that? Hailey rested her hand over Austin's balled fist on the arm of the couch. "I—I care about you too."

He played his thumb over her knuckles, leaving a trail of heat. "I don't want to go back to my room." He stood. "Let me stay with you, Hailey."

She licked her lips as nerves fluttered to life. Uncertainty twisted her stomach into a thousand knots. She didn't want to make a fool of herself again. Did Austin want another movie marathon or something more? "I'm not sure...What are you..." she closed her eyes, her heart slamming in her chest as he skimmed his knuckle along her cheek. "Austin, I..."

He lifted her chin with the touch of his finger, taking her mouth before she could finish. Sighing, she absorbed the hungry pressure of his lips and brought her arms around his neck.

Austin's tongue sought hers as his fingers glided along her shoulders and down her back, leaving her shivering in their wake.

He deepened the kiss, drugging her with need, as his

hands lingered at her waist, brushing, tickling, before he pulled her fully against him. Breasts pressed to firm chest as she rested her hands on his solid shoulders.

Austin's mouth left hers to wander to her jaw. "I want you, Hailey," he murmured, as his lips skimmed her neck, teeth nipping at her shoulder, making her suck in a sharp breath. "I want you like crazy."

Everywhere he touched, tingled. "I—I...mmm," was the best she could do when his tongue left a steaming trail along the flaming skin of her collarbone. Her head fell back with the anticipation of his next touch.

Austin's hands wandered into her hair, combing through her light brown tresses, wrapping his fingers around the ends, tugging gently as he nibbled her top lip.

Hailey opened her eyes, staring into his, completely absorbed in the dark green intensity. She took his mouth this time, wanting him as much as he wanted her.

Spurned by need, she unbuttoned his navy blue shirt as fast as her unsteady fingers could manage, eager to feel his skin against hers. She peeled the fabric away, only to come to another layer.

Biting her lip, Hailey stifled a groan of frustrated pleasure as she looked her fill. Austin's powerful build filled out his white t-shirt and cargo shorts gloriously. He was magnificent, and hers for tonight.

His eyes never left hers as he removed his holster, setting it over the back of the whicker chair, then pulled the crewneck over his head, letting it fall.

She took a step forward, played her fingers over his powerfully muscled chest, down his firm stomach, watching his jaw clench. Growing bold, she snuck a finger into the waist of his jeans. A grumble erupted in Austin's throat.

Out of nowhere, a twist of nerves slammed into Hailey. Her belly roiled with the familiar sensation that threatened to ruin everything, as it had the two other times she'd been with a man.

Fighting her anxiety, struggling to dismiss the urge to step back, Hailey moved her fingers up, pressing her palms to Austin's hot skin. His muscles quivered as he drew in a deep breath through his nose then tugged her closer, his mouth seeking hers again.

Hailey battled her doubts, attempting desperately to lose herself in the mind-numbing sensations she'd all but drowned in moments before.

She fought not to stiffen as Austin pulled at the strings knotted at the base of her neck, loosening her halter dress. She clutched her fingers at the waist of his shorts, on the verge of frustrated tears.

He tugged at the thin fabric covering her breasts, cupped them. His thumb found her sensitive nipples and traced slow circles over them, making her moan with the delicious thrill.

You're a whore, Hailey Roberts. Nothing but trash like the slut who bred you. Tensing, Hailey fought Mother Frazier's words running shrilly through her mind, words that had poisoned every intimate moment she'd ever tried to have.

A body like yours was built for sinning. A man will never see anything more. Just like your mother, little tramp. Hailey shook her head, clutching her fingers against his belt loops.

He pulled her top down to her waist and stared at her small breasts filling her sheer black bra. Groaning, Austin's mouth moved to suckle. Wet heat laved across her skin and her breath caught, then came out with a shuddering whoosh.

This is where she wanted to be, this is what she wanted to *feel*—Austin touching, tasting. She caressed her hands up his back, triumphant in the moment sensation finally overruled Mother Frazier.

Austin pulled at the front clasp of her bra, catching sensitized skin with his callused palms, pressing gently, rubbing circles that barely made contact, teasing. Her breast ached with pleasure as a dull throb started low in her stomach. She strained, trembling against Austin's hands, wanting more as she moaned.

As if he'd read her mind, he took the lobe of her ear in his mouth, sending scatterings of goose bumps along her spine. "Yes, Austin," she whispered.

He smiled slowly, and her rapid pulse accelerated. She wanted this, wanted him. It was going to be different this time. With a snap of Austin's wrist, he sent her dress to the floor. "Hailey, my God." He stared, taking her in, devouring her.

A body like yours was built for sinning. The phrase she heard every day for three years echoed like a nightmare. Nerves flooded back and she covered herself.

Austin frowned. "What are you doing? What's wrong?"

She tried to relax her arms. "Nothing."

He caressed her shoulders. "You sure?"

Why did this always happen? Why couldn't she be normal? She sunk into despair as hopelessness took over. Here Austin stood, the man she'd wanted for three years, and she was ruining everything. "Yes. Just kiss me, Austin. Please."

Still frowning, he stared into her eyes.

"Please." She moved forward, capturing his mouth.

He gripped her arms before his hands settled against her hips.

Hailey struggled not to push him away, but it felt as though the room were closing in on her. The pleasure of the evening vanished as seething frustration replaced her embers of passion. This wasn't how it was supposed to be. Her tongue met his mechanically as she readied herself to fail sexually in Austin Casey's arms.

Austin eased back and brushed his finger over her cheek. "Hailey, what is it? I lost you somewhere along the way."

"No, you didn't. I'm right here." She wanted nothing more than to be right here, in this moment with him. She moved to kiss him again but he evaded her.

"Hey." He pressed his lips to her forehead. "If you don't want to do this…"

She closed her eyes as tears came back. "I *do* want to do this. I've wanted you for so long and you're *here*." She opened her eyes, moved her head so Austin no longer touched her. She fiddled with her fingers, staring hard at the floor. "I'm not very good at this." Taking a step back, she waited for him to leave. "I'm sorry, Austin, I'm really just not very good at this," she repeated.

He took her hand, pulled her against him. He lifted her face to his, his thumb under her chin. "You're doing fine."

"I can't relax."

He brought her fingers to his lips and kissed each one, knotting her stomach with yearning.

"Austin, I—"

"Come with me." He walked with her to the bed. "Will you lay with me for awhile?"

She nodded, pathetically grateful he hadn't rushed out the door.

Austin kneeled on the mattress, then lay down. Hailey lay next to him, fighting the urge to cover herself.

He turned on the TV, flipping through channels until he found a music channel. Sarah McLachlan's easy crooning poured from the speakers. Austin set the remote down and pulled her close. He combed his fingers through her hair. "I want to kiss you, Hailey. I want to be with you." He met her lips, gently, tenderly. "Let me touch you. Relax. Think of the way you feel when I put my hands on you." He hypnotized her with his eyes, with his deep voice, as he skimmed her breasts again.

He traced her nipples with the pads of his fingers, making her shudder as he brought his mouth back to hers, drawing the kiss out until she gasped from the heat.

His lips left hers, trailed over her chin, her neck, her chest, her breasts once more. His tongue flittered over aroused skin, his eyes never leaving hers as he applied more pressure and gently suckled.

Hailey closed her eyes and bunched her fists at her side, powerless to do anything but feel. The tug and throb was back, deep in her center, stronger, as Austin continued, relentless.

Small, throaty purrs escaped her throat. Unable to be still, she slid her fingers through his hair, traced his ear, lost in the sensations Austin brought.

He moved to straddle her thighs, his hands spanning the sides of her waist, his touch sending her system raging. Bending, he nibbled her stomach, around her bellybutton, down her hips. She moaned as his fingers snuck under her panties.

As excitement built, as their intimacy increased, Hailey tensed, waiting for Mother's words, certain they were just a thought away.

"Look at me, Hailey."

The gentle demand in his voice left her no choice. She met his eyes as he pulled her panties down her legs. Everything but Austin vanished. He sent the black fabric to the floor, snagged her foot in his hand, skimmed her arch with his fingers, started his way back up, stopping at her anklebone, his mouth exploring. His tongue and teeth left her reeling as he teased the back of her knees. Her breath came in pants as his eyes promised more.

He stopped at her thighs, caressing her trembling legs. She was ready for madness, pulsing, waiting, wanting him inside.

"Austin, I'm ready."

He flashed her one of his killer grins. "Let's see." He ran two fingers over her scorching flesh, missing both marks. Her brows furrowed as she groaned her frustration. She needed him to *touch* her. Her body ached from the agonizing wait. "Austin, please."

The pad of his thumb found her, then began to trace, to rub in slow, torturous circles.

She gasped, grabbed the sheets, fisting them in her hands as a flood of electric heat built, filling her with sensation. Whimpering, she begged, ready to burst.

He added more pressure, keeping his lazy pace. Her hips gyrated out of control as she grasped for the peak, just out of reach. Husky moan after husky moan filled the room, as she climbed higher until white-hot flames careened through her center, through her core, and sent her over the overwhelming edge. A long, loud cry escaped her lips as she quivered, shuddering with the shock that swept her body.

She was sure she couldn't take anymore until Austin brought her a new sensation. His tongue flicked and she arched to meet it. "Austin. Austin," she moaned, losing her thought as he slipped, slid, suckled, probed over and over until she tensed, convulsing against his mouth.

When Austin relented, Hailey sat up, craving one thing only—to feel his body cover hers, to feel him moving inside. Her gaze trailed over him, stopping at the bulge in his shorts as he undid his button, as he tugged at the zipper. He yanked off his pants, pulling his boxers with them.

Hailey stared. Holy dear God, he was huge. She swallowed as he crawled toward her.

He met her in the center of the bed and took her lips. As tongue played against tongue, she moved her hand, touching him hesitantly at first until he groaned. "Wrap your hand around me," he said against her mouth. She did, and he tipped his head back on a rough sigh. Hailey slid her hand up and down, slowly, until he panted and his stomach muscles quivered.

Bringing Austin to the edge left her heady with power. She sped up, sinking her teeth into his chin as he shuddered.

He pushed her back on the bed, covered her with his body, leaving hurried, hungry kisses along her neck, her jaw, as he nestled himself between her legs. He pressed at her center. Shivering, she came to her senses. "Wait, Austin." She pushed at his shoulders. " Do you have anything?" she asked, struggling as he ravaged her mouth. "I'm on birth control, but I only started it a couple months ago. I'm a little nervous about free diving."

He sat up, breath heaving, reached for his shorts. He dug into his wallet and removed a gold-foiled package. "I made a quick stop off while we both showered and changed for dinner—thank *God*."

She smiled, flattered that he had thought ahead to this, that he had been wanting her as much as she wanted him.

Austin ripped the package open and took the rubber from the foil.

"Let me." She nibbled her lip as his gaze shot to meet hers.

He handed her the condom. She grasped him and he clenched his jaw. Her eyes stayed on his as she rolled the condom over him.

He pushed a strand of hair from her face. "Hailey, I need you, right now."

She'd never heard anything better. She held out her arms, welcoming him.

Their mouths met and he laid her back. His weight pressed against her as he settled himself between her legs again. He suckled at her bottom lip before his tongue sank deep, leaving her breathless. She played with his hair, reveling in the feel, as the kissed turned hungry.

Austin pushed himself forward, slowly entering her. She gasped, clamping her fingers around his powerful forearms, holding on as twin spears of pleasure and pain catapulted through her. She whimpered from his size with each gentle thrust.

"Hailey, oh my God, Hailey," he said on a strangled gasp. "You feel so good."

She sucked in a breath, sure she couldn't handle him.

"I'm trying to be gentle." His voice was strained.

"I know."

"Just relax, Hailey." He pressed his forehead to hers, moved his hand down, finding her. He stopped thrusting, concentrated on her, until she no longer felt the tight fit of having him inside.

Her fingers tensed and relaxed against his shoulders, in time with his rapid circles. When her breath shuddered in and out, he plied her with kisses. Her hips moved, urging him on, as the tingling heat traveled deep inside, through her stomach, making her shudder.

Austin began to move again, slowly at first as she gasped. She tried to speak but words failed her as she let out a strangled cry of pleasure. Dear God, what was he doing to her? How was it possible to live through something like this? As his finger sent her over, he quickened his thrusts.

She arched her head back and called out for him. She clutched around him in spasms, her body trembling uncontrollably. Each time he thrust, she contracted, shuddering on an endless moan.

Her hands grasped his shoulders, his arms, as her shattering orgasm consumed her entirely.

Austin took her mouth, once, twice, in between her gasps and his. He mumbled something unintelligible before he rested his head against her shoulder and thrust himself deep, tensing with a strangled groan.

CHAPTER 14

AUSTIN KISSED HAILEY'S SHOULDER, WATCHING the pulse pound in her neck. Her breath still shuddered in and out as his did. He lifted his head and stared at her. Hailey's eyes were closed, her cheeks rosy, the hair around her forehead damp. She was beautiful.

Austin touched his lips to hers and her lids flew open. He smiled as he settled his weight on his arms. "You gonna make it?"

"I'm not sure. That was...insanely amazing."

He grinned. "That doesn't hurt my feelings."

She beamed back. "Doesn't hurt mine either." Hailey pulled his face to hers and kissed him.

"I have to get up."

"No, stay here." She wrapped her arms around his waist.

"I'll be back. If I don't get to the trash, the whole purpose of the condom will be null and void."

"Oh, yeah. Right." She released her grip, and he pulled himself free.

"Be back in a second." He went to the bathroom and came out to find Hailey snuggled under the covers. "You're cold?"

"Mmm. I just had a *major* workout. I did a lot of sweating. Now I'm chilly, a little weak, a little shaky. But it was definitely worth it." She wiggled her brows, smiling.

Damn, he couldn't get enough of her. "I see." He crawled under the blankets, and pulled her closer, needing to touch her skin.

She snuggled in, sighing.

Austin looked down as she closed her eyes again. "Are you ready to call it a night?"

"Hmm?"

He shut off the music pouring from the television and her lids fluttered open.

"I wouldn't mind watching TV. Maybe there's a movie on."

"In a minute." He was curious about the little hiccup in their evening. "Hailey, what happened a while back?"

"What do you mean?"

He played his finger over her cheekbone, over her ear. "I'm trying to figure out what I did to make you uncomfortable."

"You didn't do anything to make me uncomfortable."

"For a couple minutes there, I wasn't sure."

"You did everything right." She picked up his hand, played with his fingers. "This is the first time I actually feel normal afterwards."

He frowned. "I'm not following you."

She slid her hands along his arm, but wouldn't meet his eyes. "I can count the number of times I've had sex on three fingers. This is the first time I actually enjoyed it."

Austin's frown deepened. Another layer to Hailey he hadn't expected. She was stunningly hot, so incredibly outgoing and confident. He noticed the way other men looked at her. He'd just assumed her more experienced. Thinking back, he remembered her covering herself as she told him she couldn't relax. "How come?"

She shrugged. "Some people aren't very good at sex."

He tilted her face until she met his gaze. "Do you hear me complaining?"

"You're too much of a gentleman."

"I promise you that the thoughts I'm having about you right now, about what I want to do to you this very second, are anything but gentlemanly."

Her eyes widened and he smiled. He drew her bottom lip into his mouth, traced her top lip with is tongue. "I'm not always a nice guy, and I'm definitely not always gentle. You make my blood run plenty hot, Hailey. Remember that."

"I—I..." she let out a whoosh of breath. "What am I supposed to say to that?"

He chuckled. "Nothing. It's simple truth. Maybe the man you were with was a dick."

"Men, Austin. I've been with two different men before you. When you can't get into it with either, you have to start looking for common denominators. That would be me."

"Sometimes there aren't any common denominators."

A small smile ghosted her mouth. "Maybe."

There was more to this story; he wanted it. "You're a puzzle. Just when I think I have you figured out, I find another piece."

She shrugged. "I'm not that hard to figure out."

"For the most part, no. But then we get back to those pieces. I want them, Hailey."

"Why?"

"Because you fascinate me."

Her brow winged up. "I'm not that fascinating."

He rolled on top of her. "We'll have to disagree there." He brushed the hair back from her face, trailed his fingers along her jaw, her neck. He couldn't stop touching her. "Tell me your story, Hailey." He pressed his lips to hers. "You trusted me with your body; trust me with the rest."

"You're asking a lot."

He kissed her again, drawing out the wave of contentment that came from holding her close. "I know." Something changed as he lay over her, looking into her honey eyes. This was no longer about *wanting* to know—

he needed to.

Hailey closed her eyes and, pressed her lips together, took a deep breath. "After I left Jeremy in the hospital, I went to my temporary foster house. I can't say it was a home; it was just the place where I ended up stuck for three years. I hated it there as much as Mother Frazier hated having me."

He curled a strand of her hair around his finger. "She was your foster mom?"

Hailey opened her eyes. "She was my foster parent. Loraine was my mom."

"Sorry." He kissed the tip of her nose.

"No, I am." She sighed.

This was painful for her, but he pushed, wanting to understand the deepest parts of her. "Why do you think Mother Frazier disliked you?"

"I don't *think*, I *know*. And she didn't simply dislike me. She hated me. She made that point clear from the beginning. I was a sinning slut like the whore who made me."

The embers of rage burned low in his belly as he listened. Her body, relaxed moments ago, grew tense beneath him. He was about to stop her, but she continued.

"I'd always loved school growing up. I was involved in *everything*. But then my parents died. After, I wasn't allowed to stay and participate in anything, but the six-and-a-half hours I was there, I relished. I didn't have to clean the house or take care of Mother Frazier's biological children and her two other foster kids. I didn't have to get down on my knees and pray for hours to 'wash away my sins'. But most of all, I didn't have to listen to Mother Frazier's rants about my sinful beauty or slutty body."

"For Christ's sake, Hailey." He could hardly stand to listen to what she'd lived through. "Did you tell someone?"

"No."

173

"*Why?*"

"Because there wasn't any point. The State would've done an investigation—maybe—and it would've made my life more of a living hell when they found nothing substantial. I was fed, clothed, and sent to school every day, where I made top marks. They weren't going to take me away from the Fraziers', and, she would've made me pay."

He rested his forehead against hers and clasped their fingers together. The woman he held was a miracle. How did someone who lived through that stay so sweet and kind? It would've been so easy to be eaten up by bitterness. "I'm so sorry, Hailey."

She shrugged. "There's nothing to apologize for."

He took her face in his hands. "Yes, there is. I'm apologizing for the social workers who let you down, for that Frazier bitch who didn't see you for who you are."

Her eyes filled. "Please, Austin." A tear slid into her hair as she sniffed. "It doesn't do any good to get upset about something that happened so long ago."

He shook his head, still seething. She pressed her palms to his cheeks, a gesture of soothing, when he should've been the one providing comfort.

"It wasn't all bad. One of my teachers—I think she must've known what was going on—made it so I could take accelerated classes during the summer months. When I left Redding behind, I took my high school diploma with me. If I hadn't had Ms. Berry looking out for me, I would've left a dropout. I think she knew I was biding my time, waiting. When I turned eighteen, I was leaving one way or the other. I'm lucky I got to leave the way I did."

Hailey gave him a small smile as he stroked her shoulder.

"I also had so many wonderful years with my parents. For the most part, I was able to ignore Mother Frazier. On the days or nights I thought I couldn't bear it a second longer, I would remember how proud my parents had been. I would remember the person they wanted me to be. It almost always helped, but I didn't leave the Frazier house unscathed. Her words stuck with me."

"Of course they did."

"For a long time after I walked out their door, I was terrified I would end up a whore like my mother. On the couple occasions I did get intimate, the fear would gnaw at me. What if I liked sex too much? What if I turned out like her? I mean, what makes a person choose that lifestyle?"

Everything made sense now—her hesitation, her inability to relax. "God, Hailey." How could he heal years of emotional abuse? She'd been strong, but she still suffered. He pressed his lips to hers tenderly. "I love having sex. If you do it right, you should. That doesn't make me a whore. It makes me human."

She frowned. "I never thought about it like that. It's so simple and so true, but for some reason, I never thought of it that way." The troubled look cleared from her eyes, and she smiled.

He touched her lips again. "I want to be with you."

"You do? Already?"

"Hell yeah."

She chuckled.

He wanted her lost in him, to push away her painful past he'd brought into the bed they shared.

She smiled. "Thank you."

"For what?"

"For giving me this. For giving me a piece of myself back. I've never had anything like this before, this type of trust with anyone." She pulled his mouth to hers and took a piece of him with her.

Trust. She trusted him, and he'd been dishonest. As Hailey wrapped her arms around him, he tried to dismiss the guilt worming its way into his conscience. He'd lied to her earlier about the man who had been watching her, bringing Project Mexico into the picture when it had nothing to do with the danger she was in. If he told her the truth now, he had no doubt she would confront her brother...that she would end up dead.

He'd always liked Hailey, had always cared for her, but as they lay twined together, her warm body arousing his, he knew there was so much more here. This lie kept her safe. He wouldn't lose her now.

❦

Jeremy sat at the bar, nursing his beer, his stomach clenched with anxiety. He set the bottle down, tempted to tip it back, to drain the clear glass of its dark brew. But he couldn't afford to dim his wits now. Donte had given him and Mateo an order.

His long finger traced circles in the condensation of his beverage and his foot bumped up and down against the uncomfortable stool. The dive he sat in didn't exactly consider cushioned seating to be top priority. He glanced at his watch, his muscles clenching tighter. Fucking A, could they get on with this already?

He'd done a lot of...interesting shit while living on the streets after he ran away from the boy's home, but this was goddamn insane—not as bad as offing the pig, but still crazy.

He glimpsed his watch again, met Mateo's gaze across the dimly lit room, waiting for the nod.

Jeremy took another pull of beer as he eyed their targets—dusky skin, long black hair, even longer legs, and definitely not over eighteen. The girls were *hot*. Donte was sure to be pleased—his life depended on it.

Moments later, he looked at Mateo again, catching

the barely perceptible movement of his head as the ladies headed for the door. Mateo stood, throwing a few pesos next to his empty glass. He followed through the doorway into the night.

Jeremy took one last sip before he got to his feet, leaving an average tip by the half-empty bottle. He walked out, casually, carefully, always remembering to remain unsuspecting and unnoticed.

He picked up his pace as he made his way to the car. Mateo turned the ignition over as Jeremy slammed his door. "What the fuck took you so long, man? Do you want me to lose them?"

"Relax. They're shitfaced. They aren't going anywhere fast."

"Relax, homie? *Relax*? You gonna find us two more bitches to take back to Donte? You're too fucking cocky. It's gonna get you killed."

They drove away from the dive, surrounded by abandoned buildings and poverty. Before long, they spotted the girls, in short, tight skirts and black halter-tops, in the beam of headlights. Mateo pulled ahead of them and jerked the car to the side.

"Let's do this," Jeremy said, finding this assignment far more appealing than the last. He and Mateo bumped fists and got out on either side of the car.

The girls were already backing up, girls with identical faces. Fucking-A, they'd scored Donte twins, a detail he'd missed in the smog of cigarette smoke. "Where you going, lovely ladies?"

"They don't understand you, dumb ass." Mateo shook his head. "Why do I get stuck with the newbies? Grab one before they decide to scream."

Jeremy advanced on the girl hurrying away on the right. "Not so fast, honey. You're keeping me alive tonight," he muttered.

Crying, she clutched her sister's wrist as they turned to run.

Jeremy grabbed her around her small waist and slapped a hand over her mouth as Mateo did the same to the other sister.

"Where you going?" He clutched tighter, inhaling cheap perfume, cheaper whiskey. "Where do you think you're *going*? You're coming with us." He dragged her toward the car.

She struggled and tried to kick her foot back, aiming for his jewels.

He stopped and yanked her hair, making her cry louder against his hand. "Be still or die," he said in poor Spanish.

When he made it to the vehicle, Jeremy opened the door. The girl kicked and punched as he shoved her inside.

The click of Mateo releasing the safety on his weapon quieted the hysterical crying. "Be quiet," he snapped, aiming the pistol at their reluctant passengers.

"Jeremy, cuff them together, then to the seats."

Jeremy found the cuffs in the center console. He snapped wrists together, then hooked their other wrists to the handle on the door.

"Now let's get out of here."

He and Mateo took their seats, bumped knuckles. "Pretty damn smooth."

"Not bad. Not bad," Mateo conceded. "Let's get back to Donte."

Mateo pulled onto the street as a movement caught Jeremy's eye.

A bum slipped into the shadows. "Stop. We've got a witness."

"What?" Mateo slammed on the breaks. "Where?"

"Hiding over there." Jeremy gestured with his head.

Mateo pushed closer to the windshield. "I don't see

nothin', man."

"He's there. Trust me."

"Then go take care of it."

Fuck. Snapping up a couple of loose girls was one thing, but this killing shit was another. "You do it. I proved I could. That's enough."

Mateo cut the engine. "Your heart starting to bleed, homie? It takes more than one kill to prove yourself to the Zulas. Get your ass out there."

Jeremy shoved the door open, sick of taking orders. He pulled his new Zulas-issued pistol from his belt holster, released the safety with an exaggerated flourish, and stalked away from the car. Maybe if Mateo wasn't careful, he'd find a bullet in *his* head.

As Jeremy walked further into the shadows, he found the thin, elderly man crouched against a crumbling brick wall.

"Please, no. Please, no," the bum begged as he covered his face with trembling, arthritic hands, crying.

Jeremy raised the gun. "Should've stayed out of the way. I don't have a choice. Gotta stay alive." He fired without thought. The man slumped forward, a mess.

Glancing at the pistol, then at the old guy and back, he nodded—much easier this time.

He secured the safety, put the gun away, walked to the car, and got in.

"You do it?" Mateo asked.

"Did you hear the shot?"

"That don't mean shit."

"Look for yourself." He glared, insulted.

"Just messing with you." Mateo laughed. "Fuck, man, you're too sensitive."

"Whatever. Let's go." Jeremy visualized yanking the gun free again and popping Mateo. His senior partner better watch his step.

Mateo started the car and drove toward the shore where the small motorboat waited to take them to Donte.

An hour later, Jeremy and Mateo were shown to an elegantly decorated office below deck. Donte stood by his well-stocked wet bar. "Gentlemen." He inclined his head, exuding power. He poured them each a brandy. "Sit down, please." He handed them their drinks.

"Thank you," Jeremy said.

Donte sat in a leather chair. "I've personally... inspected the girls you've brought me. Your choices please me tonight, gentlemen. You've done good work."

"Thank you, Señor," Mateo said as Jeremy nodded.

"They are a bit...shy yet, but they will come around. All of my men work hard. They will be rewarded with fine entertainment while we are here. The ladies should suit them well. You are welcome to enjoy their company at any time." Donte took a sip of amber liquid. "Our plans for next week are almost finalized. I will fill you in soon." He moved to stand.

"Um, excuse me, Señor," Jeremy spoke up. "I'm wondering if I might ask a favor."

Donte raised an eyebrow, took his seat again. "What favor do you ask?"

"I'm having trouble with someone—someone who has the potential to cause our organization big problems."

Donte swirled the brandy in his glass. "Oh, and who is this?"

"His name is Austin Casey. He's a bodyguard who'll be working with Project Mexico. He's already here and very nosy." Jeremy's eyes narrowed as he remembered Austin shoving him to the ground, telling him to treat Hailey right.

Donte opened a drawer, pulled out a file. He set the manila folder on his desk, opened it. A slew of photos lay inside, many from the resort. "I believe many of these pictures are of your Austin Casey."

Jeremy swallowed as he saw picture after picture of Hailey: on horseback, jet ski, walking the beach with Austin, dancing with Austin, dining with Austin, kissing Austin. "Yes, the man in all these photos is Austin." Jeremy continued through the photographs, slowing as he studied several close-ups of Hailey's beautiful face. A flicker of guilt surfaced, but he quickly squashed it. As long as he played by the rules, Hailey would be safe.

"Your sister is a stunning woman, Mr. Kagan."

Jeremy met Donte's stare. What was he getting at? "Yes, she is."

"She smiles a lot, laughs a lot. She intrigues me. I would like to dine with her here on my yacht."

Jeremy thought of the girls in a room down the hall, who were being used as the yachts personal whores.

"Just dinner, Mr. Kagan. You will join us, of course, and Austin Casey will be warned—very sternly. You will bring me your sister on Thursday night, and I will make sure Mr. Casey understands he is to mind his own affairs."

Jeremy licked his lips. "I was thinking maybe we could just kill him."

"Death is not always the best option. Making someone pay until they wish they were dead is often better, especially when the person in question is a highly decorated member of the United States Navy's SEAL Team Six. We can't afford media attention during this early stage of our operation, Mr. Kagan; his murder would certainly bring it."

"Yes. Thank you." A good beat-down would have to do.

"I look forward to Thursday."

How the hell would he get Hailey here? They weren't even speaking. How was he going to get Hailey away from Austin? "I'll do my best, Señor Rodriguez."

"You will do better than your best, Mr. Kagan. I will

have dinner with your sister Thursday evening."

"Yes, Señor." More orders—but these he would follow without argument.

Donte got to his feet. "That will be all."

Jeremy and Mateo stood as well. Mateo opened the door. Two armed guards flanked the exit, with two more at each end of the hallway.

As Jeremy wandered toward the stairwell, he heard the faint whimpers and pleading of the girls through the door.

"Ah, it sounds as if our new ladies are enjoying another round. Please, gentlemen, enjoy yourselves."

Mateo grinned. "Thank you, Señor." He opened the door and walked in, eliciting a scream from the girl he'd grabbed.

"Do you not want to join in the fun, Mr. Kagan? This is part of my gift to you."

He'd guilted women into sex before, had lied, said he'd loved them to get them in the sack, but he'd never actually gone this far. "I'm thankful just to have Austin taken care of."

"I'm a generous man. I will take care of Austin Casey and allow you to enjoy the pleasures of my new entertainment. They will only be here for a little while before we ship them off to one of our brothels." Donte opened the door for him.

"Thank you." With little choice, Jeremy stepped inside.

The prisoners were tied to the bed, crying. Mateo's pants were down around his ankles as he readied himself to enter the girl Jeremy had shoved in the car. "Dive in, Kagan." He grinned, then plunged in. "Oh, yeah, y*eah.* I love my job. Come on, Kagan. Get your dick wet. Unless you're not cut out for this."

Jeremy unbuckled his pants as he made his way to the other option, slightly ashamed, but more than that—

excited. She was so fucking hot.

The girl crawled backwards. "No, Señor, no, *por favor,*" she begged.

"You lucky bastard. You got yourself a fighter," Mateo puffed out. "I'm having a go at her next."

Jeremy pulled on her trembling legs, bringing her forward, taking another step down the path he'd chosen. Whatever he had to do to stay alive, right?

He stared dispassionately at the young, pretty girl with the terrified eyes. If she hadn't been dancing like a whore in the club, she wouldn't be where she was right now. Guilt tried its hand again, but he ignored his conscience. This was his life now; he might as well enjoy it. "I'll make you love it," he said, ramming himself deep as the girl sobbed wildly.

CHAPTER 15

"I DON'T THINK I'VE EVER BEEN so relaxed," Hailey said as she shut the door and flopped on the bed. "If I could have a massage every day, I would—absolutely, without a doubt."

Austin collapsed next to Hailey, enjoying loose muscles after ninety minutes of pure heaven. He settled his hands behind his head, stared up at the whirling fan. "That was pretty awesome."

"I had no idea our spa session would be *outside*. The rush of waves feet from the massage tables...the warm sun on our backs." She sighed and closed her eyes. "Is it Thursday already? Does vacation really end in forty-eight hours?"

"Afraid so. But it isn't over yet." Austin rolled to his side. Hailey's eyes were still closed. A hint of a smile touched her lips. He brushed his fingers through her soft locks; there was more blonde than light brown after a week in the sun.

They hadn't spent a moment apart since their first evening at the restaurant. He loved being with her, talking, laughing, laying on the beach, skin diving, making her crazy in bed. He didn't care where they were or what they did; he just wanted to be with her.

"I think we should make the most of the time we have left." His gaze tracked over her sinful body, knowing how they could start. He moved his hand to her shoulder, trailing his palms over her satin skin, stopping at her elbow, making her smile widen as she groaned. He brought his fingers back up, detoured to her breast, circling, tracing, until her nipple hardened beneath her light blue cotton top. "So, what do you think we should do first? Any ideas?"

Grinning, Hailey opened her eyes and turned to her side. "Well, I know what you want to do, but first I want a shower. The oils were amazing while they rubbed them into our muscles, but now it feels kinda gross."

He hooked an arm around her waist, pulled her closer, traced her mouth with his tongue. "Mmm, a shower." He suckled at her top lip, then her bottom one. "Perfect."

She eased back. "You want to shower together? Austin, I..."

He grinned as she stared at him. There was that hint of shyness again. They'd spent the last two nights wrapped in each other's arms, yet every time they came together, he'd had to coax away layers of inhibition. Before they were finished, he would have her without restriction. That Frazier woman didn't get to put herself between him and Hailey. "Yes, shower together." He nuzzled her neck. "What's wrong with that? We sleep in the same bed, see each other naked, have sex. Let me wash your back."

A slow smile spread across her lips. "I've never had anyone wash my back."

"We should definitely fix that." He sat up with her, pulled her shirt up and off. His cell phone started to ring, but he ignored it. Whoever it was could wait. Austin tugged at the tie holding Hailey's bikini top in place. He hummed his appreciation as the white fabric fell away. God, she was beautiful. He traced her tan line, careful to skim her hardened nipples, his gaze never leaving hers.

Hailey's fingers found their way into his hair, down his neck, and over his shoulders and biceps, her touch a whisper against his skin. "I thought we were showering."

The phone rang again. His hands hesitated on her waist as he glanced toward the edge of the bed. "We'll get there."

She pressed kisses to his chest. "Maybe you should answer."

"Later." Austin scooped her up in his arms and drew her breast in his mouth. When Hailey moaned, snagging her lip between her teeth, he had to fight the urge to lay her on the hardwood floor and take her right there.

"I want you," Hailey whispered next to his ear as she nipped at his lobe.

Shuddering, he set her down by the glassed-in shower, reached in, and twisted on the jets. Instantly, water began to spray in cross-streams. Austin took Hailey's mouth, ready to eat her alive. He leaned her against the thick pane as he untied the loose knots holding her bikini bottom at her hips. He pulled his mouth free from hers and stared into eyes, already heated with passion. "You ready to get wet?"

She yanked his swim trunks down. "I'll let you decide."

He groaned as he gathered her close, walking her back into the warm water, pressing her to the tile, pulling her arms over her head. "God, Hailey, I'm going to—"

The loud knock at the door cut him off.

They stared at each other, their breath heaving as water poured over them. "Ignore it. They'll come back later." He crushed his mouth against hers.

The knock came again, louder this time. Hailey stiffened. "Austin." She pushed at his shoulders as he continued to run his lips over her neck.

"They can come back." He simmered, frustrated, realizing he was losing her. He laid his forehead against hers, trying to think past his sexual haze. "Somebody has really bad timing." He wrapped his arms around her and cupped her butt, hoping to distract her. He *needed* her.

Knuckles rapped on the door again and he yanked himself away. "Goddamn. I'll be *right* back. Stay *right* here."

She smiled. "I will. *Right* here."

Austin slung a towel around his hips and hurried to the door, leaving small puddles with each step. He twisted the knob with an irritated yank.

The staff member jumped back, her eyes popping wide. She politely kept her gaze level with his. "Good afternoon, Señor. I'm sorry to interrupt, but I'm looking for a guest named Austin Casey. It was thought he might be here."

Austin reined in his aggravation. It wasn't this poor woman's fault. "I'm Austin Casey."

"The front desk received a call from a Señor Ethan Cooke. He asked that you call him immediately."

Ethan. Son of a bitch. "Thank you."

"Yes, Señor." She backed away.

"Uh, wait. Wait just a second." Austin hurried back into the room and dug through his wallet, unearthing an American twenty. "Here you go. Sorry."

"Oh, no, Señor."

He didn't want to stand here and argue; he wanted to get back to Hailey. "Please, Señora, I was rude. I would feel better if you'd take it."

She hesitated before she took the bill from his hand. "Thank you very much."

"You're welcome." He nodded and shut the door. Austin hurried past the bed, pausing to glance at his phone. Son of a bitch. He picked up his cell and dialed Ethan's number.

"Where the hell have you been, Casey?"

"On vacation. What do you want? I'm busy." Glancing at the bathroom door, he listened to sheets of water run off Hailey's smoking hot body.

"Well, while you've been soaking up the sun, some of us have actually been working."

"Yeah, yeah, yeah. What is it?"

"You're kinda bitchy. Got a hot date?"

Hell yeah he had a hot date. She was wet, naked, and waiting. "Just tell me what you want."

"I want to know when you were planning to tell me about the dead bodies and missing girls."

"Dead bodies and missing girls? What dead bodies and missing girls?"

"It's all over the Mexican news channels. A cop's body was found strewn about the island, and two seventeen year old sisters vanished early Wednesday morning."

"I haven't heard a thing about it."

"Doesn't surprise me, actually. I imagine the resort is trying to keep it hush-hush. Dr. Lopez, the Site Director—"

"Yeah, I know who Dr. Lopez is," Austin snapped as he glanced toward the bathroom again.

"Wow, forget the 'kinda.' You're extra bitchy. Anyway, Dr. Lopez called to tell me as the news was breaking. I've been watching ever since. To top it off, the landlord called Dr. Lopez, reporting suspicious activity around the apartment building Project Mexico will be using. People he hasn't seen before seem to be casing the joint. He was pretty worked up about it when we spoke. Lopez was kind enough to call the Dean and share the same news. I've spent the last hour trying to reassure the head of the university that he doesn't have to reconsider sending his group down, that my men are more than qualified to handle the situation. It sure as hell would help if you answered your goddamn phone."

"What the fuck, Cooke? I'm on vacation. I called you, didn't I?"

"After I had you messaged. Consider your vacation over, Casey. I want you to go over to the apartments and see what in the hell is going on. The landlord will meet you at six thirty. I also want you to see what you can find out about the girls so I can talk to the Dean again. I want to reassure him none of the women partaking in Project

188

Mexico will meet the same fate. As to the chopped cop... I think we both know what happened there."

"Yeah." Austin glanced at his watch. He had an hour. "I'll head out in a few minutes."

"Austin," Hailey called. "The water's getting cold."

He walked closer to the bathroom. "Uh, I'll be right there."

"Was that Hailey?" Ethan's voice brightened. "Is that the shower running? Well son of a bitch, Casey. Just what is it you two are doing?"

"Fuck you, Ethan. I'm hanging up."

"Wait a minute. Don't get your balls in a twist."

"*What?*" He couldn't wait until their next boxing match. "Call me when you get back with an update."

"You know I will. Goodbye."

"Wait."

He muttered another curse. "*What?*"

"Enjoy your shower, Stud. Wait 'til I tell Sarah about this."

Austin pressed "end" as Ethan's chuckle echoed through the phone. He threw his cell down with a frustrated flick of his wrist. Two girls were missing, a cop was dead, and something screwy was going on with the apartment. *Fucking great.*

He darted a glance toward the bathroom again, to where Hailey waited for him. This was the first time he could ever remember feeling like the rope in a tug-of-war between a woman and his job. He wanted his last two days with Hailey—alone. By some miracle, Jeremy and Mateo hadn't bothered them, but work was about to bring his week with Hailey to an abrupt halt. He stared at his cell for a moment, then headed to the bathroom. Steam hung in the air; the peach blossom scent of Hailey filled the room. Austin dropped his towel and stepped into the shower. He wrapped his arms around Hailey, nuzzling his face against the back of her shoulder. "Sorry."

She turned and clasped her fingers at the back his neck. "That's okay. Is everything all right?"

He didn't want to talk about it. He wanted to *want* her again, but work was already crowding his brain. Austin pulled her mouth to his, taking her into a deep kiss.

Hailey placed her hand against his cheek, easing away. "Austin, what's wrong?"

"Apparently, my vacation's over."

She frowned. "But we don't pick up Jackson and the other Project Mexico members until Saturday afternoon."

"I just got off the phone with Ethan. A couple of teen girls vanished from the island. They haven't been seen since early Wednesday morning." He would keep the information about the cop to himself for now.

Concern filled Hailey's eyes as she took his hand. "Oh my God. That's terrible. What can we do to help?"

Wasn't that just like her? He wrapped her in a hug, leaning forward to shut off the water. "You're amazing, Hailey. Here I'm bitching because I can't sit in the sun for the next two days, and two kids are missing. They're sisters. Their family must be a mess."

"Austin, you worry about other people's welfare three-hundred and sixty-five days a year." She kissed him. "You're allowed to mourn the loss of your not-even-weeklong vacation."

"Consider the mourning period over." He took her face in his hands. "I'm not going to have quite as much time as we've had over the past few days."

"That's okay."

He sighed, wanting to stay here with her. "I guess it'll have to be. When we get back from Project Mexico, will you go away with me, just the two of us for a couple of days? We'll find someplace without phones."

She stared at him, blinking. "Uh, yeah, sure."

"I've enjoyed this, spending time with you—everything about you."

"I'm...really surprised." She smiled. "I'd pretty much given up hope you would ever notice me, and now look at us."

"Oh, I noticed you. I guess that makes me an idiot for taking so long to figure out the rest." He skimmed his knuckle against her skin. "I hate to cut this short, but I really need to get going." He wrapped the towel he'd dropped around his waist again and grabbed one for Hailey.

She knotted the thick cotton at her breasts. "Where are you going?"

"There've been a couple of problems at the apartment we'll be staying at. I need to go check in with the landlord."

"I'll go with you."

He shook his head, immediately dismissing the idea. He wanted her with him, but she was safer here behind her locked door or up at one of the crowded restaurants. "No. I think it's better if you stay put until I sit down with the landlord and figure out what's going on. The sun's starting to set. I'm not taking you downtown in the dark." He pulled a pair of khaki shorts and a white t-shirt from one of Hailey's drawers. He hadn't been back to his own room except to get more clothes.

Hailey pulled a lilac sundress over her head. "But what about you?"

"I'll be fine. The faster I go, the faster I'll be back. If I'm lucky, I'll only be a couple hours." He settled his holster over his shoulder, grabbed the gun from under the bed, shoved a full clip into the magazine well.

"Can't you wait 'til morning?"

He glanced at her as he secured his Glock in the holster. Hailey stared at his pistol, a small line of worry creasing her brow.

"Hailey, this is my job. This is what I do."

"I know what you do, Austin." She evaded his eyes before she turned away, grabbing the bottle of lotion from the bedside table.

"Then what's up?"

"Nothing." She squirted cream into her hand, placed her foot on the bed, and began to rub lotion over her delicately muscled leg.

What was this? She'd seen him with his weapon a hundred times before. He sat on the edge of the bed, puzzled. "Are you upset I'm wearing my gun?"

She poured more lotion into her hand, repeated the process with her other leg. "No, of course not." Her voice was casually stiff.

Austin took her arm. "What's going on?"

She looked at him briefly, then turned her attention back to her leg. "Things are different between us now. What you *do* means something different to me now. I don't want anything happening to you. I'm a little worried, that's all."

"Hailey," he pulled her into his lap, nuzzled her neck, "I'm going to be fine."

"I know. I'm being silly." She tried to stand.

"Not silly, sweet." He moved so he could cradle her. "What do you say we schedule a movie marathon? We've tried the last two nights, but for some reason, we never get around to it."

She smiled. "I wonder why?"

"Let me go talk to the landlord—get a closer look at our digs for the next three months, then we'll movie marathon it. Ladies choice, of course."

"Ooh, chick flicks it is."

He winced. "I thought you wanted me to hurry back."

Smiling, she pulled his mouth to hers, kissing him lightly, sweetly. "I do."

192

He pressed his forehead to hers. How could such a simple gesture undo him so completely? "I want you to stay in the room while I'm gone, with the door locked. Or I can walk you up to one of the restaurants and pay an attendant to walk you back if you'd prefer."

"You're worried about the men who've been watching us."

"Not worried so much as cautious." So far they'd kept their distance, but he also hadn't left her alone.

"I don't think we have anything to worry about. They've seen we aren't here to cause problems."

"I still want to play it safe. I don't want you out walking around in the dark by yourself at least until we have a better idea of what's going on with the kidnappings."

"I'll stay in. I'll order in some room service, catch up on my emails, probably call Sarah and check in on the girls. I miss them."

"I bet they miss you too." He ran a finger down her nose before he kissed her again and set her on the bed beside him. "I have to get going. The landlord will be waiting." He stood and grabbed a maroon short-sleeve button-down from the small closet. He concealed his weapon with each button, shoved his cell in his pocket, and headed for the door. "I'll be back as soon as I can."

She hurried over to him and gave him a hug. "Careful, 'kay?"

"Okay." Austin pulled her against him, taking in her scent once more, then let her go. He stepped into the brilliant sunset, wishing he could stay to watch the sun sink below the horizon with Hailey. He shrugged off the regret. His job had begun again; there wasn't much he could do about it. It was time to step back into reality. "Lock up."

She smiled, nodded, and closed the door.

The bolt slid in the lock. Satisfied, Austin started down

the steps. He paused when he spotted the man by the dock, smoking his signature cigarette. Austin hesitated, wanting to go back, but knew he couldn't. He would have to hope everything was okay while he was gone. There was nothing else he could do.

Hailey watched Austin walk up the path to the hotel. As he disappeared from sight, her gaze wandered to the docks. The man who all but camped by the water stood in his typical spot, smoking. She snapped her curtain closed, turning away with a shiver. She rubbed at the goose bumps puckering her arms. The discomfort of being watched heightened now that Austin was gone.

She walked to the door, tested the lock, then hurried over to the bed, scooping up the remote. She turned on the TV. The canned laughter of the American sitcom comforted her. She needed to get busy before her imagination got to work.

As Hailey settled with her laptop, her cell phone vibrated against the side table. She picked it up, grinning as she read Sarah's text message. *Heard through the grapevine Austin's shower is broken. So nice of you to let him use yours. I'm also proud of your dedication to the environment—saving water by showering together?!? I'm missing some major details!!*

Hailey texted back. *I'm afraid I don't know what you're talking about.*

Her phone vibrated again. *Morgan's coming over tomorrow night. We need a conference call!*

I think that can be arranged. How about six thirty?

Let me set my alarm!!

Hailey chuckled.

By the way, Sarah texted. *I'm so happy for you.*

Me too. He's everything I never thought I could have.
I'll let you go. Love you. Miss you. Can't wait to chat.

Ditto. Kiss my beautiful girls for me. Hailey set her phone down, still smiling, and sighed. Is this what 'truly happy' felt like?

Hailey still couldn't put her finger on how she and Austin ended up in this unexpected, wonderful place. At the end of the day, it didn't matter. He was here; he was hers. She was going to treasure this miracle for as long as it lasted. She wasn't a dreamer—or not much of one, anyway. She didn't have any unrealistic expectations or hopes that her relationship with Austin would last forever. If she began to wonder what it would be like to wake with him every morning, or what it would be like to make a family with him or grow old together, she quickly dismissed the thought. Austin wasn't looking for long-term—at least not with her.

He came from a traditional, close mid-western family. He had parents still married after decades, successful brothers and sisters married to successful husbands and wives, all with adorable children. A foster kid who'd descended from the likes of a drug addicted street whore didn't exactly round out a pretty picture for the Casey Family.

If she felt a slice of pain, she shrugged it away. She wasn't foolish enough to let her past define her, but she wasn't stupid enough to believe it didn't define her for other people. Austin might not have a problem with where she came from, but that didn't mean the rest of them wouldn't.

Hailey struggled to push the unhappiness away. Nothing would change what was. She adjusted her laptop on her legs, pulling it closer, logged in, and ran a search for articles on the missing sisters from Cozumel. As she read the vague details on the girls' disappearance, her mind wandered back to Austin.

In less than a week she'd found herself more than a little in love. Was it possible? Could someone really fall so quickly, or was she making too much of her feelings? She thought of the way Austin looked at her, of the way they snuggled on the lounge chairs by the ocean waves, of his patience as they worked on her diving skills, of their long, quiet talks while they lay naked in each other's arms at two o'clock in the morning.

She pressed her hand to her fluttering stomach as her pulse quickened. Oh, it was possible to love so quickly, because she did.

Hailey stared at her screen, no longer seeing pictures of the missing teens, no longer seeing the words. What was she going to do? How should she handle this?

A knock sounded at the door, distracting her from her thoughts. Frowning, instantly tense, Hailey got to her feet, and peeked through the security hole.

Jeremy. They hadn't spoken since their argument outside the hotel lobby.

She flipped the lock, turned the knob.

Jeremy stood in his swim trunks, the bruising on his ribs almost completely faded. "Hi."

"Hi." Hurt and anger surged to the surface as he smiled at her. His words had cut deep when he made reference to her abandoning him, as he'd done on more than one occasion. He wasn't about to get away with it.

"Can I come in?"

"I don't know. Can you be nice?"

Jeremy's brow rose. "I can if you can." He started forward.

Hailey held up her hand. "I'm serious, Jeremy. You really hurt me the other day. You don't get to do that."

"Do what?"

"Throw our past in my face whenever you feel like it.

Remind me that I had to leave you in the hospital hurt and scared. I thought of you every day, Jeremy. Every single day." The loneliness she'd felt all those years without him still pained her.

"I'm sorry." He tried to step forward again.

Hailey didn't see any trace of regret as she looked at him. She held up her hand again. "Are you? Because this isn't the first time you've made a reference to me walking away—as if I had a choice. You were all I had left too, but sometimes I don't think you remember that."

"I don't want to talk about this, Hailey."

At the moment, she didn't care what he wanted. She was sick of putting Jeremy's feelings first—always. Right now, she would take care of her own. "Then leave. I've had enough. I've spent the last ten years sacrificing for you, and you don't give anything back. You'll start now, or I *will* walk away—this time with a clear conscience, because I know I've done everything I can to try to have a relationship with you. I've tried to help you the way Mom and Daddy would've wanted me to."

Jeremy stared at her, his eyes full of shock, before they darted down. "Why didn't you come get me?" he demanded. "I spent three-and-a-half years in a hellish boys' home waiting for you. I marked your birthday on a calendar the year you turned eighteen, sure you would be there the next day. You promised. I tried to be good and succeeded sometimes, but it wasn't enough. I waited six months, but you never came. By then, I gave up hope and took off with a couple of older kids. I was homeless for years because you lied, because you didn't keep your promise!"

Tears coursed down her cheeks as Jeremy broke her heart. His eyes met hers with the same vulnerability she'd seen all those years before, when he had begged her not to leave him. Hailey stepped back from the door.

They stared at each other until Jeremy finally walked inside.

"We've tip-toed around this since you came back, so let's stop." Hailey wiped at her eyes. "I tried to find you, Jeremy; I did. I walked out of the foster home I lived in the day I turned eighteen, collected my inheritance from the bank, and took a bus to L.A. After I found a job, I contacted a private investigator. I ended up taking a second job cleaning at the university to pay for him. He never found you. Even when he told me he'd done all he could, I wouldn't let him stop. You vanished from the system—a runaway. There was nothing more I could do."

"You tried to find me?"

"*Yes*, I tried to find you. I've told you that on the few occasions we've actually tried to talk about this, but I guess I should've told you everything. The PI tracked down the address of the boys' home you'd lived in, but we were two weeks too late. You had already run away. When he gave me the news, I was still hopeful he would find you, but as the days and weeks went on, I started to realize it was hopeless."

She grabbed a tissue, blotted her eyes, blew her nose. "Some days I was afraid you'd forgotten about me. Other days I was afraid you hadn't. You were so little when I had to leave you. Sometimes memories fade."

Hailey breathed out a deep shudder as she confessed one of her most troublesome secrets. "There are so many wonderful things I remember about Mom and Daddy, but sometimes I have to work hard to remember Mom's laugh or the way Daddy's eyes looked when he smiled. I'm so afraid I'm going to forget some small detail, some small something that meant everything to me as a child."

Jeremy handed her another tissue. "I don't remember as much as I wish I did, as I want to. I remember impressions more than anything—Mom and Dad making me feel safe. I remember their kindness, but I didn't have as much time with them as you did. We got screwed—big time. We should've had more time with them, Hailey."

She balled the tissue in her hand. "I know. I wish we had. I wish they were still here. Everything might be different."

Even as she said it, staring at the brother she'd longed for, she couldn't fully regret the events life had thrown their way. Austin's clothes hung in a closet next to hers. His bathroom supplies lay jumbled on the counter with hers. If she breathed deep, she caught a whiff of him on the air. Would she be standing here right now if the last decade had played out differently? Her time with Austin had been worth every moment of anguish she'd encountered over the last ten years. For the first time since she'd sat in the car with her parents, warm under her blanket, content with her family, she felt home. Austin had given her a small slice of what it felt like to be home again.

As the thought struck, she glanced at Jeremy, realizing she could live without him. She loved him and always would. She wanted him in her life, but he needed to prove he belonged there—family or not.

Over the last two-and-a-half months, and his visit prior, he'd done little to show her. He'd stolen from her, lied, had been deliberately cruel. She wouldn't tolerate such behavior from anyone else, so why from Jeremy? It was time to lay it on the line. Hailey took a steeling breath, realizing he might walk away after their conversation. "We need to talk."

"Uh oh." He tried a smile.

"Come sit down." She sat, patting the cushion on the couch next to her.

He sighed. "All right. What's up?"

"What's up is I can't keep doing this with you, Jeremy.

You've been back in my life for almost three months now, and parts of it aren't working for me."

He rushed to his feet. "What the fuck does that mean?"

"Don't curse at me." She struggled to stay calm. Jeremy's volatile temper always made her uneasy. "Sit down and *talk* to me like an adult for once."

He exhaled sharply, then took his seat again.

This wasn't easy. Sighing herself, Hailey glanced at the ceiling. "I can't go on like this, Jeremy. Your snarky comment Tuesday morning was the last straw."

"Is this because of Austin? Did *he* put you up to this?"

She narrowed her eyes as her own tempter heated. "This has nothing to do with Austin and everything to do with me. Maybe this isn't going to work. I've wanted you back in my life since the moment I had to let you go, but things have to change. We're both adults. I can't keep looking at you as if you're a helpless nine-year-old, and you have to stop looking at me as the almost-adult who abandoned you. We're here now. We're both grown. This is where we have to start."

"This is where I want to start." He fidgeted in the seat. "I knocked on your door because I want to take you to dinner."

Her eyes flew to his, surprised. Hope tried to sneak into her heart, but she guarded herself against it. "I think I've heard that one before."

"I mean it this time. My boss wants to meet you. I've been bragging about my big sister since I started working for him."

Despite the turn their relationship had taken, Hailey couldn't help but smile. "It'll have to be tomorrow night. Project Mexico begins Saturday afternoon."

"Actually, I was thinking tonight."

"Tonight? Jeremy, I'm not dressed for a night out. I can't meet your boss right now."

"Oh, come on. You're beautiful. I'm proud of you. Let me show you off a bit."

She smiled again, but shook her head reluctantly. "I told Austin I would stay in."

"What, is he your keeper?"

The vehement dislike in his voice, in his eyes, surprised her. She swore she saw a flash of hatred before it vanished. "No, Austin's not my keeper. He's a bodyguard who happens to care about me. He doesn't want me out alone until they find out more about the kidnappings."

"The kidnappings? That happened miles away."

"How do you know? I couldn't find much in the news."

"The locals talk." He shrugged, dismissing it. "Come on, Hailey. I know I'm not some fancy over-muscled bodyguard, but I won't let anything happen to you. I really want you to meet my boss. I want to show you what I've done, what I've accomplished. For once, I can actually back it up. Call Austin if it makes you feel better. Tell him you'll be with me."

Despite their conversation moments before, she saw glimpses of the sweet little boy she remembered years before. He was so eager to please, so desperate for approval. "Oh, all right."

He grinned. "Do you want to call over to Austin's room?"

"Oh, he's not here."

Jeremy stood and played with the hem of the pale green curtain. "Where is he?"

"At work. He had to meet with the landlord at the apartment we'll be using for Project Mexico." Jeremy's small smile puzzled her. "I'll just leave him a note."

"We won't be gone too long."

She got to her feet. "I need a few minutes to get ready. How about fifteen?"

"Better yet, I'll give you sixteen." He winked. "I'll be back after I shower and shave." He pulled her into a long hug. "This is going to be awesome, Hailey."

She wanted it to be. If nothing else came from tonight, she would finally see for herself what Jeremy did, who he hung around with. Hopefully she would be able to put the doubts Austin had planted about his gang and drug affiliations aside and could stop feeling guilty for wondering.

Jeremy gave her a last squeeze, kissed her cheek. "Fifteen minutes."

"Sixteen." She said with a smile.

Hailey locked the door behind him. As Jeremy wandered back to his own room, Hailey hurried to the bathroom. She was finally going to have dinner with her brother.

CHAPTER 16

HAILEY PULLED A WISP OF hair from her updo, twisting it around her curling iron. Counting to five, she released it as she scrutinized herself in the mirror. Not bad for eleven minutes. She'd played up her eyes, making them appear huge with a trick of eyeliner and a few sweeps of mascara. She applied clear gloss to her lips and studied herself a moment longer before hurrying to the bedroom to slip on her backless white sandals.

As she was scrawling a quick note to Austin, a knock sounded at the door. "Hailey, it's me."

"Hold on. Coming," she hollered. She grabbed a wrap from the closet and opened the door. Jeremy stood before her in dark gray slacks and a white collared shirt. He was so clean-cut, so handsome. "You look amazing."

Grinning, he pulled a tropical bloom from behind his back, handed it to her. "So do you."

She beamed, touched by his sweetness as she took the only flower he'd ever given her. "Thank you. It's beautiful." She hurried to the bathroom, sliding the blossom in her hair. The delicate petals were accented by pale shades of purple—a perfect complement to her sleeveless sundress. Hailey wandered back to the bedroom.

Jeremy smiled. "Awesome. Are you ready?"

"Yeah. Let me hang this note for Austin, then we can go." She secured the white sheet to the door and locked up. Smiling, she looked at her brother. "I'm really looking forward to this."

"Me too." Jeremy held out his arm.

Hailey looped hers through as they headed down the steps. "So, where are we eating?"

"It's a surprise."

He steered her away from the hotel path and kept going down, toward the water. As they approached the dock, she noticed the man usually standing close by was now gone. Frowning, she peered over her shoulder. Where did he go? He was *always* there, no matter the time—day or night.

Jeremy followed her gaze. "What's wrong?"

She shook her head. "Nothing."

"You sure?"

"Absolutely."

They stepped on the dock, and her frown returned. "What are we doing, Jeremy?"

"Just trust me."

That wasn't necessarily easy, but he was trying. "Okay."

As they walked closer to the water, she spotted the powerboat docked to the wood post. "What—"

"*Trust* me, Hailey. You love the water, right?"

"Yes, of course. You know that."

"Exactly."

In the darkness she could make out the form of a man standing at the driver's seat. Hailey stifled a gasp. It was *him*, the one who nodded at her by the palm tree, the one who stood on the sand day and night, always watching.

"Hailey, this is Desi. Desi, my sister Hailey."

"Hello, Hailey," the large, muscular man said in a thick Spanish accent. She wanted to take a step back, to tell Jeremy she'd changed her mind. Instead, she clutched her brother tighter. "Nice to meet you, Desi."

"Let me help you aboard." Desi lifted her from the dock to the boat much the way Austin always did, as if she weighed nothing. "Please sit and relax. Señor Rodriguez is glad you can come tonight."

She stared at Desi, confused. Perhaps he hadn't been watching her after all?

Jeremy hopped down and sat beside her.

Hailey bent close to her brother's ear. "Uh, who is he?"

"He works for Donte."

"Yeah, but..." The low, powerful rumble of the motor drowned her out.

Jeremy shook his head. "What?"

She didn't want to shout her questions. "Nothing." She glanced around again. What did a powerboat have to do with dinner and Donte Rodriguez? "I'm trusting you, Jeremy, but I'm seriously confused," she said louder.

He smiled. "You'll see."

"Hold on, please," Desi called over his shoulder.

Hailey did as she was told. They pulled away from the dock, gaining speed on the water. The sweet racer cut across the waves as if the swells were nothing. Hailey closed her eyes, smiling, enjoying the wind on her face, caring little that her updo would probably be ruined by the time they arrived wherever they were going.

"What do you think so far?" Jeremy shouted.

Grinning, laughing, Hailey opened her eyes, meeting Jeremy's in the deep dusk. "I think this is *amazing.*"

The boat cut closer to the bright yacht, eating up the distance quickly. "Look how pretty, how festive it is with the lights ablaze. I wonder what it must be like to stare out at the ocean from the decks."

"Maybe we should find out."

"That would be so awe—" she stopped, her eyes widening as she met Jeremy's. She took his hand, gripping it. "Are we having dinner there? Did Mr. Rodriguez make arrangements for us to have dinner on that yacht?"

"Hailey, Donte *owns* that yacht."

She gaped as she stared at the small cruise liner lit up like an elegant white Christmas. "I—I can't believe this.

Holy crap!" She grabbed him in a hug. "Thank you for inviting me tonight."

He hugged her back, kissed her cheek. "You're welcome."

She'd thought herself happy an hour before, but now... She shook her head as she smiled, staring at the magnificence of the yacht. Jeremy certainly hadn't exaggerated Mr. Rodriguez's wealth.

In a week's time, so many wonderful things had come together. She had Austin in her life; Jeremy appeared to be on the straight and narrow, building himself into a man her parents would've been proud of. If everything Jeremy and Mateo told her was true about Donte Rodriguez's charitable causes, he could only be an excellent influence in her brother's life.

She couldn't wait to share this with Austin. He'd made a mistake, had run with the wrong information, but that was over now.

Hailey sighed, perfectly at peace for the first time ever.

Desi cut the motor. The boat drifted toward the back of the yacht. Two large men walked to the edge of the launch, both of them heavily armed.

Hailey gasped, grabbed Jeremy's arm. "Jeremy, look at the guns. Are those machine guns? Why do—"

"Relax." He took her hand, squeezed. "Donte is extremely wealthy and lives out on the open water. This is just a safety precaution."

She stared at the weapons and the serious men holding them. A wave of uneasiness twisted her stomach as she nodded, unsure.

"They won't hurt you, Hailey. I've been on this boat a dozen times and I'm still here, right?"

"Yes." She glanced back to shore. They were miles from the flicker of lights in the distance.

As Desi stepped from the boat, he reached for Hailey's hand, pulling her up with him. Jeremy stepped up next to them.

Hailey stared at the circular hot tub and pool combo glowing in the eerie lights several feet away. Her gaze swept up the flight of stairs, leading to two more decks. She then looked back at the men standing close by, still holding their massive guns.

She gave one of the leering guards a small smile, nodding as the dull unease in her stomach grew to a full bloom. She looked down at the black pumice slip-proof tread she stood on, telling herself that the man eyeing her was a bodyguard, just like Austin, only working for Mr. Rodriguez instead of Ethan. She peeked at him again under her lashes, studying him further. No, the man staring was nothing like Austin. There was no kindness in the deep brown of his eyes.

A man descended the steps from the second deck. He was sleeker, less bulky than the others, wearing slacks and a button down. The gun resting at his hip was much less intimidating in its side holster. Was this Donte Rodriguez?

"Good evening, Mr. Kagan, Ms. Roberts."

The guard she'd stared at, the one with the harsh brown eyes, stepped forward, yanking her purse from her grasp.

Hailey gasped. "What are you doing?"

"If you will excuse us, Ms. Roberts," the sleek one said with a smile, "—a small precaution."

The guard searched through the contents before he handed it back.

Hailey snatched it with a huff, then turned to look at Jeremy. She glanced at the shore again, remembering there was no way back to her room. "Jeremy, may I speak—"

"Ah, so you have finally arrived."

Hailey blinked in surprise as another man descended

the stairs. He was movie- star-handsome with his dark good looks and boxer's build. She relaxed a degree, certain that this was Donte Rodriguez. He exuded wealth and power in his designer suit. He was so young, probably early thirties at most. She'd pictured Jeremy working for an older man.

He took the last step and stood before her. "Jeremy." Mr. Rodriguez nodded at her brother. "Ms. Roberts, I presume."

"Uh, yes." Good grief he was handsome.

"It's lovely to finally meet you." Mr. Rodriguez took her hand, kissed her knuckles in an elegant gesture. "You're brother speaks of you often—and very highly."

Relaxing further in his easy charm, Hailey gave him a friendly smile. He seemed nothing like his security staff. "Thank you for having me, Mr. Rodriguez. I've been eager to meet the man Jeremy works for. He clearly admires you."

He gave her a regal bow. "You are too kind. Please, call me Donte, and come with me." He led her gently by the elbow as they climbed the steps to the second story deck. Another hot tub bubbled in the corner by the smooth, glossy railing.

The large, glassed-in dining area was elegantly decorated. Lush tropical plants and flowers highlighted creamy shades of brown. Dozens of white candles flickered in crystal throughout the room. A table set for three was beautifully arranged with fine-bone china, silver, and more crystal.

"How beautiful, Mr. Rodriguez."

"Thank you—but it's Donte. Please."

She smiled her apology. "Yes. Donte."

"May I offer you a glass of champagne? Jeremy?"

"Sure, please. I'll take a glass," Jeremy said.

"I would love a glass." She would take small sips. The

last thing she wanted to do was embarrass Jeremy or herself with her low tolerance for alcohol.

"Very well." Donte guided Hailey to the marble-topped bar nestled in the corner of the dining room.

Hailey watched Donte pull a bottle of Cristal from the small wine fridge. His eyes never left hers as he peeled away the golden foil and popped the cork. She struggled not to fidget in his penetrating stare. This was a powerful man—a man who always got his way; of this, Hailey had little doubt.

"If I may be so bold, Ms. Robert's—you are quite stunning."

What was she supposed to say to that? "Uh, thank you."

A smile spread across his lips. "I have made you uncomfortable."

Horrified she had somehow offended Jeremy's boss, she placed a hand on his arm. "Oh, no, no. You didn't. And please, call me Hailey."

"Please, relax, Hailey. My only goal is to make you comfortable as my guest this evening." He handed Hailey her glass.

"Thank you."

Smiling again, Donte walked to her brother, handing him his flute of golden bubbles.

"Thanks." Jeremy set his glass down. "I have to use the restroom. I'll be right back." Jeremy opened a door and started down the hall. Apparently he knew his way around the place.

"Would you like to join me—" Donte's phone began to ring on his hip. "If you will excuse me for a moment, I need to take this."

"Sure."

Donte stepped from the room to the sleek, polished wood of the deck. Hailey wandered to one of the windows facing the shore and stared at the lights. If she squinted, she could just make out her cabana, and to the right, Austin's. Was he okay? Was he back yet? As much as she was enjoying her time on Donte's yacht and a chance to sit down to dinner with her brother, she wanted to be with Austin more.

"What do you mean?" Donte snapped.

Hailey's gaze slid to the deck at Donte's sharp tone. She focused on the view as Donte continued on in short, harsh bursts of Spanish. Someone was getting an earful. For a moment, Hailey wished she knew what he was saying. She caught a word here and there—*idiots, tonight, now*—but in the end, she had no idea. Even with her practice, she would never be able to keep up with the speed at which he spoke. Moments later, Donte came back.

Hailey turned. "I hope everything's all right."

He raised his eyebrow a fraction, but his eyes stayed cool, not reflecting any of the anger she'd heard seconds before. "I apologize, Hailey. I had a business venture go sour this evening. I do not like to lose in business."

She searched for something to say. "I'm sorry," was the best she could come up with.

Jeremy stepped into the room, a short, older woman following behind. "Dinner is ready, Señor," she said in very poor English.

"Thank you, Maria." Donte took Hailey's hand, led her to a seat, pulled out her chair. "Let's put business away for tonight. I hope you enjoy lobster."

"I love seafood." Hailey still puzzled a bit over Donte's phone call but smiled as she sat, pushing herself in.

Donte and Jeremy took their seats as Maria brought in three elegantly presented shrimp cocktail.

"Again, Donte, how beautiful."

An hour later, Hailey dabbed her napkin against her mouth, full and simply charmed by the man sitting across from her. She savored one last bite of moist cake in a rich chocolate sauce before she set her fork down. "That was amazingly delicious. Compliments to your chef."

Donte sipped his coffee, then chuckled. "My chef will have a mighty head if I compliment him as many times as you've raved about him."

She grinned. "He deserves every good word sent his way."

The beautiful clock across the room rang out the time with each deep bong. Nine o'clock. She glanced out the window to shore. Austin was surely back by now.

She'd had such a wonderful time learning about Donte's several charitable organizations, getting to know her brother better through the work he'd been doing for Donte. Jeremy was indeed in good hands. She'd been so proud when Donte told her he saw a bright future ahead for her brother.

A whippy thrill coursed through her system at the anticipation of getting back to Austin, of sharing her happiness with him. She wanted him with a sudden desperation that took her breath away. Movies wouldn't make the agenda again this evening if she had anything to do with it. Tonight would be the perfect night to surprise him with the little blue number Morgan had bought her for her birthday.

She hugged this moment of happiness to her, excited she would be going home to Austin, thrilled Jeremy worked for a man she could admire.

"I've lost you, Hailey."

Her attention snapped back to Donte and her brother. "Excuse me?"

"You were someplace else, lost in pleasant thoughts."

She sent her brother a look of apology, reached for Donte's hand. "I'm sorry. I was just thinking how happy I am. You're a very good man, Donte, with the work you do, for taking my brother under your wing and giving him a chance to start fresh." She smiled at Jeremy. "Mom and Daddy would be so proud of you. I'm sorry I had any doubts about you over the last few weeks."

He met her eyes, then glanced down. "That means a lot, Hailey."

The door opened to the hallway. The sleek man with the gun at his hip stepped into the room. "Pardon the interruption, Señor, but I must speak with you."

"Let me say good night to my guests. I will be right with you."

Jeremy and Donte stood, and Hailey followed suit.

"I'll walk you to the boat. Desi will be happy to take you back."

They walked down the stairs to the launch.

"Thank you for coming." Donte shook Jeremy's hand.

"Thank you for having us." Jeremy stepped into the boat.

"I would like to see both you and Mateo first thing in the morning."

Jeremy nodded and took his seat.

Donte's warm hand captured hers. "Hailey, I cannot express how much I've enjoyed getting to know you." He kissed her knuckles. "Please tell me you'll come back again soon."

She was sure that if she weren't in love with Austin her pulse would've pounded with the feeling of his lips against her skin, but her heart rate proved unaffected as it continued its slow, steady beat. "I would love to. I had such a nice time. The food and company were top-notch."

"You are simply spectacular. Come back again."

She nodded as he kept hold of her hand while Desi helped her onto the boat.

"Goodbye." She smiled.

"Goodbye."

Austin took his seat in the cab. After an hour-long attempt to gather information on the missing teens, he still had nothing. No one was talking—*no one*—which left him wondering. What was scaring people silent? Or better yet, *who* was scaring people silent?

Usually cash made people chatty, but American twenties, fifties, and even crisp one hundred dollar bills weren't worth the price of a few words. He did learn the girls were natives of San Miguel, Cozumel's small island town, but that tidbit came via the news.

And wasn't it strange that when a picture of the young ladies flashed on screen and their mother's pleas echoed through the speakers, the bartender turned the TV off? Why wasn't everyone searching? It was interesting that no one felt compelled to help the distraught local family get their twin daughters back.

The cabbie drove away from the busy, tourist-filled streets, taking Austin further out of town. With each turn, they left more of the hustle and charm of beachside Cozumel behind, entering third world conditions most guests usually didn't see.

Streetlights were fewer and farther between, until they vanished altogether. Buildings that hadn't seen fresh paint in years held security bars in their crumbling doors and windows. Junkies leaned or sat against the sad looking structures while prostitutes stood in the blue and red glow of bar lights. The signs encouraged patrons to enjoy hot, ready women along with a shot of tequila.

Frowning, Austin peered out the windows. Had they taken a wrong turn? Did the University really plan to put twelve college kids up in a place like this?

The cabbie took a right, traveling a mile further.

Homes began to appear along the sidewalks again. The small, concrete blockhouses were far from luxurious. Security bars still lined windows and doors, but it was a huge improvement. A little paint and a few plants would make this area cleaner and somewhat respectable. The block they'd come from was beyond hope.

The cab turned once more, and came to a stop.

Seriously?

The two-story property was little more than a pile of dilapidated shit. The lamp across the street flickered in a half-hearted attempt to light the buildings around it, throwing the apartment in shadows.

Austin's instincts hummed as he stared at the darkened house. He was ten minutes late for his meeting. Why wasn't the landlord here waiting?

Austin unbuttoned his maroon shirt, unfastened the snap over his weapon. Something wasn't right.

"Will you wait for me?" he asked the cabbie in Spanish. "I'll compensate you well."

"No. This is not a safe place. New trouble is brewing. It's dangerous."

"What danger?"

The man stayed silent, white-knuckling the steering wheel, staring straight ahead.

There wasn't any point wasting time on questions he already had answers for. He knew what the new trouble was. The cabbie was smart to keep his mouth shut, but Austin tried once more. "Do you know of the girls who vanished?"

Still no response.

There had to be a connection between the girls' disappearance and the Zulas. He *knew* there was. What else would bring such fear to an entire island? "Will you drive by again in forty-five minutes? I'll more than triple your wage if you pick me up." Everyone had a price.

214

"I will see what I can do." The streetlight blinked off, sending their surroundings into darkness.

Austin gave the cabbie an American fifty, a supremely generous payment and tip. "If you're back in forty-five minutes, there will be another." The cabbie would make more in forty-five minutes than he did in two weeks.

"I will be here."

That's what he thought. "Thank you." Austin stepped from the car and the cabbie drove off. On full alert, Austin looked around, his instincts screaming that danger lurked close.

He walked to the apartment door, gave it a testing shove. The lock barely held. "Well, Jesus." He shook his head in disgust as he wandered to a window and yanked on the black security bar. The steel didn't move. "That's something, at least." He tried a couple more. The bars were solid.

As he scanned the area, he realized he and Jackson would have their hands full. He and Ethan had been foolish to take the landlord and site director at their word when they told them the apartment was up to par for their stay.

Austin crouched, shoved his finger in a gaping crack in the disintegrating foundation. His gaze tracked up to the decaying roof. He was starting to wonder if the pictures and diagram he'd received of the interior were even from this residence. Muttering a curse, he stood and turned into the dark alley.

A skitter of unease ran down his spine, warning him to flee. He wanted to turn and go, to get home to Hailey, but he had work to do. There was no way he could allow twelve college kids into this house, into this section of town, if these were to be their accommodations for the next three months.

Austin wiped at the sweat pearling his brow, pausing

CATE BEAUMAN

mid-step at the scurry of sound coming from the large trash pile. His heart bumped against his ribs as he drew his weapon, breathing through his mouth. The stench was unbelievable. He held his gun with both hands, bracing his arms close to his shoulder, ready, scrutinizing the shadows the flickering lights played over the dark.

The clatter came once more.

Austin settled his finger on the trigger as he braced himself against the peeling white paint of the concrete wall. The noise came again as he moved forward, slowly, silently, ready for the trap.

His pulse throbbed in his throat, in his head, as he stopped, all but on top of whoever was there. A mountain of trash bags and construction debris separated him from the other side. Austin lifted his leg, gave the garbage a powerful kick. Black bags and wood planks toppled down with a huge crash. An orange alley cat let out a frightened screech as it ran off in the opposite direction.

"Fucking cat." Leaning back against the wall, Austin relaxed his grip on the gun and took a deep breath, which he regretted immediately. "Goddamn, this sucks ass," he muttered. He breathed in again, stood straight, this time alert to the putrid stench of rotting flesh. The smell was unmistakable.

Something was dead and it wasn't small. Austin pulled the corner of his shirt over his mouth and nose, hardly able to tolerate the wretched odor. He stepped over several of the bags he'd sent tumbling, stopping short and turning away when he found the source. "Fuck. Fuck. Fuck."

Austin brushed his arm over his tearing eyes, struggling not to vomit. Someone had had their head blown off fairly recently, and their remains still sat slumped against the wall, bloated, rotting, partially eaten by rodents and probably that alley cat.

216

Bracing himself, Austin turned again. *"Fuck."* The deceased was a man, but he could tell little else from the rapid decomposition. A dirty, beat up duffel bag lay in the corpse's lap. The victim had probably been homeless.

He had to get out of here, had to get back to the cabana and give Ethan a call—figure out how they should handle his discovery. "Shit." Stomach shuddering, Austin started through the piles of trash toward the front of the building. He glimpsed at his watch. The cab would be back in twenty minutes, but where was the fucking landlord?

Even as he thought it, his gut told him the owner of the apartment wasn't on his way and never had been. He'd been in this business too long not to recognize a setup. But who wanted him here, and why?

He didn't plan to wait around and find out. It was time to get the hell out of here. Trouble waited—somewhere. He wanted to run far and fast.

Austin took a step toward the street as something whizzed by his ear, crumbling the chunk of concrete just to the right of his face. Years of training had him crouching and rolling before it fully registered he was being shot at.

Another bullet pinged off broken cement, this time just centimeters from his shoulder. "Shit." Austin increased the speed of his roll, no longer worried about the stench of garbage. The trajectory of the bullets came from somewhere above.

Two more bullets winged passed him, barely missing their mark as he scurried to his feet, hurrying around the corner of the building. Austin lost his breath as he collided with a solid wall of muscle and fell backward, dropping his gun.

The hulk of man pulled Austin up by his shirtfront, smirking. "Where you going, punk?"

Without hesitation, Austin slammed his forehead

into Hulk's face, making contact with his nose. The guy loosened his grip on Austin's shirt as he crumpled forward, blood spurting like a gory fountain.

"You broke my fucking nose!"

Austin plowed his elbow against Hulk's neck, sending the asshole to the ground. "Yeah, well I knocked you out too." He whirled for his weapon, ready to make a swift exit.

Another thug in a green skullcap picked it up and pointed Austin's own Glock at him. "Not a good idea, homie. We came with a warning, but maybe I'll kill you instead."

Austin held up his hands at chest level as he scanned the area, looking for something to use as a weapon. "I think I'll take the warning."

A humorless smile creased Skullcap's face. "A smartass."

"Sometimes." Spotting a glass bottle out of the corner of his eye, Austin took a step back, bringing his arms up in a defensive posture, as if someone stood behind Skullcap. "No!"

When the man glanced over his shoulder, Austin stooped, grabbed the empty bottle, and swung. Glass shattered as Skullcap dropped the gun and began clawing at his eyes. "I can't *see*! I can't see anything!"

Austin stooped down for his gun this time, turning to leave as two men came out of the alley across the street. *What the fuck?*

"You wanna play games with us, big boy?" The man in front of Austin menacingly tapped brass knuckles against his palm as he advanced. "Let's play."

Austin glanced over his shoulder as the guy in a wife-beater rushed him with a two-inch blade.

Austin whirled, firing his gun. The bullet tore a hole through the man's palm, knocking the knife from his hand. While the man screamed, Austin bolted down the street.

Brass knuckles took chase. "You're fucking *dead*."

Austin sprinted, ducking down the first alley he saw. He hurtled a metal trashcan, then hooked a left when he came to the next building's end. Brass Knuckles no longer followed, but Austin kept his pace steady.

He ran three more blocks, stopping to catch his breath in the shadows of an abandoned business. In his haste to get away, he'd run toward the seedy bars he'd left behind not that long ago.

He needed to breathe, needed to think. Austin wiped his brow with his filthy forearm, feeling a singe of pain radiate across his bicep. Frowning, he looked down at his shirt, noticing the hole. "What the hell?" Lifting his sleeve, he swore again. Blood oozed from the gash in his skin. He'd been grazed. At some point, they'd gotten a shot off on him. Austin slid his sleeve back in place, trying to keep his wound as clean as possible until he got himself out of this mess.

Who the hell were these guys? They had to be locals someone paid. He had a feeling he knew who was sending a message, but why?

He would have to figure that out later, after he got back to the resort. If he ran straight, he would eventually come to a better section of the village. The island wasn't that big. The glow of the busy oceanfront wasn't far away. He just had to get there.

Feeling steadier and more prepared, Austin turned the corner and took a solid block of brass in the gut. The shock of pain stole his breath. Coughing, Austin fought for air, as the fist came back, catching the edge of his jaw. He saw stars as he staggered to the side of the building, fighting not to pass out.

"Not so tough now, homie. You messed up my boys. We came here to remind you to mind your own business, but now I'm gonna kill you." Brass Knuckles picked up a filthy two-by-four, ran forward, swinging wildly.

Austin straightened before the board connected with the side of his skull. He took the sharp impact in the shoulder. Brass Knuckles pulled back, came at him again, aiming for his head for the second time. Austin grabbed the thick piece of wood and kicked forward, planting his foot in the man's gut.

"Maybe I'll kill you first, fucker." Austin yanked the plank away and smashed it over Brass Knuckles back. The man collapsed to the ground, unconscious. "But you're not worth it."

Austin rolled his stiff shoulder as he struggled to ignore the stabbing pain radiating through his jaw. He kept his back to the wall, listening, making certain there weren't others. The bawdy laughter of a hooker filled the quiet as she left the bar with her latest john.

Bracing for another blow, Austin stepped from the shadows of the building, leaving Brass Knuckles where he fell. As Austin crossed the street, he spotted a cop car cruising close by. He held his breath and casually ducked his head, concealing his pistol by pulling his button-down together.

Two officers manned the vehicle, one driving, the other talking on a cell phone. Austin picked up his pace when the officer on the phone did a double take and the car slowed. He glanced over his shoulder, seeing break lights glow bright in the dark as the car came to a stop.

Shit.

The officer on the passenger's side stepped from the vehicle. "Stop," he yelled in Spanish.

Austin kept walking, inching closer to the next alley. The cop hollered again. Austin turned the corner and ran for his life. He had little doubt that the cops chasing him were on the Zulas' payroll. If they caught him, he wouldn't be alive in the morning.

He took the next right, listening as the patrol car accelerated. When the vehicle kept moving down the street, Austin doubled back the way he came. Sirens from another vehicle wailed in the distance, heading in his direction. Damn, this wasn't good. If the police were smart, they would cordon off the next three blocks and have him surrounded within minutes.

With few options, Austin ran further away from where he wanted to go. He turned the corner, all but colliding with the taxi he'd left not even an hour before. Austin raised his arms, waving for the man to stop, more than happy to see the toothless cabbie behind the wheel. The driver slammed on his breaks, and Austin ducked into the backseat. "Let's go."

A cop car rushed by.

Austin ducked, then sat back, closing his eyes as he rested his head on the seat, fisting his hands together to stop them from shaking. "Take me to the water."

The driver looked back at Austin with uneasy eyes.

Austin looked at his own arm, at the blood trailing from the wound on his bicep. He met the cabbie's gaze in the mirror, took his gun from his holster, not intending to fire, but to frighten the man into helping him. "Take me to the water," he said with more force. He pulled two hundred-dollar bills free. The cabbie yanked the cash from Austin's hand, looked straight ahead, and drove away. Minutes later, the driver stopped at an ocean lookout.

"Wait for me." Austin stepped from the cab, holding his pistol by the muzzle, using his shirt to wipe the weapon free of his fingerprints. He threw the gun far into the distance, deep into the water. He got back in the car and settled himself. "Back to the resort."

The cab pulled around the bright circular drive of the Grand Spa. Austin didn't want to be seen getting out. If worse came to worst, he planned to deny every event that happened over the last hour. "Not here. Further down. In the dark."

The cabbie met his gaze in the mirror. Austin raised his brow and the man drove forward. As the cab rolled to a stop, Austin pulled another hundred from his wallet. If the man hadn't come back when he said he would, Austin would be dead. "Thank you."

Austin handed off the bill and stepped from the vehicle when he was sure the coast was clear.

CHAPTER 17

USTIN HURRIED DOWN THE PATH to the cabanas, staying hidden in the shadows. The lights blazed bright in Hailey's suite, and he relaxed a bit. She was in her room—safe, waiting for him.

He wanted to storm in and hold her close, but he couldn't. He smelled like shit, had blood on his clothes, and a wound on his arm. He didn't want to scare her. More, he didn't want to explain.

With little choice, Austin made his way to his own room for a quick shower and a phone call. He and Ethan had big problems and less than two days to solve them.

Austin reached for his keys, still revved from his night from hell. Surely Donte knew by now his "warning" had been a waste of time. Austin had no doubt Donte issued the message. He couldn't put his finger on what he'd done to warrant the attention of the Zula's leader, but he was going to find out.

Austin unlocked his door, reached for his gun, swore. He'd hated tossing his Glock. Unarmed and on edge, he turned the knob and kicked the door open. He waited, using the exterior wall as protection, unsure if someone waited for him here as well. Pivoting, he went inside; there was no one. Austin shut the door, locked it, and did a thorough sweep of the rest of the suite until he was certain he was alone.

He wandered back to the bathroom, flipped on the light, peeled off his filthy clothes, threw them in the small trashcan. The rotten stench was putrid enough to clear the room. He closed the bag and tied it off, unworried about the likely nosey staff. The smell left little desire for curiosity.

Austin brought the shower to life. While the water warmed, he examined the cut across his upper bicep. A stitch or two probably wouldn't hurt, but that wasn't an option. Doctors would recognize a bullet wound, and he wasn't about to answer any questions. They would be obligated to call the cops, and in the end, he would be turned over to the Zulas anyway.

He studied the deep bruise blooming on his left shoulder, the tender purple welts in the center of his stomach from the blow of brass knuckles. He wiggled his jaw, wincing at the sharp ache. Son of a bitch, that pissed him off.

Bending his arm, he scrutinized his bicep again. As he flexed, blood dribbled down the mound of muscle. Hopefully, if he cleaned the shit out of it, it wouldn't get infected. The last thing he wanted was an infection in fucking Mexico.

Austin stepped into the spray, turned the heat up with a twist of the nozzle. He held his wound in the water, hissing out a breath from the sharp sting. He eyed the bar of soap wearily before he picked up the small cake and rubbed it over the gash. "Goddamn. Son of a *bitch,* that hurts!"

Certain he'd cleaned his injury as well as he could manage, Austin scrubbed the rest of himself quickly, then dumped a glob of shampoo in his hair, wondering if he would ever get the smell of rotting garbage off his skin.

After a second wash and rinse, Austin shut off the water and toweled himself dry. He hustled to the bedroom, pulling fresh clothes from the drawer, eager to get his call in to Ethan and get back to Hailey. He'd *missed* her.

At some point along the way, the idea of cuddling up with Hailey, of wrapping himself around her and getting lost in what they could bring each other, had become more important, or at least equally as important as his job.

In less than a week, Hailey had changed everything. The lines of what he thought he wanted had become skewed. She had somehow gone from casual friend to *the* woman. How the hell did that happen?

Austin pulled on a gray t-shirt and black mesh shorts, then picked up his phone and dialed Ethan's number.

"Cooke."

"If you didn't want me on your payroll, why didn't you just say so?"

"It went that well, huh?"

"Oh, even better."

"What did the landlord say?"

"Not much. He never showed up, but I did get shot at and grazed—"

"*What?*"

"I'm not finished...had to beat the shit out of several assholes, and that was before I ran from the cops. Oh, and let's not forget the dead body. You don't pay me enough, man."

"What the fuck happened?"

"I walked into a trap. The corpse was just a bonus." Austin rubbed his hand against his jaw, swearing when his fingers connected with the tender welt. "Either the landlord has his hand in organized crime or someone else entirely called the Site Director to set up a 'meeting' with me. They'd planned to mess me up, and I can't figure out why. One guy said they were warning me off, that I needed to mind my own business. I didn't get the chance to ask him to explain."

"What's your initial impression?"

"I haven't got a clue. Other than asking a few questions about the kidnappings, I've been occupied with my vacation." *And Hailey*—he kept that thought to himself.

"My 'meeting' was arranged before, so I don't think that's the connection."

"Tell me about the body."

Austin sighed as he flashed back to his gruesome find. "I don't think discovering a decomposing corpse was part of the game plan. Some poor sucker's missing a large majority of his head. I think he was homeless. I don't know if there's a Zulas connection or not. I'm not calling it in. I'll let you handle that from the States. The cops are bought. As far as I'm concerned, I never left my cabana this evening."

"Do we need to get you and Hailey out of there?"

"No, I think my little adventure was exactly what my attackers said it was—a warning. And besides, where the hell would we go? Even if I took Hailey to the safe house they would find us eventually if they set their mind to it. They're too well-connected. There's only one way out of this, Ethan. You and I both know it."

"Yeah." Ethan's sharp exhale carried over the line. "So what do you want to do?"

"Sit tight. They won't be back again—at least not this group. They fucked up, embarrassed the organization. I would've killed them if I had to, but I have little doubt they'll be taken care of by whoever sent them." Austin stretched, attempting to loosen the tension coiling his muscles tight. Seconds later, a warm trail of crimson tracked down his arm. He eyed his wound, then walked to the bathroom, grabbed a length of toilet paper. He pressed the wad to his injury.

"If things heat up, say the word. We'll pull you both. Hunter, Jackson, and I will be on our way."

"Let's see what happens. I don't want to leave unless we run out of options." He walked to the window, stared at Hailey's room. This project meant so much to her, both personally and academically. She needed these free credits. "We have other problems. Our accommodations for Project Mexico are a joke."

"Were you expecting the Hilton?"

"No, but I was expecting more than a heap of rubble. A door that actually locks would be a nice start."

"The Site Director assured me we were all set. The Dean signed off on it."

"It'll be hard to provide protection for a dozen people in a place like that. The university either needs to release more funds for another agent or find us something else."

"What a goddamn mess," Ethan grumbled. "We don't have time to dick with this. Let me call the Dean. I'm threatening to pull you and Jackson. That should get a few results."

"Keep me informed. Oh, and I'm short a weapon. I had to toss mine—didn't have time to grab the casing after I fired."

"Can you hold off until Jackson arrives?"

"I'd like to think so.

"Watch your back."

"I'm planning to." The line went dead. Austin shoved his phone in his pocket, opened the door, peering outside, wary of another trap. When he figured the coast was clear, he locked up and jogged over to Hailey's cabana. He knocked on her door. "Hailey, it's me."

He waited.

Austin knocked louder, assuming she'd finally gotten around to enjoying the huge bathtub. A slow smile spread across his face; perhaps he would join her. "Hailey, come on."

Still nothing.

His smile faded as he pounded against the door again. Unease roiled his belly. "Hailey, open up." He glanced over his shoulder, toward the docks, down the beach. Had they gotten to her? What if his "meeting" had been a diversion?

His heart pounding, he backed up, ready to bust down the door, stopping just before his shoulder met the wood. He needed to think, not overreact. Hailey had probably gotten sick of waiting. She was probably up enjoying the hotel's nightlife.

Even as Austin sprinted back to his cabana for the spare key, he knew he wouldn't find her among the other guests. She said she would stay in her room. She said she would wait for him there. God, if something had happened to her... A sheen of cold sweat slicked his body, his stomach sinking further as he thought of the things they could've done to her—or might be doing now. The Zulas were known for their brutal, if not barbaric retaliatory tactics.

Austin shook his head, unable to stand it. Hailey was fine; she had to be.

He hurried back to Hailey's cabana, fumbling with the lock, his fingers unsteady. The fear rushing through his system, devouring him whole, was a new sensation. He'd never cared for anyone the way he was coming to realize he cared for Hailey.

Finally, the key gave and he threw the door open. "Hailey!" He checked the bathroom, the closet. "Hailey!" She wasn't here, but he already knew that.

Austin glanced around the room, spotting her cell phone on the bedside table. He had to sit from the fresh wave of terror weakening his knees. She wasn't here, and she didn't take her phone. Hailey *always* took her phone.

Austin pressed his fingers to his brow, commanding himself to think. If he wanted to find her, he needed to pull it together. His heartbeat pounded in his chest, echoing like a drumbeat in his temples. *One step at a time, Casey. Take it one step at a time.*

He stood again, attempting to gain a tenuous grip

on his emotions. He closed his eyes, took a deep breath, unclenched his fists. Austin counted to ten, opened his eyes, then glanced around the room, now in professional mode. Everything appeared as it had before he left. Hailey's laptop lay open on the bed, a pen and pad of paper next to it. If the Zulas took her, she hadn't struggled.

Austin picked up Hailey's cell and searched through her information.

She'd responded to a text from Sarah less than three hours before. "Not so long ago," he muttered, trying to reassure himself. They had three hours on him. As a SEAL he'd rescued hostages that had been missing for days, weeks even.

He scrubbed his fingers against his forehead as fear cracked his shield of cool. Three hours was a lifetime. Austin shook his head. This type of thinking wasn't helping.

Forcing himself back to work, he scrolled through the conversation Hailey and Sarah had, looking for something that might tell him where she could be. Austin stopped dead as he read her thoughts. *He's everything I never thought I could have.*

Austin sat down again, surrounded by pieces of Hailey. Her peach blossom scent filled the room. Her smiling face nestled cheek to cheek with Kylee's filled the screen on her computer.

Somehow Hailey had become everything he never knew he wanted.

In defense, Austin looked away from her laptop and scrolled through her phone once more, making certain he hadn't missed anything. There was nothing.

He searched her computer's history next. An article about the teen girls' disappearance was the only activity.

Austin got to his feet and dialed the front desk.

"Front desk."

"Yes, this is Austin Casey down in the cabana suites. I'm having trouble locating my…girlfriend, Hailey Roberts. Has she signed up for any events tonight, or have you seen her around?"

"Let me check for you, Mr. Casey."

"Thank you." He paced the floor. The wait felt like an eternity.

"Mr. Casey, I'm not seeing that Ms. Roberts signed up for any of our activities, and I haven't personally seen her pass through the main lobby here this evening."

He closed his eyes. "Okay, thank you."

"Is there anything else I can do for you?"

"No, thanks." He hung up, barely suppressing the need to slam the receiver back in its cradle. Where the hell *was* she?

Austin dialed Ethan's number next.

"Hel—"

"I can't find Hailey."

"What?"

"You heard me; I can't find Hailey." He spewed his helplessness in a wave of heat. "She said she would stay here and wait for me, but she isn't *here*. Her phone is, so's her laptop, but there's no Hailey."

"Did you check in with the hotel?"

"Of course I did." He paced about, his fear winning again as he heard the concern in Ethan's voice. "I'm just telling you now so if I don't find her in the next hour, you'll be ready to get your ass down here." He ran his fingers through his hair. "My God, Cooke, do you know what they could be doing to her? What am I going to do if—"

"Pull yourself the fuck together and do what you're trained to do," Ethan snapped. "Go look for Hailey. This isn't helping her."

"I'm leaving now." He hurried to the door, flung it open.

Hailey gasped, her hand flying to her chest as she stepped back. "Oh, Austin, you scared me half to death."

Austin stared as relief warred with sharp, ripe anger. "Everything's fine, Cooke." He pressed "end," tossed the phone on the bed, dragged Hailey against him. "God, Hailey, my God. Where have you been?" He closed his eyes and breathed her in as he nestled her head to his shoulder, brushing back the soft locks of hair escaping her up-do.

Her arms came around his waist, washing away the worst of his mad.

He opened his eyes, pressed a kiss to her forehead. "Where have you been?" He eased her back, needing to see again that she was truly safe. "I've been half sick..." He saw Jeremy then, dressed in slacks and a button down, standing in the shadows of the porch. Barely masked surprise filled Jeremy's eyes as he looked away. Immediately, Austin knew. Here was the connection to his "warning" from the Zulas. Jeremy had something to do with it. It was written all over his face.

Fury rushed back so fast Austin all but choked on it. He gripped his hand against the doorframe, afraid that if he let go, he would start pummeling Hailey's brother and wouldn't be able to stop. He struggled not to lash out as he glanced back at Hailey's puzzled expression. "Where have you been? I thought something happened to you."

Her frown deepened. "Didn't you get my note? I taped it right here to the door." She pointed to the spot behind him.

"No, I didn't get it."

She rested her hand over his tensed one, squeezing. "I'm sorry, Austin. I didn't mean to make you worry."

Worry? Worry didn't even come close. If only he knew what to do with the barrage of emotions raging through him. He wanted to hold her close as stirrings of what might be love smothered him. He wanted to push her away in sheer frustration from her inability to see her brother for what he was.

"I was with Jeremy." She smiled over her shoulder. "We had dinner together—finally." She turned back. "I had the most amazing time." Her beautiful smile deepened.

Austin nodded. It was the best he could do.

"Give me just a second, 'kay?" She skimmed her finger over Austin's knuckles, then walked to Jeremy, who was still standing silent in the shadows like the coward he was. Hailey wrapped him in a hug. "Thank you. I had so much fun. This was such a special night." She kissed his cheek. "I'm so proud of you."

He whispered something close to her ear and she chuckled.

She eased away from her brother, pressing her hand to his cheek. "Thanks for the adventure. I'll never forget it."

"Me either." Jeremy's eyes flicked up to Austin's before he looked back to his sister. "I'm going to head out. Mateo wants to meet up at the casino."

"Okay. Have fun. I love you."

Austin clenched his jaw until it ached. He turned back into the room, unable to take anymore. When was Hailey going to fucking *wake up*? Maybe she never would. Maybe she couldn't. Where would that leave them? He would never be able to turn a blind eye to who Jeremy was, not even for Hailey. He rubbed his hand over the nape of his neck, wincing from the ache in his battered shoulder.

The door closed. Hailey walked up behind him and wrapped her arms around his waist, pressing her cheek to his back. He was instantly surrounded by her peachy scent.

"Austin, again, I'm so sorry about the note. The wind must've caught it."

Or someone took it down, was his guess. He didn't

touch her, couldn't turn around and look at her yet. He couldn't think straight when he stared into those big honey eyes. "You didn't bring your phone."

"I know. I forgot."

Austin stared at the wall, trying to control the anger he couldn't shake. "All of this could've been avoided with a simple call, Hailey. They didn't have a phone at the restaurant?"

"Actually, I didn't eat at the resort." Her voice burst with excitement. "Jeremy's boss wanted to meet me. I had dinner on that big, beautiful yacht."

He whirled, unable to believe what he was hearing. "You had dinner with Jeremy's boss? On the yacht?"

"Yes." She beamed. "It was wonderful and exciting and pretty much just absolutely amazing. The food was divine and…" she trailed off, her smile vanishing. "Austin, why are you looking at me like that? Are you mad at me?"

Mad? Was he *mad*? He thought of her out on the boat, surrounded by the Mexican Mafia, dining with the leader of the most notorious drug gang on the North American continent—defenseless—while he fended off thugs hunting him by the same man's order. He stepped forward, grabbing her arms, ready to explode. "You were out on that yacht with Donte Rodriguez and you want to know if I'm mad? I'm way passed mad, Hailey. I'm in a whole other stratosphere. What were you *thinking*?" He turned away and marched to the bathroom.

"What do you mean, 'what was I thinking?' I had dinner with my brother and his boss," she tossed back. "What's wrong with that?"

He whirled. "Everything!"

"Why? Why is everything wrong? Donte is superbly nice. He's a great man. Jeremy finally has a good influence in his life. How is that wrong?"

"You don't know *that* man, Hailey. You know absolutely

nothing about him." He rushed to her again, holding her face in his hands. "Why can't you *see*? Why *won't* you see?" He pivoted away. "My God, Hailey. I was sick, *sick* with worry. Now you're standing here safe and I'm sick all over again."

"I don't understand you." Her voice broke as she pressed her palm against her forehead. "What do you want from me, Austin? I don't see what you're talking about. I met Jeremy's boss and saw a man of great wealth. I saw a charming individual who involves himself in several charitable causes. I saw a person who has the potential to change my brother's life for the better. If you want me to see something else, then by God, Austin, spell it out." Tears rushed down her cheeks. She didn't give him a chance to fire back. "You hint at things, but you never say anything outright." She pointed accusatorily. "I know you don't like Jeremy; I get that. You've made yourself very clear on that point. Quite frankly, he doesn't like you either, but why does it have to matter?"

She turned toward the huge picture window, heaving out a shaky breath. "The entire time I was on the boat, I thought of you." Her voice grew quiet. "I wanted you. I couldn't wait to come back and share everything that happened. This was the first time I actually saw a glimmer of hope for Jeremy, and the only person I wanted to share that with was you." She moved to the edge of the bed, not meeting his gaze, and sat, shoulders slumped, elbows resting on her thighs, hands covering her face.

Why did she have to go and say that? Austin's anger vanished as he stared at her, so sweet and pretty on the bed, so miserably unhappy. Layers of frustration still remained, some for her, but most for the sucky situation in general. He wanted to tell her about Jeremy, Donte, and the Zulas, but he didn't dare. They were most definitely on Zulas turf. If Hailey said the wrong thing, gave the impression she knew anything about their operation, she would be dead before she took her next breath.

Austin sat next to her, resentful that he would have to swallow this round—again—instead of allowing the people who deserved it to take the fall. He skimmed his finger along her soft, naked shoulder, down her shoulder blade.

Hailey jerked away from his touch. Her back went from slouched to ramrod straight in a blink.

Austin sighed out a weary breath. "I don't know why we keep ending up here, but I hate it."

She stared ahead as tears dried on her cheeks.

If this was how it had to be, he would give her the only truth he could. "You—you scared me."

Hailey slid him a glance, then stared straight ahead again.

"I didn't know where you were. I didn't even know where to start looking. I thought you'd been taken. I've never been so afraid."

Hailey looked down into her lap and fidgeted with her fingers.

He moved closer, until arm touched arm, thigh brushed thigh, expecting Hailey to tense, to pull away, but she didn't. "Tonight helped me realize something I hadn't fully grasped." Taking another chance, he slid his knuckles over the satiny skin of her cheek. Hailey closed her eyes, leaned against his hand as a tear trailed down her cheek. Austin caught it with his thumb. "Please don't cry," he said softly, wrapping his arm around her.

A slice of pain radiated from his wound, but he ignored it. "Please don't cry," he repeated as he pulled her against his chest, cradling her close. "Nothing destroys me the way you do, Hailey." He kissed the top of her head. "Nobody makes me feel the way you do. When I couldn't find you... I never felt so helpless in my life." He eased away until she looked at him. "When we first—"

"Your jaw," Hailey interrupted, frowning as she touched her fingers to his bruise.

"It's fine." He took her hand, held it in his. "Let me get this out. When we first got to the island, no—" he shook his head, correcting himself "—long before that, I knew I wanted you, but I didn't see the point. We're so different. Then we had this week to ourselves, this opportunity to be alone, and I wanted to be with you in a way I didn't think I had a right to be."

"What—"

"Let me say what I need to." He took her face in his hands. "I need to tell you this."

"Okay."

"I figured we would have some fun, enjoy each other's company, and when the week was up, well, the week would be up."

Hurt flashed in Hailey's eyes as she tried to draw away.

"No, wait." He held her still. "Why can't I get this right? I'm trying to tell you that somewhere along the line that changed. I don't want what we have to be over on Saturday at checkout. I want to see where this can go, see what we can make of it because, Hailey, when I thought I might never find you, when I thought I might never get you back, I realized I love you. I can't say when it happened. Maybe when we were riding horses or when you told me your story or maybe when I held you close and watched you sleep that first night." He shook his head. "In the end, it doesn't matter, but I wanted you to know; I needed you to know because I read your text to Sarah. You told her I was everything you never thought you could have, and I'm telling you, you're everything I never knew I wanted, but I'm so glad you're here."

Her lip wobbled; her eyes filled. Before he took his next breath, he had his arms full of Hailey. "Austin." She hugged him hard. "I love you too. I think I loved you the first time I laid eyes on you at Ethan's company barbeque all those years ago. I still remember. I was holding Kylee. She was so little then. I turned and there you were—all big and handsome—and I had to sit down." She laughed, drew back, and planted a kiss on his lips. Hailey's smile faded as she stared into his eyes, playing her fingers through his hair. "I love you, Austin. I'm so glad I can finally say it out loud."

He wanted her. Austin pulled her close, kissed her gently, slowly. As the kiss drew out and deepened, Hailey's hands wandered from his wrists to his forearms and up. He hissed out a breath, pulling back when her fingers connected with his tender wound.

"What is it? What's wrong?" Hailey gasped as she stared at her bloodied hand. "Austin, you're bleeding." She yanked his bloody sleeve up. "Oh my gosh, Austin, what happened to you?"

"I got a little banged up when I was out." He stood and made his way to the bathroom for another wad of toilet paper.

"That's more than a little banged up." She followed, concern ringing in her voice. "You need stitches."

"No. No stitches."

"Don't be silly. You need medical attention. Let me call for a cab." She turned, heading for the phone.

"No, Hailey. Stop." He winced at his terse command. She turned, stared at him.

"Sorry. I don't want to go to the hospital."

"Why?"

What the hell was he supposed to tell her? He shrugged. "The medical care around here isn't exactly first class. I would rather treat this myself. Maybe we can scrounge up a few band-aids from the little store they have in the hotel."

"You're going to get an infection."

"Hopefully they have peroxide too. Will you help me?"

She huffed out a long sigh. "I really think you need a doctor, but since I can see your point, I'll call up to the front desk and ask if they have what we need."

He yanked a long train of toilet paper from the role, dabbed at the blood running down his arm. "Thanks."

"Don't thank me yet. If they have peroxide, I'm using it generously." She turned away and went to the phone.

Minutes later, there was a sharp knock. Austin rushed from the bathroom as Hailey opened the door. A man in employee dress smiled. "Your medical supplies, Ms. Roberts."

"Thank you very much." She took the white plastic bag he handed her before she signed off for the supplies and a tip. "Thank you again. I really appreciate this."

"You are welcome, Ms. Roberts. Have a nice night."

She closed the door and turned to Austin, holding up the bag. "Go sit down on the toilet."

Austin took his seat as she peeked in the bag. "Oh, good. They had everything we'll need." Hailey set a small box of butterfly stitches on the counter, followed by a baggie of cotton balls, gauze, and next, the dreaded peroxide. "All right, let's get you taken care of."

He pulled up his sleeve.

"No, just take your shirt off. It'll make this easier."

He didn't want to take off his shirt. He remembered what his other shoulder looked like—and his stomach. Hailey was going to freak.

"Come on, Austin. I want to get you cleaned up. Shirt off."

"Aren't you bossy." He was stalling.

"Just concerned." She stood hipshot, arms crossed, waiting.

With an inward sigh, he eased his top up and off. Before the shirt was over his head, Hailey gasped and dropped to her knees.

"Austin. Austin, what in God's name happened to you?" Her fingers feathered over the purple welts. "Look at your stomach. Oh, and your shoulder. Your jaw. Were you in a fight?"

He resolved to give her the truth, or mostly, as she stared at him, brows furrowed, eyes full of concern. "I got jumped when I went to meet the landlord."

"Why didn't you tell me?"

"There's not a whole lot you can do for bruises."

She examined his shoulder closely. "Still, you should've told me. This happened at the apartment?"

"Yeah."

"Did the landlord help you?"

"He never showed up."

"I thought you had a meeting."

He shrugged. "So did I."

"One person did all this?" Her eyes moved over his injuries again.

Austin's brow winged up, his ego suffering. "Do I look like a weenie?"

"How can you joke right now? How many were there?"

He shrugged again. "A few guys."

"A few... Oh, Austin." She took his hand, closed her eyes, and pressed her lips to his knuckles.

"Hey, I'm fine." He cupped her chin, meeting her gaze, touched by the depth of her concern. "Help fix me up. We have a movie marathon to get to."

She gave him a small smile, nodded, and stood again, all business. "We need to get you cleaned up and iced down. Rest your elbow on the counter." She tipped the antiseptic bottle, soaking a cotton ball. "Hold your breath."

God, he wasn't looking forward to this. If soap hurt... "Holy *fuck*, Hailey." Bunching his fists, he blew out puffs of breath between his teeth as the cotton ball made contact with the gouge in his arm. "That *hurts*."

"I know. I'm sorry. I'm almost finished." She dabbed at the wound again, and he closed his eyes, waiting for the torture to be over.

"Okay, there."

He opened his eyes as she threw the blood-soaked cotton away.

"Let me bandage you up, then you should be good." Hailey pulled three butterfly stitches from the box. A small line formed between her brows as she concentrated, applying each bandage gently, with competence. She set the last strip in place, pulling slightly before she attached the top piece to his skin. "Okay, I think you're all set."

He took her hand. "Thank you."

"You're welcome. I'm going to wrap gauze around your arm before we go to sleep. I don't want to undo everything we just did." She pulled him to his feet and they wandered to the bedroom.

"Lay down. I'll get you some ice for your shoulder and stomach."

"Hailey, I'm fine."

"Let me take care of you." She hugged him. "I want to take care of you, Austin. I need to."

He kissed her forehead before he let her go and lay on the bed. Hailey walked to the small fridge and pulled the ice catcher from the top section. She went to the bathroom, came back with two Ziploc bags.

"Where'd you get those?"

She smiled. "I put my shampoo and other stuff in them, just in case they exploded on the plane."

"Resourceful."

"Absolutely." She filled the bags, put more ice in a bucket, then crawled on the bed beside him. She traced her fingers over the bloom of bruises on his shoulder. "This doesn't look like it came from a fist."

240

"It didn't."

"How then?"

He hesitated as he pushed the hair back from her forehead. "A two-by-four."

She closed her eyes. "Oh, Austin."

"Hey, I'm a little sore, but I'm fine. They're in much worse shape than I am. Promise."

"I hate that I was out on the yacht, enjoying a nice meal, while you were in danger. I hate it, Austin."

He took her hand and played with her fingers. "Even if you'd stayed in your room, this still would've happened. Nothing could've changed it." He dragged her down, nestling her into the crook of his arm. "You're here with me now, taking care of me. We're together, Hailey. That's all that matters."

She sat up on her elbow and rested the ice against his shoulder. "Look at your stomach." Her voice dripped with anguish as she traced the four squared welts with her icy fingers. The heat of her lips replaced the cold as she kissed each wound gently. She sat up, her eyes locking with his.

His hand wandered to her hair, releasing the clip holding her up-do in place, sending tresses of light brown hair tumbling over her shoulders. He sat up as he curled a streak of gold around his finger, tugging until she moved forward, until her mouth was inches from his. He didn't want to think about his injuries. Hailey was here. Safe. She was all he wanted. "I love you." He kissed her temples, her nose, her chin.

"I love you too," she murmured.

"Let me show you how much." He eased forward again, capturing Hailey's mouth. His tongue sought hers as he massaged his fingers over the nape of her neck. As the kiss heated, he grabbed her around the waist, settling her in his lap.

Hailey wrapped her legs around him, humming her pleasure as he pressed his lips against the pulse pounding in her neck, then moved them across the smooth skin of her shoulders.

Hailey's fingers trailed through his hair as her teeth nipped at his chin, at his ear, sending goose bumps over his skin. Something was different this time. She was different.

He took Hailey's face in his hands, staring into her eyes, studying, and fought back a groan. Passion glazed her eyes. The shyness he typically had to coax away was absent. This is what he'd been waiting for. Hailey was with him, lost already, free of her inhibitions.

He slid her top down, traced the small swells through her bra before he unclasped the front hook, sending her breasts into his palms. She pressed her hands against his, snagging her lip between her teeth as she moaned, smiling.

He kissed her again, his mouth heating hers, thinking he might go mad. Hooking his arm around Hailey's waist, Austin got to his knees and laid her down. As her head rested on the pillow, he swept his tongue against the soft skin of her breasts, circled, tracing her aroused nipples.

Arching, she purred, skimming her palms along his waist, into his shorts, grabbing his butt. Her fingers trailed around, caressing, teasing before they took hold and began to move. He sucked in a sharp gasp, blew it out in a rush through his teeth. "God, Hailey, you're making me crazy."

She smiled again. "I want to make you crazy."

"Show me. Show me what I do to you."

She sat up, pushed him back. Her tongue circled and stroked him before her hot mouth set a rhythm that had his hands fisting in the sheets, then her soft hair. He groaned as she brought him to the edge.

HAILEY'S TRUTH

"Not yet." He pulled her up, the reins on his control snapping. "Not yet, Hailey." He sat her on his stomach, too aroused to feel pain against his bruises, yanked her sundress over her head, ripped her panties at the seam. He gripped her hips and jerked her to him, smothering himself in her heat—licking, plundering, until her thighs trembled, her stomach quivered, until she tensed, arching back, and cried out for him as she came.

"Cum again."

"I can't..." she gasped as he plundered. Her arms wrapped around his knees, her nails clawing into his skin as she erupted, rocking wildly. When she sagged back, he scooted her until she sat in his lap.

He pushed himself up, brushed her sweat soaked hair from her forehead. "We're not done yet." He took her mouth. "I'm not finished with you."

"I'm ready. I'm ready," she panted against his mouth. "Right now, Austin."

Their skin slipped and slid from the heat they'd brought each other. He grabbed a cube of ice from the bucket, traced Hailey's lips, trailed the melting piece over her chin, down her neck, her breasts, circling her nipples, making her gasp.

Cold dripped from his fingers as his mouth followed the journey the cube had just taken. He leaned her back, suckling, tasting salt and Hailey, until she begged on desperate moans.

"Please, Austin. Please." She rocked, her center rubbing against him.

Grabbing her ass, clutching, he lifted her, sitting her on him. He let out a staggered grunt as her wet warmth closed around him.

She stared into his eyes and all urgency was lost. Moving slow, torturously slow, Hailey wrapped her arms around him, resting her hands on his shoulders. He

243

snagged her top lip with his teeth, kissed her deep as her body tensed. Her breath shuddered as she climbed, as he climbed with her.

Taking her face in his hands, Austin's thumbs brushed against her skin. "I love you, Hailey," he panted.

She moved her hands to his wrists, tensing as her breath rushed out on shuddering sobs. He felt Hailey clutch around him, felt her rhythmic waves pull him to the stunning brink and over. Her eyes held his as they came together.

CHAPTER 18

USTIN LAY SPRAWLED IN THE back of the cab. He held Hailey close, his arms wrapped around her waist, his chin nestled on top of her head.

"I can't believe vacation's over," Hailey sighed. "The weather's perfect and vacation's over."

"Yup, back to the real world." But the real world was better than it had been a week before. The scent of Hailey's shampoo crowded Austin's nose; her body lay nestled against his. This was just what he wanted.

She glanced at her watch. "They should be here in about fifteen minutes."

"Hopefully they'll be on time. I wanna get everyone settled at the new location and go over the rules."

She looked up. "Someone's a party pooper."

"I'm not a party pooper." He smiled and twisted her nose. "There're twelve of you and two of us. Ethan set us up in much better digs, but Jackson and I are still responsible for everyone's safety." Now for the part Austin had been avoiding. "Hailey, I wanted to talk to you about something."

She sat up and leaned her arms against his chest. "Okay, what's up?"

"As you know, Jackson and I plan to break the team into two groups of six. It'll be easier to keep everyone accounted for, at least when we're out and about. I think it'd be better, all around, if we put you on Jackson's team."

"Oh." She sat up straighter, her body no longer resting on his as her brows furrowed.

Austin took her hand. "I'm concerned about my ability

to do my job if we're in each other's space all the time." He kissed her fingers. "I love you, Hailey. I can't be objective when it comes to you. You distract me."

A slow, knowing smile spread across her lips. "Well, when you put it that way..."

Grinning, he pulled her back. "You make me crazy," he murmured against her neck, making her chuckle. "Absolutely, mind-numbingly crazy."

Hailey had all but turned his brain to mush an hour before checkout. Breakfast had been forgotten, along with their last walk on the beach, when she'd pulled him, fully clothed, into the lake-sized tub, and took advantage of him. The bed had been next, followed by the whicker couch. The coup de grace had been Hailey pressed against the door, her legs wrapped around his waist while she moaned his name.

He no longer worried about her ability to relax when they were together. Hailey's shyness had disintegrated. She'd turned into a maniac—not that he was complaining.

The cab pulled around to the busy drop-off. Austin held Hailey close a moment longer, knowing that once they stepped from the vehicle, everything would change. Life was about to get hectic for both of them. Austin handed the cabbie his fare and tip. He and Hailey got out, both of them dressed in jeans and black Project Mexico tees. With luggage in hand, they started toward the sliding door of the airport.

They removed their sunglasses as they stepped inside, stopping in front of a monitor.

"Wow. They might actually be here a few minutes early. Does that really happen? I should take a picture of this." Hailey held her phone up to the screen and snapped a photo.

Austin shook his head and chuckled.

"I wonder if that's them." Hailey pulled him to the large

window as a 747 made a circle toward the runway. "I hope so." She turned, beaming, vibrating with excitement. "I can't wait to get started. I've wanted to do this since I read about it my freshman year."

"Well, get ready, because I don't think you'll sit down again until March. Our schedules are jammed tight."

Hailey's smile dimmed a bit. "We're not going to see each other much, huh?"

"Not like we have this week, but we'll see each other. We'll be living in the same house."

"I know. It'll be different though." She nibbled her bottom lip as her eyes filled with worry.

"It's only three months." He played his fingers through Hailey's ponytail. "How much can change in three months?"

"Yeah, I guess you're right." She gave him a small smile.

"We should probably head to baggage claim. Wait for everyone there. You ready?"

She stared out the window. "Mmmhmm."

"Let's go." Austin snagged Hailey's hand, watching her out of the corner of his eye as they walked. She'd lost some of her sparkle. Austin spotted a hallway, pulled her into it, and pressed her against the wall, resting his hands on her hips. "Hey, what's wrong? I thought you were excited."

She shook her head. "Nothing's wrong. And I am excited."

He nibbled her jaw. "What's eating at you all of a sudden?"

"I'm not sure." She avoided his gaze. "I can't put my finger on it."

"For some reason, I'm not buying that." He eased her chin up until she had to look at him. "Tell me about it."

"It's silly, I guess." She gave him a jerky shrug. "But what if this changes us? What if things aren't the same between us after we're finished here? There're times I wake up next to you and can't believe you're mine. How did this happen, Austin? How did I luck out and get everything I've ever wanted? Sometimes I'm afraid it's too good to be true."

"I have more faith in us than that. I want you to as well."

"No one..." She shook her head and looked down.

He brushed his fingers over her cheek. "No one what?"

"No one ever stays. Everyone goes away."

He rested his forehead against hers and closed his eyes. Hailey's vulnerability always brought him to his knees, especially when she tried to be so strong.

"Hailey." He framed her face, waited for her to look at him. She met his stare and wrapped her hands at his wrists as she always did. "I love you." Austin needed her to see he meant everything he said. "I *love* you, Hailey. Nothing will ever change that."

A hint of doubt still lingered in her eyes.

"I'm not going anywhere." He pressed his lips to hers. "I'm not going anywhere," he repeated, before he kissed her again and lost himself in her.

Flight 458 from Dallas/Fort Worth was announced, and Austin eased away. "I love you."

"I love you too." She hugged him tight.

He rested his cheek against her hair, playing his fingers through her ponytail. As passengers deplaning from a nearby flight walked past, Austin noticed a black-suited man standing close, recognized him as a bodyguard.

Lifting his head, tensing, Austin counted at least a dozen more. He glanced around before his gaze stopped dead on Donte Rodriguez. Donte stood across the room, surrounded by a wall of muscled protection. He watched as the Zulas leader's eyes locked on Hailey's arms wrapped around him. Austin tightened his grip, holding

Hailey closer, recognizing the small smile of challenge lighting Donte's face.

Austin had no doubt he held what Donte wanted most.

❦

Project Mexico participants shuffled in from the jetway, all of them dressed in jeans and black Project Mexico t-shirts. Hailey closed her eyes, holding Austin a moment longer, knowing she had to let him go. But she didn't want to. Something told her that as soon as she did, nothing would be the same.

She tried to hold tight to Austin's reassurances that they would be just fine, that he wasn't going anywhere. Austin was right after all: She wasn't putting much faith in what they had. Although their relationship had changed, they had a strong foundation—a three-year friendship. That meant something. He wanted her—*loved* her. That meant everything. Hailey took a deep breath and released Austin from her grip. "I guess it's time."

His gaze snapped to hers. "Huh?"

She raised an eyebrow and smiled. "I said, I guess it's time."

"Yeah, I guess so." He touched his lips to hers.

Hailey savored the warmth, knowing it would be some time before she felt his mouth against hers. She'd read between the lines when Austin told her they would be on separate teams. Both were officially in professional mode; public displays of affection were a thing of the past. She drew away. "Well, here goes nothing."

They stepped from the hall. Austin held her hand a moment longer before he gave her fingers a gentle squeeze, then let go. He moved toward the sea of black t-shirts, making his way to the front where Jackson waited as Hailey immersed herself among the Project Mexico members she'd met at the get-to-know-you session the University held two weeks before. She exchanged smiles and hellos with most of the group.

"Hailey, right?" The pretty, smiling redhead stopped in front of her.

"Right." Hailey smiled back, enjoying the enthusiasm in the redhead's bright green eyes. Her name was on the tip of Hailey's tongue: Machaela, Mickey, Marsha...

"Mia." Mia held out her hand.

"*Mia.*" Hailey beamed and rolled her eyes as she accepted Mia's handshake. "Sorry."

"No problem. I can't believe we're here." Mia glanced around. "I've been ready for weeks."

"I know. I think we're going to have a great—"

Someone tapped her shoulder. Hailey turned to find herself standing face-to-face with Donte Rodriguez. "Donte! What a surprise." Her smile warmed. "What are you doing here?"

"Hailey, I'll see you around."

Hailey glanced at Mia as she wandered into the crowd. "Nice to meet you again, Mia." Hailey directed her attention back to Donte. "Sorry."

He brushed her apology away. "There's much confusion at a time like this. I remembered you telling me Project Mexico would start today. I wanted to come welcome your group personally." He took her hand, kissed her knuckles. "And tell you again how much I enjoyed our evening together."

"Oh, well..." she looked at Austin across the room. He stared at her, his eyes intense. Hailey politely freed her fingers from Donte's grip. "Thank you. I had a wonderful time."

"Will you join me for dinner? Perhaps tomorrow night?"

Hailey glanced at Austin again, studying the clipboard Jackson had handed him. "Um, Donte, I'm flattered—very flattered. But I'm actually seeing someone."

A smile lit his face. "You misunderstand, Hailey. I think of you as a friend. A beautiful friend with a sharp, fascinating mind."

Hailey felt the blush rush to her cheeks. "I apologize." She closed her eyes, mortified. "God, this is embarrassing."

Donte chuckled. "You delight me. You have no reason to be embarrassed."

She relaxed seeing the humor dancing in his eyes. She smiled. "You're very kind." She touched his arm. "I hate to say no twice, especially after making a fool of myself, but the Project has strict rules about us staying together as a group. I'm afraid that for the remainder of my stay in Mexico, I have to keep close to my team and our guards." She looked at Austin again, caught his eye, sent him a small smile that he didn't return.

A gorgeous blonde stepped close to Austin and said something. He turned to her, smiling. Hailey squashed her knee-jerk insecurity as she watched Austin and the blonde carry on a conversation. The woman was so stunning, so classy. *Definitely better suited for Austin.*

Hailey clenched her hands. No, she wasn't doing this. Austin was surrounded by beautiful women on a daily basis. It was pretty much a job requirement when working with the Hollywood set. She refused to make herself crazy over something so petty. Austin either wanted Hailey or he didn't, but thoughts like that would stop right here.

Hailey returned her attention to Donte. "Donte, if you'll excuse me, I should get back to the group. Thank you for stopping by, for supporting our cause."

"You're very welcome. I hope you won't mind if I pop by the sites on occasion. I enjoy nothing more than watching people give back. It's truly beautiful."

As Hailey studied the handsome man in front of her, she still couldn't see the bad in him that Austin kept insisting was there. Why did he dislike Donte so much? "I couldn't agree more. We would love to have you whenever you want." If Austin would try to get to know him, he would see that Donte was a kind, generous person.

"Go enjoy your friends, Hailey. Enjoy your time here in Mexico."

"I will. Thank you again." Hailey skirted the crowd and walked over to Jackson Matthews.

"Hey, there." He enveloped her in a bear hug. Jackson was as solid as Austin, as stupendously hot with his bold blue eyes and dark golden hair, but about five inches shorter than Austin's six-foot-two stature.

She hugged him back. "I'm glad you're here."

"So, I hear we'll be spending a lot of time together. Thank God I like you." He nudged her in the side.

Hailey grinned. She'd always enjoyed Jackson. Not only was he easy on the eyes, but his great sense of humor kept her in smiles. They'd had a chance to get to know each other when he accompanied her and Kylee to London during Sarah's nightmare stalker experience.

"So, who's the hotshot you were talking to?"

"Oh, that was Donte Rodriguez. He's my brother's boss. I had dinner with him the other night."

Jackson frowned. "I thought you and muscle man," he tilted his head toward Austin, "were an item."

"Word travels fast."

"Especially when it comes from the horse's mouth."

"Austin and I are 'an item.'" Hailey made air quotes as she smiled. "I had dinner with Donte *and* my brother. It was strictly business."

"I'm just messing with you." He winked and nudged her again. "I'm happy for you. For both of you. I think you're good for each other."

She grinned. "I think so too."

"I don't know about you, but I'm ready to get the hell out

of here and get to our new and improved accommodations."

Before Hailey could agree, Jackson whistled through his teeth, bringing everyone to attention. "All right, guys, let's get this show on the road."

Twenty minutes later, two noisy, chattering groups wandered to the vans waiting at the edge of the main building. Austin led from the front, serious, official, in work mode, as Jackson stayed to the back.

Hailey attempted to hurry ahead, wanting to talk to Austin. He'd barely spared her a look since her conversation with Donte. She wanted to make sure he hadn't gotten the wrong impression.

"Excuse me." Hailey smiled as she hurried by another teammate dragging a bulging suitcase. The commotion and screams of the lead group stopped her in her tracks.

"Get them back inside," Austin shouted to Jackson.

Jackson rushed forward, herding frantic and confused members to the sliding doors. "Everyone in. Let's go."

As the crowd dissipated, Hailey stood frozen in her spot, horror-struck. Right in front of her were four bloody bodies, limbs or heads missing. Their torsos had knives sticking out of them and huge letters charred into pale, dead skin—"ZU." A hand sheathed in an ornate pair of brass knuckles lay next to one of the van's back tires. A blood soaked wife-beater on an upright torso had "PAYMENT FOR YOUR FAILED WARNING" painted across the chest. The lone head among the carnage, garbed in a green skullcap, sat impaled on a stake among the tropical flowers in front of the van's parking spots.

Hailey's breath rushed in then wheezed out as she gripped the handle of her luggage. The gore was like nothing she'd ever seen.

"Get her in." She heard Austin shout through the fog of her mind.

Hailey's gaze traveled from the slaughter scattering

the ground to the sobbing blonde in Austin's arms.

"Come on, Hailey." Jackson turned her away and put an arm around her, escorting her into the airport. "You don't need to see this."

The nervous babble of Hailey's group members floated around her as she watched cop cars arrive, lights blazing, and screech to a halt outside the sliding doors. Jackson joined Austin as he spoke to an officer just inside the airport.

"Hailey, come on." Mia, pale, and trembling, came to Hailey's side. "We're all pretty shaken up. Let's get a water, sit down, and wait."

"Yeah, okay, I'll be right there," she said, pressing a hand to her shuddering stomach as Mia walked off with the group.

Mia called for her again but Hailey couldn't turn away. Austin still held the gorgeous blonde against his chest, speaking close to her ear as she clutched at his shirt.

CHAPTER 19

FOUR WEEKS LATER, HAILEY LAY in her bunk, exhausted, frustrated, and alone. She was definitely earning each credit the university would cough up. The fourteen-hour days were grueling, but she was loving every second of her experience—the volunteering, her group members, the resilient hearts of the Mexican people.

So, why was she so unhappy?

Hailey rolled to her side, sighing, and stared out at the moon. She knew exactly why. Austin. They'd barely seen each other, had talked even less. When she was coming, he was going.

After their horrific first day at the airport, teams one and two had been virtual strangers. She still hadn't cleared the air after her brief conversation with Donte. Each time she saw Austin, Jen wasn't far away.

Hailey tried to remind herself it didn't matter that the classy, rich blonde was more suited to Austin's character. She tried to remember their amazingly romantic week at the resort, their last moments in the airport, but all that seemed so far away—almost as if it had been a dream.

Had she dreamed it? Hailey sat up with a start. Was she suffering from some weird form of grandiose hallucinations?

Shaking her head, she rolled her eyes, sick of her own racing thoughts. Hailey blew out a frustrated breath and lay back down. She'd had enough psychology classes to realize she was attempting to distract herself from the real issue: her fear of losing Austin. As the first month flew by, she'd worried that what they'd had was slipping through her fingers.

Hailey gripped the sheets and pulled them to her chin. What would she do if she lost him? How would she get through that kind of pain again?

She tossed the covers back. This was exactly why she'd avoided serious relationships. The deep feelings left her insecure, vulnerable. She *hated* it.

She had Sarah and Ethan, Morgan and Hunter, the girls. They were her family, her constants. Hailey never once worried they would leave, that they would make her feel fourteen and defenseless, lost, and more than anything, alone.

Sick dread weighed heavy in her stomach. For the first time since her parents' deaths, she cocooned her heart behind a self-protective wall. She'd been hiding behind the numbing layers of her fortress for weeks. Nothing and no one had ever hurt her the way she'd hurt when she lost her family. A part of her was preparing for the same crushing pain that would come if Austin changed his mind.

Ugh, why am I doing this?

Hailey restlessly flopped to her other side. She blinked in the dark, listening to the members of her group breathe deep with sleep. Too keyed-up to lie still, she sat up to stare out the window again. She wrapped her arms tight around her knees, trying to lose herself in the relaxing ebb and flow of the waves against white sand.

The beach was twenty steps from her bunk. The moon shined bright on the water, yet she couldn't find the comfort the sea usually brought.

The door creaked open. A sliver of light illuminated the room. Austin peeked in and Hailey's heart stuttered. "Hey," he whispered.

"Hey." She gave him a half-hearted smile.

"Do you mind if I come in?"

"No." She clutched at her knees as butterflies battered her nervous stomach.

Austin made his way to her bunk and sat down. Waves of love consumed her as she stared at his handsome face bathed in moonlight. This was too much. If she lost him, she would lose it all.

"I thought I would come by. See if you were still up." He traced his finger down her arm.

"Here I am." She moved slightly, out of his reach.

"I've missed you."

"I've missed you too." She wanted to hug him to her, to breathe in his familiar scent, but instead she sat where she was, hands clutching, paralyzed, too terrified to take the first step.

"You okay?"

"Yeah, I'm fine." She blinked as tears pricked her eyes. For the first time in her life, she felt like the poster child of what everyone believed a foster child to be— emotionally unstable, broken, too far gone for anything resembling normalcy.

"You don't seem fine."

She got to her feet, smothering in her own hopeless frustration. Why was she doing this? Austin had come to her. He wanted to be here. "Really, I am. I'm just overtired. I should lie down, try to get some rest."

"Can I lay with you for awhile? It feels like it's been ages."

She wanted to reach out but took a mental step back. "I don't think that's a good idea. You should go."

He stood, studying her in the shadows. "If that's what you want."

Don't leave me. "Yeah, it is. Goodnight."

As Austin walked to the door Hailey turned, staring out the window, tears blurring the moon.

The door opened, closed. She rested her forehead against the glass, shut her eyes as the first tear fell, followed by another and another. *It's better this way.*

She gasped as strong arms wrapped around her waist. "I've been watching you the past few days, Hailey, when I actually get the chance." Austin pressed a kiss to her temple. "I've been watching you push me away. Do you think I'm going to let you? Do you think I would walk away?"

Yes. Her throat tightened as a sob threatened to escape.

He turned her into his chest and brushed his fingers through her hair. "All these years have done a hell of a number on you. I don't know what I have to do to make you realize I'm right where I want to be, Hailey."

She'd said nothing, yet he understood perfectly. Hailey tightened her grip, treasuring this gift that had walked into her life. "I'm sorry, Austin. I'm so sorry. I don't want to be like this, but I can't seem to help it."

"You don't want to be like what?"

"Like this." She emphasized with her hands. "Unstable. Insecure. Really messed up. I thought I was handling everything well. I've been trying to." She huffed out an unsteady breath. "This is so big. So important."

"I love you just the way you are." He kissed her. "Even if you're a little weird." He smiled.

She smiled back.

"You keep life interesting. Come here." He took her hand, pulled her to the bed. "Come lay down with me. I miss waking up with you."

"I don't want to make things awkward. I know we're both going for 'professional' while we're here."

"Screw it. I'm off the clock—unless someone comes in the house guns blazing. Fall asleep with me for awhile."

She lay down.

He snuggled in beside her, played with her hair. "I really have missed you, Hailey."

She smiled again, his words a soothing balm against her insecurities. "I've missed you too."

"Are you having fun? Is this what you thought it would be?"

She stared into Austin's kind eyes, breathed him in, and just like that, her world settled. She turned into him and wrapped her arms around his waist as he did the same to her. "I'm having a blast. I love everything about this experience. I love the people, appreciate their struggles."

"I've heard good things about you."

She frowned "You have? What do you mean?"

"Dr. Lopez is quite taken with you. 'Señorita Hailey is a Saint. She is well-loved wherever she goes,'" Austin imitated in a very passable accent.

She chuckled. "It is easy to be loved when one loves deeply, when one has passion for her cause," she fired back in her own Spanish accent.

He grinned. "Not bad, Roberts."

She beamed back. "Thanks."

Austin took her mouth suddenly, urgently. Instant waves of desire catapulted her heart into overdrive as his tongue slid against hers. He rolled on top of her, pushing her arms above her head. She reveled in the weight of his muscular body pressed to hers. It had been a month since his lips met hers, since they'd been together—a lifetime.

He feathered fevered kisses along her neck. His hands flew beneath her shirt, sending shivers over her skin as he cupped her breasts. "God, Hailey, I want you," he said against her ear. "I need you."

She didn't care where they were, didn't care that Mia slept above her, and two more roommates slept to her side. Hailey pulled Austin's shirt over her head, desperate to feel his skin, eager to taste. Their ragged breaths mingled as they stared at each other. She wanted the flames, the mindless pleasure he brought her with a simple touch. "Take me, Austin, right here. Right here."

His mouth crushed against hers savagely. He snagged her lip with his teeth, pulled, before he soothed with his tongue.

She reached for the button on his cargo shorts and yanked the snap. "I want you in me. God, I want you in me."

He tugged at her pajama bottoms as their mouths met again, the anticipation almost more than she could bear. She already throbbed, ready.

The door opened; lights blazed bright with the flip of the switch. Jen stepped in the room. "Oh my God. Oh my God. I'm so sorry." She flipped the switch and shut the door with a hurried snap.

"What the *hell*?" Mia moaned.

Hailey stared at the slats of the top bunk, struggling to catch her breath. "It's okay, Mia. Jen didn't know we were trying to sleep."

"*Trying* to sleep? Some of us *are* sleeping. Or *were*," she groaned. The bed jiggled as Mia turned over.

The heat of Austin's breath feathered Hailey's neck as they lay statue still. Eyes wide, she looked into Austin's grinning face, her lips pressed together before she mouthed 'oops.' He chuckled, despite the awkward situation.

"I guess the cats out of the bag," she whispered against his ear. "I imagine everyone except for Mia, Tess, and Charlie are aware we're half-naked on the bottom bunk."

"I think you're probably right."

"What about your job? Are you going to be in trouble with Ethan?"

"I'll handle it." He kissed her gently this time, drawing it out. "We have to do better than this, Hailey. I need to be with you—soon. Very, very soon."

"I second that." She brushed her fingers through his hair, treasuring this rare moment. "Can you stay for a while or do you want to go clear the air?"

"I'm all yours."

She settled her arms around his waist, warm, content. "Just the way I want it."

Austin sobered as he brushed the hair from her forehead. "Seriously, I'm all yours. I know the last month's been hard, but this is it. You're it. I want you to remember that. This is me promising you, right here, right now, that I'm yours, Hailey."

It was almost too much to believe, but she did. She absolutely, unequivocally believed Austin meant what he said as he stared into her eyes. Happiness filled her to bursting.

For the first time since she'd lost her parents, Hailey let herself believe someone—Austin—truly loved her, cared for her, needed her as much as she did him—and he wasn't going anywhere. "All of this is so new for me. It's hard for me—scary—to let go of this... I don't know how to describe it—but this little piece I hold back for myself, this little piece I can crawl back to when somebody lets me down. I've always had it, thought I would need it, but that's not fair to you or me. I'm giving you everything, Austin. Please take care." She'd stripped herself bare, for the first time, the only time.

"My God, Hailey, I love you." He rolled off her, pulled her against him.

"I love you too."

"Fall asleep with me."

She closed her eyes. Safe. Content. Whole.

Austin brushed a kiss against her neck and she pulled him closer, drifting off with the waves crashing outside the window, with the full moon shining bright. With Austin in her arms.

Austin stood in the corner of the small, crowded building, watching, fascinated by Hailey. Even after hours of endless work in the windowless, stagnant office, she still smiled.

Both groups finally had the chance to venture out together. Austin was loving every second. He'd never had the opportunity to observe Hailey in her element. He'd seen her with Kylee a million times—and she was great—but this was different. Here, she was business-like, efficient, yet she exuded a warmth, an empathy that attracted others instantly.

Dr. Lopez hadn't exaggerated; Hailey was well-loved wherever the group went. This was the third stop of their day, and no matter the situation, people were drawn to her. How could they not be? Here was her passion. Here was her gift.

The family Hailey had been helping stood from their folding chairs. Hailey placed a hand on the young woman's arm and leaned in to whisper something in her ear. The woman smiled and hugged Hailey before she turned with her two children and left.

Hailey looked up, met Austin's gaze, grinned.

Austin loved Hailey as he held her the night before, but after today, he somehow loved her more. She was beautiful, stunningly so, but she was so much more—a miracle. She should've been a mess of damaged goods, yet she was so normal. Sure, her childhood left a few scars, but at the end of the day, she was remarkably kind, remarkably sweet, and she was his.

Hailey called out a number in her ever-improving Spanish. A mom and her two children made their way to Hailey's table. The toddler held out his arms. Hailey picked him up and snuggled him into her lap.

Glancing up, she sent Austin another smile before she took her pen in hand and started filling out relief forms with the woman sitting across from her.

As Hailey worked, Austin watched Mia and Jen do the same. Both women were kind, both were effective, but they sure as hell weren't Hailey.

Austin leaned against the concrete wall, relaxed, perfectly content with life in general—although he was ready for this assignment to end, ready to be back in L.A. He wanted to sleep in his own bed, wanted to wake up with Hailey next to him. Sneaking out of her bunk before dawn wasn't cutting it.

He wanted her in his apartment, in his home. It would be convenient having her down the hall, but it would be better if she moved in with him. It was a big step, a fast step, but it was right. What they had was exactly right, so why wait? He would talk about it with her after everyone went to bed.

A black-suited man stepped into the office space, followed by two more. "Son of a bitch," Austin muttered, standing up straight, crossing his arms, sending a look to Jackson across the room. Only one person required such ceremony in a derelict area like this. As he thought it, Donte walked in.

The families waiting in line grew silent. Mothers picked up children; men pulled their wives closer.

Two more bodyguards walked in behind Donte, one of them closing the door.

"What do you wanna to do?" Jackson voice buzzed in Austin's earpiece.

"Sit tight for now." They couldn't very well usher their group of twelve out the door when so many families traveled across the island for their chance to receive aide.

Hailey was oblivious to Donte's arrival, until Donte

made a beeline for her table. Austin clenched his jaw as she glanced up from her paperwork and gave Donte a huge smile. She stood, the toddler resting on her hip, and took his hand as she accepted the kiss he brushed on her cheek.

Donte said something as Hailey sat down. He settled in the seat next to hers, spoke to the small boy Hailey cuddled in her lap, making both Hailey and the young child smile.

Hailey wouldn't be smiling if she knew Donte was the one responsible for the "presents" left by the vans a month before. The message had been for him, but Donte had chosen to involve Hailey and eleven other innocents in his need to prove a point. Everyone was fair game. It didn't matter who the Zulas hurt.

Donte turned his attention to the mother at the table. The murmurs of his voice carried through the room. The woman cupped a hand to her mouth as Hailey's eyes grew wide. The young mother took Donte's hand, shaking it wildly, and hurried to her feet. "This man is a gift from God!" she shouted in Spanish. "A gift from the Heavens above!"

The room grew loud with chatter.

Donte stood. "Ladies and Gentlemen," he said, and everyone went silent. "It is with great honor I am able to stand before you today. I would like to offer each person here, and the families that have already left for the day, the assistance necessary to fix your homes ravaged by the hurricane many months ago."

Wild applause broke out.

He smiled and raised a hand for quiet. "Aide has been slow coming to Cozumel. I've spent the day touring the more rural areas of our great island. I see that this issue can no longer wait, can no longer be ignored. I have construction crews traveling this way as we speak. Funds will be released tomorrow morning to begin work on your homes. If you have experience as manual laborers, please tell my friends at Project Mexico as they help you fill out your papers. I will guarantee pay for those of you who lend a hand, as well as new homes for each and every one of you by month's end."

Community members rushed forward, crowding Donte with offers of thanks. His bodyguards struggled to keep people back.

Austin exchanged another look with Jackson. If they didn't help, someone was bound to get hurt, or worse. Donte's men were used to shooting first and sorting out the details later. "Let's get these people out of here before we need body bags."

Austin moved in, inching his way to Hailey.

Donte spoke close to Hailey's ear, his arm around her waist. She beamed at him and kissed his cheek.

Austin clenched his fists, tempted to knock Donte out right here. Stepping closer, he heard Hailey's voice above the din.

"We're all so grateful to you, Donte. I don't know how we can possibly thank you."

"Have dinner with me."

She shook her head. "I'm afraid I can't."

"Then sit with me at the parade this afternoon."

"You're going to the grade school?"

"I'm a huge supporter of education. Be my guest of honor."

She laughed. "Now that I can do."

"Then I am a happy man." Through the small crowd, Donte's gaze locked on Austin's, lingering, challenging.

Austin fought hard not to rush forward and grab Hailey from Donte's hold. That wouldn't be the way to handle this.

Mateo opened the door; Jeremy stood next to him.

"Attention," Mateo said in Spanish. "Please pick up a basket of fresh food and water after you've completed your paperwork inside."

Those that had finished rushed through the door. Austin followed as some of the Project Mexico participants left to help. He couldn't stand to listen to the bullshit a moment longer.

~~~

Two hours later, the vans pulled up to the small primary-secondary school in the center of town. Colorful banners blew in the island winds, welcoming the members of Project Mexico as well as Senor Rodriguez.

Austin suppressed an eye roll, just barely, as he exited the passenger side.

"I'll do a quick sweep," Jackson said, stepping from the other vehicle, walking the perimeter of the white building equipped with barred windows.

Austin stayed between the two vans, tense, waiting for the "all clear" in his earpiece—a practice that had become necessary as the violence erupting on the island continued to increase. Drive-bys were common; the death count was rising in this once-peaceful vacation spot.

"Looks good," Jackson said. "But I haven't seen King Donte pull up in his limo."

Austin grinned. "Oh, I'm sure he'll be here before long. He'll want to make a grand entrance, so it'll be a few minutes yet."

"What a douche bag," Jackson scoffed.

Austin smiled. "Copy that." He popped his head in the vans. "Okay guys, all clear. Let's get inside."

Everyone filed out and into the front entrance of the school. As the group wandered to the gym, cheers and applause broke out.

"Welcome, Project Mexico." The man at the small podium smiled, waving a hand. "Come in, my friends, and meet the children of our wonderful school."

More raucous applause followed from the surprisingly large group ranging from tiny tot to high schooler.

"The students look forward to the week you will spend with us. We would like to share our appreciation by entertaining you, we hope," the principal winked, "with a few surprises from the children."

Everyone from Project Mexico clapped for the kids.

"If you would kindly follow your guides to our play yard, we would like to get started." Fourteen children stood from the floor, walked forward, and took a hand of each member of the group.

Austin grinned when a tiny little thing with big dark eyes clutched his fingers. She couldn't have been more than five or six, he guessed. "Welcome to our school, Señor," she said, struggling with her English in an impossibly small voice.

"Thank you for having us," he replied in Spanish.

Her eyes widened and she smiled. "You speak Spanish," she said, reverting back to her native tongue.

"Yes." His heart all but melted. "What's your name?"

"Anna."

"I can't wait to see the show today, Anna."

She smiled again as she led him to the playground.

Small fabric squares on pavement awaited each guest. "Please, take your seat, Señor," she gestured grandly, "although you are very big. Do you think you will fit?"

He chuckled. "I think so. Anna, do you see the woman in the purple shirt?"

"Yes, Señor."

"Could you tell your friend to have her sit in the square next to mine? She's very pretty."

Anna giggled. "I will be right back, Señor."

A loud round of applause erupted in the gym. That could only mean one thing. "I think the man of the hour arrived," Austin said into his earpiece. "Let the curtsies begin."

Jackson chuckled in his ear.

Austin breathed deep as three black-suited men stepped outside. Donte followed behind moments later.

Before Anna could make her way to Hailey's side, Donte moved in and took her hand. Unlike everyone else, Donte rated a chair, or had insisted on one, was probably more like it. Hailey sat in the seat he gestured to, next to his.

Anna turned and met Austin's gaze. Sheer distress paled her pretty little face. Austin gave her a grin he didn't feel, a casual shrug. Anna smiled in what could only be relief as she waved and hurried back into the gym.

Jen plopped down next to him. Austin was instantly surrounded by a hint of perfume that fit its owner well—expensive and subtle sex. "Whew, what a day. I'm exhausted."

Austin glanced at Hailey as she laughed at something Donte said. He wanted her here, next to him. Instead, he focused his attention on Jen's pretty blue eyes and corn-silk-blonde hair. "It's been a long one."

"The children are so cute, so well-mannered." She smiled.

"Yeah, they are." He smiled back as he thought of sweet little Anna.

"I'm looking forward to spending the week here. I was going to be a teacher, but I changed my mind. Sometimes I think I made a mistake."

"Oh, I don't know. You're pretty great at—"

"They are coming!" An older man ran up to the chain link fence separating the schoolyard from the main road. "They are coming," he shouted urgently in broken English

"They come for all of you. It is here. The war is here."

Austin shot to his feet. "Jackson, let's get everyone back—"

Three cars screeched to a stop inches from the fence. Before Austin said another word, all hell broke loose. Project Mexico participants screamed, sprinting for the shelter of the gym amongst the spray of machinegun fire.

The man who had shouted their warning lay bleeding, dead.

Austin's first instinct was to run for Hailey, but Jen stood, gaping, as bullets hit the blacktop around them. "Get down, Jen!" Yanking her to the ground, he rolled with her behind the large metal structure, part of the playground, close to the gym doors.

"Everyone's inside," Jackson's breathy voice buzzed in his ear. "Wait. Hold that. Fuck. Where's Jen?"

"I have Jen."

"What about Hailey? Do you have Hailey?"

Cold fear clutched Austin's stomach. "You don't have Hailey? Stay here," he shouted to Jen. Bullets were still hitting the pavement but all he thought of was finding Hailey. Where the hell was she?

As abruptly as the chaos had started, it stopped. The cars squealed off, leaving the stench of rubber in their wake. Half of Donte's men took chase. The other half remained flocked around the man himself, standing guard at the cement wall sectioning the bathrooms from the play yard.

"Hailey!" Austin shoved as close as the dozen men would allow him. He watched, heart pounding, as the guards moved. Hailey lay on the ground, safe, shielded by Donte.

Austin's relief was so huge, he could only be grateful, until Donte skimmed his fingers over Hailey's cheek, until he remembered they were in this situation because of the Zulas leader in the first place.

"Is everyone okay? Did anyone get hurt?" Hailey glanced around, shell-shocked.

Donte still lay on Hailey, still stroking her skin with the familiarity of a lover. "You're safe."

Hailey struggled to her elbows. "What about the children? What about Austin?" She scrambled to her feet. "Austin." She shoved through the wall of bodyguards, rushed into his arms, shaking. "Austin. Oh, you're safe. You're safe."

He held her against him, pressed her cheek to his chest, relieved, not only that Hailey was out of harm's way, but that she seemed unaffected by Donte's touch. "I'm okay." He drew her back. "Are you?"

She nodded. "Yes, I'm good." Her gaze wandered to the small crowd of teachers and community members surrounding the man by the chainlink fence. "That man. That poor man. Will he be okay?"

Austin said nothing and sorrow filled her eyes. He pressed Hailey's forehead to his chest, played his fingers through her hair, struggling to concentrate on his job. "We need to get inside, get you all back in the vans and get out of here. Jackson, let's load everyone—"

"Mr. Casey, perhaps you should take more care." Donte stopped in front of Austin, eyes blazing.

He didn't have time for anything this fucker had to say. "What's that supposed to mean?"

"While I was protecting your woman, you were protecting another." He gestured to Jen, who was still huddled by the playground equipment, crying hysterically as Jackson helped her to her feet and brought her inside.

"Oh, it's okay Donte," Hailey turned away from Austin and laid a hand on Donte's shoulder. "We're all safe." Her gaze darted to the dead man as she clutched an arm around Austin's waist.

"No, quite frankly, Hailey, it was not okay." Donte took her chin in his hand. "You are a precious soul who deserves to *always* be first. *Never* second. Your man chose another instead of choosing you." Donte's ruthless stare bore into Austin. "You do not deserve what you have, Mr. Casey. If you will excuse me." Donte left for his limo.

CHAPTER 20

HOURS LATER, DONTE'S WORDS STILL burned Austin's ass. Fists bunched, simmering, he stared through beachfront doors at the waves crashing on the shore. Hailey was first in his life and always would be. Did she know that? Did Donte's comments bother her as much as they did him?

Unable to put it away, Austin rushed down the hall. He spotted Hailey playing cards with Mia and Charles in the crowded living room, took her hand, and pulled her up. Conversation stopped as all eyes wandered to them.

"Austin, I'm in the middle of a game."

"You can finish later." He all but dragged her through his bedroom and into the bathroom, shut the door, and locked it. "You're first, Hailey." He paced the large space.

"Huh?"

"I couldn't leave her standing there, staring, while bullets landed at her feet."

"Austin, I—"

He grabbed her arms, stared into her eyes. "I love you."

"Austin, I know that. Is this about Donte? About what he said?"

"Yes," he bit off.

She wrapped her hands around his wrists. "He was wrong. Donte was absolutely wrong. He and his men whisked me away so quickly; I had no idea what was going on. Then it was over."

"It should've been me." At the heart of it, that's what bothered him most. "I should've kept you safe."

"You did your job, Austin. You saved Jen's life today.

One person died, but one lived. She's here because of you."

That did little to soothe him. He grunted.

"What would we've told Jen's parents if you had come running after me? I was well-protected. She wasn't. You did exactly the right thing, Austin. I wouldn't have been able to live with myself if she had died because of me."

He stared into Hailey's eyes, knowing she made perfect sense, but he wasn't ready to drop it. "I don't like him, Hailey." He spun away. "Donte's bad news."

"You're angry with the situation in general."

"No, I'm not. Yes, I am," Austin corrected, squeezing his fingers against the tension at the base of his neck. "But there's more to it."

"He can't be all bad. You were at the office today. You saw what he offered to do. He's going to rebuild all of those homes. He donated the baskets of food and water, and those will feed families for days. Despite how you feel, Donte does good things. I can only be grateful."

"I don't want you to be grateful," he tossed back, frustration seething in every word. It was on the tip of his tongue to tell her Donte was the reason for the shooting at the school, that they were gunning for him because he was head of the fucking Mexican Mafia. Instead, he fumed in silence. "I want you to stay away from him."

"Why? Austin, I think—"

He whirled again. "I want you to stay away from him," he repeated, meeting Hailey's gaze, staring at the questions, the confusion in her eyes. "This isn't caveman, macho shit, Hailey. There's more to him than you think."

Her brow winged up and she crossed her arms. "Such as?"

"Just trust me."

She huffed out a breath. "See, there you go again. You give me pieces, then you evade. I want real answers."

"I'm asking you to trust me. I know that's not fair—"

"No, it's not."

"Hailey, just for a little while." Austin took her face in his hands, rested his forehead against hers. "Please, I wouldn't ask if it wasn't important."

She sighed. "I know." Her fingers gripped his wrists and he relaxed. "I'll stay away from Donte."

"Thank you."

"You're welcome." She pressed her lips to his. "I won't be patient for those answers forever."

"Yeah, I know."

"You also know I love you, right? I'm only interested in *you*." She snagged his lip between her teeth.

"That isn't what this is about."

"I only want you, Austin." Her eyes heated as her voice thickened with desire. "You're all I've ever wanted."

He stared, captivated, as Hailey said what he'd been thinking himself. "Move in with me when we get home," he blurted.

She dropped her hands. "What?"

Pulling her against him, he locked his arms around her waist. "I said move in with me. Let's live together."

"Uh...I'm...wow. You want to live together?"

"I'm pretty sure that's what I just said."

"I'm trying to catch up." She beamed. "I can't believe this. I can't believe this is really happening. Okay, yes. Absolutely. I'll move in with you." She kissed him quick. "I'm so happy." Hailey threw her arms around him in a hug.

He stroked his hand down her back, relieved. "Me too."

She met his gaze and brushed her fingers through his hair. "I love you, Austin."

The heat was back in her eyes, in her sultry voice. She was knotting his stomach with need. "You should probably show me."

274

"Mmm, I probably should." Hailey sunk her teeth into his chin, bringing pleasure and pain as she pulled at the snap on his jeans and tugged on the zipper.

Ready to explode, Austin yanked Hailey's t-shirt over her head, threw it to the floor, had her bra following seconds later. He walked her back to the wall as his mouth captured her perky breast, savoring her sweet taste, the feel of her taught nipple against his tongue.

Whimpering, her fingers tightened on his hips, kneading.

"I have to have you," he said, his declaration muffled against hot, soft skin. "I have to have you right now, Hailey. Right now."

She dragged at denim, at boxers, until he was free.

Cool fingers clamped around him, stroking. He groaned against her neck. If he didn't take her, he would erupt in her hand. In defense, he snagged her wrists and lifted them above her head. He yanked the snap on her shorts, at the zipper. Khakis slid down her legs. "I want to be in you." He snuck two fingers under her panties and shoved them deep.

Hailey gasped, stiffened, moaned. He took her mouth, swallowing the throaty sounds of her orgasm. He wanted to hear her scream the way she had in the cabana, but the group was just down the hall. Even so, he continued to play his fingers in a steady rhythm as his thumb pressed, circling, sending her flying again. Pouring, she contracted around him, tensing and letting out a strangled cry.

He strained against the need to fulfill them both, but held out. Who knew how long it would be before he had her like this again.

Austin picked her up, and Hailey twined her legs around him. He tortured them both by shoving himself into her heat.

They groaned in unison.

Clutching her hips, he rammed, once, twice, leaving her on the brink as he set her on the edge of the counter. He craved to keep going until Hailey was satisfied, until he was empty, but instead he pulled out.

"What-what are you doing, Austin?" she strangled out with hurried breaths.

In answer he got on his knees, yanked her to him, finishing her off with his teeth and tongue. Fingers clutched in his hair as her head fell back. Despite her desperate attempts, she cried out.

"Austin... Austin..." she panted. "I—"

"More, Hailey."

He stood again, ravaged her mouth as the need to bring her higher consumed him. Pulling her from the counter, Austin set her on her feet and turned her until they both faced the long mirror. "Watch. I want you to watch," he huffed against her ear.

Bending her forward, gripping her shoulders, he shoved himself up, staggered by the whippy thrill as Hailey's brows furrowed, and her mouth opened to let out a shuddering moan. Thrusting, Austin pressed his hands to her breasts, played, massaged aroused nipples as Hailey stared back in the mirror.

Her legs trembled, her head rested against his chest as she clasped her arms around his neck, gulping for air.

"More." Austin took Hailey's hand and moved it to her front, used his fingers to press hers to herself, circling, until she sobbed, until she went rigid, her eyes glazing as she pulsed against them both.

"Oh my God, Austin," she gasped. "Oh my *God*." She sunk against him as her legs buckled, as she quivered, spent. "Austin, please, please go over. I—I can't take anymore."

"Not yet." But it was a struggle. Watching Hailey lost in ecstasy brought him to the brink. This wasn't how he intended to finish. He'd brought them both to fevered pitch, but he wanted her slow and long. "Not like this, Hailey."

Yanking their towels from the chrome bar, he laid them on the bathroom floor and took her hand. They kneeled on the green cotton of his towel, the white of hers. He kissed her, gently, tenderly this time, changing the mood of their lovemaking. There was always so much flash, so much fire, but there was another way that he hadn't shown her often enough.

Austin laid Hailey back, his mouth never leaving hers. Her hands skimmed up his waist, over his shoulders, along his neck, into his hair.

Staring into her eyes, he brushed his knuckles over her cheek. "I love you."

She smiled slowly, beautifully. "I love you too."

He touched his lips to hers again, pushed himself into her. Hailey's fingers clutched at his back as she gasped. He clenched his jaw from the rush of staggering sensations.

Each thrust was unhurried, each brush of lips full of meaning. He clasped his fingers with hers and rested his arm beside her head.

With every push forward, she rocked, until she moved faster, her body taking over. Hailey urged him to hurry as she wrapped her legs around him, but he refused.

His breath caught in his throat as he slid against her tight, wet smoothness, unable to hold back. Heat coursed through him as Hailey let herself go. He followed, coming as she came, swallowing her moans as she swallowed his.

"Same as before, homie," Mateo said, as he turned over the ignition and shot out of the bar parking lot.

Jeremy sat back in the passenger seat, ready, more

relaxed than the last time.

Donte was getting tired of the playmates they brought him last month. He was ready for fresh meat.

Jeremy had watched their newest picks grind against several men while they tossed back shots of tequila. He'd fought his erection for two hours, fantasizing about his turn with the eager hotties.

Hopefully Donte would give them first dibs this time. It would be his pleasure to initiate one of the Zulas' newest prizes. He would be sure to do it right—gentle at first—show her he wasn't going to hurt her. Let her relax, let her get juicy, then turn up the heat.

That's what he'd learned to do with the ladies they had now. The girls still screamed and cried when the guards used them but he was pretty damn certain he made Angelica cum this afternoon. All it took was a little finesse; something his partner here sorely lacked.

Jeremy shook his head, growing more intolerant of his "mentor." Donte needed to wake up and buy a clue. He was so much better at this shit than Mateo. Maybe he would talk to Donte, convince him he was ready for more responsibility.

"There they are." Mateo slowed as he turned down another deserted, rundown street. "Shit. Who the hell are those two?"

Jeremy leaned closer to the windshield, scrutinizing the men walking with the soon to be Zulas women. "Beats me. They weren't at the bar."

"New plan. We'll take them out, then grab the girls. Be careful not to leave marks. That's for Donte." Mateo smiled.

That was the plan? "How're we taking them out? Which one am I grabbing?"

"What the hell kind of question is that? Fucking shoot 'em. Grab the taller one. It ain't rocket science."

As Mateo muttered his disdain for the 'newbie,'

Jeremy freed his gun, struggling not to press the barrel to Mateo's temple right then and there. If Mateo wasn't so well-liked by Donte, he would do it; he really fucking would. The whole organization would be better off.

"Let's go." Mateo traveled past the group and yanked the car to the side, tires screeching. Jeremy and Mateo stepped out, guns raised, firing, as the two men reached for their own weapons.

"Anton! Emilio!" the girls screamed as the men fell to the ground.

"Get 'em in the car," Mateo ordered, yanking on the shorter female's arm as she shrieked for the men—their brothers.

The tall girl crumbled between her siblings, clutching at their limp hands. "Anton!" She shook the older of the two men as his wound stained his t-shirt red.

"Come on. Let's go." Jeremy grabbed her under the arms and pulled as she gripped her brother. She wasn't very big, but grief made her strong.

"Hurry up, homie. She's making a fucking racket."

"I've got it. Get in so we can go." Jeremy shoved the tall one in the back and forced the cuffs around her slender wrists before he slammed the door, quieting the din inside. "What're you doing?" He looked over the roof of the vehicle as Mateo stared at him. "Get in. Let's fucking go."

"Don't tell me what to do, homeboy. Remember who's in charge here. Go make sure they're dead."

Jeremy glanced at the pools of blood surrounding the motionless bodies, shaking his head. "They couldn't be any deader, man."

Mateo raised his gun and pointed it at Jeremy. "I said go fucking check."

Sweat bloomed against Jeremy's skin, dripping in a cold line down his spine, as he stared at the barrel of

Mateo's gun. The hard glint in Mateo's eyes made it clear he would be more than happy to pull the trigger. Anger bubbled up, roaring, pulsing in his head. Jeremy yanked his pistol from the holster and pointed it at Mateo. "No."

Mateo fired, missing by inches. "Go check on those bodies, or I'm pulling this trigger. Then I'll find your sister. I've been fantasizing about getting all up in that pussy. I wonder if she'll taste as sweet as she smells." He smirked.

Hand shaking, Jeremy holstered his weapon. If he missed his shot, not only would he be dead, but so would Hailey—and she would suffer first. Mateo would *pay* for this. Stuck, Jeremy pivoted away from the car, walked to the bodies, and gave them a solid kick.

Nothing.

"See? They're gone. We shot 'em in the fucking chest."

Mateo opened the trunk and pulled out a machete. "Cut off their heads."

"Why?"

"Because you're the newbie. You do what I want, homie, and I want you to cut off their heads."

Why did everything have to be so damn gory? Jeremy yanked the knife from Mateo's hand, holding the handle like an ax. Using his rage, he bent over and hacked until the head rolled from the body. "You satisfied?" he spat.

"Nope. Next one."

Jeremy crouched over the next corpse, chopping, listening to the muffled screams and pounding from the sisters in the backseat. "They're gonna break the fucking glass, man. We're gonna to get caught."

"You let me worry about that. I'll let you worry about dealing with Donte when I tell him his newest member doesn't know how to take orders."

Jeremy's eyes snapped to Mateo's. "What, you worried, *homeboy*?" He spit one of Mateo's words back at him.

"Donte wants my sister. He's not about to hurt me, not when I can help him get her. Hailey thinks he's fucking prince charming."

"Just finish."

Jeremy made his final slice, then stood, covered in blood. Staring down at himself, he smiled. "Looks like I've done all the dirty work tonight. Wonder what Donte will think of that?" He leaned down again and cut the shirts off the men. "If we're doing this, we're gonna do it right."

Crouching, Jeremy carved deep, branding the chests with a huge "ZU." The stench of raw, bloody flesh choked the air, and he struggled not to gag. Finished, he stood back and examined his work. "Hell, yeah. The Zulas were here. Let's go."

Jeremy tossed the knife in the trunk and looked once more at the mess he made before opening the passenger side door to the shuddering gasps of the bereaved girls.

Had to do what I had to do. Gotta stay alive.

Jeremy took his seat, free of the guilt that typically plagued him. He stared at the smaller sister in the rear mirror, horror in her eyes, tears streaming down her cheeks. She was his tonight; he would demand it.

CHAPTER 21

AUSTIN SHUT THE DOOR AFTER the last member of his group walked into the air conditioning. Damn, it had been a long one. Fifteen hours of manual labor in ninety-five-degree temperatures left everyone weary and eager for their turn in one of the three showers.

Austin walked to the fridge, pulled a water from the shelf, drained the entire bottle within seconds.

"Feeling better?" Jackson asked, standing on the other side of the counter.

"I might feel human again after my turn in the shower."

"Hot day today. How's the rebuilding going on the northern point?"

"Good, considering..." He glanced around the room at members of their two teams lazing about in front of the television or sleeping where they had dropped on the rug. "Where's Hailey?"

"Do you have a minute?" Jackson gestured to the glass doors leading to the porch.

"Sure." He tossed the plastic bottle in the trash.

They stepped outside. Jackson shut the door.

"What's up?" Austin could already tell he wasn't going to like it. "Where's Hailey?"

Jackson leaned against the rail and casually folded his arms. "She's in the bedroom. Jeremy stopped by again. He's been here a couple hours."

Yup, he definitely didn't like it. Austin steamed a breath out his nose. "Why? Twice in a week? What does he want?"

Jackson shrugged. "Hell if I know. I'm assuming he

came by to visit his sister."

"That fucker doesn't do anything without an angle."

"He's pretty slick." Jackson cleared his throat. "There's more."

Austin waved his hand in a "go ahead" motion as he stared out at the bold pinks of the setting sun, his shoulders tensing by the second.

"Two more girls disappeared last night."

His gaze snapped to Jackson's. "*What?*"

"Two more girls. Seventeen. Locals. Same physical features as the others: long black hair, nice bodies. Pretty. Their brothers were murdered—carved up, decapitated."

"Well, Jesus. Do they have any leads?"

"Not that I'm aware of. The police seem to be doing as little investigating as they did the first time around."

"The Zulas own them—that's why."

"You're probably right."

"I know I'm right."

Jackson shifted, then leaned back again. "There was also another shoot-out over by the place you got jumped."

"It's like the damn wild west around here."

"Not far from it. I talked to Ethan an hour, hour-and-a-half ago. The Dean's rumbling about closing down, sending everyone home. It's not a half-bad idea if you ask me. I know the people here need help; everyone's working for a good cause, but I'm concerned with our ratios. Six to one or twelve to two, puts us at risk. We could use another agent. I keep replaying the shooting at the school the other day. If we hadn't been as close to the gym as we were, we would've had a serious problem."

"I've thought of that myself. I'll call Ethan, see what he wants to do."

"Before you do, he sent us something. He's been hacking. Said it was very interesting."

"Let's take a look."

"I'm not finished raining on your parade."

Austin slid him a glance. "Oh, goodie."

"Donte showed up at our site today."

Austin jammed his fingers in his pockets. "I was waiting for you to say that."

"I don't have the authority to ask him to leave, so I didn't do much more than observe. Our hands are fairly tied here."

"I know."

"He was all over Hailey."

Jaw clenched, he met Jackson's stare.

"I know you and Hailey talked about her keeping her distance last week. It seemed like she tried, but Donte's fucking persistent. He spent a good hour with her at our Humane Society stop, petting his fare share of puppies and kittens. Of course, he donated money, towels, and a five-year supply of dog and cat food while he was there."

The familiar rumble of fury snuck up to devour him whole. "*Goddamn*, I've had about all I can take of him. I need to get Hailey away. I need to get her out of here before something happens. There're bound to be more attempts on him. I don't want her near him when they go down."

"This whole situation sucks." Jackson slapped a supportive hand on Austin's shoulder. "Let's take a peek at what Ethan sent us? We'll go from there."

Austin nodded.

They walked past most everyone laying around, snacking, watching a movie. Jen popped up from the floor and stepped up to Austin, smiling. "Bathrooms free. It's your turn."

"Ah, I'll clean up in a few minutes."

"Just so you guys know, the group has unanimously decided to have a smallish party in about twenty minutes—a couple beers, some cards, music, video games. We've earned one after today. I hope you'll join us." She smiled again, looking up from under her lashes.

"Yeah, probably." Austin shrugged, uncomfortable, aware that Jen was hitting on him. "Jackson and I have something to do first."

"Okay. See you in a bit."

Mumbling his assent, he and Jackson continued down the hall, shut themselves in the second bedroom, and locked it.

"I'll see you in a bit," Jackson repeated in his best imitation of Jen as he batted his lashes and flounced his imaginary breasts.

Despite the turn in their day, Austin laughed. Jackson's sense of humor was never far from the surface.

"You do realize she wants to tag your ass." Jackson batted his lashes again and touched his tongue to his top lip.

Austin grinned. "Yeah, well, she'll have to look somewhere else."

Jackson sobered. "Things are pretty serious between you and Hailey."

"As serious as they get. She's moving in with me when we get back."

Jackson's brows shot up. "Really?"

"She's what I want. Why wait?"

"Good for you, man. I'm happy for you, happy for both of you. Hailey's a great lady—a sweetheart."

Austin set his laptop on the bunk and sat down. "Let's see what Ethan sent us." Austin hit a few buttons and read the e-mail. *Wonder if you'll find this as interesting as I do. Call me after you and Jackson have a chance to check it out.*

Intrigued, Austin clicked on the attachment. He frowned, staring at the grainy surveillance footage from a bar, dated last night. He leaned closer as Jackson crouched down next to him.

"That looks like Hailey's brother." Jackson pointed.

"Sure does. And look there. That's Mateo. I wonder why they're at the same bar but sitting so far apart. Kind of hard to have a conversation when you're on opposite sides of the room."

"It's almost as if they're up to something."

Austin clicked on the next attachment Ethan had sent. It was more surveillance video, dated weeks earlier. He pressed a few buttons, displaying both images side-by-side. "There they are again, drinking beer across the room from one another. Holy shit." Austin pointed to the edge of the screen. "Isn't that..." he zoomed in further. "Dear God, yes...the girls that disappeared a month ago."

Two long-haired, long-legged young women danced to the music of the live band among the haze of cigarette smoke. After a while, the girls left the bar. Moments later, Mateo left, then Jeremy. "Those fucking bastards."

Austin clicked back to the newest footage, watching all twenty minutes. They didn't see the girls that vanished last night, but they did watch Mateo and Jeremy leave in the same pattern they had the night the first two teens went missing. "The victims must've stayed out of camera range."

"Seems about right to me."

Through the thin walls of the next room came the sound of Hailey's laughter, mingling with her brother's. Austin leaped to his feet. Enough was enough. They had a fucking kidnapper in the house. It was time to end this, time to give Hailey the wakeup call she needed.

Jackson stood. "What're you doing?"

"I'm going to show this to Hailey."

"Whoa, wait a minute, bro," he put a restraining hand on Austin's shoulder. "That's not a good idea."

"I've been keeping this from her. All of it. I thought she

was safer in the dark, but now I'm not so sure. I'm starting to think she's in more danger not knowing. Maybe she'll be willing to stay away from them if she realizes how high the stakes are."

"I don't know, man. I think you're jumping the gun. I'm thinking you should sit tight on this one."

Was he being rash?

Hailey and Jeremy's chuckles bounced into the room again. She wouldn't be laughing if she knew her brother and Mateo were responsible for the kidnappings of four young women, and possibly the decapitation and mutilation of two men—probably more. She would be horrified.

"Hailey keeps asking for some sort of proof. I finally have something one hundred percent definitive. What if someone takes a shot at Donte the next time he comes around? What if they take her out instead?"

Austin shook his head; he couldn't stand the thought. This was the right thing to do. It would be easier to ask for her silence than to keep her in the dark. Hailey couldn't protect herself if she was flying blind.

"It's your call, Austin. I'll back you whichever way you want to play this, but I don't think it's a good idea."

The jumpy bass of the stereo echoed down the hall, followed by playful hoots and laughter.

"Sounds like the party's starting." Jackson reached for the doorknob. "I think I'll go play chaperone."

"I'll be down with Hailey in a bit—if she's up to it. This is the right call."

"Good luck."

"Thanks."

Jackson stepped out of the room, shutting the door behind him.

Austin turned, staring at his laptop before he exed out of the screen. He sat a moment, putting his face in his hands, dreading the conversation he and Hailey were about to have. But it had to be done. Donte was popping up far too often. The odds of Hailey ending up in a dangerous situation increased each time.

Sighing, Austin scrubbed his fingers against his jaw. How would he tell her? This was going to kill her. He would take it a step at a time. Be there for her. What else could he do?

With a big breath, he stood, opened the door, and stepped into the hall just as Jeremy shut the door to the third bedroom.

"What are you doing?"

"I'm a little turned around. I thought that was the bathroom."

"Bathroom's down the hall."

"I'm heading out. I'll wait 'til I get back to the yacht." Jeremy walked past him. Austin followed, watching until Jeremy made it to the small launch down the beach.

Hailey stared out her bedroom window as she pulled her hair through an elastic, fully intending to join her new friends for videogames and cards. The past five-and-a-half weeks had been grueling, each passing day more dangerous.

The rides to the group's daily stops were tense as everyone waited, afraid of another shooting. Reports around the community kept them all one edge. Two more girls had vanished in the night. Two more bodies had been brutalized—like the ones left by the vans that first day.

While the team assisted the overworked staff at the Humane Society earlier, there had been another drive-by less than a mile away. The violence on the island was out of hand.

Jackson's easy sense of humor vanished each morning as they left the apartment. He radiated with tension by the time they stepped into the house at night. The days were wearing on Austin, too. She saw the strain in his eyes, felt his rigid muscles when he held her close in bed.

In less than two months this would be over. They would all go home. She yearned to snuggle her girls, to see Sarah and Ethan, Morgan and Hunter, to move into her new apartment. A slow smile spread across her face. Every time she thought of living with Austin, of building a home with him... There weren't words to describe her happiness. This was the real deal. Their relationship had taken her by surprise, had moved fast, but he loved her.

Hailey closed her eyes, savoring the gift, relishing her joy. Austin *loved* her, and she him. They were going to give it a go. For the first time in her life, she truly believed she could have—no—*would* have everything she'd ever wanted: the love and support of a good man, a home filled with happiness, children of her own.

Maybe she was getting a little ahead of herself, but she and Austin would get to where she planned eventually. Now that she had him, she wasn't letting go.

Hailey put her brush down at the sound of her phone ringing. She frowned at the number. "Don't know this one," she muttered. Shrugging, she hit "talk."

"Hello?"

"Hailey."

"Donte?"

"Yes. I'm sorry to bother you on your own time, but I have a request."

"Okay." She pressed her lips into a thin line. She'd tried to keep her distance throughout the afternoon, but he didn't seem to notice.

"I realize it's against your organization's rules, but I'm wondering if you might be able to make an exception and join me on my yacht for a small get-together Thursday. I have several important business members joining me, including my father. He is very fond of Jeremy. I would love for him to meet you, as I am quite fond of you."

"Oh, Donte, that sounds like so much fun."

"Good. Then it is all set."

"Well, no, actually..." She turned from the window and stared into Austin's cool gaze. *Oh, crap.* "Um, Donte, I'm afraid I have to go. Can I call you later?"

"Is everything all right?"

"Uh, yes. Definitely. I just have to go."

"Call me back when you can."

"Okay. Bye." Her heart hopped erratically as she pressed "end" and set her cell on the bed, never taking her eyes from Austin's. She tried a smile. "Hey. I was just coming out to join the fun."

"Looks like you were on the phone to me."

She closed her eyes. "I was. Donte called. He got my number somehow, probably from my brother. He invited me to some family party tomorrow night. I was about to tell him no." She snagged her lip to stop her babbling, fiddled with her fingers as Austin continued to stare, scrutinizing, saying nothing. "Austin, he called me."

"You didn't have to answer."

"I didn't know it was him. The number came up 'unknown'. I'm sorry you walked in on something that sounded like more than it was."

He grunted.

"Darn it, what do you want me to do? If I had known it was Donte, I wouldn't have answered." She walked to the door, intending to push past him.

He grabbed her arm, turned her until she crashed into his chest. "I'm sorry."

"I really didn't know. I truly didn't."

He kissed her forehead. "I believe you. I'm sorry, Hailey."

Nodding, she relaxed against him, realizing the tense moment had passed.

He played with her ponytail. "Can I talk to you for a minute?"

"Of course." She pushed the door to close it, then took Austin's hand.

He gave her a tug and caught the door before it shut. "Actually, can we talk in my room? I have something I want to show you."

"Oh really?" She wiggled her eyebrows and smiled. Her smile faded when Austin's face stayed stony. Maybe he was still mad. "What's wrong?"

"Just come with me. I want to talk."

"Okay." Stirrings of worry tied her stomach in knots. "You're making me nervous."

Austin led them to his own room, opened his door, and closed it behind them. "Have a seat on my bed if you want."

She sat on the edge, relieving legs that were quickly turning to jelly. "Austin, what's going on?"

He settled next to her and stared down at the floor. "I heard Donte showed up at the Humane Society."

And here we go again. She closed her eyes and blew out a weary breath. "Yeah, he did. He was there for an hour or so."

"That's about sixty minutes too long."

She stood. "I don't want to argue about this, Austin. I really don't. I know you asked me to keep my distance and I'm trying."

"Really? From what I understand, you were with him the entire time."

A hint of anger cut through her nerves. "So, what, are you having Jackson spy on me now?"

"No."

"You seem to know my every move."

291

"I'm just pointing out—"

"I know what you're pointing out. I told you I would stay away from Donte, but I didn't. I tried busying myself with paperwork, but he asked me to tour the facility with him. I wasn't going to be rude—especially when he donated enough food, supplies, and money to keep the place up and running for several years to come."

"Hailey—"

She held up a hand. "I'm not finished. The goal of Project Mexico is to help the people here. Donte has more than helped many of the families on this island. If he wants me to walk around and look at a few sweet-faced puppies and kittens with him, I'm not about to say no."

Austin scrubbed his hands over his face. "This is exactly why I brought you in here. I want to show you something. I've been trying to tell you that Donte's not all he's cracked up to be, that he's dangerous. Your brother too."

"I'm not going here with you again," Biting off her words, she started for the door.

Austin rushed up from the bed, took her arm. "Wait."

She whirled around, her temper soaring. "Why should I? Why should I stand here and listen to this? I've had the opportunity to watch my brother work. I've seen him interact with the women and men of this island. He's patient and sweet with the children. He sweats away each day on the rebuilds, like the rest of us. You tell me how that's dangerous."

"It's a front, an act."

Hurt and fury mixed together. "Nothing he does will ever be good enough for you." She yanked on the doorknob, but Austin held it closed. She walked away, wanting her space.

Austin wrapped his arms around her, nestling her body to him.

She struggled. "I don't want you to touch me right now."

He tightened his grip until she went still. "Let me explain," he said close to her ear. "Let me show you. Do you think I would say this to you, do this to you, for no reason? I know how much this rips you apart."

Above all else, she knew Austin would never hurt her on purpose. "Okay," she said wearily, "show me your proof that my brother is the next thing to a monster." Shuddering nausea churned her stomach as she prepared herself for the worst.

"I'm sorry, Hailey." Austin pressed a kiss to her hair, and she closed her eyes. He turned her to face him. "I'm sorry I have to do this." He touched her lips in an attempt to soothe her.

Hailey wrapped her arms around him, holding on to his strength as Austin brought her head to his chest. She took a deep breath and eased away. "Let's get this over with."

"Come here." He took her hand and sat with her on the bed. He pulled his laptop over to them, wiggled the mouse, and clicked a button. Two grainy images popped up side-by-side.

Whatever she'd expected, it wasn't this. "What is this?"

"It's footage I received today."

She stared at her brother sitting at the bar, sipping a beer, noticed Mateo across the room doing the same. She slid Austin a glance, confused, before she looked at the laptop again.

"This is security footage from last night," he pointed to the left side of the screen, "and about a month ago." He pointed to the right.

"Yes, I noticed the dates." She shook her head, growing more perplexed. "Austin, I don't see anything wrong."

"Look right here." He pointed to the images of the two young women in the corner of the video. "Do you recognize them?"

She moved closer. "No, I don't. Wait. Oh, oh, yes I do. Those are the girls that went missing."

"Exactly."

She scrutinized the screen again, watched the girls leave the bar. Moments later, Mateo got up and left. Two minutes later Jeremy did the same. Austin fast-forwarded through the second set of images before he played the footage on the right again. "Now look here."

Hailey watched as Mateo left again, and much like in the first video, Jeremy got up as well. Austin closed the laptop as Hailey pressed her fingers to her forehead. "I feel like I was supposed to see something."

"The footage on the left was from the night the girls disappeared while we were still at the resort. The footage on the right was from last night. The girls were at different bars, but in both instances the bar was the last place they were seen before they vanished."

Frustration nearly brought her to tears. "Take me to the point here, Austin. I'm clearly missing it."

"Hailey, both incidents happened on a night when Mateo and your brother went out for drinks. Although we can't see the victims in the second tape, we sure as hell saw them in the first. Jeremy and Mateo left moments after they did. We can assume the same of the second tape."

The implications finally hit home. "Wait a minute. Wait a minute." Hailey rushed to her feet, her heart thundering, her stomach sick with disbelief. "You're suggesting my brother and Mateo kidnapped four young women?"

"I'm not suggesting anything—I'm telling you." His voice was rough with frustration.

"My God, Austin. Do you truly understand what you're saying? Do you understand you're ripping me to pieces over two videos that don't show me a damn thing?"

"What are you *talking* about?" He yanked the laptop

open, played back to the part where the teens left before Mateo and Jeremy. "I see it." He stabbed his finger against the screen. "Ethan sees it. Jackson too. But you still don't. You won't."

"What do you want me to *see*?" She threw her arms out to her sides.

"The *truth*, goddamnit! I want you to see the truth."

"I'll tell you what I saw. I saw my brother and Mateo drinking a beer before they got up and left. And somehow, that makes them kidnappers?"

"If they were there together, why were they sitting apart?"

"I don't know," she shouted. "I haven't a clue, but that sure as hell doesn't make them kidnappers."

"They were staging, making sure they didn't look suspicious!" Austin rubbed his hand over his jaw, trying to gentle his voice. "Sorry, Hailey. It's three against one here. Three sets of experienced, trained eyes telling you your brother is in this up to his eyeballs."

She clutched at her stomach, struggling not to be ill. "I think you're seeing what you want to see, what you're choosing to. You haven't liked Jeremy since the day you met him. You haven't liked Donte either. This was supposed to be about Donte too, right? I guess he was driving the getaway car?" She burst into tears from the injustice. "Oh, Austin, why are you doing this? Why can't you just accept you made a mistake, that you're wrong?"

"I'm not *wrong*. I'm not. Think, Hailey. Think." He grabbed her arms and yanked her against him. "Why does Donte have well over a dozen bodyguards? And why are they armed with fucking machine guns? I'm a bodyguard. I'm a fucking former Navy SEAL. Do you see *me* walking around with an AK-47? Have you ever seen me with a weapon like that? Have you not noticed they all have the same tattoo? Mateo has it on his arm. Some of the guards have it on their necks. They're Zulas. Do you get that? Do you understand their capacity for violence? Wake *up*, Hailey. Wake up." He turned away, his voice going sharp. "The violence, the kidnappings. None of that stuff started until Donte dropped anchor here."

"Have you ever thought these could all be coincidences? Donte was at the school when we were shot at."

He whirled again. "They were shooting at *him*. He's the ringleader. He's in charge of this whole thing."

She choked out a breath as she swiped at the tears pouring down her cheeks. "So, my brother's a kidnapper and Donte's the leader of the mafia."

"Yes."

She scoffed out a humorless laugh. "I can't believe this. You're jealous. I can't believe you would do this to me. I told you I loved you, *only* you. I don't want to talk about this anymore; I really don't. Let's take a night off." She hurried to the door, ready to sob.

"We aren't done here, Hailey. Don't walk out that door." His voice grew low, dangerous.

She turned. "We need to be finished for tonight."

"Not until we get this straight. What I'm telling you has nothing to do with jealousy. Donte and Jeremy are exactly who I've told you they are."

Utterly confused, Hailey could only stare at the floor. "I'm not so sure. I'm not sure of anything anymore."

Austin sat on the bed and pressed his hands to his face. "I don't know what else to do here." He looked up and met her eyes. Something in his hopeless expression had her heart lurching. "I have the facts, Hailey. I've shared them. I've shown you, and you still won't believe me. I can't keep doing this with you."

"So what are you saying?"

"I don't know what I'm saying." He scrubbed his hand over his chin, rubbed at the back of his neck, his voice desperate. "I guess I'm telling you to choose. Me or them."

She stumbled back from the shock of his words. "You—you want me to choose between you and my brother? How can you ask such a thing?" This was so huge, too huge to truly comprehend. "I can't. I don't know how. I can't choose."

He shook his head, his eyes full of sorrow. "You just did."

"No, I—I... Austin."

"I thought we could do this. I thought we could make this work, but now I see we can't. This isn't working for me, Hailey. I can't be with someone who thinks I'm a liar."

"I don't think..." Her world dropped out from beneath her as the meaning sunk in. "Are you telling me this is over? That we're over?"

"Yeah, I am. I can't stand by and watch this anymore, be a part of this anymore. I don't want to watch you laugh and smile while you talk to him. I don't want to walk in and hear you having phone conversations with a Mafia King. I've given you the truth you asked for, and it's still not enough. They're going to hurt you; I won't be there when it goes down."

She struggled to concentrate on what he said as she fought for each breath. "*Hurt* me? Do you think they can hurt me any more than you're hurting me right now? You said you loved me. I let myself believe that you loved me."

"I *do* love you." His voice was drowning in agony.

"Please don't say that." The first sob escaped. She pressed her hand to her mouth. "Please don't. I can't stand to hear it. You promised me, Austin. You promised me, and I believed you." She reached blindly for the doorknob as she struggled to suppress the next racking shudder.

Yanking the door open, she rushed to her room, oblivious to the laughter and noise down the hall. She slammed her door, yanked open the window, and gulped in fresh air. It was too hot, too crowded in here. The walls closed in around her as she fought for each unsteady breath. She had to go, had to get out. She popped the flimsy screen from the window and lowered herself to the rocks. Jumping to the sand, she ran, desperate to escape the agony that threatened to send her to her knees.

Hailey ran for what could have been minutes or hours; she'd lost track of time, trying to outdistance her pain. She sprinted until she was dizzy and fell, collapsing to the beach. On hands and knees she panted until the first keening sob stole her breath again. Austin was gone. They had just begun, and she'd lost him.

Trembling, too tired, too defeated to stand, Hailey fell back, curling into a ball, shuddering, freezing in the balmy Caribbean air. She cried herself dry.

With her last tear she clutched herself tight, unable to get warm. Would she ever be warm again? Would she ever be whole? She'd given Austin all of the pieces. He'd promised to take care, but he didn't. He said he loved her but he couldn't, not really, not the way she wanted. Not the way she needed. If he loved her, nothing would've stood in their way. Love wasn't asking someone for the impossible. Love wasn't asking someone to choose between two huge pieces of their heart.

Lost, drained, Hailey focused on each breath in, each breath out, matching the ebb and flow of the waves crashing against the rocks beyond. The violent rush of sound competed with the thoughts racing through her mind.

Austin didn't love her. How could she have been so foolish? How could she have let herself believe he did?

She stared into the dark until moonlight faded, until the sun began its rise in the east, until her eyes finally grew heavy with the burden of true exhaustion. She slept.

CHAPTER 22

"**H**AILEY. HAILEY, COME ON. WAKE up."

"Hmm?" She blinked against the bright sunshine. "Jackson?"

He crouched beside her. "We've been worried about you."

She sat up, head aching, eyes burning, sleep still fogging her brain. "You have?"

He pressed his hand to her brow. "Yeah, we have. We've been searching for you for hours."

She glanced around at rocks, the water, confused, before reality rushed back to slap her. Hailey covered her face with her hands as her heart broke all over again. The glaze of shock no longer coated her raw wound. "Oh, God, Jackson. What am I going to do?"

He sat in the sand next to her and wrapped an arm around her shoulders. "You'll put one foot in front of the other and keep moving."

"You make it sound so easy. Even that seems like too much right now." Overwhelmed by despair, she swiped at tears she couldn't keep at bay.

He hugged her close. "It's definitely not easy. I'm not exactly sure what happened between you two... Maybe you can work it out."

She wanted to grab hold of hope, but ruthlessly squashed it. It hurt too much to believe in anything but an ending. "No, I don't think so. He told me we were finished."

"Sometimes people say things they don't mean, things they regret and wish they could take back."

Hailey met Jackson's gaze as his voice vibrated with regret, realizing they weren't just talking about her and Austin. Jackson's eyes told her he was speaking from experience.

"Did you love her?"

He looked down at the sand. "Yeah, I loved her—still do. Four years later and I still do."

Intrigued, Hailey scooted closer. "Have you talked to her?"

"No. It was a college thing. She moved on."

"I'm sorry." She rested her head on his shoulder, giving comfort as she took it. She let the subject drop, since Jackson clearly didn't want to talk about. "I'm sorry you had to be out looking for me. I didn't mean to stay gone so long. I know we aren't supposed to leave the house without you or Austin, but I had to go. It felt like the walls were closing in, like I was suffocating."

"I'm just glad you're safe."

She let out a deep sigh. "I guess we should get back." She didn't want to. She wanted to stay here where the waves were rough and wild, where the water was stunningly blue, where everything was simple.

"Yeah." He looked at her again. "Dr. Lopez wants to see you."

She winced. "That's not good."

"He likes you. You're great at what you do. I'm sure you can smooth things over."

"I hope so." It would be tough fulfilling the remainder of the semester with Austin just a bedroom away, but she wanted to be here, wanted to see this through. Being busy, helping others, would give her a purpose, would give her a reason to keep going.

Jackson stood and held out his hand; she took it. They walked up the embankment together.

"You brought the van?"

"Heck yeah. We're not far from Point North. We're about three miles from the house."

"What? Are you sure?"

"Positively."

Hailey buckled her seatbelt as Jackson pulled onto the narrow road. Each mile closer sent her pulse scrambling, her stomach clenching. She pressed her hands together tightly as Jackson turned into the small drive. Hailey stayed where she was, trying to find the courage to take the first step.

"You ready?"

"As I'll ever be." She gave him a weak smile before she got out. Jackson took her hand, walked with her, opening the door to the house. The noisy din of a dozen people fixing breakfast stopped the moment she and Jackson stepped inside.

Hailey's gaze automatically flew to Austin's, held there for a moment before he turned away. She took a deep breath, willing the tears back. "Um, I wanted to say..." her voice shook. She cleared her throat, tried again. "I want to apologize. I realize I broke the rules. I've made everyone late for our first stop today. I had to go..." her voice trembled again—along with her lip—so she stopped.

Mia came up and drew Hailey into a hug. "You scared us, girlie. I'm glad you're safe."

The gesture of support almost broke her. She grabbed hold of Mia like a lifeline, held on as the first tear fell. "Thank you." She breathed in a shuddering breath and shook her head before she pulled away. "I have to... I have to...." She gestured to the bedroom and hurried off. Once inside her room, she leaned against the closed door and shut her eyes. This wasn't going to work. She couldn't stay here.

Someone knocked.

Why couldn't they give her five minutes? All she

needed was five minutes to pull herself together. Squaring her shoulders, Hailey turned and opened the door. Her stomach lurched. Dr. Lopez stood before her.

"Hailey, I'm glad you are all right."

"Thank you. I'm sorry I left."

"We will have to talk. We have strict rules about these very things."

She nodded, swallowed. "Yes, I know."

"Please meet me in my office as soon as you can."

"If I could have a moment to change, to get the sand off me."

"Ten minutes."

She didn't miss the hint of scolding, the disappointment. "Ten minutes," she agreed.

As Doctor Lopez walked to his office, Hailey moved in the opposite direction. She passed the living room, spotted Austin on the porch and Jen right next to him. Hailey looked away, ignoring the slice of pain as she hurried into the bathroom. She couldn't let it matter.

She struggled to keep going, to keep moving through the misery. She closed her eyes and welcomed the first numbing chink in her emotional coat of armor. She stepped into the shower, rinsed more than washed, dressed in shorts and a tank top, brushed her teeth. Then she took the dreaded walk down the hallway to knock on Dr. Lopez's office door. She did it all in eight minutes flat.

"Come in."

Hailey opened the door. She tried a smile and cleared her throat. "Thanks."

"Come sit." Dr. Lopez folded his hands on his desk and sighed. "Hailey, I'm afraid we have a problem here."

She glanced down at her lap, at her fingers laced and clenched tight. "I imagine we must."

"You left the apartment, which is very much against the rules. You signed a contract with the university stating that while you were here with Project Mexico, you would abide by all that we ask—for your safety and everyone else's." He slid a copy of the agreement in front of her. The paragraph in question was circled with bright red ink, her signature scrawled several lines below.

"Dr. Lopez, I remember signing this paper. I realize I broke the rules. I can only be sorry and ask if there's anything I can do to make things right."

"Your housemates were in danger throughout the night as a result of your actions. The University was put in great legal jeopardy. It is never ideal to have only one guard, but during these violent times on the island, it is downright unacceptable."

"Yes, I understand." It appeared as though she would not only lose Austin, but also an entire semester of credits. She swallowed hard, trying to hold back yet another bought of tears.

"Although this situation is quite severe, it is not this that troubles me the most."

Hailey frowned. She'd only broken one rule, unless dating and sleeping with the bodyguard was a clause she'd missed. "Oh?"

"I'm quite troubled, and quite frankly sad that I must discuss my next point with you."

She licked her lips, struggling to keep calm as disdain darkened the doctor's eyes. "Dr. Lopez, I'm not sure what you're talking about."

He stared at her, studying. "A huge part of me believes you truly don't. I wish I could go with that. I wish I could go with my gut, Hailey, but once again, I must follow the rules."

She nodded, wanting him to get on with it already. Sighing, Dr. Lopez brought out a stack of yellow sheets from his desk. "Do you know what these are, Hailey?"

"Um, no, I don't."

"These are papers I've filled out for insurance purposes. It appears as though everyone within our apartment has had something disappear over the last few days. Everyone, except you."

"I'm afraid I don't understand..." she trailed off as his implication sunk in. "You-you think I stole from the group, from my friends? I—I can't even..." How could he believe such a thing? They'd worked side-by-side for over a month, yet he would believe that she took what didn't belong to her?

"As I said before, I have a hard time believing this of you. You have such a deep kindness. You're wonderful with the people, one of the best we've ever had here with our program. It was suggested to me that perhaps it wasn't you, but someone you know."

Her thoughts swirled so fast she couldn't keep up with the conversation. She pressed her hand to her forehead. "I'm sorry, Dr. Lopez, I didn't... Can you-can you start again?" Sweat popped against her skin. She stood, afraid she would vomit or pass out. "It's very hot in here. Can we open a window, please?"

"Yes, yes." Dr. Lopez rushed to his feet and pushed the window up.

Hailey hurried over to the breeze blowing through the window, pressing her face against the screen. They thought she was a thief. Eleven people down the hall thought she had broken their trust, had taken their things.

She clasped her hands together, breathed deep, then turned to Dr. Lopez. "I would like you to come with me. I want you to search my things. I haven't taken anything from anyone here. I never would."

"Please sit for another moment."

"Only if you agree to search through my things afterward."

"That isn't necessary."

"Yes, it is. It is to me."

"Okay. Fine. Now, please sit." He gestured to the chair. "As I was saying, Hailey, I'm not convinced you took anything, but I wonder if someone else may have—someone who visited over the last couple days."

"You mean my brother." A swift kick of anger replaced the surprise of his appalling accusation. "So, let me get this straight. Because I'm the only person who hasn't reported something stolen, that automatically means either my brother or I did it? Has it ever occurred to you that someone else has been stealing, and told you they had something taken to throw you off?"

"Yes, in fact, I did think of that, but then I did something I don't typically do. I went back through everyone's files, got in contact with a few people, had criminal backgrounds reexamined—just to be certain the university didn't overlook anything through their own."

"Well, then you would've seen that I've never had so much as a speeding ticket."

"I did note that in my report for the university. But something curious came up when I added a few more names to my list. Perhaps you would like to take a look."

Hailey snapped up the paper Dr. Lopez held out, falling into her chair as she read the report, stared at the subject's name: Jeremy Kagan.

She knew her brother had gone to jail for underage drinking and the bag of pot, but the rest was a punch to the gut—breaking and entering, *multiple* drug possession charges with intent to sell, four simple assault convictions, DUI, petty theft, possession of a deadly weapon. And he hadn't simply gone to jail; he'd done two six-month stints in California State prison.

"I take it you weren't aware of these facts."

"Where did you get this?" Her voice trembled.

"Cozumel is a small island, but I do have connections

that must remain anonymous." Dr. Lopez laced his fingers. "Hailey, I believe we should finish the business at hand."

She struggled to take her eyes off of her brother's rap sheet. "Can I keep this?"

"Yes."

Hailey folded the paper, set the page on the desk, and turned her eyes to focus on Dr. Lopez.

"Hailey, after talking with the Dean about the events of the past couple days and your disappearance last night, we have no choice but to ask you to leave Project Mexico."

Even though she knew it was coming, it didn't hurt any less. "If you think that's best."

"I do not think it's best, but it is the only solution I can come up with. As I said before, you are truly one of the best participants we have ever had in our program. You have a gift, Hailey, a true gift with people. I have enjoyed working with you very much."

She stood. "But not enough to stand with me. Not enough to believe me when I tell you I've had nothing to do with the disappearance of my teammates' things."

"The university will launch a full investigation. If it is unanimously agreed upon that you played no part in the thefts, you will only loose this semester's credits. If we come to other findings, you could very well lose all credits taken at the university."

She shook her head as she absorbed the next blow. "Are you telling me I may not be able to graduate next semester, that my entire academic record would be null and void?"

"That is indeed what I'm saying. We will expect you to vacate the premises within two hours. Because your integrity is in question, we will ask a member of the team to be with you while you pack. Please understand this was a hard decision to make. I will do what I can to see that you keep the credits you have earned."

Hailey turned to the door on legs she wasn't sure would carry her down the hall. She took one careful step at a time until she grabbed for her doorknob. As she gave it a twist, her stomach shuddered its revolt. With all the strength she could muster, she bolted to the bathroom, slammed the door, and instantly became violently ill.

When her belly finished heaving, she collapsed to the floor, staring at white tiles, brushing at the sweat beading on her forehead with trembling fingers.

Her life had turned upside-down in less than twenty-four hours. How would she get up and keep moving? Everything she'd worked for, everything she'd ever wanted was gone.

It was time to go home. She needed to go back to L.A., needed to be with Sarah, Ethan, and her sweet baby girls. She craved to be with people who knew who she was, because right now, she wasn't sure herself. Thoughts of Kylee's smiling face, of Emma's little fingers and toes gave Hailey the strength to get up. She made it to the sink, rinsed her mouth, and began the chore of gathering up her things.

Someone knocked. "Hailey, are you okay?"

Mia.

Hailey walked to the door on jittery legs and opened it. "Come to make sure I don't steal anything while I pack?"

Hurt flashed in Mia's eyes. Hailey closed her own. "I'm sorry, Mia. That was unfair and completely unnecessary."

Mia gave her a small smile. "It's okay."

"No, it's not. I'm out of sorts and spewing venom at people who don't deserve it."

"You're forgiven." Mia's smile warmed.

Hailey brushed Mia's arm and gave her a gentle squeeze before she went back to grab her tote bag and towel. She stepped from the bathroom, met Austin's gaze.

She cast her eyes down, adding more chinks to her armor.

Shaking it off, Hailey walked to her room. "I'm going to book my flight before I pack."

"Yeah, sure." Mia sat on Hailey's bunk. "Hailey, I've been hearing the rumors. I want you to know I don't believe a single one. I don't believe for one second you took anything from anyone."

Hailey closed her eyes, thankful for Mia's wave of faith, and pulled her into a hug. "You have no idea how much that means to me right now. You truly have no idea." She sniffed, fighting back tears that were only a blink away.

"Everything'll be okay. I'm sure of it."

Hailey wasn't. "I hope so."

She let Mia go, opened her laptop, and began to search for the first flight leaving Cozumel. After ten minutes, she found a plane with available seats departing later that evening. She winced at the price. That would cut into her savings. With no other choice, Hailey entered her credit card number and was quickly declined.

"What do you mean I'm declined?" She checked the number again, retyped it slowly, then pressed enter. "Declined" flashed at her again. "I don't understand. I've only charged a hundred dollars on this thing the entire time I've been down here."

Mia popped her head down from the top bunk. "Why don't you call the credit card company? There's probably something wrong with the system."

Hailey dialed the help number on the back of her card. The automated voice asked for her account number. She punched it in and waited to be connected with an operator.

"Good morning."

"Yes, good morning, I'm having trouble with my card. I just tried to buy a plane ticket and was declined."

"Let's take a look, Ms. Roberts."

Hailey stood and paced the room.

"Ms. Roberts, it seems you're over your limit."

She stopped in her tracks. "Over my limit? What do you mean I'm over my limit? I've charged one-hundred dollars while I've been in Mexico. That should be the only balance I have."

"I'm looking back through your purchase history. This does appear to be abnormal charging. I think we need to flag your account."

Nerves gnawed at her stomach, and she felt sick again. "Can you tell me where the charges were made?"

"Most of the activity took place in San Miguel and Playa Del Carmen, Mexico—mostly bar and casino transactions."

Jeremy. It had to be Jeremy. She pressed jittery fingers to her throbbing temple.

"We'll flag your card for now, ma'am. I would suggest you call the Credit Bureau, have them put a fraud alert on your profile. It'll take a few days to get this straightened out."

She didn't have a few days; she had little more than an hour. "Okay, thank you." Hailey clicked off and pressed her hand against her rapid heartbeat, struggling not to hyperventilate. What was she going to *do*? The thought of being stuck in Mexico without the protection of Austin and Jackson terrified her.

Her savings account. She could wire money from her savings account.

Hailey sat on the bed, weak with relief. She worked her way through her passwords, waiting for the screen to switch over to her balances.

She could only stare.

Overdrawn? She clicked the mouse to take her to her checking. Zero balance. Fingers shaking, breath shuddering, she exed out, tried again. This was a mistake. The bank had made a mistake. She had four hundred dollars in her checking, ten thousand in her

CATE BEAUMAN

savings account. She'd been saving little bits here and there for years.

The screen popped up again exactly as it had moments before. "No. *No.* I can't believe this. This isn't happening." She pressed her hands to her face and began to rock back and forth in her panic. She didn't have a penny to her name.

Mia jumped down from her bunk. "Hailey, what is it? What's wrong?"

"He took it. He took it all. Everything I have. Everything I've worked for. I don't know how I'll get home."

"I could lend you some money."

"No." She shook her head vehemently. "No, I can't pay you back."

"Let me get Austin."

"No," she raised her voice.

"Hailey, I know you two are—"

"No." She grabbed hold of Mia's hand before she could escape. "I don't want you saying anything to anyone about this—especially Austin. Austin and I are over. We're over." Maybe if she repeated it a million times she might believe it. She was on her own, as she'd always been, as she would be from now on. "I'll call my friend in L.A."

Mia sat next to her and put an arm around her as Hailey dialed.

"Hello?"

Hailey squeezed her eyes shut at the sound of Sarah's soft voice.

"Hello? Hailey, are you there?"

"Yes, I'm here." Tears tightened her throat.

"Oh, honey, what's the matter?"

"Pretty much everything. If you name it, I'm pretty sure it's wrong."

"Tell me what's going on."

She clutched Mia's hand. "I wish I could. I wish I could

310

tell you everything right now, but I'm in some trouble."

"What kind of trouble?"

"I need a loan." God, it pained her to ask. She'd never had to ask before.

"Of course. How much?"

She choked on her tears. It was that easy. Sarah would make it that easy. "Enough to get home. I need a plane ticket. For today. As soon as possible. I'm so sorry, Sarah. I'm so sorry I have to ask you for this."

"Don't insult our friendship. You do want to come home, right?"

She found the strength to smile. "More than anything. I need you, Sarah. I need my family."

"I'll pick you up at the airport. I'll bring Morgan too. Let me get this arranged. I'll call you right back."

"Okay."

"I love you."

"I love you too." And she knew Sarah always would. She wouldn't give her the words and take them back.

"Right back, Hailey. Hang in there."

She clicked off the call and leaned against Mia, taking the comfort offered. "My life is such a mess right now. *I'm* such a mess right now, and I don't have time for it."

"What can I do?"

"You're doing it."

"How about I give you a hand with packing?"

It was hard to admit she needed help, but she did. The turmoil of the morning had zapped her strength. "Yes, okay."

"Let's get you the hell out of here. Austin told us this morning the university made the decision to pull us out next week. I'm a little envious you get to go home today. It's scary around here."

She thought of Sarah's voice, of the soothing familiarity. "You know what? So am I. I can't wait to be home. I *need* to be home."

Her phone rang.

"Hailey?"

"Yeah, it's me."

"You're all set. Your plane leaves at one. You won't have much of a wait. It's nonstop, too."

"How'd you manage that?"

"You forget that my husband is a supremely hot computer geek."

She grinned for the first time in twelve hours. "I can't argue with you there."

"Your ticket will be at the counter. Hurry home. I'll be waiting."

And because Sarah said she would be there, Hailey had no doubt. "See you soon." Hailey set her phone down, turned, and was surprised to see that Mia had singlehandedly packed her entire suitcase. "Holy crap, Mia."

Mia shrugged. "You're pretty organized, and we only get two drawers. It wasn't hard."

"It would've been for me. Tying my shoes would be difficult today. Thank goodness I'm wearing sandals." She wiggled her toes. "Will you do me one more favor?"

"Sure, what is it?"

"Would you get Dr. Lopez? I asked him to look through my stuff."

"Hailey, don't go there. It isn't necessary. You didn't take anything."

"We both know that, but I don't think anyone else does. I can't stand having people think I'm a thief. Besides, if anything else goes missing, Dr. Lopez will know for sure it wasn't me." But nothing else would disappear, because Jeremy wouldn't be back to the apartment.

Mia hesitated at the door. "I'm not supposed to leave you alone." She winced. "I'm sorry."

Her life had really come to this. "It's okay. I'll stand in the hall."

"I'm really sorry, Hailey."

"And I'm thankful for all you've done to help me."

Mia left her standing in the hall. Austin's door was open. Hailey stared at his bunk, remembering the nights she'd curled up with him, warm, content, safe in his arms. She would never have that again. Nothing would be the same.

There wouldn't be any more casual movies at Ethan and Sarah's or play dates to the zoo with Kylee. She would never again feel Austin's lips against hers, feel his body pressed to hers. They were truly over. In little more than a month, she'd gained everything, then lost it. Unable to stand the pain, she turned away.

"Hailey, I see you are ready to leave us."

Dr. Lopez's voice snapped her out of her thoughts. She glanced up, met his gaze. "Yes."

Austin stared at the television—had no idea what he was watching. Cars blew up among the spray of machinegun fire; he couldn't have cared less. His eyes were heavy, his head pounding from sheer exhaustion. He hadn't slept in over twenty-four hours. He'd searched frantically for Hailey in two-hour shifts, trading off with Jackson throughout the night.

When Jackson took his turns, Austin sat at the kitchen table, waiting for Hailey, willing her to walk through the door. He'd sipped coffee, filling his system with artificial energy while he replayed their argument. Everything had gone so wrong. He meant to show her the truth, but ended up tossing out ultimatums instead. He regretted it as soon as he did, but when she didn't choose him—wouldn't choose him, was more like it—she'd hurt him in a way he didn't know was possible.

And then, she was gone.

Austin glanced up as Hailey's stiff murmurs trailed down the hall. Her hair was pulled back; her ghostly pale complexion accentuated her devastated honey eyes.

Austin balled his fists in defense, fighting the need to rush up and go to her, to stand by her side. He'd listened to the whispered rumors swirling through the apartments, the unfair accusations. It wasn't hard to see she was holding on by inches. Her pride was all that kept her standing.

When Dr. Lopez had come to him in the wee hours of morning, Austin tried like hell to convince him Hailey wasn't a thief. He'd given him the information necessary to cast suspicion where he knew it belonged, but Dr. Lopez had been unmovable. Although Dr. Lopez hadn't believed Hailey a thief, she had broken her contract with Project Mexico. Rules were rules, and Hailey hadn't followed them.

Her world was falling apart around her, but Austin stayed where he was, glued to his seat in the common room. If he got up, he wouldn't let her go, but nothing would've changed. Jeremy would still be in the background, ruining her life, putting her in danger. Donte wouldn't be far behind. The resentment would always be there—along with the worry—eroding at their foundation. So he stayed on the couch, muscles tense, heart breaking, letting Hailey deal with the decisions she'd made for the life she had chosen.

Brakes squeaked in the driveway; someone honked.

"Hailey, your cab's here," Jackson said. "I'll walk you out."

She nodded.

Mia grabbed her up in a quick hug. "I'm going to miss you, Hailey. I'm going to miss your kindness." She drew away. "We'll find out who took everyone's stuff," she glanced around the room, glaring, "because it certainly wasn't you."

Hailey hugged Mia to her again, kissed her cheek. "Thank you," she whispered, closing her eyes. "Thank you so much for everything."

Austin clenched his jaw, fisted his hands tighter as her voice wavered with tears.

Jen took his hand, covered it with hers, squeezed. He accepted the lifeline, fearful he would crumble himself without something to hold on to.

Hailey opened her eyes, met his, holding, before her gaze landed on Jen's fingers clutching his. Flinching, she looked away, picked up her suitcase, and started for the door.

Jackson wrapped his arm around her waist. Austin tried not to resent his friend for offering the comfort he no longer could—no longer would.

Hailey reached for the knob as two of her team members walked down the hall, whispering, "...about her past. What do you expect from a foster kid? They're all bad news..." Courtney trailed off, her eyes widening in horror as she glanced around the silent room.

Hailey paused mid-step, her fingers tightening on her suitcase before she kept going, never looking back.

Jackson pulled her closer and looked over his shoulder at Courtney, eyes hard as he walked Hailey out the door.

Austin rushed to his feet, simmering with rage. Hailey didn't deserve that. No matter how upset he was, how hurt, he knew she had never ever done anything to deserve that. "That was fucking bullshit, Courtney."

He walked to his room, ignoring Courtney's sputters, as he shut the door and stepped to the window, watching Hailey leave.

Jackson tipped her chin up with his finger and said something. Hailey nodded, gave him a small smile. She hugged him and closed her eyes as Jackson's arms came around her. Hailey held on, clutching at his shirt, her face radiating with pain.

She eased away, walked down the drive to the taxi.

God, this was killing him. She looked so small, so broken, so alone. Austin blew out a breath and rubbed tense fingers over his forehead. He'd wanted to take care of her, was coming to realize he'd intended to ask her to marry him, but he'd broken his promise. He let her down. Now Hailey had to face the world on her own—as she'd done too many times in the past. Jeremy certainly wouldn't stand by her.

But neither was he.

His gaze flew to the window at the realization. He wasn't any better than anyone else who'd left her behind so easily. Austin yanked his door open and rushed down the hall, slamming into Jackson on the outside steps.

The cab turned the corner; it was too late.

"Goddamn. I need to go after her. When does her flight leave?"

"At one. You have two hours, man."

Austin hurried into the house, barely registering everyone standing around the television.

"I can't believe this. Another shooting, and only two blocks away this time."

Austin paused with keys in his hand. "What's going on?"

"There was another shooting. Two families were killed about an hour ago." Mia sniffed. "They had small children."

Dr. Lopez stepped in the room. "Austin, where is Jackson? I need to speak with you both, immediately."

Austin squeezed the keys, warring between his need to go to Hailey and his responsibilities to his job. "Let me get him." If they hurried, he could take care of both.

Jackson stepped inside as Dr. Lopez started down the hall.

"Dr. Lopez needs to see us. I'll be right there." Dashing to the bedroom, Austin picked up his phone and dialed Hailey's number. He swore—her cheery voice was telling him to leave a message.

"Hailey, it's Austin." God, where did he start? He sat on the edge of the bed, searching for the right words. "I really need to talk to you." He heaved out a sigh. "I've made a hell of a mess of things—let you down. I want to fix it, need to fix it. Please call me when you get this." He closed his eyes and rested his forehead in his hand. "I—I love you, Hailey. I love you so much. Please call me." He hung up.

Jackson rapped his knuckles against the door, stuck his head in.

"Come on in."

"You okay?"

"No." Austin pinched the bridge of his nose, trying to relieve the building pressure.

Jackson stepped in the room and closed the door. "She loves you, man. You guys'll work things out."

"I don't know. Why did I show her those fucking videos?" He rubbed his chin, stood up, restless. He bunched his fists, wanting to use them to pummel out his frustration. "I lost my cool...let her down like everyone else."

"You fucked up a little. I bet you can patch it up when we get to L.A. Dr. Lopez just got off the phone with the Dean. They're evacuating us tonight, tomorrow morning at the latest. Everyone's packing. As soon as they find us a flight, we're out of here."

The idea of being back in L.A. was very appealing. He would track Hailey down as soon as they landed. They would sit down and talk everything out. Jeremy would still be a problem, so would Donte, but he had to fix things with Hailey first. "Let's get packed."

Austin put his phone in his pocket, still hoping Hailey would call him back.

CHAPTER 23

AILEY PULLED HER PHONE FROM her purse and glanced at the readout. *Austin.* Her thumb hovered over the "talk" button, trembling. Her heart hurt with each beat. She stared at his grinning face filling her screen as the jumpy rhythm of her ringtone continued. He wore his black ball cap backwards, accentuating the green of his eyes, the white of his straight teeth.

She had taken the picture moments before they suited up for her first official scuba dive. Austin had taken her hand, holding tight as they tipped back into the depthless blue. Unable to stand the memory, she shoved her phone in her bag, ruthlessly ignoring the double beep that told her he'd left a message.

The cab took a right, heading to the airport. Hailey was ready to board her plane and leave her "opportunity of a lifetime" behind. Her six weeks in Mexico had been an experience, one she would never forget, but nothing had ended the way she planned.

Hailey rested her weary head against the window, staring out at the impossible blue of the Caribbean. Miles out, Donte's yacht gleamed in the bright sunshine. Jeremy was there—probably lying, possibly cheating and steeling. Her brother had played her for a fool. Even after Austin's warnings, his pleading, she hadn't wanted to believe the worst in him. But Jeremy's rap sheet spoke for itself. There was no way to misinterpret his long list of criminal activities the way she had the videos Austin showed her. It still hadn't sunk in that Jeremy wasn't the man he pretended to be. She'd watched him do so many wonderful things over the last five weeks, but it was all a lie. Austin had been right, absolutely right, and now he was gone.

Hailey reached for her cell, retrieved Austin's message, hesitated, unable to put the phone to her ear. What if his voice was flat and cold—the way his eyes had been in the living room minutes before?

Stomach churning, head pounding from the pressure of unshed tears, Hailey dropped the phone back in her bag. If she heard his deep voice before she was a little stronger, a little steadier, she was afraid she would crack into a million pieces.

She needed home, Morgan and Sarah, needed to rebuild a life she no longer recognized. In a month's time she'd allowed Austin to become everything. She'd believed in the possibilities, in him wholeheartedly, and as a result had no cushion, no defense against the hurt, nothing left for herself.

Her money was gone, her academic career potentially lost, and the man she loved didn't want her in his life. How would she come back from that? Where did she begin?

Hailey glanced at her watch, pressed her lips firm, and looked over her shoulder at Donte's yacht fading in the distance. "Senor, stop please. We need to turn around. I have to go to the docks."

The driver glanced in the mirror and sighed, muttered something, then made a u-turn. It was time to take a step, a giant leap, and begin the process of moving on, of rebuilding.

The taxi pulled up to the dock. Hailey paid the driver, grabbed her suitcase, started toward the launch. She recognized Desi by the small powerboat, glanced at his machinegun. She swallowed her unease as she remembered Austin's questions about the need for such a weapon.

"Hello, Desi. I was wondering if you could bring me out to Donte."

Desi's brow shot up. All traces of the gentlemen he'd appeared to be the night she had dinner with Donte were gone.

"It's very important," she added.

Desi turned and spoke into his radio in rapid Spanish.

Hailey strained her ears, focusing on his words, only able to pick out a few.

Desi turned back. "Donte will see you. Come." He took her arm, pulled her onto the boat more than helped her. "Your luggage will stay with me."

She nodded. "I won't be staying long in any case. I have a plane to catch."

The motor rumbled to life and they were off. Hailey pressed her sunglasses more firmly against her nose as the warm breeze rushed up to meet her. She closed her eyes and breathed deep, trying her best to relax her shoulders. She would miss this—the speed, the wind in her hair, the tropical air.

Minutes later, Desi eased back on the throttle, slowing the boat. Hailey opened her eyes. They were almost there. It was time to face Jeremy.

The engine rumbled, idling, as they moved closer before Desi cut it altogether. Waves slapped against the sides, kicking up spray, misting Hailey with small drops as the boat coasted to the slip on the yacht. Another guard grabbed the rope thrown to him and tied off.

Desi turned. "Your purse."

She rolled her eyes. "You've seen me with Donte several times. I'm not going to hurt him."

He held out his hand. "Your purse."

With a huff, she handed it over to be searched. Within seconds, her bag was given back. Desi took her arm and shoved her to the platform. Hailey skidded forward and caught herself against the railing.

"Easy there, Desi. That's my sister you're roughing up." Jeremy smiled at her.

She stared at Jeremy, looking her fill at the man who was more a stranger than a brother. He'd entered her life broken and helpless, so precious and sweet when their parents brought him home. Now he was grown and still broken, but no longer helpless, no longer a victim. The man before her was a lie, an insult to the man their parents had wanted him to be.

"I need to talk to you." She glanced at the three guards standing close. "Alone."

His smile disappeared. "Okay." He took her hand.

She pulled hers free. "Don't. Just don't." She couldn't stand him touching her.

Heat flashed in his eyes as he nodded. "After you," he gestured grandly, sarcastically, to the upper deck.

Anger built with each step Hailey took as she thought of what she'd lost, of what she still might lose because she'd welcomed him back in her life. When her foot met polished wood, she whirled. "How could you? How could you, Jeremy?"

He crossed his arms. "How could I what?"

She laughed without humor as she stepped back from him. "Where do I start? Lying, stealing, the *extensive* criminal record you failed to mention. And worst of all..." She caught herself before she blurted out her knowledge of his connection with the Zulas. Something told her that her life depended on staying quiet. She shook her head instead.

"Worst of all, what, Hailey? *What?*" He advanced on her.

Shaking her head again, she backed away. "Nothing." Hailey glanced over her shoulder and briefly studied the guards, their machine guns, the ornate 'ZU' tattoos on their necks. She looked back at Jeremy to meet his cold stare. What had she been thinking coming here on her own? "Just forget it. I should go." She moved toward the steps, but Jeremy grabbed her. She cried out from the bite of his fingers against her skin.

"No. You came out here with things to say, so say them."

"You're hurting me," she said between her teeth, more frightened than she wanted to let on. "Let *go*." She yanked free and saw bruises already forming.

Jeremy stared at her arm, brushed his fingers through his hair. "Sorry. I'm sorry. You know I have a temper."

"Save it." She backed up another step. "There's always an excuse for your actions, even when they hurt other people."

"It must be hard being so damn perfect."

"I'm not perfect, but I'm not a liar either."

"Neither am I."

Hailey yanked a paper from her pocket, unfolded it, shoved the page at him. "Let's start with this. You told me you had a brush with the law over some underage drinking and a bag of pot. I guess you kinda forgot to tell me about the rest." She pressed her fingers against the throb in her forehead. "Prison. You've been to prison. Twice. *Twice*, Jeremy."

He shredded the paper, let the wind catch and carry the pieces away. "So what? I did my time. I've changed. You see the work I've been doing with Donte."

More lies. "No." She pointed her finger. "Don't insult me this way. I've been asked to leave Project Mexico because of what you did."

"What—"

"Shut up." She couldn't stand any more deception. Any lingering fear of her brother vanished. "Shut up until I finish. I foolishly thought you came to visit me this week because we were finally getting somewhere. I thought we were regaining some sort of connection, but that wasn't it. That wasn't it at all. You used me to steal from the people I lived with, the people I considered my friends."

He glared, his voice growing quiet. "I didn't steal from anyone."

She kept going, full steam ahead, ignoring his denial. "I'm on the verge of losing everything. *Everything.* Do you get that?" She pushed him back a step. "Austin's gone. You took every dime I have—had," she corrected. "I very well may lose all of my college credits because they think I'm a thief."

Jeremy shook his head as he looked to the sky, smiled. "You're unbelievable. I'm not doing this with you, Hailey." He turned and started walking away.

She followed. "You're right. You're not. I'm finished. I'm finished with you. You've used me for the last time." Despite everything, it still hurt to say it. Flashes of the small boy gripping her hand in the hospital played through her mind.

He stopped, pivoted around. "Walking away again?"

"Yes. But this time I'm leaving because it's *my* choice. It wasn't before. You don't get to do this to me anymore— lie, steal, manipulate. I love you, but I've had enough— more than enough."

"You don't love me," he smirked. "You love some figment of your imagination—the person you wanted me to be."

"No, I loved who I knew you *could* be. We all have choices to make. You made yours, now I'm making mine."

"Spare me your sanctimonious bullshit, saintly sister." Shaking his head, he turned and climbed the stairs to the third deck, never looking back.

Her eyes filled as she looked at her brother for the last time. She grabbed the railing, ready to leave.

"Hailey, what a wonderful surprise." Donte stepped from the dining room she'd eaten in a month before.

"Donte." She sniffed, blinking back tears as she smiled cautiously, remembering what Austin had told her. Somewhere beneath the handsome, classy exterior lived a brutal monster. She took a step toward the stairs. "I was just leaving. I have a flight to catch."

"A flight?" He tipped her face to his, concern bright in his eyes. "What do you mean, Hailey?"

She gripped her purse and willed Donte to drop his hand. His touch made her skin crawl. "I'm going back to L.A."

"But Project Mexico has just begun."

"I know. It didn't work out."

He held her a moment longer before he let go. She glanced at her watch, more than ready to be on the boat back to the dock. "I hate to be abrupt, but I really have to go. My plane leaves in half an hour." She would be lucky if she made it.

Donte's brows drew together as he stared into her eyes. "You are troubled, my beautiful friend."

"No," she said too sharply, and his frown deepened. "I'm sorry." She shook her head. "I'm just tired and ready to be home."

"I have something for you before you go. I know you're in a hurry, but would you be so kind as to wait? It will only take a moment."

Why wouldn't he let her leave? She looked down at the small powerboat, then at Donte. "Okay."

"Just one moment," he said as he held up a finger, smiled, and dashed away.

As Donte hurried off, Hailey turned, let out a shuddering breath, and braced her trembling hands on the glossy rail. She had to get out of here. A rush of panic consumed her with her need to be gone.

The buildings of San Miguel were so far away. She wanted to be there, waiting for her plane among the hustle of tourists. It was tempting to rush down the steps and demand Desi take her back, but she doubted he would leave until Donte gave him the okay.

Hailey took a deep breath, growing impatient as one minute turned to two, then three. Where was he? She stepped into the dining area. "Don—" she stopped abruptly when she heard a woman's muffled cries and a man shouting through the door.

Hailey took a step back, inching toward the deck. She heard the unmistakable sound of a slap. The man's voice grew angrier as the woman cried harder. Hailey rushed forward and pressed her ear to the door, listening as the sobbing grew faint. Biting her lip, she turned the doorknob slowly, quietly, peaking down the long hall.

Hailey gasped and stumbled back. She saw one of the missing girls disappear around the corner with... "Mateo," she whooshed out on a quivering whisper. "Oh God. Oh my God." She hadn't recognized his voice. He'd sounded so callous, so cruel. She inched away, terrified he would see her. She needed to get to shore, needed to get help.

When she was far enough from the door, she whirled, hurrying to the deck, all but slamming into Donte. "Oh." Her hand flew to her mouth, stifling a scream. "You scared me."

Donte took her arms. "Hailey, you look as if you've seen a ghost. You're shaking. What's wrong?"

"Nothing. Nothing." She tried to steady her breathing. "I just need to be on my way. I'm going to miss my plane."

"We can get you another flight, my love. I want you to meet my father. He was delighted when I told him you stopped by. He'll be just one more minute."

Donte touched her again, and she struggled not to cringe and yank away. Each gentle stroke of his finger felt like a snake slithering across her skin. Fear clawed at her until she was certain she would start screaming and not be able to stop. "I'm not feeling well. I need to go, Donte." She gave a gentle tug, attempting to free herself. "I really need to go," she repeated. "Perhaps I can meet your father another time."

His jaw tensed, his eyes challenged. "Will you have lunch with me when I travel to L.A.? I'll be in the area next week."

Not on your life, she thought, but she would say whatever he wanted to hear. "Yes. Yes, I would love to." She yearned to untangle herself, to run down the stairs, but that wouldn't get her off the yacht. This was a power struggle. She'd more or less told him 'no.' It was becoming clear no one told Donte Rodriguez 'no.'

"Let me walk you to the boat."

"Thank you," she said almost desperately as they started down. Hailey's legs trembled with each weighty step. She was almost there.

"Until next week then." He kissed her cheek when they stopped by the launch.

She gave him a small smile as he stared at her. If she didn't find a way to calm down, he was going to figure out she knew something. She struggled to focus on their conversation, on the need to play it out. "Until next week. If your father is still visiting, I would love to have lunch with him as well."

Donte smiled, relaxed. "I think that can be arranged."

"Good. Good."

He took her hand, kissed her knuckles as she stepped on the small watercraft. She struggled with her need to weep with relief as he released her and she took her seat. It was over, finally over. She was free.

"Desi will accompany you to the airport and help you with your bag. He'll stay with you until you board your flight."

There was nothing she wanted less. She wouldn't have time to get help. "Oh, no. That isn't necessary, Donte. I'll be fine."

"It will make me feel better to know you arrived safely. Beautiful women shouldn't travel alone."

Another power struggle. "Thank you."

Desi jumped on the speedboat, his massive weight rocking it slightly. He spared her a glance as he turned over the engine and reversed from the launch. The boat powered forward, picking up speed.

Hailey looked over her shoulder, gave Donte a half-hearted wave. She glanced up as a movement caught her eye on the top deck. Jeremy leaned on the rail, staring down. Hailey dropped her hand and turned away from her brother.

She made it. Hailey sagged against her seat, weak with relief. Closing her eyes, she breathed deep, steadying herself. She needed to think. Lives depended on it. If Donte had one girl, she was sure he had all four.

Hailey pulled her phone from her bag.

Desi turned. "No phones," he demanded.

She gripped her cell and stared at his unyielding face. "Oh, I'm not calling anyone. I'm just checking to see if my flight's on time."

"No phones," Desi snapped again. He took his hand from the wheel as if he was coming to her seat.

"Okay." She shoved her cell in her purse and held up her hands. "Okay, sorry." If he took it, she would lose precious time. Hailey couldn't shake the sense of urgency as she thought of the girl crying, of the sound of a huge hand cracking against her young, pretty face. They needed help, and they needed it now. She wouldn't have time to sneak off to the bathroom and call if she wanted to make her flight. The police weren't an option.

Several recent news reports on the island had suggested corruption—and at least one reporter had ended up dead.

She couldn't make a call now, but she might be able to pull off a text. Hailey trained her eyes forward, sneaking her hand in her purse. Her first instinct was to try Austin, but what if he ignored her message? Instead, she risked scrolling through her contact list until she found Jackson's number.

Desi turned and Hailey pretended to rummage through her purse. Thinking fast, she pulled out a stick of gum, unwrapped it, and popped it in her mouth. Cold sweat beaded on her skin as he stared at her for what felt like a lifetime. When Desi finally faced the horizon, Hailey let go of the breath she'd been holding and tried again.

She tipped the phone away from the glare of bright sunshine, saw Jackson's information still displayed and slowly, carefully typed out the message: *D yacht. 4 kidnapped. HELP.*

Desi whirled. "What are you doing?"

Startled, she gasped. "Nothing."

Desi let go of the steering wheel and the boat jerked. Her purse went flying. Hailey stared in horror at the phone clutched in her hands.

Desi rushed toward her. "Give me that."

Hailey pressed send as she got to her feet. She glanced around, instinct urging her to flee, but there was no place to go. Out of options, she stumbled forward and dropped her phone in the sea.

Desi grabbed her arm as she watched her only tie to the outside world sink beneath the water. "You stupid little bitch. What are you up to?"

"Nothing. You scared me. I tripped." She prayed her message went through. Getting rid of her phone was the only way. If Desi had read what she typed, she was certain he would've killed her right then and there. At least now she had a chance.

"I don't believe you. Sit down." He shoved her with such force she had to grab hold of the seat or fall out of the boat. "We're going back. Donte can deal with you."

"I'll miss my flight," she argued, but it would do no good. She stared at the island as the boat zipped in a fast circle. The shore grew more distant by the second.

Her only chance was Jackson—and Austin, she hoped. And herself. Through sheer terror, Hailey reminded herself she was on her—for now. If she could convince Donte that Desi had misunderstood, she might live to see another day. In the meantime, she could do nothing but wait.

❧

Austin waited impatiently for the eleven remaining members of Project Mexico to gather their luggage and head for the sliding doors of the airport. Luck had been on their side when Dr. Lopez rushed into the main house, telling everyone they had ten minutes to finish packing for their three o'clock flight.

Twenty-five minutes later, they finally arrived at Cozumel International. If everyone would hurry the hell up, he might be able to catch Hailey, but it was doubtful. Her plane was due to take off in ten minutes. She was probably already sitting in her seat, buckled and ready to go.

He huffed out a frustrated breath. It was better this way. They had a lot to talk about, and it wasn't going to happen in ten minutes or less.

As soon as he set foot in L.A., they were hashing this out come hell or high water. If he knew Hailey—and he did—she would be with Sarah and Morgan. In nine hours, he would pull through Ethan and Sarah's gate, grab hold of Hailey, and never let go.

Austin turned, tensing, as an argument broke out by the airport entrance. One panhandler accused another of stealing from his collection, following his accusation up with a fist to the face.

Weary murmurs spread among the nervous Project Mexico participants as the last bag was tossed from the roof of the van.

"It's okay, guys. Get your stuff. Let's go inside." Austin nodded to Jackson at the back of the line, picked up his own suitcase, rubbed at his aching neck with his free hand. He couldn't shake the tension settled there.

Something wasn't right. Scanning their surroundings, Austin searched for the source of unease, but everything appeared status quo: tourists rushed in and out of the airport, cabs picked up and dropped off their passengers. He looked over his shoulder. The sooner they were in the air, the better.

The skirmish settled down as the group passed into the building. Austin glanced at the sketchy characters with their cardboard signs and plastic cups and could only be thankful Hailey's plane was leaving first. His responsibility was to the university, but there was no way in hell he would've left Mexico before he was sure Hailey had gotten out.

With everyone safely inside and heading to check their luggage, Austin pulled his phone from his pocket, making certain it was holding its charge. He'd left Hailey a message almost two hours ago; surely she'd gotten it. Despite their angry words, he thought she would've called.

Fear began to claw his belly. Was he too late? Had he broken her trust beyond repair? There was so much between them—too much to walk away from.

Austin dialed the first three digits of Hailey's number, then stopped. Harassment wouldn't win her back.

Consumed by helpless frustration, Austin shoved his phone in his pocket. The nine-hour waiting game would drive him crazy. He picked up his suitcase and started toward the check-in line.

"Casey, you need to see this."

Austin stopped, alerted by the sharp tone of Jackson's voice. "What is it?"

Jackson held out his phone.

Austin ripped the cell from his hand as he read Hailey's message. *D yact. 4 kidnapped. HELP.* Goosebumps puckered his skin as ice cold fear rushed through his heart. "She sent this five minutes ago."

"I know. I felt it vibrate on our way inside. I just got around to checking it. I tried to text her back, but I didn't get an answer."

Austin glanced at the flight screen, confused. The monitor flashed "flight closed." He hurried to the window, and watched the Air America plane back up from the jetway. "What the hell is going on?"

"Hell if I know."

Austin's fingers flew over the keys as he tried to text Hailey again. *EXPLAIN??? CALL OR TEXT NOW!!* Seconds ticked by as Austin stared in agony. His pulse throbbed in his throat as one minute turned to two. It felt as if he waited a lifetime. "Something's wrong, man. Something's wrong."

"Hailey's obviously trying to tell us Donte has the girls on the yacht, but how the hell does she know?"

Austin said what he knew in his heart. "She's not on the plane. Donte has her." He passed a look over the Project Mexico participants standing around, waiting. "You have to take them back. I'm staying here. I'll go talk to the woman at the kiosk. Maybe she'll tell us if Hailey boarded her flight." Austin shoved Jackson's phone in his front pocket and hurried to the line, cutting past angry

331

tourists as he made his way to the Air America counter.

"Hey, where the hell do you think you're going, pal?"

Austin spared the balding jerk in the tacky orange Bermuda top a glance as he passed him by.

"Yo, asshole, I'm talking to you. Get in line."

Austin whirled, walked back to the dick with the big mouth, and grabbed him by the collar. The man's wife gasped as her eyes popped wide. "You listen to *me*, asshole," Austin said between clenched teeth, letting his fear and anger spew. "My girlfriend is *missing*. So what you're gonna do is shut your mouth and let me find out what the fuck is going on." He yanked the guy higher. "Are we good now?"

The man sputtered as he tried to peal Austin's fingers from his clothes. "I'm having you arrested."

"Yeah? Go ahead and try." Austin removed his hands, trying to find his calm through waves of helpless terror. He was wasting time. When he turned, everyone stepped back, letting him pass.

The woman at the front desk eyed him wearily. "Good afternoon. What can I do for you, sir?"

"My friend—client," he corrected quickly, "was supposed to board flight 5525 to Los Angeles. I'm hoping you can confirm that for me." Austin opened his wallet, flashed his badge. He knew it didn't mean jack shit, but that didn't mean this woman did.

"I need to get my supervisor. Hold on please."

"Can't you just call up the flight list and tell me whether or not Hailey Roberts boarded the plane?"

Her mouth tightened with impatience. "I'm sorry, sir, not without my supervisor's permission. I'll just be a minute."

Austin drummed his fingers on the countertop as he watched the second hand spin around the clock face. He was losing precious minutes. Hailey was more than likely on a boat with the leader of one of the world's most brutal cartels. Somehow, she'd stumbled on the four missing teens.

Donte wouldn't treat her the way he had the night he wined and dined her. Had they killed her already, or were they enjoying her the way he knew they were enjoying the girls? It was too much to think about. Austin's stomach pitched as he continued his torturous wait.

He heaved out a sigh as a man in a suit walked to the counter. "Sir, can I help you?"

"Yes." Austin flashed his badge again. "My client was supposed to board flight 5525 to Los Angeles. I'm hoping you can confirm she made it to her plane."

"May I see your badge again, sir?"

Austin clenched his jaw as he dug his wallet back out. He wasn't going to get very far with this guy. He handed over his identification.

"You're a bodyguard?"

"That's right. Hailey Roberts, one of your passengers, is my client. It's imperative I know her whereabouts. I believe she's in danger."

The man shook his head. "I'm sorry," he glanced at the ID, "Mr. Casey, but we're legally obligated to keep all of our passenger's information private."

Austin struggled to hold on to his patience as the supervisor refused him with a sunny smile. "I understand, but as I said, I believe she's in extreme danger."

"As much as I would like to help, I'm afraid I can't."

"Well, thanks for nothing." He yanked his wallet out of the manager's hand and walked off. It was time to call Ethan. He dialed and waited as it rang twice.

"On your way home?"

"Not yet. I need you to do something."

"What's wrong?"

"I think Donte has Hailey. I want you to check if she

got on her plane."

"Give me a couple minutes." Ethan tapped away at his computer. "Damn firewall," he muttered.

As he heard Ethan's fingers flying over the keys, Austin heart pounded, his fist clenched. Answers were moments away; the wait was utter agony.

"Okay, I'm in. Let's see. Flight 5525, non-stop to L.A. There's record Sarah bought Hailey her ticket."

"Sarah? Why did Sarah buy Hailey's ticket?"

"Jeremy cleaned her out—maxed out her credit card, overdrew her checking, wiped out her savings. Took every damn dime. She called here a couple hours ago. Sarah said Hailey was as upset as she'd ever heard her."

"Goddamn." Austin struggled to keep his fist from connecting with the concrete wall as another layer of helpless anger piled on top of the rest.

"I'm into the next screen. Shit. Shit, man. Hailey never boarded the flight."

Austin pressed trembling fingers to his temple. "Donte has her on the yacht. I want to get her now, storm right out there and get her, but I know I can't. I need your help. Hunter's too."

"Let me charter a jet. Hopefully Collin's friend will let us use his plane. We'll be in the air in forty-five, tops." He tapped computer keys again. "I'm sending out an all call to Hunter, Collin, and Tucker Campbell too."

"I don't care who you bring. Just get here." He pressed the side of his fist to the wall, rested his weary head against it. "I love her, Ethan. I won't be able to stand it if we're too late."

"We won't be. Go keep an eye on the yacht. We'll be there in seven hours, and we'll arrive with a plan. I'll call you before we land."

"Okay." Austin tried to hold on to hope. "Hailey texted Jackson. Donte has the girls too. Looks like we're doing a five-person extraction. We have to end this."

"I know. I'll take care of everything. Let me go so I can get there."

"Hurry." Austin hung up and walked to the sliding doors.

"Casey, wait up," Jackson called, jogging to him.

Austin stopped. "What are you doing? You need to take the group back to L.A."

"They board in an hour. They're grown adults scared enough by the violence they've seen to stay where I told them and get their asses on the plane. Jen said she'd call me when everyone's on board. I'm not leaving you here to deal with this yourself."

How could he express his gratitude? "Thank you." Austin held out his hand.

Jackson took it and shook. "You're welcome. Now, let's get out of here and go get your girl back."

Austin nodded as they stepped outside. It was time to start their surveillance. This was what he'd spent years doing as a SEAL. He was about to use his training to save the most important person in his life.

CHAPTER 24

DESI PULLED BACK ON THE throttle and cut the engine. Hailey's stomach lurched with the up and down motion of the boat as it drifted to the yacht's launch again. Desi glanced over his shoulder, eyes narrowed, as he picked up his radio and spoke into it. The head of Donte's security team descended the stairs as the speedboat was tied off.

"Ms. Roberts, you're back so soon."

"I didn't have much of a choice," she said cooly as she eyed the Sleek One. "Clearly, there's been a misunderstanding."

Desi fired off in heated Spanish as the head of security nodded, staring at Hailey. She tried not to shrink under his impenetrable gaze. Instead, she lifted her chin, determined to play this out despite the way her heart thundered in her chest. It would be a miracle if she survived the day. She would do her damndest to increase the odds.

"You should come with me," the Sleek One said.

Hailey stayed where she was, swallowing her terror. "I have to get back to the island. I missed my flight. I need to make arrangements for a new one."

"Now, Ms. Roberts."

Sighing, she stood up, trying to hide the trembling in her legs. "I don't think Donte will be pleased."

"I imagine you're right." His eyes glittered as his voice cooled.

Her knees buckled with her first step. Hailey grasped the plush seat as she made her way to the front of the boat. "Donte has always treated me with such kindness, such respect. I don't understand what's going on."

"Respect is earned through loyalty. Right now, I question yours." The Sleek One nodded at Desi.

Desi grabbed hold of Hailey's tender arm, squeezing the bruises Jeremy had left not long ago. She gasped from the pain as Desi lifted her from the boat and shoved her, hard.

She lost her footing, skidded on the black tread, and went down with a thud on hands and knees. The burn of hot pumice scorched her skin.

"Get up," Desi said between his teeth as he yanked her up by the elbow.

Hailey stared at her hands, down at her knees, wincing, as the gouges throbbed with each heartbeat. Blood oozed down her legs, dripped from her palms.

"She bleeds well." Rio, the guard with mean brown eyes, stepped forward, grinning with madness. "I spotted a fin. Perhaps we will feed her to the sharks."

Rio pulled Hailey to the edge of the boat and jerked her arm over the water, squeezing the wound on her hand until bones popped. Whimpering from the radiating pain, she watched drops of blood disappear into dark waves. Rio held her tight as he knelt down, splashed his fingers in the water. "I think this is how you shall die today, little bitch," he laughed.

Few things terrified Hailey more than sharks. She fought to keep quiet against her need to cry out and beg.

Moments later, the fin Rio must've seen glided their way. Rio all but fell off the boat with his mirth as he splashed harder. "I will enjoy this. I really will."

He stood as the shark swam closer, until Hailey stared at beady black eyes. She tried to scurry back in her panic, but Rio held her firm, yanking her arm out again, squeezing. Pain no longer registered over the bright hot terror coursing through her veins. Her breath came in gasps until she grew dizzy with hyperventilation.

Rio lifted her then, holding her over the water as another fin joined the first, swimming close. Hailey screamed, clasping his wrists, struggling to hang on to the burly man. "Please! Please stop!"

Rio stooped, dipping Hailey low, sending her legs knee deep. The shark charged forward. She slammed her eyes shut, waiting for the unspeakable pain of being ripped to pieces. Her stomach twisted when Rio pulled her up quickly, laughing hysterically as the massive fish crashed headfirst into the yacht.

"That's enough, Rio," the Sleek One said. "You've had your fun. Take her to Donte's office." He turned and climbed the stairs.

Pride forgotten, Hailey dropped to her knees on a keening sob. She trembled, from pain, from fear, until she was sure her bones would break.

Rio chuckled as he grabbed her arm again, wrenching her to her feet. Gasping, she collapsed to the deck, her legs too weak to hold her.

"Get up, little bitch." He yanked her up, bringing her elbow back with such force that she yelped. Hailey staggered forward as Rio pushed her to a flight of stairs leading below deck.

She tried to stop. "Please, I need a moment to catch my breath."

Rio clutched her tighter. She whimpered as her arm began to tingle.

A slow smile spread across his face. "Stop again and I'll break it in half." He twisted his wrist, wrenching her elbow until she cried out.

Blinking back tears, Hailey refused to cry anymore. She averted her gaze from Rio's cruel eyes and stared ahead, waiting to be brought to Donte.

Rio dragged her down the steps and through an elegant hallway. The wood paneled walls gleamed with polish; her sandals sank deep in plush carpet. She glanced behind her and closed her eyes, wincing as she stared at her bloody footprints staining the creamy white. Would they punish her for that?

Rio stopped at a door, opened it, and sent her flying with another harsh shove before he shut her in. She heard a lock click into place.

Hailey took in the masculine space—the maroon leather couches and office chair, a glossy solid oak desk, state of the art office equipment. Her gaze paused on the telephone.

She flicked a glance over her shoulder, moistened her dry lips with a swipe of tongue, and moved forward. She needed to try Jackson again. Her hand shook as she grabbed the receiver and she pressed in his number. The line connected and rang. Her breath streamed in and rushed out.

"Hello."

"Austin?" Her voice broke at the sound of his.

"Hailey, thank God."

"I—I need help," she struggled to talk through the tears strangling her throat.

"I know. Where are—"

The lock on the door turned. Hailey dropped the handset back with a clatter as she hurried away from the desk, leaving a trail of blood as she went. It was too late to do anything about—Donte had stepped inside.

She wiped her cheeks, drying her tears, and took a deep breath, trying to keep herself from sobbing. Hearing Austin's voice undid what little grip she had on her composure.

"Hailey. You're back, I see." He gave her a guarded smile.

"Yes." She closed her eyes, trying desperately to push

Austin from her mind. He knew she was in trouble. She needed to do her part and survive long enough for him to come get her. "Yes, I'm back. I'm not sure why."

"Desi said you used your phone after he asked you not to."

She nodded. It was better to give him the truth or most of it. "I was checking my flight information."

He moved further into the room. "But he asked you to put your phone away. You could have waited until you reached shore."

She nodded again. "I know, but I'm so eager to go home." She shuddered out a breath on the verge of tears. God, she wanted to go home.

Donte walked forward, stopped in front of her. "You are very upset."

Give him the truth, she reminded herself. "I am." A tear escaped. Before she could wipe it away, Donte caught it on his thumb.

"You are too beautiful to be upset."

"Rio's crazy," she blurted out. "He was going to feed me to the sharks."

Donte stared until she struggled not to squirm. "Come sit down. Let's clean you up." He held her elbow, leading her to one of the plush leather chairs facing his desk.

She relaxed a fraction when he crouched down and frowned at her raw, bloody knees.

"This looks very painful."

She gave him a small smile. "It stings."

"Did Rio also do this?"

"Desi shoved me."

"He has been too rough. Especially over a simple misunderstanding." Donte skimmed his finger down her calf, following the dried trail a bloody drop had taken. He opened her palms, pressed his lips above her wounds.

She took his hand and clutched it. "Thank you for

your kindness, Donte."

"It is easy to be kind to an angel." He tucked a piece of hair behind her ear, moved forward, and brushed his mouth against her cheek.

Hailey closed her eyes, fighting the urge to move away. He might let her go if she didn't resist.

Donte eased back. "Let's get your wounds bandaged."

She smiled. "I would like that. Will I be able to go to the airport after?" She held her breath, afraid she'd pushed too far.

He stared at her. "I will take you to shore personally."

She hugged him in her relief and let out a watery laugh. "I can't tell you how much I appreciate this. I can't wait to be back in L.A."

"I'm sorry you are so happy to leave me here in Mexico."

It wasn't hard to play the part of the grateful victim. "Only for a little while." She hugged him again. "We're having lunch next week with your father."

He took her hand and kissed her knuckles. She winced as the movement opened the wound on her palm. Blood pooled, then dripped. Donte turned to the desk. Hailey's heart thudded as she watched his eyes trail over the drops of blood. She spotted the box of tissue behind a large plant. "I—I was going to help myself to a tissue. I was making a mess on your carpet."

He stared a moment longer before he turned to face her again. "I think we can do better than a tissue." He stood as his phone rang. "Let me get this, then we will take you to the kitchen. Maria will clean your scrapes and bandage you up before we go."

"Okay." She got to her feet as Donte walked around his desk and answered the phone. He spoke in Spanish while Hailey wandered to the large porthole window. She stared out at the cloudless sky, the blue water, the island she would set her feet on again very soon—hopefully.

Her mind wandered to Austin, to the sound of his voice on the phone just minutes before. She would call him when she was safely at the airport. That would probably be the last time they would speak—except for the awkward conversations they were bound to have at Ethan's company barbeques or other times when they were forced to interact. They should've thought of that before they dived into something that was never meant to last. Thanksgivings and New Years Eve, birthday parties and weekend getaways were forever going to be uncomfortable—and painful—now that they had made such a mess of things.

Hailey realized the room had gone silent. Donte no longer spoke on the phone. She turned, took a step back as he stared, his eyes hard and dangerous.

Something happened; something had changed. She sent him a smile. "I didn't hear you hang up." She cleared her throat, attempting to vanish the nerves from her voice. "I was lost in my thoughts." Her skin crawled with icy fear when he said nothing, his heated gaze trained on her. "Donte—"

"I just received a very interesting report, Hailey."

"Oh?" She fiddled with her fingers, but stopped when he followed her movements.

Donte stood. "One of my most trusted men just informed me that Austin Casey and Jackson Matthews chose not to board their flight with the Project Mexico group."

She frowned. "Project Mexico? I thought they were leaving next week."

He grinned, but his eyes remained cold. "You are very good, Hailey. Very good."

She shook her head, unable to speak.

Donte took a step closer. "Why do you think Mr. Casey and Mr. Matthews never boarded their flight?"

"I—I don't know." But it was clear Donte did. She

inched closer to the window.

"Oh, I think you do. I very much believe you do."

"Donte—"

He rushed forward and slapped her.

Hailey fell back, the pain a shock against her cheek.

"You betrayed me, Hailey. Made a fool of me." Donte advanced again. She saw stars as he pulled her up by her ponytail, cringed as he held up his hand. "Look! Look at my palm. It is covered with blood. *Your* blood. Do you know why, Hailey?" He yanked back on her hair until she gasped, until she met his angry stare. "Do you know *why*?" he said between clenched teeth.

Terror clogged her brain as she sucked in a rush of air. Was it better to answer or keep quiet? "I—"

"Shut up. I will talk, and you will listen." He jerked her forward. "Because you used my phone." He let her go, chuckled without humor as he shook his head. "Reaching for a tissue. You lied to me. Not once, but several times. First, you make a call from the speedboat and tell me you were checking your flight information; then, you call from my yacht and tell me you needed to clean up your wounds."

"No—"

He squeezed her lower jaw until she was sure he would break her bone. "Shut *up* I said."

Tears trailed down her cheeks as she trembled.

"It does you no good to deny your deceit. I *know* you placed a call to Mr. Matthew's phone right here from this very yacht." Donte struck her again, stinging her tender cheek. "Right here from this room. From this phone. My phones are monitored, Hailey. Your bloody hand and fingerprints don't lie as your mouth does." He smeared his wet palm over her throbbing cheek, pressing hard against her wound. "You are sloppy, Hailey. Sloppy and stupid. For that alone, you will die. Because you lied, because you're a traitor, you will die painfully."

She slammed her eyes shut as the first pitiful sob escaped her throat. Donte dragged her to his desk. Hailey watched as he pulled a long knife from his top drawer.

Oh, God, it was over. It was over. As she stood waiting for the plunge of blade, she thought of Austin. Only Austin.

Donte raised his hand, and she closed her eyes. Her breath tore in her throat until Donte laughed. "Do you think it will be that easy?"

She opened her eyes as he cut at the fabric of her tank top, at the strap of her bra. She struggled against him. "Please, no."

"Oh, yes. Yes indeed, Hailey. I planned to do this all along. Kinder of course, gentler when I thought you were someone else. But now I'll use you as you've used me. Be still."

She struggled.

"Be *still.*" He brought the blade to her throat.

Because she had no choice, she did as she was told.

Donte set the knife on the desk. "I've wondered what you look like, what you feel like, what you taste like. Today I will finally find out." He skimmed his finger along her collarbone, pulled at the tattered strap of her bra until her breast tumbled free. He smiled. "You are indeed beautiful." He brushed his palm over naked skin, against her nipple.

She clenched her fist, wanting to scratch at his face, wanting to grab the knife and plunge the blade into his heart.

"You can try, Hailey. You can try to take that knife, but it will be the last move you ever make. If you satisfy me, I might keep you around until I get tired of you."

"I would rather die."

He pinched her nipple between his fingers. "Oh, you'll

die all right, but not until I've had all I want from you."
Donte pressed his lips to hers.

Hailey refused to respond.

Donte's teeth sunk into her lip, until she was sure he
would bite it off. The bright, sharp pain and metallic taste
of her own blood pitched her stomach, and she vomited.
Hailey stared in horror as yellow bile mixed with blood,
staining the pristine white of Donte's shirt.

"You little bitch." He shoved her back.

Hailey's head connected with the corner of the
heavy leather chair. Her vision dimmed, going gray, as
Donte leaned forward and cracked his fist against her
cheekbone. "We're not finished here. We'll pick up where
we left off when I can stand the sight of you. Rio, get in
here. Get her out of my face."

Rio burst through the door and yanked her up as he'd
done several times before. He dragged her down the hall,
opened another door, pushed her through, shut it, and
twisted the lock.

Hailey lay on the floor, hurt, trembling, terrified, but
grateful to be alive. She stared at the door, attempting
to plot her next move, but she couldn't think. Her brain
was fuzzy. Somewhere, in the back of her mind, she knew
shock was setting in.

She closed her eyes, desperate to get a grip on her
scattered thoughts. Sheer exhaustion took her under
before she could take her next breath.

Hailey blinked, sucking in a breath against the pain.
She pressed her fingers to the throbbing in her temple, to
her tender cheek. *Where am I?* She sat up quickly, closed
her eyes, fighting a rush of dizzying nausea. Slowly, she
opened them again and scanned the room, taking in the

elegant periwinkle curtains draping large windows, the beautiful dark wood of the bedroom furnishings, the plush bed she hadn't had the energy to crawl to.

Hailey rolled to all fours, instantly regretting it. The raw wounds on her hands and knees stung with the pressure of her weight. As quickly as she dared, she eased herself up on watery legs and gasped.

Four girls—the teens from the missing posters, huddled in a corner. Huge haunted brown eyes stared at her. Long, tangled black hair hung against stained shirts. Purple welts and bruises marred their beautiful olive skin.

Compassion flooded Hailey as she took a step closer and all four flinched. "Um, hello." She shook her head, had to clutch at the bed as the movement made her woozy. "*Hola. Me llamo* Hailey," she continued in poor Spanish. "I want to help you."

One of the girls started to cry.

Hailey stepped closer. "It's okay. Everything will be all right." She struggled to make sentences from the handful of phrases she'd used on a daily basis with Project Mexico. Another girl began to sniffle. Hailey crouched in front of them, making her knees sting. "Help is coming. We must stay strong and quiet."

"Who will come?" one of them asked, trembling.

"My friends. One was a policeman, the other a..." she didn't know the word, so she saluted like a soldier.

"When?"

"I don't know, but soon. They told me before Donte hurt me."

The girls all shrunk when she said Donte's name.

Hailey got to her feet, wincing as her body ached. She wandered to the window, stared out at the island—a sight that must've been pure torture for the girls. Home was so close, but so far away.

She had to believe Austin and Jackson were out there,

coming up with a plan to rescue her. Had she been clear enough in her text? Did they know Donte held her on the yacht? Were they looking at the massive boat right now? She studied the horizon, the light fading as night swallowed day. How long would Donte wait before he wanted her? Would he kill her after he finished raping her? She glanced at the island again, hoping Austin and Jackson could *feel* where she was being kept. There had to be something she could do. She couldn't cower in the corner and wait to die.

Hailey glanced around the room, searching for a solution. What could she do to save her own life and the lives of the terrified girls behind her? Her gaze stopped on the light switch as she remembered a movie she'd watched one night in Ethan's game room. Austin had been there too, sitting on the opposite side of the couch, so far from her reach, but not nearly as far as he was right now.

Hailey turned to the girls. "Does the guard come in here?" She gestured to the shadow of feet under the door.

"Not unless he wants to have us."

Hailey nodded. "Can you bathe? Are there towels in the bathroom?"

"Yes, they let us shower. Sometimes they watch," the smallest girl said, sniffling.

Hailey dashed to the bathroom and stared at the dirty disorder as she grabbed a filthy towel. She brought it to the bed, rolled it, and walked quietly to the door.

"What are you doing?" One of the girls rushed to her feet. "He will kill us if he thinks we are trying to escape."

"What is your name?" Hailey asked.

"Angelica."

"Angelica, I'm trying to help us. I want to make it easier for my friends to find us."

Angelica hesitated before she nodded and stepped back.

Hailey carefully moved closer to the door, crouched

down, and laid the towel against the wood, covering the crack.

She hustled to the window again, peered left and right, checking for an armed guard on the deck below. No one was there. Cold sweat dripped down her back as she hurried to the light switch. With trembling fingers she flicked the lever off and on, differentiating her pattern, hoping to draw attention to anyone who might be watching from shore. They were miles out, but it was worth a shot in the fading light.

Hailey continued for several minutes, until Angelica's twin burst into tears. "Please stop," she sobbed. "Please—they will find out, and we will die."

Hailey looked over, realizing the young girl was shaking in sheer terror. "Okay. I'll stop. I'll stop." Either Austin and Jackson had seen her signal or they hadn't.

Hailey tossed the towel back in the bathroom, turned, and gasped as she caught her own reflection in the small mirror. She hardly recognized her own face. She skimmed fingers over her dark purple cheek, swollen double its normal size. Her eye was nearly sealed shut, her lip a mess of puffy, bloodied skin.

She glanced at her arm, at the three sets of welts Jeremy, Rio, and Donte's hands had made on her skin. From shoulder to elbow, she was black-and-blue.

This was the brutality Austin spoke of. This was what the men on this boat were capable of—and surely more. They were truly monsters, and she had defended them, time and time again. Closing her eyes, Hailey sighed. She was the worst kind of fool. She'd lost Austin for this.

The thought sunk her spirits so low she had to force it away. She couldn't let Austin enter her mind, or she would crumble. The young girls in the next room needed kindness—a gentle touch. She would be there until help came to take them away.

CHAPTER 25

AUSTIN SAT IN THE BLACK of night, listening to the water lap against the boat as he stared at the bright lights of the massive yacht a mile away. He and his team had been floating for hours, waiting to move forward with their plan to extract five hostages. It was easier to think of her that way: not as Hailey Roberts, the woman he loved, but as a faceless individual in need of help.

Austin had shut himself down, methodically, ruthlessly, after he'd received Hailey's brief phone call. The terror strangling her voice had all but undone him. Her breathy shudder as she said his name, as she told him she needed help, even now, tried to slip through his barrier of cold. Austin closed his eyes, feeling helpless, but opened them just as quickly, too afraid to take his eyes from Hailey's window.

When she hung up abruptly, his mind catapulted him to the worst-case scenario. He'd been certain the guards discovered Hailey trying to save herself and killed her for her trouble. Grief, so sharp, so all consuming, had threatened to smother him as he hid along the dilapidated docks, running surveillance on the yacht.

It had taken all he had to put the binoculars back to his face, to let himself hope that Hailey was still alive. Twenty minutes later, when the lights flashed on and off every few minutes in the bottom row of windows, Austin had struggled with tears, knowing she had to be.

He and Hailey had watched a movie—months ago—in Ethan's game room. As the credits rolled they'd argued over the realism and effectiveness of using a light switch as a distress signal.

"Donte and his top men just took their seats in the dining room," Jackson said into his transmitter.

"Copy that," Tucker Campbell said from another boat anchored a mile west. "From my standpoint, I'm counting ten guards total on port and starboard side and an additional four at bow and stern. We're in for an interesting night."

Jackson started the engine, accelerated them three-quarters-of-a-mile—the closest they would get and hopefully not draw suspicion from the guards. "Hunter, Austin, are you ready to go?"

Hunter stood in his wetsuit, zipped himself up. "Let's do this."

Austin checked their air gauges again, then handed Hunter his tanks. "Remember, no lights, due west, dive deep the closer we get to the yacht. We'll separate, plant the explosives, and regroup. Thirty minutes to extract. Failure's not an option. Tucker, you ready?"

"I'll be watching for you."

Ethan glanced up from his computer. "I'll wait for your signal before I jam the electronics. You should have radio silence for approximately ten minutes before someone figures it out. I can't guarantee you more."

Hunter sat on the edge of the boat. "All hell will break loose after that."

Jackson slipped his phone back in his pocket. "Collin just checked in. He's fueled up and filed the flight plan. If the shit hits the fan, we meet at the airport in exactly one hour."

Austin joined Hunter on the edge. "Stay together until I signal."

Hunter nodded as Ethan stood and handed off two bags. "Careful, boys."

Austin and Hunter bit down on their regulators and leaned back into the water.

Austin was engulfed by black warmth. He and Hunter both pressed on their underwater navigators. Dim neon lit the space around them. Hunter gave Austin a nudge on the arm, the signal that the cord attaching them for their blind dive west was still intact.

It didn't take long to reach the glow of lights radiating from the yacht. Austin glanced to his left, met Hunter's eyes through their masks, and gave a thumbs up. Hunter detached the cord at their weight belts and dove deeper as Austin did the same. They separated, Hunter heading to the stern, Austin moving toward the bow.

When Austin estimated he was at center, he unzipped his bag, carefully freed an explosive, and mounted it against the yacht's bottom. He moved several feet to the left, planting another charge opposite the plastic he'd already secured. Swimming to the bow, he repeated the process, wired the device, and set it. He glanced at his watch. They had exactly thirty minutes.

Austin swam quickly to the stern, knowing Hunter would be waiting. Within seconds, he spotted Hunter's thumbs up as they rose to the surface, ready to begin the next phase of their plan.

Austin spit the regulator from his mouth before he pulled himself into the small powerboat anchored off the yacht, took the key from the engine, and zipped it into his bag. With his task complete, he eased soundlessly into the water, swimming to Hunter's side. He pulled the regulator from his mouth again. "You ready?" he whispered.

"As I'll ever be."

They both splashed around the edge of the launch.

"What the hell is that?" one of the guards moved forward.

"Maybe it's one of the sharks you're always fucking with," guard number two chuckled as he crouched next to the first.

Austin glanced at Hunter as they replaced their regulators and sunk under water. When both guards inched to the edge, Austin punched his fist forward, giving Hunter the signal. Hunter and Austin reached from the water in unison, gripped the guard's wrists and necks, and pulled them into the water. Austin used the momentum of the fall to drag his opponent deeper.

Austin dodged a slow motion fist to the face before he found purchase on the incredibly strong man's wrist again. He wrenched his arm behind his back. The guard attempted to fight, one handed, until Austin did the same with his rival's other arm. Austin held on, ruthlessly, until the man expelled the last of his air and went still.

Without mercy, Austin let the guard go and shoved him deeper. He glanced over, watching Hunter's man sink into the dark depths.

Hunter gave the signal to surface. They held on to the yacht, yanked the pieces from their mouths, breathing hard. "Son of a bitch," Hunter said.

"You getting soft, Phillips?"

"Fuck you."

After several deep breaths, they removed their tanks and clipped them together. Austin sucked in a gulp of air and sank under the water again. He tied the breathing devices to a long rope Hunter had secured to the launch, then ascended.

"Let's get this done," Hunter said as he hefted himself up.

Austin did the same, scanning the area before he stood, watching for more guards. He hurried to the interior of the deck, waved his hands about, hoping Jackson and Ethan were paying attention as Hunter did the same for Tucker's benefit on the opposite side.

"Look what our friends weren't wearing when we

dragged them under." Hunter handed over a fully loaded M-4. "These fuckers have no business with weapons like this."

Austin held his up and peered through the site, testing the weight of his new weapon. "This sure as hell isn't a Glock-17." He would've preferred his pistol, but this would have to do. "If they haven't moved the hostages, they should be on this deck. Let's finish this."

He and Hunter moved in silent unison with the skill of elite military men. They stood at opposite sides of the door. Austin peered around the corner, then held up a fist to signal for Hunter to cover him. Hunter dropped to his knee, sighted his weapon, ready to fire. Austin slid around the edge of the wall, leading with his gun, watching, waiting for someone to surprise him. He stared at plush, creamy carpet, noting the trail of blood. Someone lost enough to make faded footprints along the threads. The outline was fairly small—a woman's sized shoe.

When Hunter joined him seconds later, Austin pointed to the floor, at the trail stopping by a door on the right before it continued down the hall, turning left.

Hunter nodded and they kept moving. They communicated through hand signals as they made their way down the long hall, opening door after door, covering one another, coming up empty with each room they swept.

Austin approached the door where the footsteps stopped. He attempted to twist the knob, but it held firm. He and Hunter had to check the location. Hailey—the hostage, he corrected immediatcly, could bc in there.

With little choice, he raised the butt of his gun and slammed it hard against the gleaming brass. The noise was loud enough to have them hustling inside the instant the knob gave.

The room was cloaked in shadows. Light shined through the curtainless window. Austin stared in horror at the patches of blood scattered about the floor. What had they done to her? What would he and Hunter find when they finally opened the door leading to Hailey?

Hunter gripped his shoulder, yanked hard. "Pull yourself together, goddamn it," he whispered tersely. "You keep it together or we're all fucking dead."

Austin found a slippery grip on his control and turned away from the gore, taking several deep breaths. He concentrated on the movement of the florescent second hand on his watch. They were running out of time, and they didn't have Hailey—the hostage, he corrected himself again. He and Hunter had five hostages to extract. That was all he could think about. "Twenty minutes," he whispered, nodding, letting Hunter know his head was back in the game.

As Hunter twisted the doorknob, Austin raised his gun. Hunter yanked the door wide. There was no one there. They hustled down the hall, stopping at the end, still following the trail of dried crimson.

Austin stood opposite Hunter as they spotted their newest obstacle—the guard walking past the glass deck doors. If the guard came back too soon, he would see them as they made their way down the long hall.

Hunter peered around the corner and held up a finger before he pointed to the blood and made a stopping motion with his hand.

Austin nodded, interpreting Hunter's signals. They had another guard to deal with, and the blood stopped at the door where the guard stood.

He and Hunter needed to create a diversion, but nothing that would tempt the guard to call into a radio with no signal. Hunter motioned with his head until Austin moved to stand next to him.

Hunter scraped the butt of his gun against the wall, making a scratching sound. He repeated the action until the guard down the hall moved away from the door.

Austin and Hunter creeped back as the man's reflection bounced off the pristine glass to the right of them. As he turned the corner, the edge of Hunter's palm connected with the guard's windpipe. The man's eyes flew wide as he clutched at his throat, fighting for air. Hunter followed his brutal blow with another to the man's temple. Austin caught the bulky man as he collapsed forward.

"Son of a bitch," Austin whispered as he struggled to keep his balance.

Hunter grabbed the man's legs. "Come on, let's go." They carried him down the hall, struggling slightly with the deadweight of his massive size.

A voice traveled from the staircase to the left as they made it to the door where the bloody footprints stopped. Hunter dropped the guard's feet, yanked the door open, and hurried to help Austin drag the guy inside.

Four girls trembled in the corner, crying. Austin scanned the small space. Where was Hailey? One of the twins sobbed loudly. Austin dropped the guard, leaving Hunter to drag him to the bathroom as he walked closer to the victims. With each step, they shoved themselves further back, clearly terrified. "Shh," he whispered. "We are here to help you," he said in easy Spanish. "We are going to take you home to your families, but you must be quiet or we'll get caught."

"You are Hailey's friends?"

Austin's gaze whipped to the tallest girl's on the end. "Yes, I'm Hailey's friend. Where is she?"

"She said you would come. She said you would help us."

Austin struggled to be patient as he looked into four pairs of eyes too weary, too traumatized for their young, pretty, bruised faces. "I need to find Hailey. Where is she?"

"She is so kind. She has helped us."

He inched closer as he checked his watch. They were down to fifteen minutes. "Help her too. Tell me where she is. We're running out of time."

"Mateo brought her to another room." The tall girl started to cry. "Donte has someone bring us there when he wants to rape us."

"Where is it?"

"At the end of the hall; the last door on the right."

Austin stood and whirled so fast one of the twins let out a stifled scream. He hurried over to Hunter. "You need to get them out of here, Phillips." He unzipped his bag and handed Hunter the key for the powerboat.

"We all leave together. That's the deal."

"That was before. Hailey's down at the end of the hall."

"As soon as I step outside with them and turn the engine, it's all over."

"I know. If we don't do it this way, it's still over but seven people die instead of two." If Hailey wasn't going to live, he didn't want to either. "We're wasting time, Phillips. Get them out of here. Go pick up Tucker; have him drive while you man the gun, because they'll come after you. Get yourselves to the airport. Tell Ethan Hailey and I will meet him back at the boat. That's what the scuba gear's for—Plan B."

Hunter stared at him, then nodded. "I can't speak Spanish for shit. Tell them they have to follow my lead."

Austin turned back to the girls, knelt down close to them, looked them each in the eye. He couldn't be gentle, only frank. "It's time to go. If you want to live, you will be silent. Do exactly what Hunter tells you. Get in the boat, lay on the floor, and say nothing. You cannot cry. You cannot scream, even if you are afraid. They will hear you. They will shoot you. Do you understand?"

"Yes," they said in unison.

"Be brave."

"What about Hailey?" the tall and courageous one asked.

"I will get Hailey. We will see you at the airport."

"The airport? But I want to go home."

"You can when it's safe. Donte has bad men everywhere. If they know you are alive, they will kill you and your families. If you trust Hailey, trust me. I love her."

The girls looked at each other and stood.

"Go. Hurry. Follow Hunter."

Hunter stopped at the door, held up his hand, and signaled for the group to stop. He opened the door a crack, peering out before he made a "go ahead" motion with his hand. The girls clutched each other's hands as they followed Hunter down the hall. When they turned the corner, Austin moved in the opposite direction. Eleven minutes would go quickly, but he had less time than that. Hunter would turn over the ignition in less than two.

Austin continued forward, stopping outside the last door on the right. He put his ear to the wood, nearly crumbling with relief as he heard the unmistakable sound of Hailey's voice. She was alive.

Austin put his hand on the knob, twisted slowly as Hailey spoke to her brother. He inched the door open, unsure if Jeremy was armed.

"Why won't you help me, Jeremy? Why won't you even try to get me out of here?"

"How do you expect me to do that? We're surrounded by guards. If I step out of this room with you, they'll kill us both."

"I'm going to die anyway. At least let me try."

"I can't, Hailey. Let me think. I'll find a way to get you out."

"My hero," she said with biting disdain. "What about the girls? Can't you at least help them? They're so young,

357

so traumatized."

"I don't want to talk about them."

Austin peered in as much as he dared. Jeremy stood with his back to him in the expansive, luxuriously decorated space. Hailey was too far in the room for him to get a look at her, to get an exact idea of where she was located. He readied his gun, waiting for Hunter to make his move.

"Did you really do it? Did you really kidnap them? Take them away from their families?"

"What choice did I have? I do as I'm told or I'm dead."

"But you knew what the men would do to them, and you did it anyway. Don't you have a conscience?"

"Son of a bitch." Jeremy stormed forward; Austin inched back. "Do *you* understand I'm as much a prisoner as you? The same penalties of betrayal apply to me as they do to you."

Austin eased ahead again, took his stance again.

"You *chose* this life, Jeremy. Those girls didn't. I sure as heck didn't, but you took me along with you anyway." She moved to sit on the edge of the bed. Her knees were raw red wounds, her palms just as bad as she fiddled with her fingers, but still, he couldn't see her face unless he took a chance and inched further into the room. It wasn't worth the risk.

"All this time I wanted to help you. All this time I've done nothing but love and defend you, but do you know what I've come to realize? The boy you were ceased to exist ten years ago. The boy I loved died the night our parent's did. You died right along with them, Jeremy."

"I'm out of here." He turned and headed to the door.

Austin hurried to the side, waiting.

"So, you're just going to—"

A rapid stream of gunfire broke out—Austin's cue to get him and Hailey the hell out of there. He burst inside and punched Jeremy in the face, sending him crumbling to the floor. Austin turned, staring as he rushed forward. "Jesus Christ, look at you." His heart broke as he ran his hand over Hailey's left arm riddled with welts. "Look what they did to you." His fingers traced over the right side of her face as he studied the bloody bulge of her bottom lip. The bruising was so bad, the swelling so severe, her wounds almost looked fake.

"You came." Hailey clutched at his wrists, her hands trembling.

"Of course I did. I wasn't going to leave you." He pulled her against him once, for the briefest of seconds, before he stepped back. "We have to get out of here."

As they turned, Jeremy crawled to his radio. "Hostage—"

Austin whirled. "You son of a bitch." Waves of rage radiated through him as he ripped the walkie-talkie from Jeremy's hand and threw it against the wall, shattering it. "What the hell do you think you're doing?" He plowed his fist into Jeremy's face again, sending blood pouring from his nose. "You let them do this to her, goddamn you." He followed his punch with a shove, sending Jeremy halfway across the room. "Fucking coward."

The pounding of feet rushed over their heads as the pepper of gunfire continued.

"Come on. We have to go right now. Stay behind me." Austin peaked into the hallway as a guard came around the corner. Raising his gun, he smashed the butt of the weapon into the man's face. "Let's go, Hailey." He grabbed her hand. "*Run.*"

They took off at full speed down the long corridor.

"Sissy!"

Hailey slowed.

"Help me, Sissy," Jeremy gasped, crawling from the bedroom. "Take me with you." He held out a hand, fell forward. "Don't leave me, Sissy."

Austin pulled Hailey harder as she hesitated. "I have to help him."

"We don't have time."

Feet clamored down the staircase in front of them.

Austin yanked Hailey around the corner as bullets splintered the wood above his head. Hailey let out whimpering screams as the guard turned into the hall, charging after them. Austin lifted the M-4, firing randomly until the man fell. Within seconds, more men followed.

Austin carried Hailey up the flight of steps, used his shoulder to shove them through the outside door. Warm, muggy air met them. "Duck and keep running, Hailey. Keep running. We're almost there." They skirted the deck as bullets poured from above, from the side, landing all around them. "We're almost there," he said again, as much for his own benefit as hers.

They descended the last flight of stairs to the launch. "Stay close to the wall." They made it to the spot where he and Hunter had gained entry. "Take my hand. Hold on tight. We have to jump."

"Jump? No! No! I can't go in the water. I can't."

"We have to."

Hailey screamed as a plank of wood disintegrated at their feet. Another bullet landed within inches of the first.

"Come on, Hailey. We have to." He yanked his small dive bag open, pulled their masks free.

"Sharks. I saw sharks," she whispered in terror.

"Look at me. Look at me," he demanded.

She tore her glassy gaze from the water.

"We're going to *die*." He handed her the mask he'd bought her for her birthday. "Now you put that on and jump. Trust me, Hailey." He slid his mask on as she did the same, took her hand, and gripped it tight. "Hold my hand and jump with me."

She nodded, took a deep breath, and they jumped feet

first off the side. The water glowed eerily from the lights. A steady spray of bullets pinged into the depths. Hailey clutched his fingers in a death grip as he pulled her with him to the tanks he'd tied off several feet below. He twisted on the oxygen, took a small breath before he handed the regulator to Hailey. Repeating the process with Hunter's tank, Austin helped himself to his own supply of air. He quickly unfastened his flippers, pulled them on with the ease of experience, and clipped his dive bag to the tanks.

A relentless wave of bullets poured into the water as he focused on the knots holding the tanks in place. He struggled to pull Hailey's tank loose as she clung to his waist, fighting to keep herself from floating to the surface. He'd forgotten her weight belt. Without success, Austin fiddled until finally the knot slipped free.

Hailey shouldered the tank and waited, still clutching at him. Glancing at her, he met her eyes as they darted left and right in terror. The tight mask against her swollen face had to be excruciating. He moved his hand up and down slowly, signaling for her to try to regulate her breathing. She nodded and closed her eyes.

Austin looked at his watch. Seven minutes. They were out of time. He attempted to loosen the second tank, but the knot wouldn't budge. They would have to leave it. Austin gave Hailey the signal they practiced weeks before, alerting her to the need to buddy breathe. He took his last breath from Hunter's tank before he grabbed Hailey's hand, pulling her deeper into the darkening depths, bringing them to thirty feet, well out of bullct range.

His lungs screamed for air. He motioned for Hailey to give him a turn. He sucked oxygen in, blew it out, sucked it in, blew it out, in again before he handed the regulator back.

They continued the tedious process of sharing air as they swam further east, further into the dark, until

361

Austin had no choice but to use a small dive light. The pace was slow, painfully so. With each kick, he began to ascend—twenty-five feet, twenty, fifteen, keeping them steady, letting their bodies release nitrogen as they made progress toward Ethan and Jackson. Everything would move fast when they surfaced. The last thing Hailey needed was decompression sickness.

He checked the gauge on their air supply. They were running lower than he liked. Hailey was breathing too fast. Her fear of what swam in the dark was eating up their oxygen. He had no way to reassure her as they continued forward.

Two minutes later, he rechecked his compass and their air gauge. With an eighth-of-a-mile to go, they had no choice but to surface. Hopefully Ethan and Jackson were watching for them. Austin tugged on Hailey's hand to start their ascent.

Within thirty seconds they surfaced. Austin flashed his dive light in the direction Ethan and Jackson should've been waiting. He sighed with relief at the rumble of a motor, the acceleration of a boat in the distant east. "It's almost over, Hailey. Hang on."

"I'm trying. I'm so tired."

"I know."

Austin held the light up again like a beacon. He glanced behind him at the yacht, listening as powerboats charged toward the launch. Donte was going to escape, and the guards were going to come after them.

Jackson cut the engine and let the boat glide up next to them.

"Here, take her. Get her out of the water."

Jackson and Ethan leaned over the side, grabbed Hailey's hands, tugged her into the boat.

Ethan and Jackson leaned over again, clutched him under the armpits and pulled. "Son of a bitch, Casey.

You're fucking heavy."

As soon as Austin's ass touched the boat, he scrambled up, breath heaving, grabbing the pair of binoculars by the steering wheel. Donte and his father were running down the last flight of stairs to the launch. The bombs wouldn't ignite for another sixty seconds. By then, it would be too late. They would be gone and Hailey would always be looking over her shoulder. "My dive bag. Where's my dive bag?"

Ethan unclipped the small pack from the tanks next to Hailey, handed it up.

Austin yanked at the zipper and pulled the detonator free. "Hunter and Tucker?"

"They're good. They're safe." Jackson said as he sent the boat flying.

Hailey stood, clutching the seat at her side. "Austin, what is that? What are you *doing*?" She pulled on his arm. "Austin, what—"

"What I have to." Without regret, Austin pushed the safety up with his thumb, and pressed the button. The light glowed green seconds before the massive explosion lit up the sky. Orange flames plumed up as huge chunks of yacht rained into the water.

"No!" Hailey screamed as she rushed to the back of the boat. "No! Jeremy! Jeremy!"

Austin hurried after her as she wailed in agony, collapsing to the seat. He pulled her rigid body against his in a hard hug until she struggled away. "You did this!" She shoved and clawed. "You killed him! You killed my brother!" she spewed on wild, primitive screams before Ethan came back, took her around the shoulders, sat her in his lap in the captain's seat.

Austin listened to Hailey wail against Ethan's shoulder, heard Ethan's soothing murmurs as he stared at the flaming remains of the Zulas, wishing he felt sorry for ending them.

CHAPTER 26

HAILEY STRUGGLED UP THE STAIRS of the large private jet. Her trembling legs weighed a ton. It felt as if she walked through mud, making each hurried step agony. Sheer will pushed her forward, fearful that Austin would make good on his threat to carry her.

She didn't need to be carried; she just needed to rest, to lie down and close her eyes. Surely she would wake up from this nightmare and be back in her bed. Her clothes would be dry instead of cold and dripping with seawater. Her face and arm wouldn't throb with each beat of her heart.

She stepped into the luxurious cabin and glanced at Collin, Hunter, and Tucker, registering their surprised looks, then at the girls she'd shamefully forgotten about over the last half hour.

"Hailey. Oh, Hailey. You are safe." Angelica rushed up from her seat and grabbed her in a hug. "I was so afraid for you."

Two older women stood, hurrying forward, crying as they engulfed her. "Thank you. Thank you so much."

It took all Hailey had to return their grateful embraces. Now that she was safe and on her way home, fatigue ruled, threatening to pull her under right where she stood. Her mind and body simply couldn't take anymore. "I have to sit down." She staggered to a leather seat.

Hunter hurried forward as Austin stepped on the plane, engaging the door after Ethan and Jackson entered. "My God, you look like hell." Hunter pressed his fingers to her pulse. "Hailey, are you okay?"

"I don't know. I'm so tired." Her eyelids grew heavy, so heavy she couldn't force them open.

"Of course you are. Let's get you strapped in so we can go." He wrapped the straps around her hips and secured the buckle.

The voices of Austin, Ethan, and Jackson floated through the fog.

"Everyone take your seats. Buckle in," Collin said as the whirl of the engine filled the cabin. "They'll ground flights before long. The island'll shut down until they figure out what the hell happened on the water."

Urgency rang sharp in the passengers' whispered murmurs. Tension suffocated the cabin, yet Hailey couldn't make herself open her eyes.

"Tower, this is flight 244 requesting permission to take off."

Proceed. Cross runway one-niner.

"Roger that." The jet accelerated, traveling the long runway, the engines screaming, ready for take-off. "Flight 244 is ready," Collin said.

Go ahead, flight 244.

The plane jolted, hurtled forward, gaining speed.

Flight 244, this is the tower. Throttle back. I repeat, throttle back. All flights are grounded.

"Negative, Tower, I'm at flight speed and running out of runway."

Silence filled the space.

Proceed, flight 244.

The plane tilted, lifting off the ground. A cheer went up through the cabin. Hailey fought her eyes open and stared into the green of Austin's.

"Go to sleep, Hailey," he whispered, brushing a finger over her cheek. "We'll get you changed and cleaned up when we reach altitude. Sarah packed you some clothes."

She wanted to reach out to him, to say something, to

feel something, but she couldn't. Her lids fluttered as the tunnel of exhaustion reached up to grab her and took her under.

⁓ↀ⌘⌐

Hailey opened her tired eyes to everything familiar, to everything home, as Ethan's Rover sped along the 405 toward the Palisades. Somehow she'd lost hours. The last thing she remembered was staring into Austin's eyes as the jet soared into the sky.

She glanced at her clothes, surprised that her sopping tank top and jean shorts had been replaced with a baggy t-shirt and loose gray sweat shorts. And her wounds were bandaged.

Austin's deep voice carried from the front as he spoke to Ethan quietly. She stared at his handsome profile and was staggered by a wave of love.

Still talking, Austin peered over his shoulder, stopping mid-sentence as he held her gaze.

His green eyes captivated her as they always did, but it was different now. Everything was different now.

She stared at the scruff of beard covering his chin, the tension clenching his jaw, the purple bags of exhaustion marring his skin. Austin had risked everything to protect her, to save her—but he had killed her brother.

Somewhere deep, below the flutters of anger and well of misery, she knew he did it for her, but the myriad of mixed feelings were too much to handle.

Her stomach twisted and her heart pounded as she trembled in her seat. Tears rumbled below the surface, like a volcano ready to blow, but they wouldn't come. She wanted the relief, the cleansing they would bring, but the painful emotions were stuck under layers of repression, a skill she'd honed too well. In defense, she looked away.

It hurt too much to think, to feel.

With the last of her will, she tightened her chinks of armor and focused on the rising sun, watching the fiery reds silhouette the mountains and skyscrapers of Los Angeles.

Resting her head on the corner of the seat, her eyes grew heavy again as Ethan merged onto I-10. In utter defeat, Hailey turned herself off.

Minutes later, she sprang awake as the car rolled to a stop. The sprawling wood and glass of Sarah and Ethan's home spread out before her. The cedar edge of Kylee and Emma's swing set peaked around the side of the house. Here was comfort and love; here was everything she never thought she would see again.

Morgan and Sarah ran from the house, racing to her side of the car. Sarah yanked her door open. "Oh, honey, look at you. *Look* at you," Sarah repeated as she crushed Hailey in a hug and held on.

"Let's get her inside," Morgan cooed, her eyes swamped with sympathy. "Can you walk?"

"Yes, I can walk." Hailey swung her leg out of the vehicle and quickly realized her limbs still felt like two-ton weights.

Sarah supported her on one side, Morgan on the other, ignoring Ethan and Austin as they started toward the house. Hailey breathed in Morgan's dark, flirty scent, the meadow flowers of Sarah, and felt the first tear fall.

"You need a warm bath, something light to eat, then you're off to bed," Sarah soothed.

Hailey nodded; her throat was too tight.

"It's okay, sweetie. You're going to be all right." Morgan gave her a reassuring smile that didn't dim the worry in her eyes.

"I'm calling my dad after we get you settled. We'll have him come give you a once over." Sarah opened the front door. Bear and Reece shimmied with excitement as their tails whipped back and forth wildly.

"My boys." Hailey leaned forward and pressed her face in soft fur. "I'm home."

Kylee hurried down the hall, blonde hair tangled, cheeks flushed, eyes sleepy. "Hailey!" She stopped short, staring, gasping. "Uh oh, you have a very bad boo-boo. I will kiss you and make you all better." She extended her arms to be picked up.

"Oh, not right now, honey," Sarah said, starting forward.

"It's okay." Hailey scooped Kylee up, her muscles protesting as she held Kylee tight, breathing in baby shampoo. "It's okay," she repeated.

Kylee's little mouth feathered against her tender skin. Reece's tail smacked at her leg with each enthusiastic wag. Her armor crumble. Hailey pressed her good cheek to Kylee's as she struggled with her rapid intake of breath, her quick, shuddering exhale. "Oh God."

Ethan walked over and plucked Kylee from her arms. "Hey, big girl. Come have breakfast with me."

"Hailey's crying," Kylee's voice vibrated with concern.

"She'll be all right." He kissed her cheek. "So, are we having Cheerios or should we try to make pancakes?"

"Pancakes," Kylee's enthusiastic shout carried down the hall as she and Ethan disappeared around the corner.

Everything here was so normal. Everything was exactly as it had been when she left, but still, nothing was the same. Nothing about her life was the same. Hailey took two steps and fell apart. The stunning weight of grief sent her to her tender knees as her body racked with tearing sobs.

Sarah crouched next to her and ran a gentle hand over her back. "Oh, sweetie, let's get you upstairs."

"I..." She wanted to, but she couldn't find the strength to stand.

"Enough of this." Austin bent down, picked her up, and cradled her close.

If she hadn't been at her breaking point, she wouldn't have clung to him, she assured herself; she wouldn't have rested her head in the crook of his neck and found comfort.

Morgan hurried up the stairs ahead of Austin. "I'm going to draw your bath." She dashed down the long hall.

Sarah followed behind, hesitating when Emma's fitful wails started in the nursery. "Let me get Emma. I'll be right there."

Hailey and Austin continued down the hall alone. When they reached her bedroom door, he stopped. "Hailey, I'm so sorry. When you're feeling—"

Morgan stepped from the bathroom. "Oh good. Why don't you bring Hailey in here and I'll get her settled."

Austin nodded as he walked through the bedroom, into her bathroom.

Hailey breathed deep. Her bathroom smelled of her favorite peach bubble bath. Soothing violin bath music filled the room. Seafoam green candles were lit around the tub. A soft, plush towel was folded close by, waiting for her. "Thank you," she whispered to Morgan as a fresh wave of tears came.

"Oh, honey, you're welcome. Come on, let's get you in the tub. You can soak your troubles away and tell Auntie Morgan all about it."

Hailey let out a watery chuckle. She'd missed this. She'd missed Morgan and Sarah so much.

"Austin, you can set Hailey down. Sarah and I will take good care of her." Morgan rubbed Austin's shoulder.

Hailey felt his hesitation before he set her on her feet. "If you… I want to…"

"Look who came to say good morning." Sarah came in holding Emma.

Hailey stared into big blue eyes, brushed her fingers through soft black hair. Emma was a perfect blend of her mother and father. "Oh, look how much she's grown. I can't wait to get my hands on you."

"Bath first," Morgan insisted.

Sarah followed Morgan's command with a firm nod. "Emma needs her breakfast first anyway."

Austin jammed his hands in his pockets.

Sarah turned to him. "Honey, why don't you go down and get yourself something to eat. I think Ethan and Kylee managed to make pancakes without burning them. The fire alarm hasn't gone off like it did last week." She took his hand and gave him a small smile. "We'll take good care of her."

"Hailey, I..." He shook his head, turned, and left.

Hailey stared after him, heartbroken. She sighed and looked at Morgan and Sarah. "It's such a mess," she said shakily. "Everything's such a mess."

"We'll have to help you clean it up," Morgan said. "Now shirt and shorts off. Get into that water before it gets too cold."

Hailey did as she was told. She pulled her shorts off, then her panties. Her shirt went next, followed by her bra. She stood in front of her friends naked. Both Sarah and Morgan sucked in a breath as they stared.

"Those monsters," Sarah said with heated exasperation.

Monsters. That's exactly what they were. That's exactly what Jeremy had been.

"In you go." Morgan took Hailey's arm gently, leading her to the tub, peeling off the tape and gauze covering her wounds.

Hailey stepped into the warm bathwater, eased her weary body down, wincing as she felt the sharp sting in her knees and palms. She sunk to her chin and sighed as her muscles instantly relaxed. "Oh, this is heaven."

"Of course it is. We'll fix you an omelet, toast, and a fruit salad after this. You'll feel like a whole new woman."

She gave Morgan a small smile. Would she ever feel the same again? Rocky emotions sank and bubbled to the surface so fast she couldn't keep up.

Emma began to fuss. Sarah pulled over a chair, put Emma to her breast, and the baby instantly quieted.

For the first time since Hailey arrived, she studied her friends. Sarah played with Emma's fingers, smiling, as she stared down at her daughter. Morgan's breasts were fuller, her tummy rounded slightly on her compact bombshell body. Her face positively glowed with impending motherhood.

Hailey looked away, shamed that her friends' happiness brought her a stab of pain. Not even a week before, she'd believed she would have everything Morgan and Sarah did. Somewhere down the road, she and Austin would've ended up in exactly the same place. She'd wanted to be his, had wanted so desperately to carry his child—their child. Now, that would never be.

Austin had risked his life to save her. They had *all* risked their lives to save her. Would Austin resent her even more for that? He'd warned her—too many times—of what her brother had been, of what Donte had been, but she didn't listen. And even though they left Mexico Austin's life was still on the line. If the authorities were able to connect what he'd done to set her free from the Zulas—because surely, that was what he'd done—he would go to prison forever. Or worse.

Their relationship would be different—awkward, tenuous. There were layers of hurt. Trust had been broken on both sides. Surely too much to recover from. They'd started their affair with intensity, with passion, and ended it the same way. Nothing would ever be the same between them, but she certainly owed him a thank you and an explanation as to why she'd gone to the yacht in the first place—for what it was worth.

"Do you want to talk about it?" Sarah asked, brushing a piece of hair behind Hailey's ear.

"I think I have to or I'm going to make myself crazy."

Morgan pulled another cushioned chair to the massive tub. "Let us have it."

And she did.

Twenty minutes later, as the bath water cooled, Sarah clutched Hailey's hand. Morgan offered a fresh tissue.

"I don't know where to go from here." Hailey blew her nose. "I'm pretty much starting my life over. I don't know how to feel about Jeremy. On one hand, I love him. On the other, I hate who he was. My brother was a lie. I'm ashamed I feel more relief than sadness that he's gone. What kind of person does that make me?" She wiped at her streaming eyes.

"I'd say it makes you perfectly normal," Sarah said, squeezing gently on her hand. "He wasn't a nice person, Hailey. He did terrible things. He would've continued to do them. You don't have to feel bad for not being able to overlook that. God knows you tried."

Hailey nodded, finding solace in Sarah's words. She stared down at her bubbles, drew her knees up, and wrapped her free arm around her legs, her heart still heavy.

"What else?" Morgan encouraged. "There's more. Spill it all, Hailey. That's what we're here for."

She sighed. "I don't even know where to start. My college credits are in jeopardy. I don't have a single dime to my name, but above all else, Austin's gone. I've lost him. I love him so much, and he doesn't want me."

"Oh, I don't know about that." Morgan tossed her tissue in the trash. "I'm pretty sure the man standing in here a few minutes ago was falling all over himself

372

with worry."

Sarah nodded. "Austin may be upset with you, but he's still very much in love. He looks at you the way Hunter looks at Morgan, the way Ethan looks at me."

"So what should I do?" She sniffed.

"Nothing," Morgan said.

Hailey frowned.

"At least not right now," Sarah added quickly. "Give yourself some time. Give Austin some time. You've been through a lot, honey. Take a breath. Heal. Steady out a bit and find your feet again."

"Austin loves you, sweetie," Morgan smiled. "He'll wait. I promise."

Hailey huffed out a breath and flipped the lever for the drain. "Okay. I'll take care of myself for a while. See what I can salvage later." She stood and wrapped herself in the soft cotton.

"And you'll do it from here. I'm not letting you out of my sight for at least two weeks— definitely not until we get your finances straightened out."

Hailey stared at her friend. "Sarah, that's not necessary."

"I disagree. You were there for me during some of the worst moments of my life. I'm returning the favor."

Hailey's lip wobbled, her emotions still unsteady. "You're going to get me going again."

"Go in. Get dressed. We'll have breakfast on the deck downstairs."

Hailey nodded. "Okay."

Sarah and Morgan left her alone to change. For the first time in three days, Hailey relaxed, could hear herself think. She'd take Sarah up on her offer, and for once, let someone else take care of her. Of course, she'd do her share, but it wouldn't hurt to take a few days and work on putting the pieces of her life back together.

Hailey pulled a pair of sweats from the drawer, another baggie t-shirt, and dressed, ready to start the slow process of rebuilding. The first step had already been taken. She'd poured her soul out to her two best friends and was lighter for it. She would take another and go down to help with breakfast instead of crawl under her covers and hide from the world.

Austin found Ethan in the kitchen devouring a double stack of pancakes. The thought of eating soured his stomach. "I'm going to head out."

"Sit down. Pull up a chair." Ethan gestured to the seat next to his. "You look like hell."

He *felt* like hell. "Nah, I need to go." He started toward the door, unable to stop thinking about Hailey—so bruised, so broken. Her screams for her brother still haunted him.

"Hunter called."

That stopped him cold. There would be a mountain of paperwork to deal with. Maybe if he focused on the details, he could get his mind off Hailey. "What did he say?"

"Come sit down and I'll tell you. Grab a cup of coffee while you're at it."

Austin eyed Ethan. "I don't want coffee."

"Then just come sit you're a—" he glanced at Kylee, "butt down."

"Sit your butt down, Austin." Kylee repeated, making Ethan wince.

Austin chuckled for the first time in too long.

"Kylee, don't say that," Ethan corrected. "Daddy made a mistake."

"Okay." Kylee nodded. "Have a bite of my pancakes." She held out her fork to Austin, bursting with pride. "I made them with daddy."

His stomach shuddered. "Oh, no thanks, honey."

Kylee's eyes watered, her lip trembled as she set her fork down.

God, how did Ethan and Sarah ever say "no"? Kylee used that pouty look like a weapon—swiftly and effectively. "Okay. I'll try a bite."

She grinned, held the fork up again. Austin slid a small square of sweet, moist pancake in his mouth. The home cooked food settled him. "Not bad," he said as he chewed. "Not bad at all, kid."

She beamed, held up another bite. "Have more."

He obliged her and himself by taking the offering. "I think I'll have a plate after all."

"Maybe we can talk about work when you're done stuffing your face," Ethan said without heat as he looked at his daughter, smiled, and winked.

Austin piled his plate high, filled a glass with orange juice, another with milk, too at home to feel rude. He took his seat, slathered his breakfast with butter and syrup, and dug in.

"You ready now or should I make you some bacon to go with it?"

"No, this is good," he said over a mouthful. "Enough about breakfast. Let's talk business." He smirked.

"As I was saying, Hunter called. Collin just left with our new guests for the Colorado safe house. They'll be far enough into the mountains; no one should ask questions while we get everything figured out."

"What are we going to do with them?"

"I'm already working on that. After we get confirmation everyone is—" he glanced at Kylee again, "no longer with us, we'll work on setting the families up somewhere in Europe. I'm going to push for Political Asylum. It might be a stretch but many countries are willing to accept victims of sexual persecution. I'm hoping I might be able to tug some strings in Spain. We guard several government officials at our branch there. I'll put in a few calls this afternoon. Hopefully we can get the mothers work, the girls some counseling, get them into school. I don't foresee them heading into a bar again anytime soon."

Austin grunted as he swallowed down half his orange juice.

"I got a call from Dr. Lopez while you were upstairs. So far it appears our objective was a success. Apparently they found an arm floating in the water with a watch on it similar to Donte's. It'll take awhile to get the DNA back, but I don't think we have to worry. That was more than a lethal blast to anyone within a hundred yards."

Austin hesitated with his next bite as Hailey's scream echoed through his mind again. He put the fork down. "We did the right thing, right?"

Ethan frowned. "What kind of question is that? We did the *only* thing. There weren't any other options."

"I know." He scrubbed his fingers over his chin. "I know," he repeated. "She never would've been free. They would've gotten to her eventually."

"And you, my friend. Probably all of us. You know how big they were on retaliation. They would've made her suffer before they finished her. Stop for a second and think about who means more to Hailey than anyone else in this world."

Austin's gaze left Ethan's, traveled to Kylee as she happily shoved a bite in her mouth. The thought was so unbearable, so disgusting, it was almost unbelievable such cruelty existed. But it did.

"You think about that the next time you start to question yourself. Ask yourself if you could've lived with that. I know I sure as hell couldn't. I won't have any problems sleeping in my bed tonight knowing my girls are safe; my wife is safe and so is Hunter's. We did this as much for Hailey as everyone else. Those bastards are dead. I don't plan to waste another moment worrying about it. My conscience is clear. I hope yours is too."

Ethan was right, absolutely right. Everyone he considered family was safe. The woman he loved was alive. They could all move on.

So why did he still feel wretched inside? Austin flicked a glance to the stairs. Because Hailey was upstairs and she wasn't his anymore. Never would be. He'd killed her brother; Hailey would never be able to forgive him. "I need to get out of here, man. I need to clear my head for awhile."

"It's interesting you should say that."

"Oh yeah?"

"We just accepted a new contract with the Feds. I need someone to check it out before I sign my name on the dotted line. I'm thinking about sending Jackson and Tucker, but I want everything seen to first. Our little adventure in Mexico will be the first and last time we take anyone's word on accommodations."

"Where?"

"Southeastern Kentucky."

Austin's brow shot up. "Kentucky? What the hell's in Kentucky?"

"Appalachia, my friend. The first lady's new pet project. She wants to pick up where Robert Kennedy left off, and the locals aren't real happy."

Austin shook his head. "You lost me."

"Kennedy wanted to bring aide to the people of Appalachia. The poverty levels are shocking from what I've researched. The first lady is pushing for a three-year grant to bring teachers to the area—doctors, dentists, etcetera, etcetera. The goal is to get the place back on its feet. Drugs are rampant, the poverty, as I said, astounding, and several of the clans in the area aren't thrilled with being the first lady's project. They've already burned down a structure. Threatened to kill anyone who comes."

"Three years is a long time."

"Yeah, it is. I don't expect our men to stay. I'm thinking six month stints, then we'll cycle them out."

"So, you're happy with Tucker's work so far?"

"Surprisingly, yes. For someone who almost got my wife killed, he's done well. He completed all of the training at the top. Having another agent with a police background is a huge advantage for us. The clients he's worked with are pleased. I can't complain."

"Good. I like him. He's a good guy. Other than the part about almost getting Sarah killed."

"I've chalked it up to police procedure. I'm mostly over it."

"So, when do I leave?"

"Take a few days first."

"No." Austin shook his head. "I want to go as soon as possible."

"You can run, but you can't hide." Ethan said in a singsong voice as he glanced at the ceiling.

"I need to smooth it out. I really messed her up."

"Been there, done that." Ethan slapped a hand on Austin's shoulder in a show of support. "You guys'll be all right. Go home. Get some sleep. Book yourself a flight. I'll see you in a couple weeks."

He and Hailey definitely wouldn't be all right, but he left it alone. "E-mail me the details. I'll leave first thing in the morning." Austin piled his dishes, scooted back from the table.

"Get me some preliminaries. I'll send Jackson along next week."

"Sounds good." He stood and walked over to Kylee.

"Thanks for breakfast." He kissed her forehead. "You're a good cook."

Kylee smiled.

Morgan and Sarah's voices trailed down the hallway. Hailey wouldn't be far behind. He wasn't ready to see her. There was too much to say, too much on the line to get it wrong. He would take his two weeks, stay busy, and try to work it all out. Austin put the dishes in the dishwasher. "See you, man."

"Your keys are on the hook in my office."

"Thanks."

CHAPTER 27

HAILEY WALKED INTO HER APARTMENT for the second time that day. She shoved her keys in her purse and set her bag on the small entryway table as she glanced around at the boxes she'd packed throughout the morning.

Jeremy's items sat in a corner for donation, except for the two or three things she was keeping. She twisted the pretty pearl ring she discovered among the loose change scattered in his top drawer—the one she'd treasured from her mother, the one she'd given to Jeremy with a promise she hadn't been able to keep.

Among the debris in his closet, she found a tattered picture of she and him taken so many years before. She had stared at the photograph for a long time, studying the living room she remembered from her childhood; the seven-year-old boy with hopeful eyes and her herself, grinning, confident, ready to take on the world. Then she came across the three-by-seven family portrait, the last one taken before their lives were ripped apart.

Her mother had been so beautiful, so kind. Her dad so strong and sure. And their children: Hailey Roberts and Jeremy Kagan—two stunning kids—a testament to what good, loving people could do for lost souls. Or one anyway.

Over the last two weeks, Hailey had come to realize that as much as her parents tried, Jeremy had needed so much more of their time. He'd been broken, perhaps broken beyond what love was able to fix. Jeremy had been a sweet child, so full of potential, so capable of being more than he'd chosen to be. But the lights had gone out for her brother the day their parents met their fate on a dark, icy road. He'd stopped fighting the odds of being just one more broken kid in the system.

She hadn't. Life had thrown her several cruel pitches, yet she made something of herself. Perhaps things weren't turning out the way she wanted, but she would keep going because that's what she did.

The time Hailey spent with Sarah and Ethan over the last several days put life back in perspective. She'd come to terms with her feelings about Jeremy. She would always love him—or the parts of him that saved family pictures and heirlooms, the boy that had been her little brother all those years before.

Hailey had picked out and arranged for a gravestone to be placed next to her parents. The marker would offer closure and symbolize her goodbye to the young boy she had adored with all her heart. She'd done all she could to try to save him from himself, but in the end, he'd been a grown man responsible for the life he made.

Ethan had helped her resolve her financial issues. She was officially back in the black. She still had her friends—the family she'd made with the Cookes and Phillips. She still had her job. Her college career was a big fat question mark, but Hailey was prepared to fight anyone who called her a thief.

That left Austin. He was the one dark spot in her life—the one person she couldn't find any resolve for, any closure. Morgan and Sarah had assured her of Austin's love, but sometimes love wasn't enough. He vanished when they got home. She hadn't seen or heard from him since he deposited her on her bathroom floor—not that she actually expected to.

How long would it be before she could think of him and not want him, not need him? Would she ever stop mourning what they would never have? She missed him, loved him, and could only be grateful for the sacrifices he made for her—for all of them.

She needed to thank him, to apologize, to try to make things right—make everything a little easier, at least. But he had to come back first.

With a long sigh, Hailey picked up the next empty box, wandered to her small shelf of flowery knickknacks, and got to work. The decision to move in with Ethan and Sarah hadn't come lightly, but it made the most sense. She couldn't afford her apartment without a roommate, and it would be easier all around with Ethan's busy schedule and Sarah taking on jobs here and there.

She paused when she heard a knock on the door. She set down the sheet of packing paper, walked to the door, peeked through the security hole. Hailey's heart tumbled in her chest as she stared at Austin. "Holy crap," she muttered.

She wasn't prepared for this. He wasn't supposed to be home for a couple more days, or so Ethan had told her. Well, he was here now. "Okay." Hailey shook out her hands, trying to relieve her nerves. "Okay," she said again as she held a hand to her shuddering stomach, took a deep, calming breath. She pressed her lips together, twisted the knob.

"Hey." Austin gave her a small smile and shoved his hands in his jean pockets.

"Hey." Dear God, he looked good. His hair was wet from a shower. His muscles were so...mouthwatering. He smelled amazing. Hailey wanted to reach out to him, to hug him, but he was off limits.

"Ah." He rocked back on his heels.

"Oh. Oh, come on in." She held the door wider, rolled her eyes at herself as he walked through.

"You're packing. Why are you packing? Where're you going?"

She caught the hint of alarm in his voice, felt a small thrill. Maybe all was not lost. "I can't afford to stay here by myself so I'm moving in with Ethan and Sarah for a while."

"Oh." He jammed his fingers back in his pockets and heaved out a heavy breath. "Hailey, can I talk to you for a minute?"

Wasn't that what they were doing? "Yeah, sure. Take a seat." She gestured to the loveseat. "Do you want something? I think I have some iced tea or water or...iced tea," she finished lamely. God, she needed to get a grip.

"No, thanks." He sat down. "Would you mind sitting too? I think it'll make this easier."

"Okay." She rushed over to the arm of the small couch, plopped down, and sat rigid with nerves, fiddling with her fingers.

"Your lip looks good."

She pressed her finger to the lip in question. "Yeah, it's all better."

"Your bruising's almost gone too." He reached up, skimmed his knuckle across her cheek.

She closed her eyes at the warmth of his gentle touch.

"Hailey," he said quietly.

She opened her eyes. He'd moved closer. She gave him a nervous smile, eased away a bit.

"I have something for you."

She cleared her throat, swallowed. "Yeah?"

Austin reached in his back pocket and pulled out a folded envelope.

"What is it?"

"Open it and find out." He handed it over.

The university's address was stamped in the left corner. She licked her lips, opened it, and pulled out a sheet of paper. Scanning the words, her eyes widened. "Oh my God. The university isn't going to take my credits

CATE BEAUMAN

away." She beamed at him, then kept reading. "Holy
cow." She pressed a hand to her chest. "They're giving
me credit for Project Mexico. I can't believe this. I get to
graduate next semester. How in the world..." She stared
at him. "You did this. How did you do this?"

He shrugged. "The Dean and I had a discussion."

"And? Is that all you're going to tell me?"

He shrugged again and gave her a smile. "Pretty much."

She smiled back. "Well, thank you." For a moment
everything felt normal between them—easy. Hesitating,
Hailey sunk on the cushion, her thigh brushing his, gave
him a hug. "Thank you."

His solid arms wrapped around her, pulled her close.
His hand settled in her hair, pressing her face to his chest.
"You deserve those credits, Hailey. You were amazing."

Closing her eyes, she held on to him. What could
she say as her heart pounded in an unsteady rhythm,
breaking all over again? She didn't want to let him go,
but he wasn't hers, so she eased back. "You were—you
were pretty great yourself."

"Thanks." He skimmed his finger along her jaw and
stared at her lips.

Hailey's stomach twisted in painful knots. She rushed
to her feet, confused, unsure of where they stood. "Uh, I
should probably pack."

"Wait." Austin snagged her hand as she started
toward the remaining shelf of pretty knickknacks. "We
need to talk, Hailey. I figured after you got my message,
you would've at least given me a chance to explain."

"Message? What message?"

"I left you a voicemail right after you left the
apartment—in Mexico."

And then she remembered. Austin had called, but she
hadn't been strong enough to listen. "I—I never heard it.
I was going to wait until I got home, then I had to throw

my phone overboard."

Tension choked the room again as the yacht and everything that happened came to the surface.

"You texted Jackson before you tossed it."

"Yeah. I knew I only had one shot." She picked up a piece of packing paper, crumpled it, balling it tight, squeezing the wad as she vibrated with nerves.

"What does that mean?"

She shrugged. "It doesn't really mean anything."

"No matter how things were between us—are between us—were," he corrected again, shaking his head, "I would've helped you, Hailey."

She turned away, tossed the ball of paper on the floor, and picked up another sheet. "I couldn't be sure."

Austin rushed to his feet, yanked her around. "How can you say that?"

"What do you mean 'how can I say that?' Not even twelve hours before you'd told me we were through. You didn't want anything more to do with me." Sighing, she closed her eyes. Here they were again, even after some time. Any hope that they could work things out was quickly vanishing. "Look, it doesn't matter anymore." She removed her arm from Austin's grasp. "You should go."

He walked away a step, then turned. "I'm not leaving. I have things to say, things I should've said before but didn't get the chance."

"Then say them. I have stuff to do," she snapped. Shaking her head, sighing, she pressed her fingers to her temple. "I'm sorry. That was rude. I'm out of sorts. The least I owe you is the opportunity to speak." She took her seat on the loveseat again.

Austin sat as well, massaging his fingers over his chin. "I don't know how to start, so I guess I'll start with an apology."

She frowned. "An apology? Why? You saved my life."

"And took your brother's."

She stared at the hardwood floor, struggling with her torrent of swirling emotions. "I miss Jeremy." She grabbed Austin's hand as he tried to move away. "I miss the little boy I lived with so long ago. The sweet brown-eyed boy who had so much love to give, so much kindness in his heart." She met his gaze. "But he's gone. He vanished the night I left him alone in the hospital."

"Hailey." He moved closer.

"No, let me finish. I've had a lot of time to think." She pressed her lips together. "I didn't have any choice back then. I had to go, had to leave him. I was only fourteen, but I never got over the guilt, never got over the pain of losing my entire family in one night—in one way or another. I wanted to pick up with Jeremy where we left off. I wanted to believe that was possible, so I overlooked so many things. Too many things." She squeezed his hand. "And lost everything that was truly important."

He stared at her, gripping her fingers. "I don't know where to go from here."

"I'm not sure either." She pulled free of his hand.

"Maybe we could start with friends."

He might as well have stabbed her in the heart. "Yeah, maybe." She stood, walked back to the knickknacks, and began to fiddle with a pretty glass flower Kylee had given her.

"Is that what you want?"

She wanted it all. "Friends?" She picked up a piece of packing paper, afraid that if she looked at him, she would give in to her tears.

He walked up behind her, rubbed his hands up and down her arms, turned her to face him. "Is that what you want, Hailey?"

She couldn't take her eyes from his. "I—I—"

"Tell me what you want." His voice became more

gentle, pleaded.

She had to tell the truth. "Too much. I want too much, Austin." She looked down at the floor and set the flower down on a taped box before she dropped it from trembling fingers.

"I'll tell you what I want." His finger lifted her chin until she met his gaze. "I want back what we had before I lost my temper and said things I didn't mean, before I broke your trust and ruined the best thing in my life."

This was too huge, too unbelievable. She shook her head.

"About thirty seconds after you got in that cab, I realized I let you get away. I let the only woman I'll ever love slip through my fingers."

"Austin." She pressed her forehead to his chest.

"Tell me what you want, Hailey." He played his fingers through her hair.

She met his gaze and wrapped her arms around his wrists as he cupped her face. "I want you."

Austin's fingers clenched, relaxed. "I was afraid I would never hear that again." He brought her mouth to his and kissed her. "I love you. I'm so sorry I hurt you, Hailey. So sorry I broke my promise and let you down."

She locked her arms around his waist, holding tight. "I hurt you too. I didn't believe in you. I didn't believe the truth."

"If there was any way I could've ended things differently with your brother..."

"I know." She kissed him again. "I know."

"Do you love me, Hailey?"

"Of course I do. I love you more than anything."

"Good. That's good." Austin smiled playfully before he trailed his mouth down her neck. "I wanted to be sure." His lips moved to her jaw. "It's a pretty big deal."

"Mmm." Hailey closed her eyes, savoring the feel of

Austin pressed against her.

"I imagine we should probably move these boxes down the hall. To my apartment. To our apartment."

Her eyes flew open. "What?"

"I want it all back. I want you in my life, in my house, in my bed. I want you to be my wife."

She stared at him, staggered. "You want to get married?"

"As soon as possible. I just spent two weeks without you. That was fourteen days too long." He pressed kisses along at her temples. "Say you'll be my wife. Marry me."

"Yes. Yes, of course. I want babies, Austin. Lots and lots of babies."

He paused. "Define lots and lots."

"Two or three."

"How about two with an option for three?"

She grinned. "I can live with that."

"We should probably get a house first."

"Yes, I think we should." She laughed. Austin was giving her everything she'd ever wanted—him, a home, a family. "We have a lot of planning to do. A wedding."

"Later." Austin picked her up. "Much, *much* later." He walked out of her apartment, down the hall, unlocked his door, stepped inside, and kicked it closed. "Welcome home, Hailey." He kissed her long and deep as he hurried to their bedroom.

ABOUT THE AUTHOR

Cate Beauman is the author of The Bodyguards of L.A. County Series. She currently lives in Tennessee with her husband, two boys, and their St. Bernard, Bear.

OTHER TITLES BY AUTHOR

Morgan's Hunter

To read an excerpt from Morgans Hunter,
visit www.catebeauman.com

Falling for Sarah

To read an excerpt from Falling for Sarah,
visit www.catebeauman.com

7808857R00232

Printed in Great Britain
by Amazon.co.uk, Ltd.,
Marston Gate.